The Wanderer Rises

The Wanderer Rises

by

John Robertson

IGUANA

Publisher: Meghan Behse
Editor: Holly Elizabeth Warren
Interior illustrations: Ann Sanderson
Front cover illustration: Ann Sanderson
Cover design: Daniella Postavsky

 978-1-77180-325-0 Hardcover
978-1-77180-324-3 Paperback
978-1-77180-326-7 epub
978-1-77180-327-4 Kindle

This is an original hardcover edition of *The Wanderer Rises*.

Table of Contents

The Wanderer Rises

By the latter half of the third decade of the twenty-first century AD, ten years after the Paris Agreement on climate change, humankind has begun to make meaningful progress in curtailing its greenhouse gas emissions. Will it be enough to hold global warming to the agreed limit of 2.0 degrees Celsius, and ideally the more ambitious target of 1.5 degrees? Despite significant technological advancements and investment in sustainable energy production, it appears that more radical measures may be required to prevent the ever-expanding energy demands of the developing countries from countering the progress of the developed countries. As scientists and policymakers consider this dilemma, some are beginning to fear that an even more immediate and greater danger — insufficient fresh water — may overshadow the risk of global warming. Then, an unusual object approaches the Earth from the far reaches of the solar system, and there is yet a third candidate for the greatest threat that humankind faces, and one which in no way stems from either our own activities or our ever-increasing multitudes.

Acknowledgements

I have had a lot of help in creating *The Wanderer Rises*, for which I am thankful. My wife, Cathy, has been a patient and able typist. I doubt that anyone else would have put up with my barely legible low-tech penciled scribblings with copious marginal insertions and insertions within insertions. Then there was the time she left three chapters of the untyped manuscript, pages neither attached nor numbered, sitting on our bed below an open window, the day of a massive thunderstorm.

My daughter Hayleigh, who is an author herself and an English teacher, has given me several pointers along the way on the art of writing a fictional novel and has recommended useful resources on the subject.

My sister's partner, Colin Bantin, retired professor of physics at the University of Toronto, has been a great help with the mathematics of orbital mechanics, a key component of the science in the novel. I have drawn on many other published works for other aspects of the science, which I acknowledge in my list of references.

You will see with a quick page flip that the book is extensively illustrated, an aspect I feel is important both to supplement the reader's imagination of some of the awe-inspiring scenes and to clarify some of the complexities. I am thankful to my graphical artist, Ann Sanderson, and my map builder Daniella Postavsky, for their patience in working with me to transfer the images from my own mind into the story.

John Robertson

Foreword

Researching the scientific background of this novel has given me the opportunity to further explore several areas of interest and to clarify details of areas that I had some knowledge of, which has been an enjoyable process.

In addition, I've had an agenda while writing this book. This agenda arose from frustration with the polarized and politicized debate over the last two decades on the subject of climate change.

On one extreme of the debate are those who believe, almost religiously, that either the climate has not and is not changing, or if it is changing it is not as a result of human activity to any significant degree. Even some who accept that global warming exists and is due to human activity believe that climate change is too difficult to do anything about and the consequences aren't serious enough for us to make the effort.

At the other extreme are those equally intransigent believers that climate change consequences are so severe that they justify the immediate curtailment of fossil fuel consumption. They believe that it is easy to do so by moving to renewable sources of energy without significant impact on economic activity and quality of life, including the aspirations of the developing countries of the world, but that if economic sacrifices are required then they should be imposed on the rest of us for the sake of the climate. Some are prepared to take this to the extremes of engaging in falsification of information and other unlawful actions, even to the point of sabotage of energy infrastructure.

My agenda is simple: I want to bring a little more balance and context to this topic. I have tried to do this in part by putting climate change into the broader contexts of climate history, socioeconomic and demographic considerations, and other challenging and potentially more serious global issues like fresh water availability and political adventurism. I'm also positioning the issue in the broader context of the solar system and galaxy within which we deal with climate change. I have explored these topics through the fictional stories of individuals dealing with the subject as it affects their lives, rather than through an academic paper, letter to the editor, or other piece of nonfiction. My hope is that I have developed a sufficiently interesting array of characters and plotline to draw the reader through some of the more technical material.

My target audience is firstly myself, to more thoroughly ground my own views on climate change, and secondly my family and friends, to help them develop their own understanding and views. If that's as far as this ever goes, I will be satisfied. If, however, it is found worthy of broader publication and distribution, I will be pleased.

My family and friends will not be surprised that *The Wanderer Rises* is a work of science fiction, since my recreational reading has always been predominately in this genre. The type of science fiction that I have most enjoyed stays entirely within the boundaries of actual scientific knowledge except for one small tweak, and then builds the story upon the extrapolation of that tweak. I have attempted to do the same.

The scientific facts in the novel are accurate — at least as accurate as I can accomplish by cross-referencing various sources — and they are unbiased; that is, I haven't gone looking for facts to support a particular point of view. The analyses supporting the story are also all accurate based on the applicable branch of scientific knowledge, whether it is orbital mechanics or variations of the Stefan-Boltzmann law for estimating the effective temperature of a solar system body subject to changes in its surface albedo and atmospheric greenhouse gas density. The plotline of the story will likely not come to pass in reality, but based on scientific data, it certainly could.

All the characters in the novel are fictional, but I have modeled some on individuals I know or know of, and people who know me may recognize a bit of me in one character.

All the locations in the stories are real. In one case only I've created a composite of two places to create the story's setting. In several cases, I have visited and am quite familiar with the locations I write about; in others, I have carefully researched the places to ensure accuracy. Forgive me for running you along my jogging path on the banks of the Charles River between the Harvard and MIT campuses.

At one time I thought about undertaking the orbital mechanics calculations that are required to maintain accuracy in the story line. The mathematics and computer science involved are similar to those employed in my own doctoral thesis. Fortunately, however, before I started working on these elements I made a new acquaintance with someone who had much more currency with the math and physics than me and who had recently retired and had the time to fiddle with a few scenarios. In the story, these calculations are undertaken by a young mathematician at the NASA Jet Propulsion Laboratory using an orbital mechanics program named Cruncher IV, which is what I called the nonlinear optimization algorithm I developed as part of my thesis many years ago. Although there are numerous orbital mechanics programs in existence, none actually go by such a name.

Enjoy! (I hope.)

John Robertson

Chapter 1

Early June 2027
Canadian Rocky Mountains, near Golden, British Columbia

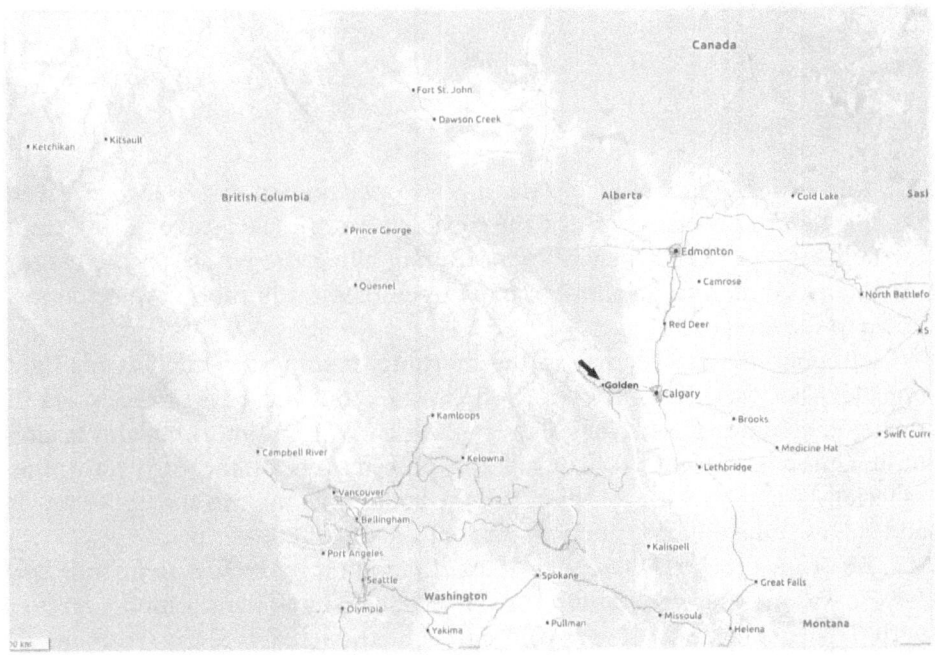

It was cold! Tom lay in his sleeping bag with just his head poking out as he opened his eyes. Even inside the tent he could see his breath. He knew it would be colder still outside the tent, with quite probably a thin skim of ice along the shoreline of the pristine mountain lake that lay just feet away.

He quietly slipped out of the warmth of the bag and into his clothes, being careful not to awaken the eleven-year-old boy whose tousled head slept on beside him. This was quite a feat as Arthur had snuggled up tight during the night, trying to capture a few degrees of warmth from his dad, which reminded Tom of Trish, the boy's mother.

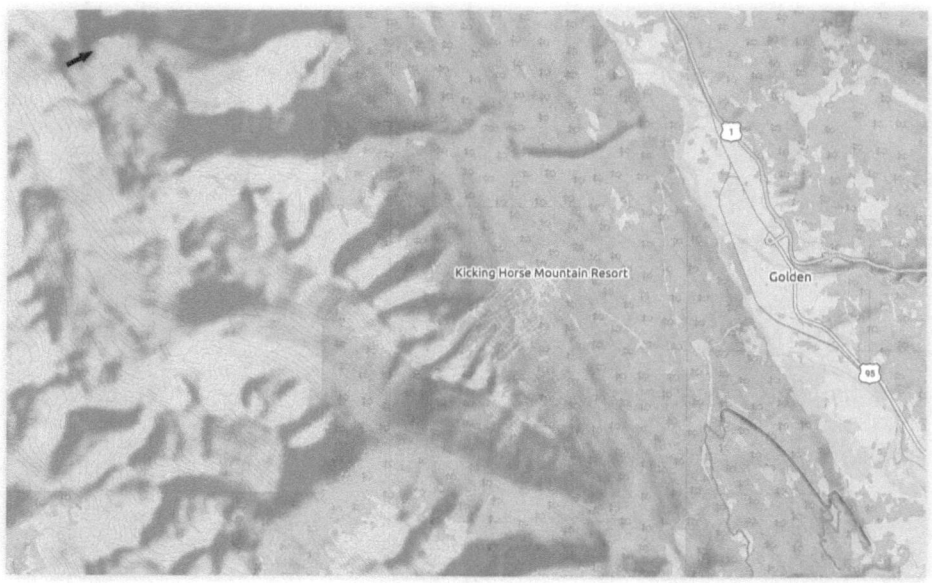

Tom extracted himself from the tiny two-person tent and briefly surveyed the splendor of his surroundings: the cobalt blue of the lake, still as glass except for faint ripples from a pair of loons gliding along the far shore; the craggy mountains climbing high above him to the southeast, still snow covered almost down to the level of the lake.

Although it was only five in the morning, there was already ample light outside. That was one of the things he loved about this part of the world in spring and summer, with long days starting early in the morning and lasting until almost midnight. Tom loved the peacefulness of the early morning, especially when, as with this weekend, he could hike up into the upper bowls and ridges and enjoy the sunrise from near the top of the world.

Yes, Tom thought, *there were a great many things he had to be thankful for.* He was making a good living as an electrician in Golden, which, together with Trish's income as a part-time nurse at the local clinic, gave them all they needed with a decent amount left over for savings. They had three great kids, Arthur and his two younger sisters, Susan and Sigrid.

Golden was a quiet little town nestled in the Canadian Rockies, well connected to the outside world by the Trans-Canada highway and the Canadian National Railway, but providing Tom with almost instant access to thousands of square miles of mountain wilderness with all the skiing, hiking, fishing and hunting one could ever want. In addition to a comfortable home in town they had a tiny cabin on a small lake they shared with a few others on the benchland, plus the high camp at Shadow Lake, a six-mile hike three thousand feet above the cabin. Shadow Lake and its surroundings were crown land open to anyone, but, with no established access trail, Tom had never seen another soul there and felt like it was his own private temple.

He and Trish regularly attended St. Paul's, the local Anglican church. Though not dogmatic, they both believed in a power and a plan behind the creation of the universe, and a creator whose prime commandments called for love between all people. So, it was quite natural for Tom, as he stood in the frigid mountain air beside the serene yet icy lake, to raise a brief prayer of thanks to God and to seek a blessing on and the safekeeping of his young family.

As he finished his prayer, Tom caught a small movement out of the corner of his eye, a few feet away from the tent. A massive shaggy form rose from the ground with a gaping mouth big enough to crush a man's leg.

"Hello, Beast," said Tom, breaking the morning's silence as the 150-pound, two-year-old Tibetan Mastiff stretched and ambled over for a pat. Beast was quite comfortable sleeping in the open at thirty degrees Fahrenheit, which was one of the reasons Tom had chosen a dog from that uncommon breed as his family's companion and protector. While Tom regularly sought God's safekeeping for his family, he also believed that he himself was God's first line of defense, and Beast was a key member of the family and a partner in that responsibility. In times to come Tom would be all the more thankful for his choice.

Tom knelt beside the ring of fire stones, which, besides the built-up bed of sandy earth on which his tent stood and a tiny biffy fifty yards upslope, were the only permanent signs of human habitation that would be apparent to a casual observer of the lakeshore. Everything else Tom and Art needed for their weekend of fishing they had carried in the four rugged miles from where they had left the family GMC Suburban and would carry back out. The route was not an established trail but rather a series of headings and distances laid out many years ago by Tom across the contours of a 50,000 to 1 topographical map, but long since committed to memory.

A few breaths brought the embers from last night's fire back to a steady glow. Tom grabbed the kindling, which Art had been tasked to collect first thing on arrival in camp last evening, from underneath the light tarp that kept it dry from rain and dew. Soon the fire was a small blaze and Tom had a pot of tea water warming and a half dozen strips of bacon sizzling.

He called to the tent — "Time to rise. Breakfast's on," — knowing that food was the only way to entice the eleven-year-old from the warmth of his sleeping bag.

Art sleepily responded, "What is for breakfast Dad?"

"Bacon and bushcakes."

Art perked up. "Bushcakes. My favorite," he chirped.

Bushcakes were really nothing more than pancakes cooked in a little hot oil in a frying pan over an open fire. The surface of the cakes tended to get slightly crispy from the deep-frying effect of the hot oil if it was allowed to get a little too hot — a regular outcome when cooking over an open fire. Tom had achieved the bushcake effect unintentionally some years ago on a family camping trip. When Trish had playfully commented that she had never had crispy pancakes before, Tom had defended his campfire cooking by stating that he was cooking bushcakes, not pancakes. Bushcakes had been a favorite of all the kids ever since.

Art emerged from the tent moments later, still in his pajamas. "Dad, it's so cold out," he said as he sat as close to the fire as he could without getting right into it. "Can you build the fire up bigger please, much bigger? I'm freezing."

Tom untied his own hooded sweatshirt from his waist and put it on the boy. It came down nearly to his knees. "I can't build the fire up while I'm cooking," he said, "but that should keep you a little warmer." He had to agree with Art though, it was darn cold. Cold was to be expected at this time of year, latitude and altitude, but this was a little colder even than normal. On the other hand, it had generally been a warm winter, rarely colder than zero degrees Fahrenheit at town level, and occasionally above freezing. For that matter, it seemed to Tom

that the winters had all tended to be warmer of late. It seemed like the minus-twenty-degree-Fahrenheit January temperatures he recalled from his youth were pretty rare these days.

Global warming was supposed to have added less than a degree to the world's average temperature in his thirty-three–year life, but it seemed more noticeable than that around here. Tom hoped that all the multilateral programs to put a limit on global warming were going to work, even if they were making a lot of things more expensive, especially fuel and power. As he looked up at the lip of the large glacier that cloaked the upper bowl to the east and fed the lake, he hoped it would still be a thing of grandeur when Art grew old enough to bring his own son here.

As he set the bacon aside to stay warm in a small pan and poured the first dollop of batter into another hot pan, he said, "In another quarter hour the Sun is going to start to peek up above that notch between the mountains," pointing to the southeast, "then it will start to warm up and we'll get our rods out and catch some trout for lunch."

Art peered in the direction his father was pointing, seeing nothing but the long shadow cast across the lake by the easternmost twin peak. "Dad, how do you know the Sun will come right into that gap? It's pretty narrow compared with the mountains on both sides. If the Sun stays behind the mountain it's going to be forever till it's warm."

Tom chuckled, "That's true, but I know it will rise pretty much right at the bottom of the vee at this time of year because it has every year I have been coming here since I wasn't much older than you. That's where it's always come up, and where it always will."

Chapter 2

Early July 2027
Sonoma County, near Santa Rosa, Northern California

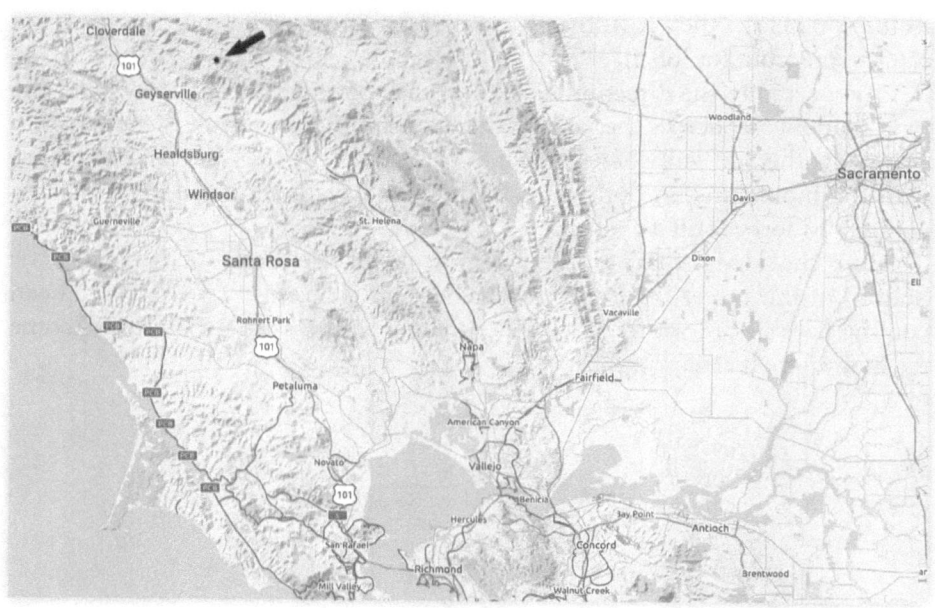

It was hot! Alyssa Morgan sat at her desk in a small office in a corner of the plant, finishing her weekly report to the head office. The outside temperature was climbing toward the daily high, probably about eighty-five degrees Fahrenheit at this time of year, but heat coming off the steam turbine and condenser kept the plant interior a good ten degrees warmer even with the exhaust fans fully on. The twenty-seven-year-old blond engineer had a small air conditioning unit that she could turn on. She didn't plan to stay in long, though, and she preferred to keep her energy consumption as low as possible.

Alyssa enjoyed a warm climate, so the Santa Rosa area suited her well, with pleasant early morning bike-riding temperatures in the low fifties warming to the high eighties throughout the day in summer. In winter it rarely dropped below freezing. By managing clothing, it was possible to be comfortable outdoors all year round, and by managing ventilation, a house could be kept at a comfortable seventy to seventy-four degrees with a little supplementary heating or cooling provided by a high-efficiency bidirectional heat pump.

She sent the report off. It was a good report and she was pleased with the performance of her little operation — a forty-megawatt geothermal power plant producing enough electricity to meet the needs of two thousand California homes. She thought of it as her operation since, as the onsite engineer, she was the only employee of the company within a hundred miles. Western Renewable Power Inc. was small, and it contracted out any maintenance to a local service company, keeping just Alyssa on site. So, it was her responsibility to monitor the central plant and the half dozen, two-mile-deep steam wells that supplied it with superheated steam, as well as the reinjection wells to return water back to the subterranean steam reservoir.

It was Alyssa's responsibility to keep the system in tune, extracting the maximum amount of electric power from the available geothermal energy resource without overpressuring the turbine or exhausting too much water vapor. Every gallon of water released in the form of steam to moderate pressure fluctuations had to be replaced with makeup water, which was a scarce resource.

Alyssa donned her headphones, safety glasses and hard hat as she stepped into the plant. Even through the sound-dampening ear protection, the wail of the turbine spinning at three thousand rpm sounded like a banshee screaming match. Alyssa knew very well that if the turbine ever came apart from a high-pressure spike, her personal protective equipment would provide very little protection from pieces of metal scattered by the equivalent of a small bomb. Even if the turbine's steel casing contained the blast, the superheated steam released in such an event would cook anyone in the plant. It was her job to make sure the plant was operating within its design capacity with all pressure relief valves in good working order, and she was confident that she had all that under control. But you never know what Mother Nature has in store.

As Alyssa checked the readings on her various pressure and temperature sensors one last time for the day, she reflected on the source of all the energy she was turning into electricity. As hot as it was inside the plant, it was like the North Pole compared to the huge lake — estimated to be nine miles in diameter — of white-hot molten magma about four miles beneath her feet. That magma was about two thousand degrees Fahrenheit and if it were ever forced upward and made its way into one of her steam wells and then to the surface, it would truly be hell on Earth.

Alyssa didn't think there was much risk she'd ever have to deal with magma, and she was better qualified than most to assess that risk. She'd gotten her engineering degree from Stanford with a concentration in geology and geophysics. Many of her classmates chose careers in research or government, but she preferred to put her knowledge to practical use. With California's legislated renewable power standard set at 50 percent by 2030 there was a great need for technical people in the renewable power industry. It was a job in which she thought she could make a difference for the better. Little did she know the challenges that her expertise and courage would soon be put to.

After completing her checks, Alyssa locked the plant building and climbed into her half-ton company truck to check each of her well sites. This involved a drive along a rough service road that snaked its way around and sometimes over the ridges of the Mayacamas Mountains, which rippled over the whole region of The Geysers in Sonoma and Lake Counties. This quiet, peaceful drive was a striking contrast to the atmosphere of the plant. She should see no one on the circuit today. There was no scheduled maintenance on any of the wells and no access to the service road other than by the locked gate at the plant entrance. If she got into any difficulty, she had radio contact with the maintenance company and emergency services. However, there were mountain lions in the hills, and so she carried a Browning 308 rifle in the truck, and knew how to use it. None of these precautions were needed today.

By midafternoon Alyssa had completed the circuit without event. She changed out of her work clothes into a light jersey and riding shorts. Alyssa didn't live at the plant, though she kept a cot and a small fridge in a corner of the office. Her home was a small house in Healdsburg, about sixteen miles back along Geysers Road, nearly all downhill on the way back. She wheeled her Garneau hybrid out of the gate, which she locked behind her. The Geysers Road was paved except for the occasional stretch of gravel, and with a 2,500-foot drop in altitude it would be an easy forty-five-minute ride. The return trip was quite another story, but that would be done in the cool of a six o'clock start the next morning.

Alyssa loved biking and both her and her boyfriend, Brad, belonged to the Santa Rosa bike club. As she crossed the Little Sulphur Creek bridge, she thought about weekend plans for the two of them. They would probably join a club ride. The weather was supposed to be good as usual, if a little warm.

The young woman felt that she was doing her part to meet the voluntary national energy conservation challenge, and she hoped the rest of America was too. She knew she could live with a few degrees warmer climate and still be very comfortable, but she also believed there would be serious consequences for many other people if global warming wasn't brought to a halt.

As she pedaled into her driveway Alyssa felt great, lucky to have such a good life, and excited to see Brad after a week apart. After a cautious start, in keeping with her personality, they had grown close both emotionally and physically, and now Alyssa saw nothing but good things in their future.

Chapter 3

Late July 2027
Washington, DC

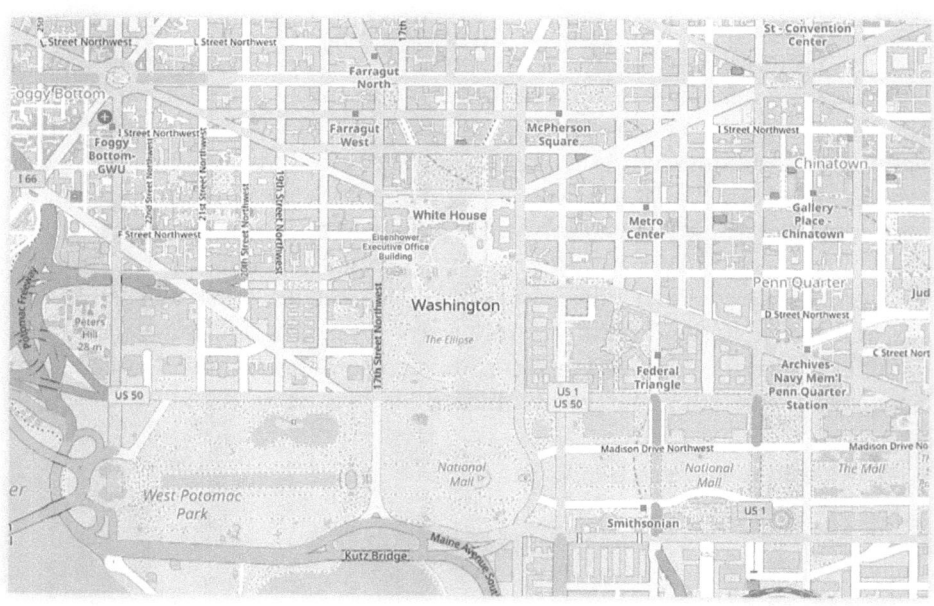

It was dark as the president of the United States came awake to the soft beeping of his Timex. The longer days of summer were waning, and his day would begin, as usual, with twenty minutes in the third-floor exercise room and another twenty minutes of jogging around the grounds before his shower and a light breakfast at six thirty. Jim shut off the alarm and slipped into his workout gear and out the bedroom door quietly so as not to awaken his wife, Julia. He greeted the on-duty secret service agent in the main corridor and jogged to the end of the corridor and up the stairs to the exercise room.

The TV was tuned to his usual news station so he could catch up on any new international or national developments before his formal briefing papers arrived at six thirty. Exercising and absorbing information at the same time was typical of Jim's double-tasking style. This morning as he worked through several short upper body sets, there was nothing remarkably new being reported, and he found his thoughts wandering to the unexpected chain of events over the last three years that had landed him with a heavy responsibility.

He was no stranger to executive responsibility and decision-making, but his background was not in politics. He was a business leader, most recently the CEO of Rockworth Construction Corporation where he had combined his cooperative problem-solving leadership style and his knack for identifying good people with a lot of hard work to build a highly respected and successful business, one of the largest in the country. Jim believed in people and their ability to rise to most challenges with the right support, though he would not hesitate to move an employee out of a role if they were struggling with it. He would never have sought it but was gratified to have been named *Fortune* magazine's Businessman of the Year in 2023.

Jim had been grooming his executive team for an eventual succession in the company's leadership but had planned on another three or four years before stepping down from that demanding, high-stress role. It came as a great surprise three years ago when he received a personal call from Tim Mahally, the Democratic Party nominee for the 2024 presidential election. Would he consider joining senator Mahally on the Democratic ticket as his vice president running mate? Several days of intense private discussions followed.

Mahally was candid about his reasons for preferring to move outside of the usual political spectrum in his choice of running mate. Mahally believed, and had persuaded the Democratic Party leadership, that a left-wing political philosophy would not succeed in the 2024 election. He was looking for a centrist to command respect and even support from the centrist elements of both national parties, who would complement his own moderate but distinctly pro-environment image. However, the senator was also firm that he wanted someone who, while being reasonably philosophically aligned, would bring a different set of experiences and capabilities than his own to the Executive Office of the President of the United States. Mahally willingly committed that if the two of them were successful, then Jim would be an active participant in assisting and advising the president on policy and major decisions.

Over the course of several days, the discussions between the political leader and the business leader ranged over many topics. In the end, the senator was satisfied that Jim, while politically inexperienced, was bright, articulate and fully deserving of his reputation as a consummate business leader. In turn,

Jim developed considerable respect for Mahally's political views and his plans to refurbish the Democratic Party's image. Jim also became convinced that a revitalized centrist Democratic Party would be a better answer to America's challenges and opportunities than the eccentric and divisive Republican leadership that had risen to power in 2016, or than a highly socialist Democratic government would, and that he could make a meaningful contribution to such a government.

Mahally's political calculus was correct. He and Jim won the election, and the Democrats gained a majority in the House of Representatives and a near majority in the Senate. Mahally was true to his word on Jim's role, and the two of them collaborated on a variety of policy measures, balancing the president's environmental priorities with practical business and economic realities. These measures had generally found prompt support in both Houses. The two of them, after two years having become both respected colleagues and friends, were just beginning to see the fruits of their efforts when Tim Mahally, President of the United States of America, died abruptly of a heart attack. James Rushton suddenly found himself truly out of the frying pan and into the fire in terms of responsibility and stress.

Jim had no plans to run again in 2028 for either president or vice president, so intended to focus all his efforts on doing his best for the country during his unexpected interim presidency. After three months in his new role, he was still largely following the agenda that he and Tim had developed, while keeping an open eye for emerging developments that might call for a course correction. Although not yet apparent, such developments were in fact emerging.

Chapter 4

August 8, 2027
White House, Washington, DC

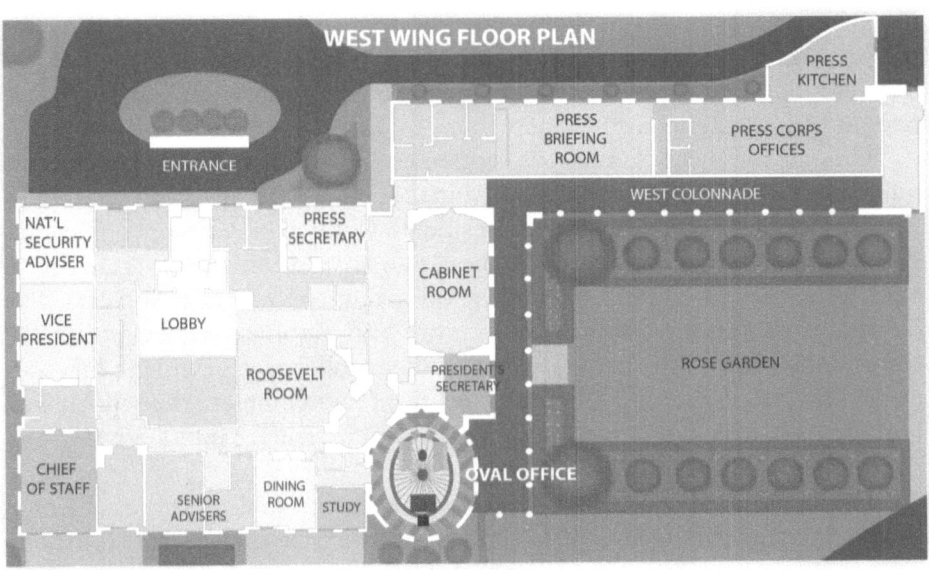

WEST WING FLOOR PLAN

The president's schedule had begun, as usual, that morning at quarter to eight in the president's study beside the Oval Office with his daily intelligence briefing by the director of National Intelligence. The National Security advisor, the Homeland Security advisor and the White House chief of staff, Will Templeton, were sitting in. Jim preferred the more informal setting of the study adjacent to the Oval Office for his own private think time and for meetings with small groups of key staff. Will generally sat in on these meetings in case anything arising from the meeting required his rejigging the president's schedule for the day. Today that hadn't been the case and the briefing was done by eight fifteen, leaving the president a few minutes to go back over the written briefing and to prepare for his eight thirty meeting with his science advisor, Dr. Eli Wayman.

During his two-and-a-quarter years as President Mahally's right hand, Jim had learned what a large group of specialists of every type staffed the Executive Office of the President of the United States. This was a group with little or no political ambition, appointed by and holding office at the president's pleasure, and existing only to assist and advise him with his responsibilities. One of the first messages he had sent through Will upon his appointment a little over three months ago was that he was fully satisfied with the existing senior leadership within the Executive Office and had no intentions of making any changes. That included Will, whose position was usually occupied by the president's closest confidant.

Jim was looking forward to his meeting with Eli, which he had been scheduling for an hour each month to keep up with any important scientific developments. It would be a one-on-one, one of few such meetings in his routine, and very relaxed — also a rarity. Jim liked and respected Eli, a sixty-five-year-old Nobel laureate with a reputation as one of the world's most creative particle physicists and cosmologists.

One of the science advisor's key roles, in addition to overseeing the multidisciplinary staff of specialists within the Office of Science and Technology, is to ensure that the United States President's Council of Advisors on Science and Technology comprises the leading minds from all major branches of science. Although Eli was outspoken on a few controversial subjects, like Israel and gun control, he was well known and highly respected within the community, with a wide network of top-caliber colleagues. Although Eli's area of personal expertise was extremely technical and complex, the scholar had both a knack and an interest in putting scientific matters into a context that the public could grasp.

Jim had told Eli about a week ago that he wanted to discuss the subject of global warming. Jim wanted Eli's condensed views; he didn't want to include anyone else in the conversation — not staff or council specialists, the Secretary of the Environment or the Administrator of the Environmental Protection Agency. He knew Eli would be well prepared, so once the two were comfortably seated he got right down to it.

"Eli, update me on the latest thinking on global warming. It is something our recent president was passionate about and I need to get my own views better defined and grounded. Let's start at the beginning — how sure are we that mankind has been heating up the atmosphere, and then how successful are we being at getting it under control?"

"Yes, Mr. President," began the science advisor, "let's take your first question in two parts. First, is the Earth's surface heating up? The answer is a pretty clear yes. In the period since 1880, when good records began to be kept consistently, the average temperature of the Earth's surface has increased by between one and a half degrees and two degrees Fahrenheit. The increase has not been perfectly steady. In particular, the rate of increase has been greater in the latter half of this period, and there have been shorter periods of faster and slower rates of increase. From the late 1990s to the end of the first decade of this century, global warming slowed considerably and very nearly stopped, but temperatures continued to rise thereafter with 2015 being a record hot year since the data have been kept, and then new records in many years since. As late as the latter part of the last decade there were still a few responsible scientists who questioned the interpretation of the temperature data, but I think it is safe to say that in recent years increasing temperatures have become accepted as scientific fact.

"The second part to your first question is whether we are confident that we understand why the Earth is heating up and whether it is a man-made or 'anthropogenic' cause rather than a natural phenomenon. It has always been a bigger challenge to explain physical phenomena than to measure them, and that is true with global warming as well. So, please stop me if I stray further afield than your time and interest can afford."

Jim, who had a notebook out and was jotting down key points, nodded encouragingly.

"Let's start with some atmospheric science facts. The air we breathe consists mostly of nitrogen, about 78 percent, and oxygen, about 21 percent. The remaining 1 percent is mostly argon, about 0.9 percent, leaving only one tenth of 1 percent yet to be accounted for. You may be wondering where carbon dioxide fits in. It is a part of that last 0.1 percent; in fact, it is currently at about 0.04 percent of the atmosphere, or four hundred parts per million as the unit of measure we use for very small concentrations. Carbon dioxide is what's called a trace gas, but it is also the main greenhouse gas. Air also contains varying amounts of water vapor which is suspended in it, on average about four thousand parts per million, about ten times as much as carbon dioxide.

"Carbon dioxide, water vapour, and certain other gases, even in trace amounts, contribute to the Earth's greenhouse effect. The Earth receives energy from the Sun in the form of shortwave radiation — what we think of as visible light. Most of this short-wave radiation readily passes through the Earth's atmosphere, including the molecules of the various greenhouse gases, and reaches the surface of the Earth, though some of that shortwave energy is reflected by the atmosphere and some is absorbed by it. Of the large portion that reaches the surface of the planet another part is reflected upward by the surface and passes unimpeded by the atmosphere back into space. The remainder is absorbed by the Earth, warming it and causing it to radiate energy in the form of heat, or long wavelength infrared radiation.

"Here's the greenhouse part. The molecular nature of greenhouse gases is such that they don't allow longwave radiation to pass through as readily as they do shortwave radiation. So, yes, a lot of the infrared radiation from the Earth's surface does make it through our atmosphere and out into space, but some of it is absorbed by the greenhouse gases and then most of that is radiated back to the Earth, as depicted in this little diagram."

Eli handed Jim a printout of the diagram so he could take a closer look, then continued.

"The higher the concentration of greenhouse gases in the atmosphere, the less infrared radiation escapes and the more is radiated back to the Earth, warming it still further.

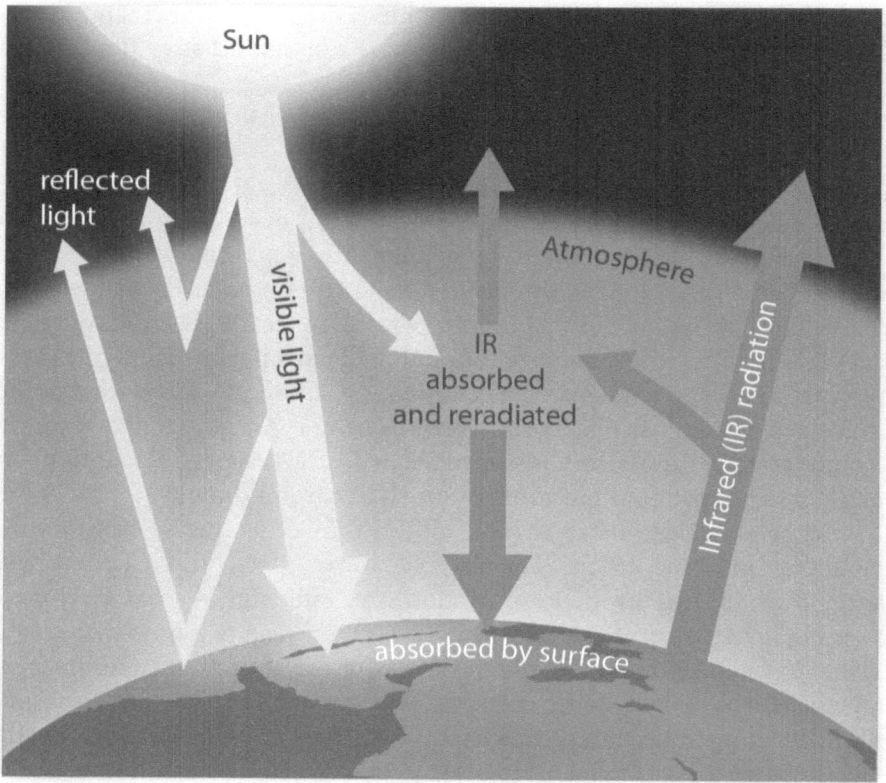

"The greenhouse effect is something we've known about for a long time, and it is a good thing. Without the heat-trapping effect of the atmosphere, the

Earth's natural average temperature would be about zero degrees Fahrenheit rather than the current fifty-eight degrees, and humankind would never have evolved. So, generally, the greenhouse effect is essential to our existence and continued survival. It is a very good thing, but of course, like most good things, you can have too much of it.

"If we go back to the early Industrial Age, the carbon dioxide concentration was about three hundred parts per million. Our models of how the greenhouse effect works predict that the increase in carbon dioxide since then to its current level of four hundred ppm would pretty much account for the increase in temperature that we've seen. These models could be wrong, as scientific models have been in the past, though the science involved is quite straightforward.

"So, it is possible that there is some other cause or causes for all or part of the recent global warming, but the best explanation is that it has been caused mainly by man-made emissions of carbon dioxide. The unfortunate corollary is that global warming will very likely continue and even accelerate unless emissions of carbon dioxide can be curtailed, with global average temperatures increasing by another four and a half degrees Fahrenheit to eight and a half degrees Fahrenheit.

"Mr. President, I know that's a lot of technical information, but I think that a little more will help you grasp the whole picture. While it is true, as best we can tell, that the change in carbon dioxide concentration in the atmosphere as a result of man-made emissions is what is causing the greenhouse effect to grow stronger in recent decades, carbon dioxide is not the largest contributor to the greenhouse effect. Most of it actually comes from the much higher concentration of water vapour, about three times more than comes from carbon dioxide."

The president responded, "So, let me see if I've got it so far. First, the Earth's temperature has been rising based on the best measurement technology that we have, not perfectly steadily but reasonably so, over the last century and a half. Second, our atmosphere acts something like a greenhouse and always has, without which the Earth would be too cold to live on, and the physics of how this works are well understood. Third, the carbon dioxide concentration in the atmosphere has been increasing over this same period, which is clearly measurable. And carbon dioxide, though not the most powerful ingredient of our greenhouse by far, is nevertheless one of the ingredients and the only one that has changed significantly."

"That's all correct, sir, but another fact to provide further context is that the Earth has in the distant past seen much higher carbon dioxide concentrations than the current four hundred ppm, or than we will ever reach as a result of man-made emissions. For example, during the Cambrian period, five hundred million years ago, the concentration was as high as seven thousand ppm. That was a very warm period with a global average temperature about twelve degrees higher than at present, about seventy degrees Fahrenheit. That period lasted about fifty million years, and by its end there was little polar ice and sea level was about three hundred feet higher than at present.

"We also understand that there have been many very cold periods in the past — so-called ice ages. In fact, we are currently, that is, for the last ten thousand years or so, enjoying a warm spell within the Quaternary Ice Age, which began about 2.6 million years ago. Within the Quaternary Ice Age there have been fairly regular cycles of cooling periods, with glaciers advancing, followed by warming periods, such as the present, with glaciers shrinking. There were also at least four other ice ages prior to the Quaternary Period. The granddaddy of them all was the Cryogenian, about seven hundred million years ago, during which ice covered nearly the entire Earth.

"While man-made carbon dioxide emissions were obviously not a factor in these pronounced cooling and warming periods, it is likely that variations in carbon dioxide and oxygen concentrations resulting from natural causes were a contributing factor, though probably not the primary cause. Other factors include episodic events like large meteor strikes and super volcanoes, as well as recurring phenomena such as solar output cycles and variations in the Earth's orbital path and axial tilt. In fact, it is the latter that appears to give rise to the cycles of warming and cooling within our current ice age.

"So, Mr. President, I don't mean at all to suggest that man-made global warming won't have some serious consequences, nor that we shouldn't be doing what we can to curtail it. However, I thought you should know that we are talking about relatively small variations in temperature compared to what Mother Nature herself has been orchestrating over a longer time frame, and likely has in store for us in millennia to come."

"Thank you, Eli," the president said, "That's a very clear refresher on what we think about anthropogenic global warming, and I appreciate the broader context you have provided. What are the consequences of continued warming?"

"Yes, Mr. President," Eli continued, "first of course there is the direct consequence — higher temperatures, not likely as high as during the Cambrian but higher than we've seen in recorded history. The U.S. lies in the temperate zone, where this increase would not be dire. In fact, the northern United States, Canada and most of Europe would have more pleasant temperatures than at present. However, in the tropic zone, in places like India and large parts of Africa and Central and South America, the impact on human comfort and health would be very serious. Ironically, these areas have contributed almost nothing to creating global warming, at least so far; and they are also the areas with the least ability to moderate the impact of higher temperatures through air-conditioning.

"Then there are secondary consequences. The most notable of these will be a rise in sea levels of as much as five or six feet. It may not sound like much, but it would necessitate extensive diking and pumping to protect coastal cities and abandoning some coastal regions and island nations. Along with the higher temperatures, we will also see more extreme weather — stronger and more frequent tornados, devastating floods, severe droughts and wildfires. Some parts of the Earth may get a longer growing season, but for the most part, the temperature and weather extremes will adversely affect food production. Then there will be the impact on the plant and animal species that are unsuccessful at adapting, with many dying off — not that large scale species die-offs were uncommon during past climate changes. The warmer temperatures will also permit various types of insects and diseases to extend northward and southward from the tropics with impacts on human health, crops, cattle and forests."

"Okay, Eli," Jim interjected, "from what you've said I am understanding that global warming is a fact, that man-made carbon dioxide emissions are likely the cause even though more significant temperature variations have occurred in the past without any human involvement; and that, even if carbon dioxide emissions are not certain as the cause, the probable consequences are serious enough that we should take all reasonable steps to curtail our emissions as a matter of prudent risk management. Have I got it pretty much right so far?"

"Yes, Mr. President, I couldn't sum it up any better than that."

"Eli, I have found this briefing very interesting and informative, but I am at my limit for absorbing the details. I would really like to hear your thoughts on how much progress is being made around the world in curtailing greenhouse gas emissions, so I will see if Will can squeeze in another short session for us next week. Thank you, Eli."

Eli Wayman walked out of the anteroom through the Oval Office and headed for his own office in the Old Executive Office Building next door. Eli found the new president respectful, cordial and attentive. He would do anything he could to help him make the world a better place, and in months to come that help would certainly be needed.

Chapter 5

August 15, 2027
Near Idaho Falls, Idaho

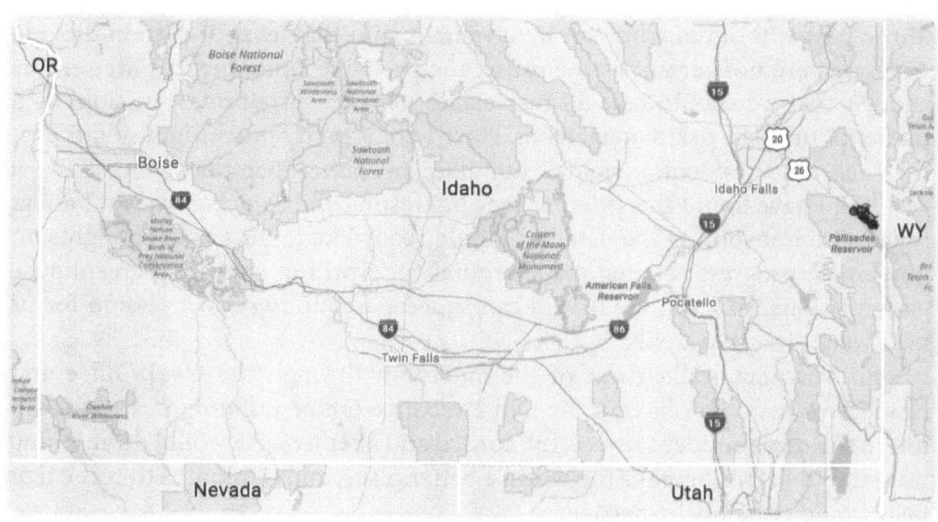

Peter was cruising peacefully northwest along U.S. Route 26 toward Idaho Falls in the late afternoon. His twin cam 95 CID Harley Softail was loafing along barely above idle at the fifty-miles-per-hour speed limit. He liked the bike for its comfortable ride, and it was reassuring in his line of work to know that he could spin it up to triple that speed if needed. Traffic was light on the Swan Valley Highway that afternoon. He could have safely cruised at double the limit, but he was taking it easy, partly because he enjoyed the scenic ride along the Palisades Reservoir and the Snake River, but mostly because he had no wish to attract any attention from the state police given the amount of meth he was carrying.

Peter Poplinski didn't think of himself as a bad man, though he certainly didn't think of himself as a good man either. In point of fact, he didn't think of himself or others in those terms at all. He simply lacked that frame of reference entirely, and always had. However, those who knew him would describe him as a very bad man who would resort to extreme violence in the blink of an eye if opposed, but also as a very smart man. An undergraduate in clinical psychology would quickly identify him as having ASPD, or antisocial personality disorder, given his disregard for the rights of others and his total focus on serving his own needs. Peter lacked a conscience and moral compass.

At age thirty-eight, Peter stood six-foot-five and weighed two hundred and fifty pounds. During his eight years in the Idaho Maximum Security Institution for voluntary manslaughter, he had invested every free minute in the gym, and he had rarely missed a day on the weights ever since. He was well built and very attractive. He looked about ten years younger than he was. He had a powerful libido, which he was usually able to satisfy with willing female companions given his extreme physical attractiveness.

Peter was the current head of Satan's Wheels motorcycle club, which was prospering under his leadership. The gang's principal occupation was to serve as a courier for drugs moving from out of state to the centers of Boise, Twin Falls and Idaho Falls as well as occasional longer runs into Portland, Oregon. The gang also took on enforcement contracts, including executions, when available.

Peter had only been sent up the once, though he was suspected in several other homicides for which no witnesses existed, or at least none willing to testify and endure the terrible reprisals that the Satan's Wheels had developed a reputation for exacting on snitches.

Peter planned to gas up and turn south on the back roads well before Idaho Falls. He wanted to avoid the traffic in and around the Falls, and reduce the risk of a fender bender or some other chance encounter with law enforcement. He had stopped for gas at a station right at the turn off up to Ririe on the way out from Idaho Falls a few days earlier, and a young girl serving gas had caught his interest. She had been wearing tight jean shorts that emphasized her firm, round butt, and a T-shirt that her young, unrestrained breasts tented out in a continuously moving double crest. Long, straight brown hair cascaded down her back to just below her waist. She was breathtakingly cute and probably not more that eighteen years old.

As Peter pulled into the station and up to the pumps he spotted the girl in an apparent wrestling match with three young gorillas that looked like college football jocks. He shut down the bike and heard her yell, "Get your hands off me, you pigs, and I'll give you your lousy change."

Peter could see one of the boys had both her arms pinned straight up above her head from behind with his left arm, while his right arm was up underneath her T-shirt having a good grope. The two others stood with their backs to Peter, holding their phones out and waiting for the T-shirt to be pulled up over her head. Peter didn't consider this behavior wrong. It was more that, in his mind, he already viewed the girl as belonging to him, and these three were handling his property.

He got off the bike and removed a short leather blackjack from a pocket. He didn't raise any warning or telegraph his intentions in any way. In ten quick steps he was on them. The first of the two with their backs to him never knew what hit him as he dropped from a slash of the blackjack across the back of his head, just above the hairline. It wasn't a killing blow, not because Peter had any compunction about killing, but because that would just create too many complications at present.

The second of the two was only beginning to turn to face the sudden attack when Peter delivered a brutal kick to the side of his knee, snapping it like a dry stick despite the powerful thigh and calf muscles above and below. Number two dropped to the pavement screaming in pain. Orthopedic surgery could perform near miracles these days, but the boy's football days were definitely over.

By this time the third boy had released his grip on the girl and was backing away, having sized up the attacker.

Although there wasn't much difference in weight between the two of them, the boy sensed the pure animal ferocity of the biker and wanted no part of it. He was surprised and relieved when Peter relaxed and commanded, "Stand still, arms out to the side and slowly pass me your driver's license."

Wondering if this frightening beast was in fact some type of law enforcement, the boy meekly complied with Peter's authoritative demand. Once he had the license, Peter instructed the boy to drag his moaning friend over to their car and shove him into the back seat. Peter followed behind with the inert form of the first one he had dropped, removing that boy's wallet and extracting his license as well. He also took the license from the moaner. Then he placed all three licenses on the car's rear fender and took their picture with his phone before tossing them into the back seat.

In a quiet but firm tone, Peter spoke in the ear of the bewildered college boy, "Get into your car and drive. Don't stop until you get to Portland. That will give you time to figure out a better excuse for how your friend broke his knee than that the three of you were beaten while molesting a young girl. I don't care what it is, but if you mention me, I will hear about it, and I will come visiting both you and your family, and there won't be anyone left to talk about that visit. The same goes for your buddies. Make sure they understand."

The shaken boy got in and drove off. Peter looked around. The whole drama hadn't lasted more than three minutes. The girl was standing about fifteen feet away, and no one else was outside the gas station to have seen or heard anything. Peter walked slowly toward the girl.

"Are you okay," he said, "Did those assholes hurt you?"

The girl replied, "No, I'm fine. I don't think they would really have done anything, and it was mostly my fault anyway. After they had me clean all their windows, and check their oil and water, they weren't giving me any tip, just rude comments, so I kept a couple of bucks of their change. Anyway, thanks for helping me out. My name is Brook. Do you need gas? What were you telling that guy?"

"Hi Brook, yes I need to fill up my cycle. Call me Stef, its short for Stephan. I was just telling him to get his friend to a hospital and to think twice before bothering a pretty girl next time."

After she topped off his gas and brought his change, he said, "You can keep that, just to show that not all of us are like those jerks. I am heading for a party now. You're welcome to join. When are you finished here?"

"I am pretty much finished for today now," she said. "In fact, this is my last day. I already have my check and was just doing those guys as my last customer before hitching into the Falls. Could I get a lift home after the party?"

Peter was amazed that it could be that easy. "Sure," he said, "I'll be happy to drop you off. What's your address? I'll just put it into my GPS."

Minutes later they were underway, the girl holding him loosely around the waist for balance. Peter backtracked east on the highway and turned south on Meadow Creek Road.

As they slowed for the turn, Brook said, "Wouldn't it be quicker to go west into the Falls."

Before throttling back up Peter replied, "We are going to a club house outside of the Falls, and this is the best way. Hang on tight."

Brook was beginning to wonder if she had made a mistake in accepting this guy's invitation. She had just broken up with her boyfriend Dan, who would otherwise have been picking her up and driving her home. They'd been dating all through their senior year at I.F. High School and she liked him but was tired of having to fend off his wandering hands every time they were alone. She had been raised as a good Mormon girl and, though she didn't follow many of the rules strictly, she wasn't ready to go as far as his hormones were insisting on. She had thought that a little cooling-off period would make him take her more seriously. This older guy was really nice, had a cool cycle that would get lots of attention in her neighborhood, and was really good-looking. At first she had thought that going to a party outside her usual crowd would further make her point with Dan. Now, she was starting to worry.

Brook's worries grew when after half an hour her ride pulled over and off the road in the middle of nowhere. She hadn't seen another vehicle or a house since just after leaving the highway. She asked, "What's going on? Why have we stopped?" As she prepared to run, though, she saw no option but to dash into the woods and hope she could lose him.

The man she knew as Stef replied, "Don't worry, we're almost there, but our club is a secret club, so guests always need to be blindfolded when we first bring them, until we know them better. It is just a club rule." And that was true, because he ran the club, and he had just made it a rule.

The man still seemed very friendly and nice. Brook wasn't sure anything was wrong. She doubted she could outrun him, and even if she could, she knew she was miles and miles away from anywhere she could get help. She was still worried but she didn't want to insult the man who had helped her out and had been nothing but pleasant to her. So she went along with the blindfold.

In fact, it was more than an hour later, after many turns and twists, before the motorcycle idled to a stop. Brook heard the man tell someone to "radio the farm and have the gate opened." Had she been able to see, she would have seen that they were on a small gravel lane beside a shed manned by two mean-looking men. Both were well armed, including a twelve-gauge shotgun and a CAR-15 with a thirty-round clip, though the weapons would have been out of sight in any case. They weren't usually necessary to persuade unwelcome visitors to turn around and go back to the farm road the lane led off of.

The bike was immediately throttled back up and they continued for another ten minutes at a moderate speed before pulling up to a noisy gathering. Stef said, "We're here, let's get that blindfold off and get you a beer."

As she got her bearings, Brook could see several houses and what looked like a large barn. There were thirty or forty people in view, mostly gathered

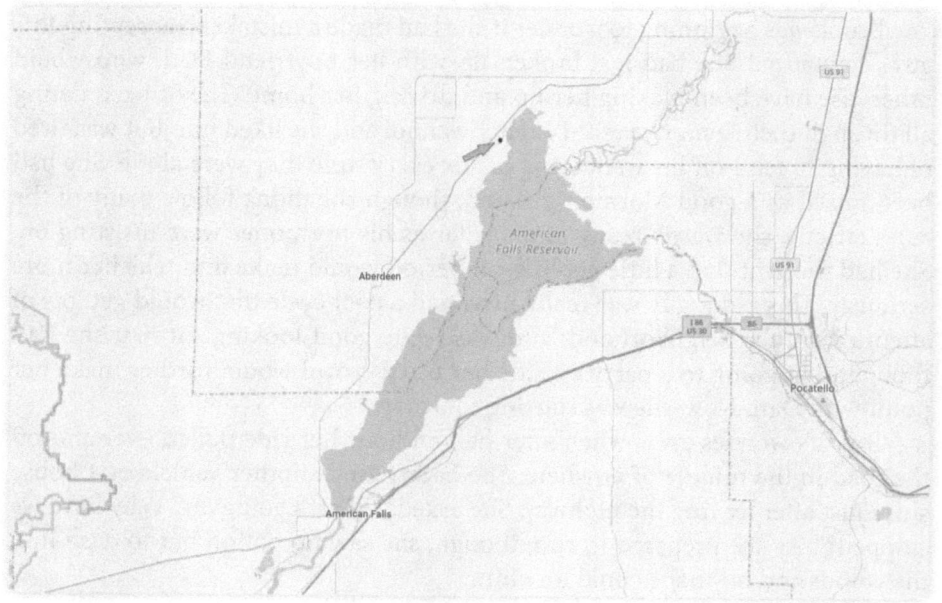

around a fire, drinking. A large iron spit was suspended over the fire by two iron posts, each with a V-shaped bracket on the top to hold the spit. The spit held a good-sized pig and was being gradually turned by a handle at one end. In the distance she could see the ground sloping away from the buildings down to what looked like a large pond or a small lake. She couldn't see enough to know she was looking out at a bay on the northwestern shoreline of the American Falls Reservoir, and she didn't see a large gate being closed one hundred yards behind her, restoring the razor wire perimeter fence line that surrounded the club on all four sides.

Peter wasn't under any illusion that his security arrangements would stand off any organized state or federal police force. His primary defense was a low profile. The location of the club house, or "the farm," was a closely kept secret that was not to be divulged to anyone outside the club, literally on pain of death. The nearest farmhouse was ten miles away, the nearest village was further. Club members were not to travel to or from the clubhouse in groups of more than three and were to use a variety of routes. There was no post box, no address, no phone line and no power. The place had an effective modern solar and battery system and a backup diesel generator. Propane and diesel fuel were trucked in using the club's half-ton truck.

Peter's secondary line of defense, if ever required, would be flight. The back side of the farm yard, toward the reservoir, had another gate that accessed myriad trails through the wooded flanks of the reservoir. The outpost and gate security were only to warn of and delay any incursion by law enforcement while the rest of the club rolled their bikes out the rear gate and down the hillside into the woods, before starting up and scattering. The security team were to shoot only to keep heads down, and to surrender after a few minutes. They would do time but would be looked after. Most of the rest would escape.

As Peter kicked his bike up onto its stand, the group around the pig roast quieted down and one of them, Peter's lieutenant Ruddy, called out, "How'd the pick-up go, boss?"

"It went just fine. Call me Stef, not boss. You can stash it in the house for now, and I'll want three teams of two to handle the drop off runs in the morning," replied Peter. "This is Brook. She is partying with us, just for the evening, so someone fetch us both a beer. By the way, where did the pig come from?"

Ruddy chuckled, "Sure Stef, we'll have to see some ID for Brook though, she sure doesn't look twenty-one! The pig was donated to our party by a farmer. Don't worry, it came from well outside your hands-off zone."

Peter insisted that his members not hassle or intimidate anyone within a distance of at least fifty miles in all directions to avoid drawing attention to their locality. In point of fact, there was no need for any extracurricular violence or robbery. The club had ample income from its activities; and bank accounts and mutual fund portfolios, spread among many locations, that would rival even the wealthiest landowners in Idaho. They could afford to buy anything they needed or wanted.

Brook remained uneasy. There seemed to be an undercurrent to the conversations around her, and from the number of motorcycles parked behind the main house it was clear that she was the guest at a motorcycle club. That wasn't what she had expected when she accepted Stef's invitation, but as she thought back through their conversation, she couldn't say that he had done anything to deceive her. She decided she had no choice but to make the best of it, sipping tentatively at her beer, and nibbling on a bun filled with barbecued pork. Her host stuck close by and soon took her toward the main house saying, "Come on, I'll show you around a bit."

Once inside, she was briefly toured around an unremarkable main floor before being led upstairs and into a room off the main corridor. As he closed the door behind them, the man said, "This is my room. It's completely private in here. You are a stunningly beautiful girl and I want you very badly." He took both of her shoulders, bent over and kissed her hungrily on the lips.

She tried to twist out of his grip and said, "No, please, I don't want this. I hardly know you. I want to go home. You said you would take me home."

The man replied in a husky voice, "Relax, I will take you home, or one of the boys will, after we've had our fun together, and it will be a lot more fun than flashing your tits around a gas station lot." He kissed her again, forced her over to the bed and snapped a plastic handcuff on one wrist, the other end of which was fastened to a sturdy pine bedpost. He then stripped her T-shirt over her head and along the cuffed arm, leaving her naked from the waist up. Her breasts were small, slightly pointed as the tips merged into the nipples, but standing out firmly from her chest without a trace of a sag, and only just fully developed. His need seized him in its own irresistible grip.

She was now bawling her eyes out and struggling ineffectually to get her T-shirt back over her head and to cover her breasts at the same time. Through her sobs she cried, "No, I'm not like that. I don't do this. I have never done anything like this. I don't want you to kiss me or touch me. Please, please, let me go and take me home."

He drew her free arm away from her chest and locked a second cuff on it, pulling a strap tight to force both arms slightly away from her body. He said, "Listen to me and listen carefully. I would prefer that we did this together, and that you enjoyed it as much as I am going to, but if not, that's okay. It will still be good for me. You can relax and enjoy it, or scream and fight, but it won't change anything. They will barely hear you outside the house, and none of them will mess with our fun. After that, there is no one to hear anything for miles and miles.

"After we are through, one of my boys will drive you home, again with a blindfold for most of the way. He will drop you a few blocks from your house, but remember, I know exactly where you live. So, keep our fun here tonight between you and me for two reasons. First, if I hear anything about it in the news or in the police reports I have access to, I will visit you and your family. I will hurt you all. I will hurt you very badly, so badly that this evening will seem like a picnic. Second reason, if you keep our little bit of fun completely secret, it will be over and will have no effect on the rest of your life. If you blab, not only will your family suffer horribly, but everyone will treat you differently from then on — the girl who ran with a motorcycle gang. Think about it carefully."

By that point she had stopped struggling, partly from physical exhaustion, partly from the exhaustion of fear. He reached over and unbuttoned her jean shorts and tugged the zipper down, peeling off the shorts and blue panties in one quick motion. She began to kick and scream but he captured one leg at a time into ankle cuffs attached to the foot of the bed.

She lay there spread-eagled on the bed, still bucking and writhing but with diminishing strength. Caught up now irrevocably in his own animal passion, he barely heard her futile pleas.

Chapter 6

September 2, 2027
Washington, DC

"Hello Eli," greeted President Rushton, "I am glad you can join me for a sandwich today so we can continue my education on global warming." The president ushered Dr. Eli Wayman along a short interior corridor to the private dining room where sandwiches and a choice of beverages awaited. "I got a lot out of our last briefing, but we ran out of time before you could tell me whether we are winning or losing in the war against global warming. Can you please pick the story up from there?"

"Certainly, Mr. President," Eli responded. "There's good news and bad news. Here in the U.S. we have made a good start and so has our neighbor to the north, Canada, and in fact, so have most of the G7 advanced industrialized nations. The Paris Agreement, which we all signed in 2016, committed us collectively to cut greenhouse gas emissions with the objective of limiting temperature increases to at most 3.6 degrees Fahrenheit and preferable only 2.7 degrees. That's a pretty ambitious objective given that we were already up by something like 2 degrees at that time. However, the likelihood of achieving even the higher limit is questionable given that each signatory was left to voluntarily set their own nationally determined contribution or NDC.

"We set our own NDC at a net emissions reduction of 26 percent to 28 percent below the 2005 baseline, to be achieved by 2025. We also set a longer-term goal of an 83 percent reduction by 2050. Back then we were producing about 18 percent of the world's emissions with only 4 percent of the population. So, in fairness, we have more of the burden to shoulder.

"In comparison, China accounted for about 20 percent of global emissions back in 2016, with about 18 percent of the population. Its NDC actually involves increasing greenhouse gas emissions by as much as 35 percent by 2030 relative to a 2010 benchmark, before peaking at that level. In 2016 India was the fourth largest emitter, producing 4 percent of emissions but with 18 percent of the population and a seemingly not very ambitious NDC, which would result in a 100 percent increase in emissions by 2030 from a 2010 benchmark. Then there's

Russia, the third largest emitter with 8 percent of the total with only 2 percent of the world's population. Russia's NDC has been described as one of the weakest put forward by any signatory to the Paris Agreement, with a 2030 emission level of about 35 percent above 2010.

"Back to our own objectives — unfortunately we missed our own 2025 target. The Clean Power Plan instituted by the Obama administration, and the even broader Climate Action Plan, would have got us there but were largely suspended or dismantled by the Trump administration. Those elements that were subsequently reinstated, and then later even reinforced by you and President Mahally, were just too late to have had enough impact by 2025."

"Just a minute, Eli," the president interjected, "I'm not really hearing much of the good news you mentioned, only the bad. Of the world's four largest emitters of greenhouse gases, three of the four are planning to continue to increase emissions through 2030. We are the only one that is targeting to decrease and even we missed our 2025 target. So, help me find the good news in all this!"

"I am sorry, Mr. President," Eli replied, "if my choice of words painted too rosy a picture to start with. Certainly, if we measure our progress against a target of limiting the temperature gain to 2.7 degrees, or even 3.6 degrees, the overall picture is not good. However, let me comment on China and India, and put their increasing emission targets in context.

"Mr. President, as I am sure you already know, greenhouse gas emissions are primarily a result of consumption of energy by people in the form of fossil fuels; either directly, as when we burn fuel to power our automobiles and airplanes and warm our homes, or indirectly, as when we use electricity to light our homes or run our air conditioners and appliances, if that electricity is generated by burning coal or natural gas as most is. Also, our consumption of most other things, from food to disposable baby diapers, requires the use of energy to produce these things and transport them to where we live. Consumption of energy is essential to the standard of living of the developed countries. We here in the U.S. have the highest standard of living in the world, which means we each use a great deal of energy and we generate proportionally more than four times the greenhouse gases than our share of the world's population. That four to one relationship between greenhouse gas emissions and population is much the same for most of the developed nations and, of course, the rest of the world aspires to our standard of living, or at least something closer to it than what they have at present.

"So, Mr. President, if China were to develop its economy to achieve just half of the standard of living we enjoy, but using the energy sources and efficiencies of 2016, they would actually have to double their emissions of greenhouse gases compared to 2016. Instead they have committed to a much tougher target of only a 35 percent increase above their 2010 benchmark — which is actually just a 16 percent increase from their 2016 level — and capping at no higher than that level thereafter. The picture for India is similar but coming from even further behind us in terms of standard of living, compounded by the most rapidly growing population in the world. So, a 100 percent increase in emissions is a pretty reasonable target after all."

"Okay Eli, I get that China and India are actually doing their bit now that you lay it out that way. I suppose that there's an explanation for Russia too is there?" asked President Rushton.

Eli paused and chose his words carefully, "Mr. President, I believe you are aware that I have been a vocal advocate of American support for Israel, and therefore I am not a fan of Russia, which has aided some of Israel's strongest opponents. So, I am perhaps not totally objective when it comes to Russia. That said, no, I don't see a benign explanation for Russia's 35 percent increase target. Russia's 2016 emissions per capita were similar to ours and the rest of the developed world. So, like us, they should have been targeting a reduction as their fair share of contribution to achieving the Paris Agreement objective. Russia certainly has its own challenges. It's a northern country so must use more energy for heating, and solar energy is much less effective at those latitudes. They are also a very large, spread-out country so must use more energy for transportation. But other developed countries, like Canada, face similar challenges.

"Mr. President, I think what it comes down to in Russia's case is that, although they were signatories to the Paris Agreement, their political leadership at that time and still today has little interest in climate change mitigation compared with their other priorities. Frankly, although their feeble efforts to limit greenhouse gases are a problem, that's not their biggest threat to global well-being by a long shot! I am sorry, Mr. President, I have strayed from the subject."

"Eli, I appreciate it when a spade is called a spade," the president said, "and I share your concerns about the true priorities of the Russian bear. So, please continue."

"Yes, Mr. President. I will try to finish on a little more positive note, now that I have laid the groundwork. I think you have gotten the point that, although curtailing global greenhouse gas emissions is the prudent thing to do, it's also a very difficult thing to do on the required scale given the linkages between standard of living, energy use and emissions. No nation is going to accept a cut in its standard of living and some of the most populous are compelled to significantly improve theirs, along with continued growth in their populations. With that in mind, here's where I think there is some good news. First, as the Paris Agreement demonstrates, there is now a global focus on curtailing emissions, with a few notable exceptions. The emission reduction targets we have each voluntarily adopted may not be sufficient to limit temperature increases below the 2.7 to 3.6 degrees Fahrenheit Paris Agreement objective, and some may not be doing enough to achieve their targets, but nearly every signatory to the Paris Agreement is working seriously on curtailing emissions. Something is being done. The nations of the world have been mobilized, and that's no small achievement.

"Second, I'd like to come back to our own track record. It is true that we missed our 2025 target, but we didn't miss it by much and our actions are now accelerating, so we could well be back on track by 2030. There are basically four broad points of attack on emissions. One is conservation, simply adopting a less wasteful and less energy-intensive lifestyle, or even a less consumption-oriented lifestyle. Our culture has actually shifted a fair bit in this direction over the last decade. I think that was reflected in the success of the election campaign that you and President Mahally recently won on a moderate but pro-environment platform. This culture shift is especially pronounced among the younger generations, but that will make an increasing difference if new generations follow in their footsteps. And that is another important piece of good news."

"Okay, Eli," said the president. "As usual, I jumped the gun before hearing the whole story. I am really glad to hear that our people, especially our young people, are changing the way that they think about life, liberty and the pursuit of happiness. You are right, that really is good news."

"Another point of attack is energy efficiency — accomplishing the same result in a better way, using less energy. This applies to all energy using activities, both by people directly and within industry. In contrast to conservation, this is a matter of technology improvements rather than culture change. Again, we are making good progress on this front.

"Then there's the third point of attack, shifting the energy mix to less emission-intensive sources. The worst offender here has been coal plants and ours will eventually all be shut down. There are some replacement energy sources that are emissions free, like hydro, geothermal, solar, wind and nuclear power. Hydro and geothermal are great in the locations where they are available, but those are limited. Solar and wind have tended to be expensive, though technological and manufacturing advances have improved their affordability. They also are not practical in locations that have limited sunshine or lack steady winds. Even in relatively good locations they need to be backed up by a secondary source of power for periods when sunshine or wind is lacking, at least until we can make further progress with low-cost power storage technology. Wind and solar power infrastructure also have their own aesthetic and environmental issues to contend with, especially as they become more ubiquitous.

"Nuclear power does not emit greenhouse gases, but there remains a high level of public mistrust with this source. So, although we are making good progress with eliminating coal burning plants, and a good part will be replaced with non-emitting renewable sources, most of the replacement power will have to come from natural gas. That is still good progress, since natural gas combustion releases only a little more than half the greenhouse gases that coal combustion does per unit of energy released, but it does limit how quickly and how far we can go to limit global warming while maintaining our standard of living.

"Then there's the fourth point of attack, which is carbon capture. The most effective way to do this is by growing forests. Other plants, including edible crops like corn, capture carbon dioxide from the air as well, but the harvesting process usually releases most of it back to the air. There is some forestation activity going on here in the U.S., but there is more potential in other countries. If fresh water were abundant, then reclaiming some of the world's deserts, including our own arid lands, would make a big difference. However, availability of fresh water is becoming as big a problem as global warming, maybe bigger — but that's a discussion for another day.

"So, Mr. President, here in the U.S., although we got off to a slow start, we are starting to make some good progress on each of these fronts. Some of this reflects voluntary conservation actions by Americans, part of the culture change I mentioned earlier, that likely would have occurred without any policy incentives. A lot of it is due to state-level policies, like renewable power portfolio standards. Some of it has been initiated by the reinstitution of many of the elements of the Obama administration's Clean Power Plan and Climate Action Plan.

"With no intent to engage in flattery, Mr. President, I think what is now giving reinforced impetus to all four points of attack is the trilateral carbon tax and credit system, which you and President Mahally negotiated with Canada and Mexico and had ratified by congress by mid-2025. That tax of $50 per ton of carbon dioxide emitted, which increases by $5 each year for the following ten years, is providing a real incentive for people and businesses to conserve, be more efficient and produce more efficient products, and use energy from lower emission energy sources. It is really working in tandem with the culture change and technology progress I mentioned earlier. Many people already want to live a less consumerist, energy-profligate lifestyle, and you've given them an increasingly strong incentive to do so. So, Mr. President, I do stand by my original statement that there is both bad news and good in our track record so far."

"Thanks, Eli," said the president, "I am glad to hear that you think the Carbon Tax and Credit Act is helping, though I think we have to give President Mahally the credit for the masterful personal leadership and persuasiveness required to get three democratic national governments on board in a few short months.

My role was limited to working with the secretaries of Energy, Commerce and Treasury, as well as the chair of the Council of Economic Advisors and the director, National Economic Council, to design the system. We wanted to provide strong incentives to curb greenhouse gases but with minimal adverse effects on employment and income. That's why 100 percent of the net revenue from the system is being applied to reduce federal corporate and personal taxes. So, even though the price of gasoline will have increased by 25 percent by 2035 at a $100 per ton carbon tax, and many other things will be more expensive too, a lot of the pain will be offset by having lower taxes, though not all of it. I only wish Tim were here to see the results.

"Anyway," the president continued, "I agree, that there is some good news as you said, it's not all bad; but where does that leave us? Are we going to be successful in avoiding global warming and its harmful effects — what is the bottom line?"

"Mr. President, I am sorry to say that it appears unlikely that the objectives of the Paris Agreement will be achieved. Although many countries, like us, are taking serious actions to curtail carbon dioxide emissions and, as a result, global warming will be less than it would otherwise have been, the collective actions do not appear to be sufficient to limit warming to 2.7 or even 3.6 degrees. The best we can achieve with current actions and technology will probably be closer to 5 degrees. The reductions in emissions required from the developed nations in order to counterbalance the growth in energy consumption by the developing nations would just be too much to accept. The impact on the economies of the developed nations and on their standard of living would be too great to be sustained in a democracy. As a species we will survive, though other species will not, and many individuals among us will suffer; however, it would be quite a bit worse in the absence of the Paris Agreement."

"Eli, I know you are being objective and spelling out the most likely outcome that science can predict, but surely there's something more we could do. What would it take? Do we have any other options?" the president asked unhappily.

"Well, Mr. President, what it would really take would be a source of energy that doesn't emit greenhouse gases, doesn't have any harmful or risky side effects, and is plentiful and inexpensive. In theory such a source exists — nuclear fusion, a different type of atomic reaction than the uranium-based fission reaction that powers our existing nuclear power plants. Fusion produces more energy than fission and doesn't leave radioactive waste behind. However, it would still encounter the same fear factor as fission does. In any case, although good people have been working on it for quite a while, a workable fusion reactor still seems a long way away. Never count technology and human ingenuity out though.

"In terms of other options, Mr. President, I would be remiss if I didn't mention the field of geoengineering and in particular, stratospheric sulfate aerosol injection. Geoengineering in general refers to deliberate manipulation of the climate, as opposed to the unintentional impacts of human activity that are giving rise to global warming. There are numerous geoengineering concepts for cooling the Earth to offset greenhouse gases. The most effective, but also controversial approach, is to inject sulfate aerosols into the upper stratosphere using aircraft. Sulfate aerosols tend to work the opposite of greenhouse gases. They reflect some of the sunlight away from the Earth, preventing it from reaching the surface rather than trapping it at the surface. It is sulphate aerosols that are the reason large volcanic eruptions tend to produce a temporary cooling effect.

"Theoretically, injection of sulphate aerosols would be a low-cost, effective and rapid way to cool the Earth, and it is reversible since they would settle out of the stratosphere in a few years if they did not get regularly replenished. However, we don't know for sure because all the work to date has been through computer simulations with no real-world test data. This approach is highly controversial, with opposition ranging from theology to concern with potential side effects to concern that it would diminish the motivation to address the human causes of global warming. Nevertheless, geoengineering is an option and could be used temporarily to buy us time for greenhouse gas curtailment, based on current and potential new technology, to take fuller effect.

"Mr. President, I think I've used up more than I should of your time again. I hope it has been worthwhile for you. If you like, I can talk more about nuclear fusion and geoengineering the next time we get together."

"Eli, thank you again for bringing me up to speed on this whole subject area. I don't think I am going to sleep any better because of it, but I do need to know what we are facing, and I will need to think on what more we should do about it. I'll let you pick the topic for our next session though. I am sure there are lots of other things that I should also be aware of." The president shook hands with the senior advisor as he let him out the front door of the dining room, directly into the main corridor and past the secret service agent stationed there. Although he didn't know it, he would soon have more pressing reasons to lose sleep over than long-term global warming.

Chapter 7

September 15, 2027
Boston, Massachusetts

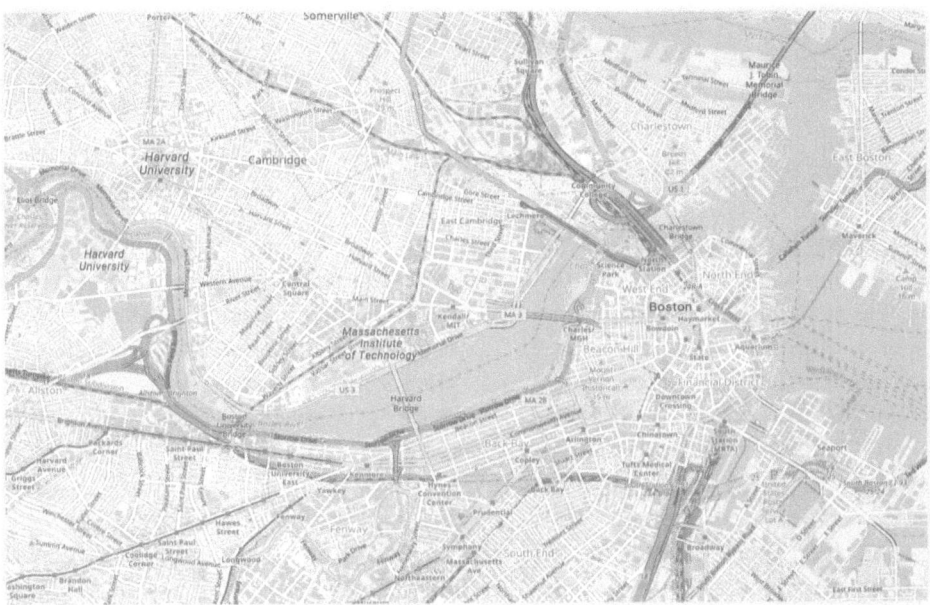

There was just enough light to make out the sidewalk as Larry emerged from Tang Hall at six o'clock in the morning, switched his phone's clock to stopwatch mode, adjusted his headlamp, and headed down Audrey Street and across Memorial Drive. He turned upstream on the path along the Charles River and settled into a steady six-mile-an-hour pace. At twenty-eight years old, Larry wasn't a huge jock, but he liked to get in three runs a week, with usually one longer run on the weekend. He alternated run days with his gym days. This morning he was eager to get back to his lab and check the overnight results, but he still planned on an eight-mile loop along the river, picking up the pace for the last two miles to get the endorphins flowing.

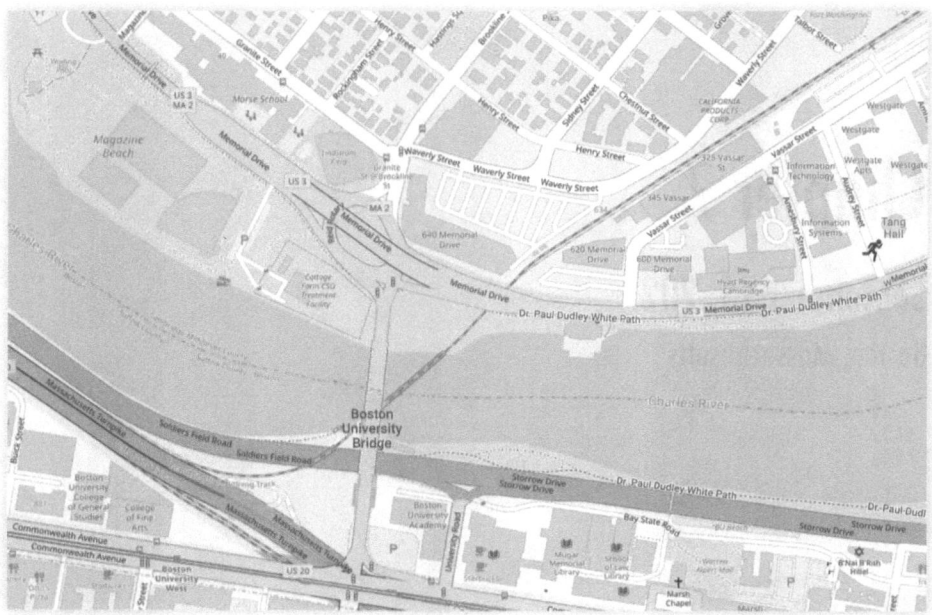

Larry Johnstone worked as a research engineer, a post-doctoral fellow under the supervision of a full professor at the MIT faculty of engineering, where he had recently graduated with his PhD in chemical engineering practice, with a minor in materials science. His passion was fresh water, as reflected in his doctoral thesis, "Cell Geometry, Membrane Properties, and Electrode Composition Impacts on Electrical Efficiency of Capacitive Desalination." He would tell family and friends that it was just a fancy way of saying "how to make fresh water cheaper."

Larry passed the Boston University Bridge, sticking to the Cambridge side of the river. He enjoyed running in the early morning — the cool air and quiet. He crossed to the Boston side at the John W. Weeks Footbridge connecting the two sides of the Harvard campus. There were a few other runners on the path as he turned downstream, and through tendrils of mist he could just make out several silhouettes of sculls warming up out on the water, both eights and fours. The crisp commands of the coxswains were audible over the dark water, contributing to the surreal feeling of the morning.

Larry's current work was a continuation of his thesis research — basically experimenting with a few different design variables, each of which would individually lower the power required to turn a gallon of seawater into a half gallon of fresh water and a half gallon of very salty brine. His objective was to unravel the nonlinear interaction of these variables to find a combined design where they would reinforce each other. He was fortunate that his supervisor

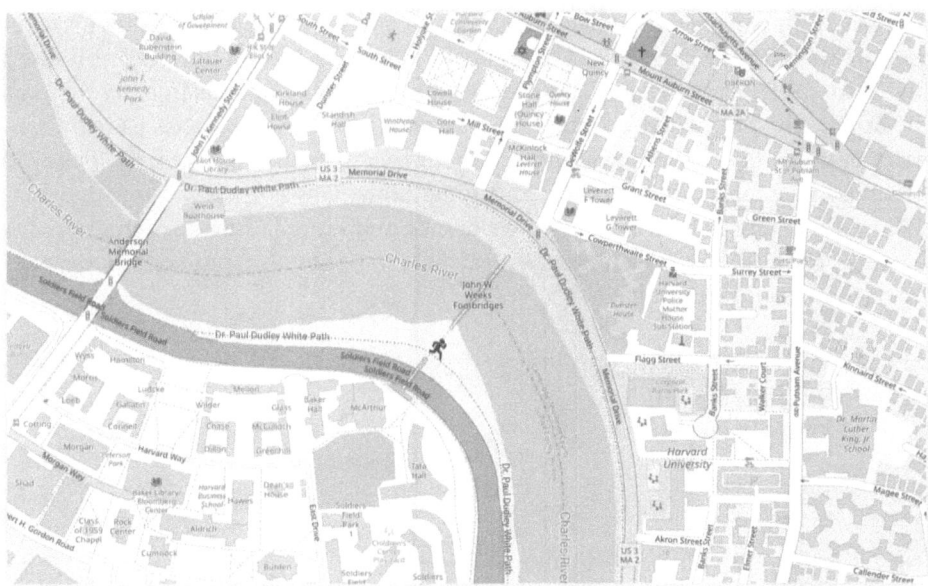

believed his work was promising enough to have secured a fellowship that provided laboratory facilities and funding for the equipment and materials he needed and allowed him to keep his small apartment in Tang Hall.

The young man was keen to make a difference for the better in the world. As he passed the Boston University Bridge on the Boston side heading toward the harbor, he reflected on what he believed was one of the greatest obstacles to a better future for mankind — probably the greatest one — the increasing scarcity of fresh water. He knew that only 2.5 percent of the world's water was fresh, and of that 69 percent was frozen in glaciers and ice fields and 30 percent was underground, leaving only 1 percent readily accessible as surface water in lakes, rivers, and swamps.

With only 1 percent of the fresh water, or 0.025 percent of total water, readily accessible, what was making matters worse was that much of that water was concentrated in geographic areas with low populations — Canada and Russia. Use of water for agricultural purposes was rapidly depleting the available supply in many countries, with acute chronic shortages prevalent in India, the Middle East and much of Africa. Some people in these areas were already dying of thirst, but many more were facing starvation due to insufficient water to irrigate the arid fields. Growing populations in these places were driving water depletion ever more rapidly toward a massive crisis. Even in the United States, regional shortages were increasing. The mighty Colorado River is a dry river bed in its southern reaches, drained to support agriculture in the sweltering Imperial Valley in California and the Mexicali Valley in Baja California, Mexico.

The Sun was peeking above the horizon as Larry reached the downstream end of his planned run at the Longfellow Bridge. He turned to retrace his steps back to the Massachusetts Avenue Bridge, gradually increasing his pace as he approached the final quarter. He was concerned about global warming, in part because he knew it would exacerbate fresh water shortages. He believed strongly in energy conservation and greenhouse gas emission curtailment as being important for the long-term welfare of mankind, but he knew that people would perish in larger numbers — and much sooner — from water shortages than they would from heat.

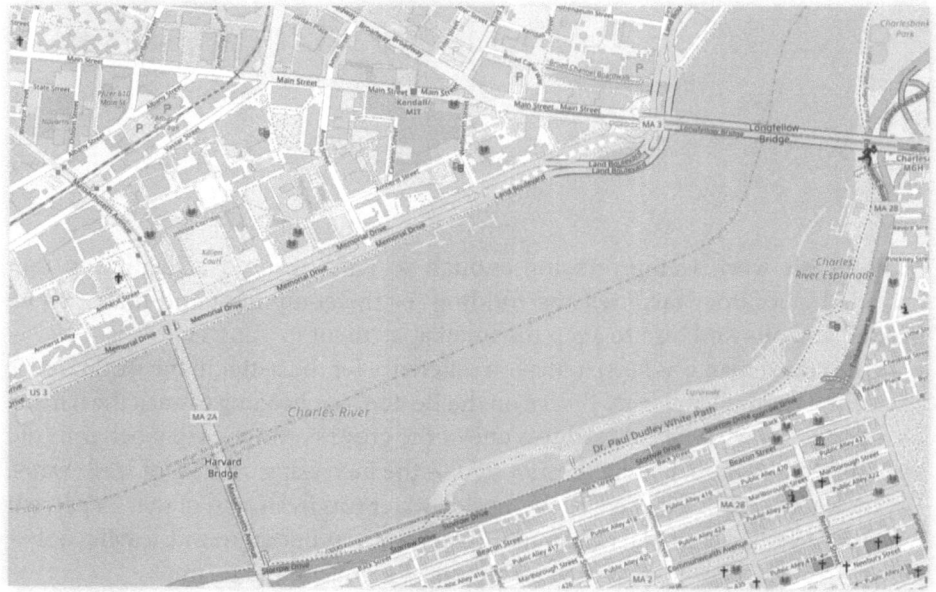

He reached the Massachusetts Avenue Bridge and crossed back to the Cambridge side, upping his pace still further for the final mile back to Audrey Street. Larry believed that water conservation was as important as energy conservation, but doubted it would be enough to overcome shortages in the hotter, drier, more populous regions of the world. However, if only a small portion of the 97.5 percent of the water in the world's oceans could be converted to fresh water economically, then there would be ample fresh water for all, at least anywhere within pipeline distance of a coast, and that was Larry's vision.

Technically it was quite possible to desalinate seawater, and that was being done in small quantities in many places to provide drinking water. However, the existing technologies were relatively energy intensive and therefore expensive and not suitable for the large volumes of fresh water required for agricultural purposes.

Larry's objective was to reduce the energy required to convert salt water into fresh water to a tenth or less of the best existing technology. At the same time, he knew he needed to avoid exotic and expensive materials for his membranes and electrodes. This wasn't cutting-edge theoretical research that would revolutionize man's understanding of the physical world, like the work of Albert Einstein or Peter Higgs or Saul Perlmutter; it was basic engineering design and process control blocking and tackling. Larry had some theoretical models and simulations to guide him, but much of his work was trial and error, building up a database of what worked well and what didn't. He knew that research and engineering had reduced the cost of computing power significantly, so he was confident that his persistence would eventually achieve a similar payoff. And he thought he was close, very close.

As he reached the foot of Audrey Street, Larry slowed to a walk and stopped his timer. He was breathing heavily after his sprint over the last quarter-mile. He checked his time and was pleased to see just over an hour — *not bad for a nerd*, he thought. He walked on for a few minutes to cool down, enjoying the moment as the early morning Sun began to light up the riverside hardwoods, with the brilliant reds and oranges of the New England autumn just starting to appear. Larry loved the Boston climate — a little cool and damp in winter but with pleasant temperatures for most of the year. He knew that the Charles had occasionally frozen solid enough to walk across as recently as the last decade, but winters were milder these days.

By eight o'clock in the morning, Larry, having showered and breakfasted, unlocked the door of his lab. A desk equipped with a high-end desktop computer took up one wall of the lab, a stainless steel workbench covered with various pieces of equipment and materials, as well as a number of microprocessors for process control and measurement, took up another two. Three open-topped thousand-gallon tanks stood in the middle of the room with various pieces of clear plastic tubing connecting them to the apparatus on the bench. One tank was labelled "salt water," one "brine," and one "fresh water." Several fifty-pound bags of salt were stacked in a corner — it was simpler to make seawater on site than to fetch it from the harbor. Each of the tanks had a hydrometer floating on the top to provide a quick check on salinity levels, though more exact and continuous measurements were being taken by in-line refractometers attached to the inlet and outlet tubing and tied into the recording microprocessor.

Larry pulled up a stool in front of the recording microprocessor and called up a summary of the overnight performance of his latest set of cell design parameters. He was already excited because he could see that his fresh water tank was almost half filled in the twelve hours since he had started the run. The summary display confirmed over four hundred gallons of production, which wasn't much in absolute terms, but it was a small laboratory-scale cell, so the amount of fresh water production wasn't as important as the power consumption, and that showed just what he had hoped — a paltry 0.6 kilowatt hours, about the same amount of power required to light a fifty-watt bulb for twelve hours. He checked the salinity level of the input stream and the brine and fresh water outputs, and all were correct, with no degradation in the fresh water purity over the duration of the run. Power consumption was also constant as was the rate of water production.

Larry switched on the recycle pumps to send the fresh water and brine back to the salt water tank and reset the measurement system to run the same test a second time. He also turned on a local radio station for background noise as he moved over to his desk to send a brief report to his supervisor. He knew he still had a long way to go, including a little further design refinement, independent verification, and scaling up, first to a pilot plant and ultimately to a large utility-scale plant, without losing the power efficiency achieved in his laboratory apparatus. Nevertheless, he was excited by the path ahead.

Larry wasn't paying much attention to the news summary, but the latest update on Carrie, an intense cyclonic system tracking from the central Atlantic west toward Bermuda and North Carolina, caught his attention. Carrie was now a full Category 5 storm and still growing in size and strength, and the computer models were showing a high likelihood that it would begin to swing north and make landfall on the New England coast with a potential surge of twenty feet or more. The newscaster said that the governors of all the coastal states were advising residents in low-lying areas to be prepared to evacuate, and all others to have sufficient food and water on hand for an extended interruption of power and services. As he finished his report and emailed it off, Larry mused on the relative risks of climate change versus fresh water scarcity. Time would tell — less time than he imagined.

Chapter 8

October 1, 2027
Washington, DC

The upshot of the president's daily intelligence briefing that day was that the Russian bear was sharpening its claws. The available intelligence pointed strongly to a ramp up in Russian activity in Libya, arming and funding one of the local factions sharing a fragile balance of power in the fragmented North African country. It appeared to be a deliberate and early test of the new president's degree of interest in the Mediterranean and Middle East, probably with the hope of making some inroads on the watch of an inexperienced, unelected president. Jim wasn't the kind of leader to stand by and let that happen, unaware that he would soon have much bigger problems to deal with.

While his intelligence advisors packed up their briefing books, Jim spoke to his chief of staff, "Will, let's have these folks run through the situation in Libya again in the next few days, bringing in the secretaries of state and defense. Once we have a response plan, I'll want to communicate with my counterparts in the UK, continental Europe, and our allies in the Middle East."

Will responded that he would get right on it. He stayed behind as the others filed into the Oval Office proper and then out. He had booked fifteen minutes for himself to go over the priorities of the next few days with the president.

At the end of their brief meeting, Will confirmed with President Rushton that he was comfortable with his itinerary. As Will prepared to depart, he said, "Mr. President, I know you are not keen to seek an elected term come next year. However, the senior leadership of the Democratic National Committee has asked to get some time on your calendar in the next while. From what I am hearing, they will ask you to consider running for the party's nomination and they will support you if you will. Mr. President, that's not an automatic conclusion on their part. It has been carefully thought out. Although you haven't yet established your own distinct presidential image, you are strongly associated with our popular late president as an important part of his successful team. They have done a lot of sounding out and are convinced that you will have broad support within the party and would win the election."

Jim sighed and replied, "Will, of course I will meet with the leadership and hear them out. You are correct though. I don't plan to run the gauntlet of the primaries and then an election campaign. There's lots of important work to be done that I will need to focus my attention on. I took on the vice presidency at the request of President Mahally, whom I greatly respected. But I'm not a politician, and as much as I liked and respected Tim Mahally, I don't really want to ride the coattails of a sympathy vote to the leadership of this country. So, I will do the best I can at this job for the next year and a quarter but then leave it to someone who is better suited."

Will wasn't surprised at this response, and he didn't capitulate, "Mr. President, you are right that the party is seeing this through a political lens and the sympathy vote is an important part of the calculation. But that's not why I hope you'll keep an open mind. I have watched you now for three years, as a campaigner, as a vice president and now as the president. You may not be a politician, but you are a leader, a very good leader, and that's what this country needs while we continue to put the extremes of our past politics behind us. I was very close to Tim Mahally, so I know you didn't join him just because he asked. You joined him because you believed in the centrist vision he espoused, and you still do. I know of no other person in the current political spectrum that is better able to carry that vision forward. Mr. President, you don't have to say yes to the party. There are still several months for you to mull it over before you will need to make a commitment. But, please don't say *no* just yet. Once you do, the momentum will begin to move in another direction and will be difficult to recapture. Please keep your options open for now."

As Will stepped out Jim noticed that he was a few minutes behind for his next appointment, another session with Dr. Eli Wayman, his science advisor, who was then ushered into the study by the president's personal secretary. "Hello again, Eli. What horrible problems are you going to educate me about today? Do you have anything up your sleeves to gain us friends and stability in North Africa?"

Eli chuckled, "Mr. President, it isn't really the role of your science advisor to bring you horrible problems. Really, I should be bringing you solutions. So, no, I didn't think we'd talk about problems today, though we can come back to global warming and geoengineering whenever you wish. Today I thought I'd run through with you the function of our Planetary Defense Coordination Office at the NASA headquarters here in DC. This is the agency through which you and I would be alerted to a risk of a significant asteroid strike on the Earth. Just to reassure you, none are currently expected, though one will come fairly close in 2029, and we will cover that."

Eli continued, "Mr. President, I know you were partly jesting about North Africa, but do you think that large volumes of low-cost fresh water could help whatever situation you are dealing with there? Coincidentally, I have heard just this week from a colleague at MIT who is overseeing some very promising research into low-cost, large-scale desalination technology. It's a little too soon to be sure, but it seems like they may have quite a breakthrough."

Rushton responded, "Yes I was jesting, but now that you mention it, maybe fresh water could help. It sure couldn't hurt. Tell me more about that when you think it is ready. Now, I am all ears to hear about the risk of asteroid strikes."

"Mr. President, let's begin with a refresher for you on what our solar system looks like, as we currently understand it, which is pretty well I think. It will help to look at a few images I've got here on my laptop."

COMPARATIVE SIZES OF SOLAR SYSTEM PLANETS

Eli angled is laptop toward the president so that he could see the screen clearly.

"This first one is just a simple illustrative depiction of the solar system with its four small solid inner planets and four outer gas giants. The size of the planets is shown pretty much to scale as they would appear if we were looking at a true image, and the planets all happened to be at a point in their orbits where they were all lined up in a row, which they never actually have been or will be. For example, Jupiter's diameter is roughly twelve times that of the Earth, roughly as it appears here.

"The distances between the planets as shown in this illustration are not to scale, however. For example, Jupiter is more than three times further from the Sun than its next innermost neighbor, Mars; whereas here it looks like it's only about twice as far out. More dramatically, Neptune, the outermost planet looks here to be only about twice as far out as Jupiter, but in reality it is way out in the cold, about six times further out. It is tricky to show the distances between the planets in an accurate linear scale because the range of distances is so great that to fit them all in one picture would squash the innermost planets together.

"There are a few other things that are worth noting here. First, the planets are all shown in one plane, like a row of marbles lying on a platter. Of course, space is three dimensional, unlike the surface of a platter, so in concept the planets could all orbit the Sun in a topsy-turvy array of different planes. In reality they do lie pretty much in a single flat plane with at most a few degrees difference between the inclinations of their orbits relative to Earth's orbit. This plane is referred to as the plane of the ecliptic. This is obviously too ordered to be an accident given the infinite number of alternative possibilities and is the result of how the Sun and the solar system formed from a whirling contracting hot cloud of gas about 4.8 billion years ago. The planets all orbit in roughly the same plane as that original cloud of gas did.

"Another thing to take note of is our apparent observer position. This picture is drawn as if we were in a space ship lying slightly above the plane of the ecliptic, looking down toward the planets at an angle of maybe thirty degrees. Of course, even the terms 'above' and 'below' are arbitrary in space, but in our Eurocentric culture we are used to thinking of the top of the world as being the north pole, which points at the star Polaris. So, we use the term 'above' in the space of the solar system to mean being on the same side of the plane of the ecliptic as is Polaris. Another common depiction would be where the observer position is directly above the plane of the ecliptic looking straight down from above the Sun. Another one is a sideways view as if our eyes are on the plane of the ecliptic. No one viewpoint is correct. It just depends on what we are trying to understand and conceptualize.

"The planets are all revolving about the Sun in their individual orbits. The direction of rotation is the same in every case, counterclockwise as viewed from 'above.' So, if this picture were animated, the planets would be swinging away from us. By the way, the Sun also spins on its own axis in a counterclockwise direction when viewed from 'above,' and all the planets except Venus and Uranus spin on their axes in the same counterclockwise direction. This common direction of revolution and rotation stems from the spin direction of the cloud of gas and dust from which the solar system originated, which then imparted the same spin to every solar body that was formed at that time. Venus, which has a very slow clockwise spin, and Uranus, with a more noticeable clockwise spin, were likely knocked off their original direction of spin by large collisions with other bodies."

Jim was again taking notes in his small notebook. He said, "That's all very interesting, and your illustration of our solar system is quite an eyeful. Please send me a copy of it."

"I certainly will, Mr. President, and I'll include the rest of the pictures that I am going to show you. Just delete any that you don't want to keep. The last thing I want you to absorb from this illustration, though, is the two circular rings of rocks that are also orbiting the Sun in the plane of the ecliptic. The first, which is called the asteroid belt, lies between the orbit of Mars and Jupiter, and the second, called the Kuiper belt, is way out beyond Neptune. These rings of rocks play a major role in the potential for an asteroid to impact the Earth. The illustration is a little misleading in that these chunks of rock are quite a bit more spread out than it appears, remembering that Jupiter is much further away from Mars than the scale of this illustration makes it seem, and likewise Neptune is much, much further from Jupiter than it looks here. There's also not as much material relative to the size of the planets as the illustration suggests. The total mass of the asteroid belt is only about 4 percent of the mass of our moon. The mass of the Kuiper belt is quite a bit larger than the asteroid belt, perhaps as much as four or five times the mass of our moon, but still far less than that of the Earth. Nevertheless, there are a lot of rocks in these rings ranging in size from pinheads up to Ceres in the asteroid belt, which is about six hundred miles in diameter, and Pluto in the Kuiper belt at fifteen hundred miles in diameter.

"Actually, it is a misnomer to call the objects within the Kuiper belt rocks. Unlike those in the asteroid belt, which are mostly dense nuggets of carbon or silica or nickel and iron, the Kuiper belt objects, or KBOs, are largely frozen volatiles such as methane, carbon dioxide, ammonia and water. If and when one of these balls of ice from the Kuiper belt, or even beyond, gets close enough to the Sun to begin to vaporize, it forms a glowing tail and is referred to as a comet.

"There is lots of action in both belts, with objects colliding with each other as well as being pushed around by Jupiter and Uranus. As a result, objects are often ejected from these belts, sometimes inward, possibly to collide with a planet or the Sun, sometimes outward into the farther reaches of the solar system or out of the system completely. In fact, both of these belts were originally much more massive than at present, having lost most of their original mass in the 4.8 billion years since the origin of the solar system.

"Although there are several other potential sources of medium to large solar system objects that could strike the Earth, these two belts are the primary sources. In fact, nearly all of the many meteorites that have been discovered on or below the Earth's surface appear to be from the asteroid belt. There have undoubtedly been collisions of comets into the Earth as well, though these appear to be much rarer and the heat from friction with the Earth's atmosphere would melt and vaporize all but the largest of comets before it could impact the Earth's surface. Much of the water on the Earth's surface has likely come from impacts of comets in the distant past. However, that doesn't rule out a comet strike in the future. We watched Shoemaker–Levy 9 plough into Jupiter in 1994, releasing massive amounts of destructive energy. Even if a large comet did vaporize before striking the Earth, the energy released by its vaporization could still leave a very destructive footprint beneath its flight path.

"Mr. President, I think that's as much mileage as we can get from this illustration, but I have a few more which I think will complete the picture of our solar system for you."

The president held up a hand and said, "Once again you are feeding me a lot of information, Eli. It's all fascinating and, so far, not too scary, but I have a suspicion that the scary part is yet to come. However, before we go on, can you come back to Pluto? You said there were only eight planets, four solid inner planets and four outer gas giants, leaving out Pluto, which was called the ninth planet when I was in school. Then, later you referred to Pluto as being part of the Kuiper belt. Why has Pluto been demoted as a planet?"

"Yes, sir," responded the science advisor. "That's a good question. Actually, the dividing line between what is a planet and what is not is largely arbitrary. Pluto is certainly smaller than any of the other planets — about half the size of Mercury and smaller even than our moon. Because it is made up of frozen gas, like the gas giants, it has a very low mass, about 5 percent of that of Mercury. The latest definition of a planet includes a requirement that it has to be big enough to have cleared the space around its orbital path of most other objects, either by drawing them into itself or flinging them away. With its low mass, Pluto has not been able to clear its orbit of the many, many Kuiper belt neighbors it has. So, back in 2006, Pluto was placed in a new category called 'dwarf planets,' along with several other recently discovered objects that are of similar size to Pluto and that have other planet-like characteristics except for not having cleared their orbits. An example of another dwarf planet is Eris, which orbits further out and is larger than Pluto. There are several more that have been identified, and probably two hundred others in the Kuiper belt that have not."

"Okay, I get the picture," said the president, "we either have eight planets or, if Pluto-sized objects are allowed to make the cut, we have dozens."

"Yes, Mr. President, which is a pretty good segue to the next picture I'd like to show you. Our solar system actually extends well beyond the Kuiper belt shown in the previous picture, and it has a lot more chunks of ice floating around than just those, like Pluto and Eris, in the Kuiper belt. This next illustration shows the eight planets, each with its orbital radius plotted

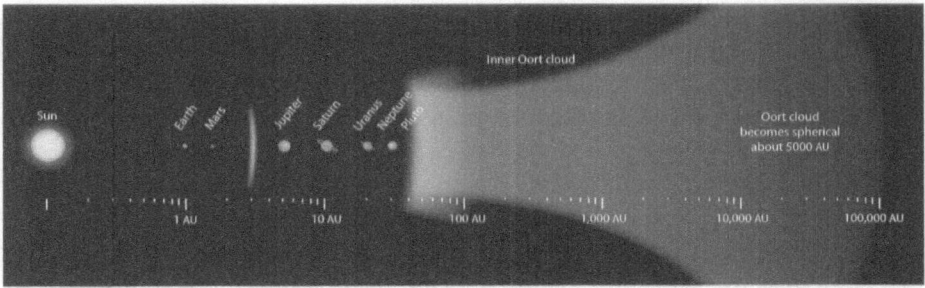

to a logarithmic scale measured in AU, or astronomical units. One AU is the distance of the Earth's orbital radius, about ninety-three million miles. Saturn is way out at ten AU, with Uranus and Neptune out quite a bit further at twenty and thirty AU.

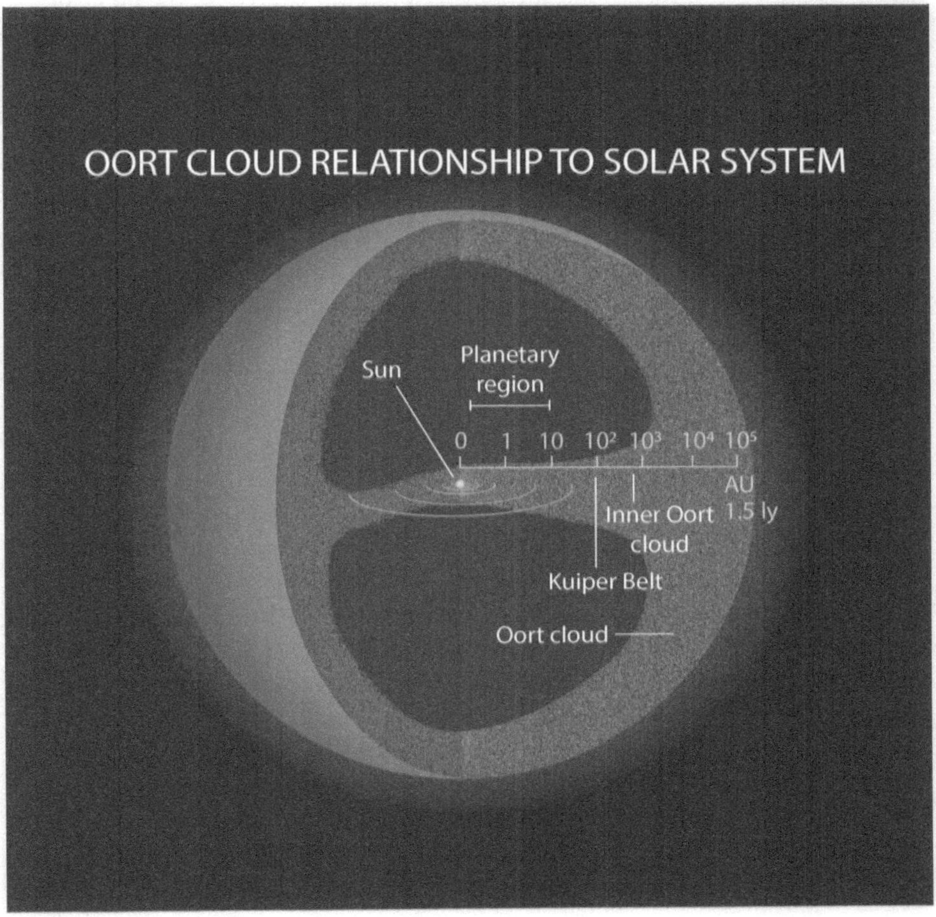

OORT CLOUD RELATIONSHIP TO SOLAR SYSTEM

"Our point of observation for this one is directly above the plane of the ecliptic, looking down. Once again, we see the eight planets, the asteroid belt and the Kuiper belt, all of which would be moving from the bottom of the picture toward the top as they revolve around the Sun in their counterclockwise orbits. What I want you to take note of is the expanding zone called the inner Oort cloud, beginning at the outer edge of the Kuiper belt at about one hundred astronomical units out, and extending way out beyond one thousand AU. The inner Oort cloud is shaped like a flat ring similar to the shape of the Kuiper belt — though much broader in extent — but the inner Oort cloud extends into the Oort cloud proper, which is actually a thick spherical shell surrounding the solar system at the great distance of five thousand to two hundred thousand AU.

"That third picture shows the Oort cloud itself in relationship to the rest of the solar system. The Oort cloud consists of about two trillion objects of varying sizes, primarily of the ice ball variety. Unlike the planets, the asteroid belt and the Kuiper belt, all of which revolve around the Sun within a few degrees of the plane of the ecliptic, the objects in the Oort cloud revolve around the Sun in a chaotic variety of different directions and planes. Unfortunately, from a collision watch perspective, this also means that they could come at us from just about any part of the sky.

"So, Mr. President, you now have a pretty full picture of the playing field. As we've already touched on, there are three broad types of things that can fall out of the sky on top of us. There are asteroids, hard rocky or metallic objects, originating primarily from the asteroid belt but at some time those that now approach close to Earth have been thrown out of the belt and into a new orbit. Most of the objects we need to worry about are of this type. A near-Earth object, or NEO, is any asteroid or comet that follows an orbital path that lies inside or reaches within 1.3 AU of the Sun. In simple terms, it is an object that can get fairly close to Earth, which itself orbits at a pretty constant distance of one AU from the Sun. Of the known NEOs, there are many thousands of asteroids but only a few hundred comets.

"Then there are the ice ball comets that come in two types. There are the short-period comets that originated from the Kuiper belt and have elliptical or elongated, rather than circular, orbits, but which lie near the plane of the ecliptic. The most well-known short-period comet is Halley's Comet, which completes an orbit of the Sun every seventy-six years or so and becomes very visible for a few weeks at its closest approach to the Sun and the Earth. Halley's Comet is due to return next in 2061.

"Then there are the long-period comets, those which take more than 200 years, and possibly millions of years, to complete one orbit around the Sun and which originate from the Oort cloud. The long-period comets have highly elliptical orbits in any and every possible plane, as depicted in that last diagram. Comet Hale-Bopp, which passed by in 1995, is a long-period comet. It was

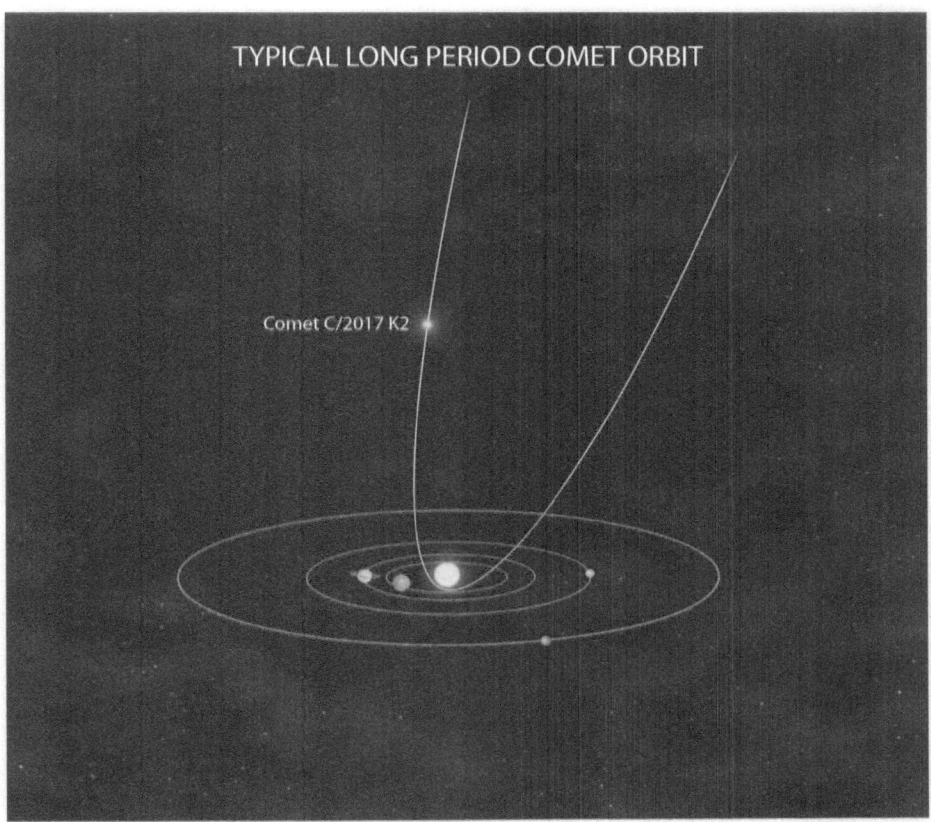

TYPICAL LONG PERIOD COMET ORBIT

Comet C/2017 K2

visible to the naked eye for nineteen months due to its unusually large size — twenty-five miles in diameter. However, we won't see Hale-Bopp again for two thousand four hundred years."

"Okay Eli," the president interjected, "I think I am going to have to live in suspense for a while. As you said, I have a good understanding now of the playing field and the types of solar objects that could come crashing down on us. You did say, I think, that no major collisions appear imminent, and I am going to have to leave it at that for now. However, maybe we can fit in another meeting in the next couple of weeks so you can complete this briefing before I forget all the background, and perhaps you could give me an update on your fresh water project at that time."

"Yes, Mr. President, that is fine. It's not my fresh water project, but I will be ready to update you at your convenience. And you are correct. I did say that no major collisions appear probable in the near term, though Apophis gave us some concern recently, which I'll tell you about at our next meeting. So, a surprise is still possible."

Chapter 9

October 13, 2027
Sonoma County, near Cloverdale, California

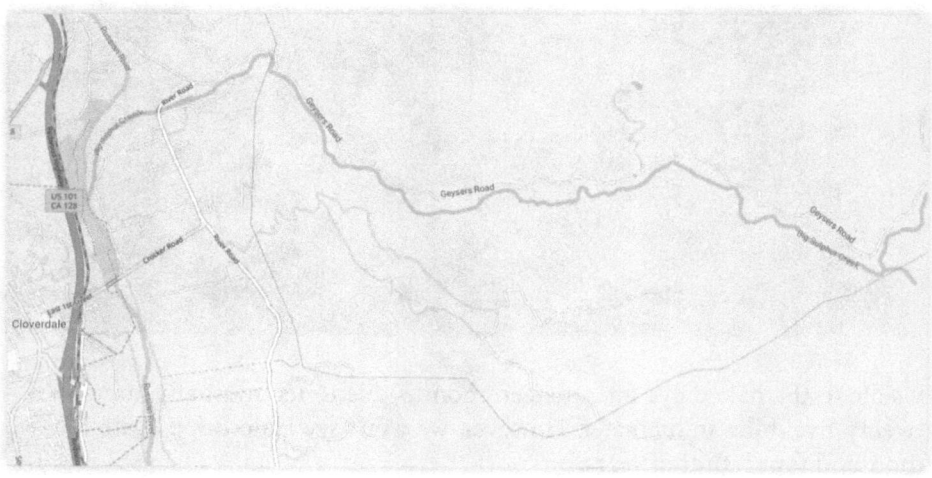

John exhaled quickly as he bobbed to the surface, sucked in a breath and scanned ahead where he could see a raging tumult of white water roaring down a steep incline studded with jagged rocks like a monstrous shark's teeth. It looked unsurvivable, and John felt his adrenaline spike to yet a new high as he was swept across the short pool beneath the fifteen-foot drop he had just plummeted over. He knew though, that with the right skill and execution he could survive, having just scouted the quarter-mile section from the bank above and picked a target route. It was all about the adrenaline spike.

Earlier that day, John and his friend Carlos had driven up to Cloverdale from the house they shared in Santa Rosa. They drove in along River Road to where it crossed Big Sulphur Creek, about a mile above where the creek emptied into the Russian River. This is where they planned to end their creek run. They off-loaded John's Kawasaki 250 dirt bike from the back of Carlos's half-ton truck and chained it to a small tree just out of sight of the road. From there it was about a nine-mile drive in along the north end of Geysers Road, which closely paralleled the creek, to their launch spot at Iron Bridge just upstream of where Squaw Creek reinforced the flow of Big Sulphur Creek.

This was a challenging stretch of white water, rated class IV–V by the organization American Whitewater, being at the upper end of difficulty. This early in the rainy season it would be at relatively low flow and therefore highly technical, requiring rapid course adjustments to avoid collisions with numerous unforgiving obstacles. The flow would not be enough to provide an easy open path, flowing around bigger rocks and helping to push the buoyant light-weight creeking kayaks away into clearer channels. It would often be essential to hit the entry to a chute in the perfect spot, not always dead center, and with the perfect directional alignment of the kayak, not necessarily straight downstream. Otherwise you risked clipping a rock, perhaps just enough to unbalance the craft and cause an upset, or landing at the bottom of the chute upright but pointed at the wrong angle to avoid the next obstacle. The durable little polypropylene kayaks could absorb a lot of bangs, scrapes and scuffs, but there would certainly be enough flow to make a full-on collision a painful experience at the least. Worse still, an upset in these waters would likely mean direct contact with the creek bottom, with no kayak intervening to absorb the shock. Even with the necessary protective helmet, this would very likely result in serious injury.

John Kirk and Carlos Campo were both highly skilled and experienced white-water kayaking enthusiasts, though Mother Nature can occasionally surprise even the best. They were also both extremely fit. Their jobs, as members of the Santa Rosa police force's small tactical team, demanded a high level of fitness, but the two young men had taken it well beyond the level required to pass their semiannual requalification tests. That extended to the hand-to-hand combat aspects of their jobs as well. Neither were very big men. John was a little over six feet and about two hundred pounds. Carlos was a little shorter but nearly the same weight. Yet both were consistent winners at the black belt level of the local karate tournaments they enjoyed. They were risk-takers craving the excitement of overcoming a difficult and dangerous situation whether on the job or in the white water, with apparently no fear of the possible consequences.

John and Carlos were not careless risk-takers though. They had carefully assessed this creek against their own abilities and had decided that they could handle it. They planned on four hours for the nine-mile descent, even though the actual running time on the water would be little more than an hour. This allowed for plenty of route-scouting from the shoreline for the more challenging sections, which they had carefully marked on their laminated topographical maps. As they had sealed their neoprene sprayskirts and pushed off from the Iron Bridge earlier that day, they were excited to be challenging Big Sulphur Creek and confident that they could master it.

John took advantage of the momentary calm, relatively speaking, of the pool below the steep drop to set himself up for the next series of gates he had to thread. He was glad that the pool had proved deep enough that he hadn't struck his stubby bow on the rocky bottom. He and Carlos had guessed it to be about six to eight feet deep from their survey from above. A fifteen-foot drop wasn't much in the white-water kayaking world. Drops of over a hundred feet were fairly common on big rivers with big waterfalls, but you had to have a deep pool to land in. A tall waterfall creates a frothy layer of air mixed with water as it strikes the plunge pool below, extending several feet below the surface of the pool and cushioning the impact with the water itself. Creeks like the Big Sulphur didn't usually produce deep enough plunge pools to absorb a drop of much more than twenty feet.

John successfully navigated another hundred yards of the cataract and was able to pull over to the right into a back eddy in a hollowed-out crescent of the creek side, which he and Carlos had identified as a safety stop. He turned upstream to watch his friend make the drop, work his way deftly through the rock maze and slide into the back eddy. They confirmed with hand signals that both were good to go; it was too noisy for speech. They had previously agreed that if either one was hurt or getting tired, they would both extract at the first opportunity, cut cross country to Geysers Road, which was rarely more than a hundred yards from the creek, and walk back to the truck or the bike.

Carlos edged back into the flow. John watched him fight has way down the rest of the cataract before pulling out himself. Disaster struck almost immediately. It was just one of those random events. As John maneuvered to take his line into the next chute, his paddle struck a shallow rock lurking just below the surface and he missed the power stroke required to push the agile craft into a straight-on descent. He still made it down the chute but at a significant angle to the flow and to the preplanned line of descent. He made a split-second decision to abandon the ideal path and take an alternative narrower cut through the barrier of broken rock obstructing the creek bed. It was the wrong decision, but there had been little choice.

As John swept toward the cut he had chosen, he realized it was going to be a tight squeeze. The cut was the entry to a small chute tight against a rock wall to his left, with the base of the wall undercut so that it leaned out into the chute. On the right a large shelf of rock flanked the chute, sloping down into the water at about a thirty-degree angle. There was a very narrow gap between the wall on the left and the shelf on the right, barely wide enough for the kayak, but water pounded through the gap, accelerated by the choke point. John hit the top of the chute dead center but a lot closer to the overhanging wall than he wanted to be. Halfway down, the kayak heeled sharply to the left as its right side mounted a little too far up the slope of the rock shelf. With the kayak canted to the left, John's head struck the sidewall a glancing blow before he could reach the bottom of the narrow chute.

Without a helmet John would likely have fractured his skull and almost certainly would have been knocked unconscious, which would have led to his death either from aspiration of water or additional severe impact injuries as he was swept down the remainder of the cataract, likely inverted most of the time and with no directional control. As it was, the blow was still hard enough that he grayed out momentarily, but fought back to alertness in time to reestablish control and regain his planned route. He navigated the rest of the way down without further incident, but his usual victory shout after completing a tough run was absent as he joined Carlos at their next safety stop.

Carlos could tell that John was shaken. "Are you okay buddy?" He asked searchingly.

John ducked in beside the creek bank and was able to grab the branches of a small bush overhanging the bank with one hand. With the other he removed his helmet, which he saw had a scuff mark but wasn't cracked. He felt around his head but found no bumps or cuts, the helmet having absorbed the impact and distributed it over the side and top of his head while preventing any lacerations. "Yeah, I got off line and took a good shot to the head from the sidewall back there. I'm okay, just a little groggy maybe."

Carlos responded, "Let's take a break and have a snack. We don't have much further to go, and there's lots of time."

Once they had pulled their kayaks up onto a nearby pebble beach and had some Gatorade and a power bar each, Carlos had a close look at John's head. He could see no sign of either pupil being dilated, and John insisted that he felt well and had no dizziness or balance problems. They both had thorough first aid training and knew about concussions and what to look for. After a half-hour break all seemed well and they resumed their descent.

After reaching the outskirts of Cloverdale, pulling out of the creek and retrieving first the dirt bike and then Carlos's truck, the two young men talked about what other challenges and adventures they might undertake as they drove home. They both enjoyed their work on the police force, but Santa Rosa was a fairly quiet city for the most part, with opportunities to exercise their firearms skills in a live situation fairly rare. They kept their arms skills honed on the police range, just as they did with their fitness and unarmed combat skills, but they were starting to feel like they were wasting the investment they'd made in developing their fighting skills.

Carlos was one of the team's sniper experts, with a Remington 700 in .308 caliber as his assigned weapon. On duty he would carry a rifle that had been carefully tuned by the police armorer, but he kept an identical personal rifle in a small gun safe bolted to the floor in the back of the truck's cab. He had placed in the top five several times at California SWAT Championships and felt he could get better with more shooting time. He wasn't a military caliber sniper with reliable accuracy at a thousand yards or more, but he was well polished for typical police actions, which were usually at ranges of less than a hundred yards, though often under challenging conditions of low light with encroaching structures and nearby noncombatants.

John was part of the assault team and when called out would carry a standard AR-15 semiautomatic rifle with high velocity lightweight .223 caliber rounds in a high-capacity twenty-round magazine. All members of the Santa Rosa tactical team carried the Kimber 1911 .45 ACP automatic pistol as their sidearm, and with terrorism continuing to raise its head occasionally, they were encouraged to carry it even while off duty. Although for TAC team members, the sidearm was a secondary weapon, rarely used in shooting situations, John and Carlos spent nearly as much range time with their pistols as with their primary weapons. They both had customized shoulder holsters for off-duty time, to keep the guns close at hand if needed but unobtrusive when wearing a light jacket. The pistols had been left behind for their white-water run, securely locked in the gun safe in Carlos's truck along with the Remington 700, but were back in their shoulder holsters for the drive home.

The talk, as usual, turned to the possibility of enlisting in one of the elite military forces, such as the SEALs, with their primary training installation on Coronado Island not far away in southern California. They knew that the admission and training process, lasting over a year, would be extremely arduous even though they could both easily pass the first hurdle, the Physical Screening Test. The opportunity for adventure, combat and service to country appealed to them. They had been drawn to the police force for many reasons, but high among them was an inherent instinct to serve and protect, which they found was only being partially satisfied in their current roles compared to what they felt they had to offer. They were attracted by what they knew from public information about the SEALs, operating in small covert groups, usually against targets with large heavily armed protective forces.

Another option they discussed was applying to a police force in one of the larger urban centers, such as the Los Angeles Police Department. They were sure they could get a strong recommendation from their SWAT captain and the chief as long as they gave them some time to fill their positions and train their replacements. It would be a much less challenging process and a surer bet, but it would also involve less intense action. Neither of them was temperamentally inclined toward an easier choice just to avoid difficulty and hardship. In fact, they placed difficulty and hardship on the positive side of the scale. Yet neither one was quite ready for the step into a new location and lifestyle. They didn't have serious romantic attachments to hold them back, but they both loved Santa Rosa and the Sonoma County area with its casual lifestyle, moderate climate and varied countryside. So, they set that discussion aside for now.

"Let's talk about a serious white water vacation," John said. "I'd like to head up north in the spring, maybe as far as Canada. I hear that the Canadian Rocky Mountains are spectacular and there is some serious white water to be had. It's a different style of kayaking than the creeking we are used to around here – big rivers, much faster and wilder, though more open and less technical. I think it would be fun for a change. There's a Kicking Horse River Kayak Festival in a place called Golden, British Columbia. I can show you some cool videos when we get home."

Carlos was quick to buy in to the idea of a road trip with some camping, hiking and a healthy dollop of white water in new scenery. By unspoken agreement, they would stick with Santa Rosa for at least another half-year or so before taking on a change in lifestyle.

Chapter 10

October 26, 2027
Washington, DC

James Rushton had already started on his chicken Caesar salad as his executive secretary ushered Dr. Wayman into the private dining room adjacent to the Oval Office. "Have a seat, Eli. I hope that plate of fruit and vegetables is what you ordered for your lunch. Can you start with the water project please before we resume our Chicken Little discussion?"

"Thank you, sir," said the science advisor, "the fruit and vegetables will do just fine. Mr. President, there's not too much more to say on the subject of water. A young post-doctoral fellow at MIT has been working in the area of desalination technology. One of the subjects I had intended to raise with you at some point is the emerging global fresh water shortage, and this young man has been trying to do something about it. I have met him now, and he is quite an idealist. I think you would like him.

"In any case, the technology, in fact several technologies, for separating salt out of salt water is well established and in use around the world; but it is relatively expensive because it takes a lot of electrical power, which, by the way, in many places means burning more fossil fuels. Larry — that's his name — is not a theoretical scientist, he is an engineering and materials scientist. He appears to have come up with some modifications to the existing technology that greatly improve its efficiency, by nearly a factor of ten. So, it could potentially produce large volumes of fresh water at close to a tenth of what it would currently cost. That would make it feasible to produce fresh water not only for drinking, but also for agricultural irrigation, avoiding eventual wide-scale crop failures."

"So, what's the catch?" said President Rushton.

"Well, it is still pretty early days," replied Eli. "My colleague, Larry's supervisor, has overseen several trials and both he and Larry are confident that the formula works at the laboratory scale. In the normal course, the next step would be an academic paper to disseminate the results, and an MIT patent application. After verification by another group using the same formula but their own equipment, MIT would likely seek a commercial partner to construct a pilot plant and, assuming no flaws show up at a larger scale, MIT would license the commercial partner to produce and market full-scale units."

"That sounds like it could take a fair bit of time," the president mused. "It would also leave the technology at least partly under the control of a business corporation. Normally I would be more than happy with that. Our whole economic system depends on business corporations to make it work. However, in this case, it feels to me like enough is at stake that the government should play a role, at least to begin with until this thing takes off — or falls apart. Eli, can you get together with Secretary of Commerce, Bruce Cartwright, and Will Templeton to work out a plan to accelerate this? I want a full-scale model up and running yesterday. Skip the pilot plant, we will fund the full-scale plant and take the risk. Bring in private sector design engineers if Larry would like some help to scale up the design. Private sector fabrication subcontractors are also fine, but I want us to remain in control of the overall project. Could you also arrange for me to meet with the president of MIT? I want to ensure we have their understanding of the national importance of the project and their full support. Can you do all that for me, Eli?"

"Mr. President, I will," confirmed the advisor. "I understand now what people mean when they say you're a thoughtful decision-maker but once you've made up your mind you move decisively and quickly. Is that enough for today, or would you like to carry on with my Chicken Little act?"

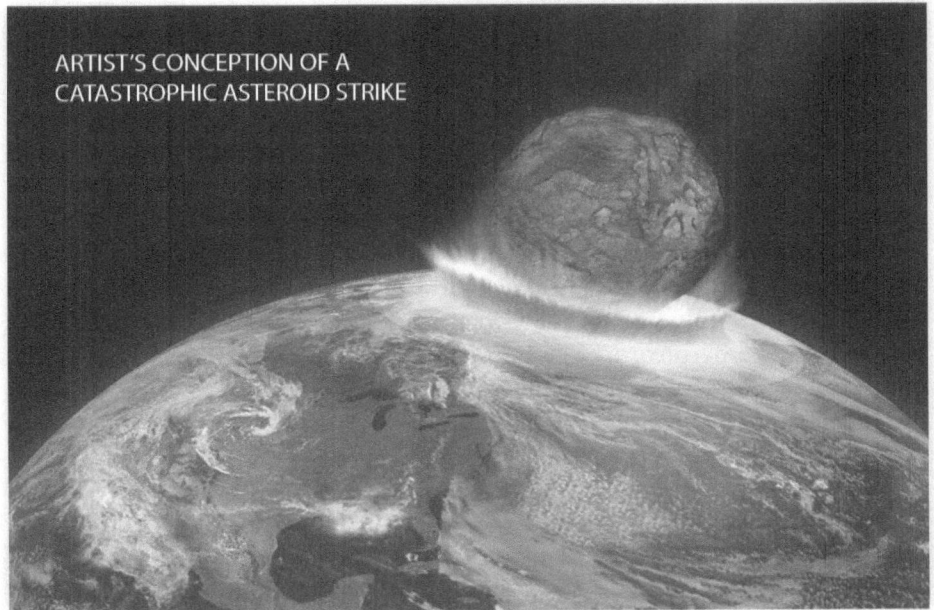

ARTIST'S CONCEPTION OF A
CATASTROPHIC ASTEROID STRIKE

"Oh, let's finish the rocks-from-the-sky story," said James Rushton. "Now that I have the background, let's get to the meat of the matter. Eli, with all those objects that come that close to the Earth, how big would one have to be to cause us real trouble, and how likely is that to happen in the next ten years?"

"Mr. President, ones that are big enough to do catastrophic damage are statistically very rare," responded Eli, moving his laptop closer to the president to display more images. "The sort of sensational event depicted in this artist's conception of a killer asteroid strike may have occurred a few times in the first one or two billion years of the Earth's history. By now, after about four and a half billion years of the Earth sweeping a path around the Sun with its gravitational attraction broom, it has pretty much cleaned up the neighborhood of objects of this magnitude, along with the other seven planets, including the four gas giants with their much bigger brooms. Yet, the potential certainly exists for an impact large enough to be catastrophic from a human perspective. The so-called dinosaur killer struck the Yucatán peninsula near the location of the current town of Chicxulub sixty-five million years ago, and the energy released changed the climate so radically that it caused the extinction of many species including all the dinosaurs. That object was an asteroid about six miles in diameter and would have released the energy equivalent of one hundred trillion tons of TNT, several billion times that of the atomic bombs that destroyed Hiroshima and Nagasaki.

"As massive as that impact sounds, for the Earth itself it was a pin prick, and not the largest it has ever experienced. However, for the life subsisting on the surface of the Earth, it was devastating beyond imagination. The initial blast and heat would have been horrific, obliterating and incinerating everything for thousands of miles. Secondary effects would have been massive over an even broader front, including reentry of enormous amounts of molten material ejected from the impact crater into space, tsunamis, volcanic eruptions and earthquakes. But the global extinctions resulted from a tertiary effect that spanned the whole world, a change in climate so profound as to make our global warming problem pale in significance. The amount of dust injected into the upper atmosphere allowed so little sunlight through that most plants died. Then the herbivores that fed on them died, followed by the carnivores that fed on the herbivores. The human race would face a similar fate to the dinosaurs, with survival possible only for small groups located at great distances from the crater, and only those who were well prepared with extensive stores of food, energy and equipment. Fortunately, this is a once-in-one-hundred-million-year event, so the risk is very low.

"More worrisome than a dinosaur killer–sized object is the risk of a smaller but still sizeable impact, say by something a half-mile in diameter. These are estimated to occur once in a hundred thousand years, so it is still a rare event

LARGE BODY RELATIVE SIZES

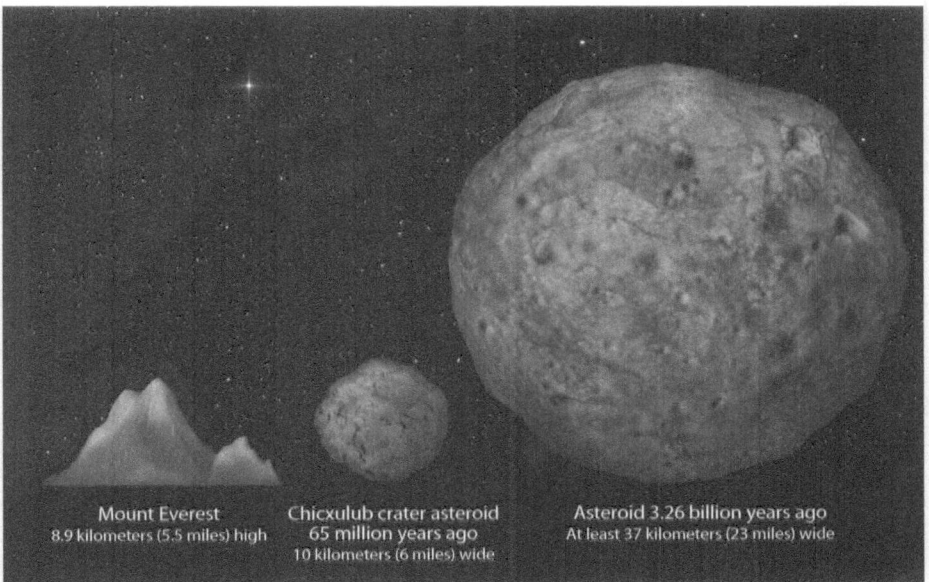

Mount Everest
8.9 kilometers (5.5 miles) high

Chicxulub crater asteroid
65 million years ago
10 kilometers (6 miles) wide

Asteroid 3.26 billion years ago
At least 37 kilometers (23 miles) wide

statistically, though much more likely than the dinosaur killer. An asteroid of this size would pack a punch equivalent to sixty thousand megatons of TNT. The largest nuclear bomb the United States has ever produced has only twenty-five megatons of explosive energy. The bomb that decimated Hiroshima was fifteen kilotons. So, the impact of a half-mile asteroid would still be terrible beyond all measure, likely obliterating a good part of whichever continent it impacted with primary and secondary effects. There would still be worldwide tertiary effects and resulting crop failures, but not as extensive or as prolonged as they were for the Chicxulub crater. Human civilization would survive and recover, even without extensive preparation, though fatalities would number in the hundreds of millions or even billions, and several countries would cease to exist as functional political entities."

The science advisor continued, "Next on the list would be an object an order of magnitude smaller still, say about a hundred yards in diameter. That is pretty small compared to the dinosaur killer, but it is still a good-sized rock, bearing in mind that it would strike at a speed of something like ten miles per second, or thirty-six thousand miles per hour. The energy release would be equivalent to about sixty megatons of TNT, or more than twice that of our largest nuclear weapons. That would still devastate a large part of any state it struck, but not an entire continent. However, the secondary effects such as earthquakes and volcanic eruptions could still adversely impact a large swath of the continent.

"I'd be most worried about an asteroid of about one hundred yards hitting somewhere in the Western United States. That impact could stir up the Yellowstone magma chamber into an eruption. Yellowstone has the potential to inject enough ash into the atmosphere to cause global climate change similar to a full-sized dinosaur killer impact, but even a much more modest eruption could throw up enough ash to eliminate agricultural production as far as the Canadian Prairies and the U.S. Midwest, in addition to the explosive double whammy to Wyoming, Idaho, and Montana over and above the impact explosion itself.

YELLOWSTONE CALDERA

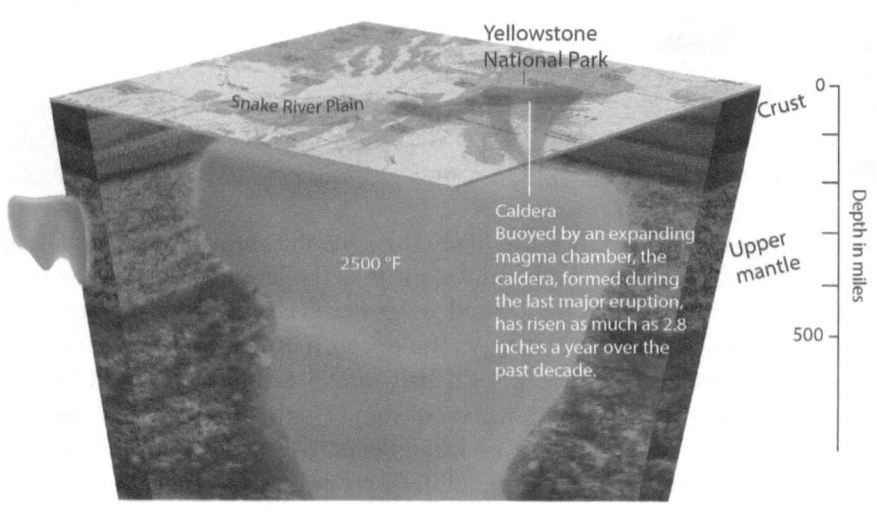

The massive molten and solid but super-heated rock lake some 300 miles wide that lies below Yellowstone.

"An impact of this size appears likely to occur about once in a thousand years, so within the ten-year period that you stipulated, still a very low risk. However, we can't predict far in advance which ten-year interval within the next thousand years will be the one that takes the hit or where on Earth it will occur. What we can do is keep a close watch on the sky and have some advance warning of a large impact and possibly be able to deflect it or at least have a prepared impact response.

"This table that I have printed out for you provides a handy summary of the likelihood of this spectrum of nasty outcomes.

ASTEROID STRIKE PROBABILITY

SIZE	NUMBER NEAR EARTH	FREQUENCY OF IMPACTS	LAST IMPACT	ANNUAL PROBABILITY OF IMPACT
10–50m	200,000,000	1 in every 5 years	Siberia, 1908: area not populated	0.2
100m	200,000	1 in every 1000 years	China, 1490: 10,000 deaths	0.001
1–2km	2000	1 in every 100,000 to 1 million years	Argentina, 3 million years ago: local extinctions and global cooling	0.00001
15km	50	1 in every 65 million years	Mexico, 65 million years ago: dinosaur extinction	0.00000002

Source: Risk Ed

"Mr. President, that brings us to the point of all this background that you have patiently absorbed. Specifically, the scientific systems that we have in place to identify potential impacts of asteroids or comets with the Earth and give us some time to respond. Do we have enough time left to cover that?"

The president had finished his lunch but encouraged Eli to continue.

"Sir, here in the United States our efforts are managed by the Planetary Defense Coordination Office of NASA, which is located right here in Washington. These are the people I would hear from if a potential situation were to develop, and of course I would immediately arrange for you to be notified and briefed. This coordinating office has overall responsibility for early detection of potential large impacts, and of leading our response to a probable threat. They oversee NASA's Near-Earth Object Observations Program, which watches the skies above us, and they work closely with the Jet Propulsion Laboratory. The JPL undertakes the fairly difficult computerized mathematical calculations required to estimate the orbit of a newly identified asteroid or comet and to determine whether and when it might intersect Earth's orbit, and where Earth will be at that time. The PDCO also coordinates with similar national agencies of other countries to share information and minimize duplication of effort.

"Mr. President, our federal government has been taking the risk of a large impact fairly seriously for several decades now, and we have some pretty sophisticated instruments keeping an eye on what is over head. The Panoramic Survey Telescope and Rapid Response System (Pan-STARRS) has been in operation for more than a decade with a primary mission of detecting impact threats. It is located high up the Haleakalā volcanic crater rim on Maui with multiple large 1.8-meter aperture scopes, one of the largest digital cameras ever built, and extensive computer processing capability. Cameras and computer processing are critical for detecting moving objects, which is accomplished by comparing pictures taken at intervals of time for any change in position or brightness, and correlating with known objects.

"More recently, the Large Synoptic Survey Telescope, located high in the Andes of north-central Chile but operated by our National Science Foundation, has now been in operation for several years. It has an 8.4-meter primary mirror and a camera more than double the size of the Pan-STARRS. These are two of the biggest but by no means all of the hardware that is looking out for us. So, we know quite a bit about the acorns out there that could fall from the sky, and I am happy to break tradition with Chicken Little and say I believe a large impact is very unlikely in the next ten years, not just statistically but based on scientific data. Of course, if that view ever changes, you will be the first to know. However, I should mention that no large impacts doesn't mean no close calls, and I should briefly mention Apophis before I finish."

Seeing a nod from James Rushton, Eli continued, "Apophis is the object that has caused the greatest level of excitement since we have been watching out for potential impacts. It is a good-sized chunk of rock, about three hundred and eight yards in diameter, so it would pack a nasty punch. It wasn't spotted until 2004, although it inhabits Earth's neighborhood of the solar system and comes fairly close to us fairly often. I think that with today's instruments and observation program it would have been detected much sooner.

"When an object is first identified, it takes several observations over an extended interval of time to calculate its path with some precision. The initial calculations, based on limited data, indicated a fairly high risk that an impact would occur twenty-five years later, in 2029, on April 13 specifically — which is of course only a year and a half from now. The combination of its size and impact-risk stimulated a lot of attention to this particular asteroid, and over time a more precise path was developed going out to 2029 and many decades beyond. So, we know now and have for more than a decade that Apophis will come very close April after next, within about twenty miles, but will not actually strike us.

"That distance is within the orbits of many of our commercial communication satellites, and high performance jet aircraft have flown above that altitude. It will be visible to the naked eye from many places, though not from here in the US.

We have been watching it very closely for the last year to make sure that it hasn't encroached on that slim margin of safety, and it has not. In order to alleviate public concern, we will be undertaking a communication program to provide assurance and factual updates, but we will still likely see some activity from the lunatic fringe.

"We won't have seen the last of Apophis next year by any means. In fact, at about the same time that an impact in 2029 was ruled out, it started to look like that near miss might alter the orbit of the asteroid enough to cause a collision on its next pass in 2036. That too has long since been put to rest, as has a collision on subsequent passes out to the end of the century.

"So, Mr. President, I hope this subject hasn't taken more of your time than it merits given that it is very unlikely I'll ever need to raise it with you again, but I thought you should be knowledgeable on the subject, since Apophis will inevitably stir up increased public interest. Now I'll be off to fast-track your fresh water program."

"Eli, once again I have found our time together interesting and worthwhile. Let's not call it *my* fresh water program though, let's call it Larry's program. When I go to meet with the president of MIT, I'd also like to meet with Larry himself. On the asteroid strike front, I am happy that the risk is so low that I won't need to think about it again, but also happy to have a good grounding to be able to handle any questions on Apophis knowledgeably before steering them your way for more details. However, I haven't missed the fact that you have carefully qualified your assurances with words like 'very unlikely' rather than 'impossible,' and that you would advise me promptly if this assessment were ever to change. So, I take it that it is something of an uncertain science?"

"Mr. President, I had planned to have the MIT contingent come here to see you, but I am sure they would be most delighted by a visit from you; and yes, all science has its uncertainties. We have well-defined orbits for a large number of asteroids and comets of a size and orbit that could pose a hazard to Earth, just about all of them that we think are out there. However, there's probably a small number we haven't spotted yet, and a chance that one of those could be a problem. The bigger risk, however, is that the solar system is dynamic. The orbits of seemingly benign asteroids and short-period comets can change because of close encounters with one of the planets, especially Jupiter, or even because of minor collisions among themselves. Then there are the long-period comets we talked about. Those are ones with highly elliptical orbits extending many hundreds of millions of miles into the outer reaches of the solar system, and potentially coming toward us from any direction rather than the plane of the ecliptic, which is much easier to monitor. One of these could be headed toward us but not yet be close enough or fast enough for us to detect. So, we do need to keep an active look out in case something new develops."

Eli gathered up his materials and left the president musing to himself. Neither of them expected to meet again on matters of astronomy, other than to discuss public communications about Apophis, but they were wrong.

Chapter 11

November 1, 2027
Canadian Rocky Mountains, near Golden, British Columbia

Tom Svenson broke trail through about two feet of light snow covering the forest service road that led to the cabin. Beast, his 150-pound Tibetan Mastiff, followed behind, pulling a large toboggan loaded with a few basic supplies. Then, in sequence came Arthur, Susan and Sigrid, with Patricia Svenson bringing up the rear. There was room on the toboggan for seven-year-old Sigrid, and Beast could easily handle the additional weight, but the Svensons expected all three of their children to manage the three-mile uphill trek. All were equipped with lightweight metal frame snowshoes. The family was planning to spend the weekend at their mountain retreat.

At an explosion of motion from just off the side of the road, Tom threw up his light shotgun and dropped a plump spruce grouse into the snow. Beast bolted ahead, toboggan and all, to gather up the bird and take joint credit for the kill. Grouse were fairly common in the area and, though not as great a prize as a wild turkey or a deer, were still something Tom would take for the pot when the opportunity arose. He thumbed another number 7½ shell into the breach of the 410-gauge Browning Citori over and under shotgun that he carried along for such purpose, being careful not to take it from the pocket holding the half dozen slugs. He'd brought the slugs just in case they encountered an aggressive cougar or wolf. Although it was unlikely they would see one, especially with Beast as part of the group, Tom preferred to be prepared, especially when the safety of his family was involved.

They reached the cabin with plenty of light still left in the day, even though dark would fall by about four thirty at this time of year. Trish got to work setting a fire in the Franklin stove that sat in the middle of the cabin between the small living room and kitchen. With a relatively small area to heat, the woodburning stove would take little more than an hour to raise the temperature inside the cabin from twenty degrees up to a comfortable seventy degrees Fahrenheit, even as the outside temperature began to fall toward an overnight low of fifteen degrees or less. If anything, the trick was not to feed too much wood into the stove and overheat the little cabin, especially the second-floor loft where the two girls would sleep. Even in midwinter, when overnight temperatures could fall to minus thirty degrees Fahrenheit, it was easy to keep the cabin at a comfortable temperature with one early morning restoking.

Tom, accompanied by eleven-year-old Arthur, got to work turning on the propane system they used for cooking and lighting, as well as refrigeration in the summer — there was no electric power in the area. Next, the two of them shoveled a clear path from the back door to the outhouse and then headed down to the lake with their ice auger. The hole in the four inches of ice would be their source of water, which they would haul back up to the cabin in pails. It would also serve for ice fishing the next day. In summertime Tom would use a small pump to pump water from the lake up to a large barrel on the front deck, but it would freeze solid at this time of the year.

Tom could install a small generator to provide power to the little mountain retreat, but he never would. The disruption to the peace and quiet of the lake would far outweigh the benefit. Tom and Trish were perfectly happy with the off-the-grid aspect of their cabin — no cell phone coverage, no electricity, no running water, hot or cold. Most of the small number of other cottage owners on the lake felt the same. Tom's one concession to convenience was the propane system. He used fifty-pound refillable cylinders, about twice the height of a standard barbecue tank but still easy to move around. One tank would last most of a year, and he kept two full ones in reserve, topping up the empty one in the summer when he could drive the Suburban all the way in.

Apart from that, Tom enjoyed cutting wood for heating and the occasional bonfire when the risk of forest fires was low enough to permit it. The area immediately around the lake was first-growth Douglas fir, never having been logged, though there were numerous logging concessions not far away. Tom never had to cut a tree down because there were ample deadfalls on his five-acre lot, which he tried to keep up with. He just needed to cut them up with a chainsaw and then split them to size with a splitting axe, or wedge and sledgehammer, depending on thickness. His current project was to cut up a forty-inch diameter giant, which put his forty-one–inch bar Stihl chainsaw to good use. The branches of the giant were a good workout for his twenty-four–inch bar chainsaw. In reality Tom had more wood split and stacked in his woodshed and under the upper deck of his bunkie than he could expect to burn in a decade. He also had most of a year's supply stacked in the basement storage area of the cabin. He could have left off further cutting for a long time, but Tom liked to cut and split wood.

Tom and Trish also had plenty of staples stored in the basement walkout of the cabin. They weren't really full-blown preppers, but they did believe in a certain level of emergency preparations. So, a corner of the basement was dedicated to about two years' worth of flour, sugar, both white and brown, syrup, pancake mix, salt and pasta of several varieties. Below the basement they had a partial subbasement, dug down below the frost level, which held the harvest of potatoes, carrots, parsnips and onions from a quarter acre root garden Trish tended in a sheltered hollow behind the cabin. The subbasement also held several cases of canned goods such as tomato sauce, vegetables and fruit, and canned meat.

Tom enjoyed hunting and fishing, and there were ample deer in the area and fish in the lake. He was confident that they would not lack for meat if they ever had to wait out a disaster of some sort that interrupted the normal availability of food from the Save-on-Foods grocery store back down in Golden.

Once the water had been hauled up to the cabin, and the grouse was plucked, cleaned and hung in the cool basement, Tom and Art joined the girls and Trish in the snug living room looking out over the lake. As darkness fell, they lit the three propane lamps and settled in for a game of *Monopoly*. The three kids sipped on marshmallow-topped hot chocolates, and Tom and Trish each enjoyed a good splash of Lamb's Navy Dark Rum mixed with Coke Zero with a squeeze of lime. Their eyes met as the kids chattered about their property-buying strategies and whether any alliances should be considered to increase the chances of beating their dad. The Svenson parents knew they were both thinking the same thing — how fortunate they were to have such a wonderful family and life, with hardly a care in the world.

Chapter 12

November 6, 2027
El Peñón summit (9,000 feet) near Vicuña, Chile

At eight o'clock at night Darya's alarm clock brought her quickly awake. She opened the blackout curtains of the single window of her small dormitory room to catch the late day sun low in the western sky as she dressed for her night's work. She completed her post-nap cleanup and tied a heavy jacket around her waist as she headed down the hall toward the cafeteria. She would be working inside, but the main observatory, open to the night sky, would be cool at this altitude and time of the day even though it was late spring, approaching summer.

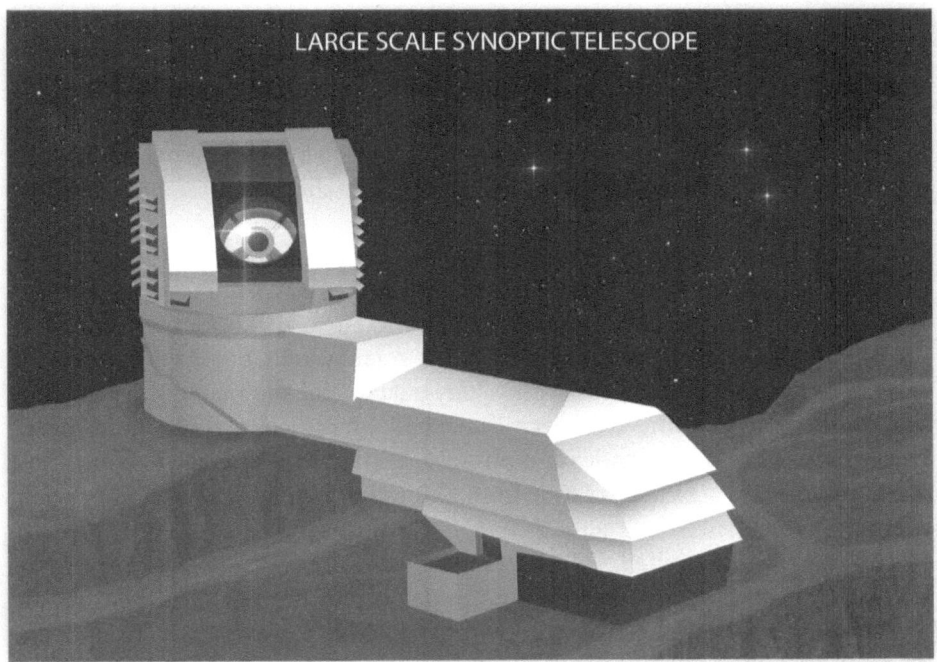

The slight, dark-haired young woman took her time eating a light meal that could best be described as brunch. Much of the work at the Large Synoptic Survey Telescope observatory occurred during the night, so the cafeteria was accustomed to feeding the scientists and technicians a selection of breakfast, lunch and dinner options throughout the day. Darya's one-hour slot on the Big Eye wouldn't start until eleven o'clock, so she had plenty of time to browse through her laptop for personal communications and world news. For that matter, she didn't really need to be present in the observatory during her time allotment. She had already fed the scanning parameters into the scheduling system after checking and double-checking all the details. The duty technicians needed no help from her to upload her parameters and initiate her scan sequence. She could monitor the scan just as effectively on her desktop computer in her small room, or for that matter she could sleep through the night and review all the results in the morning. It was very unlikely that anything that might require any intervention from her would occur. Yet she preferred to be on the spot watching her pictures of the sky as they unfolded, not that anything very meaningful would be apparent from visual inspection of the two hundred digital photographs the Eye would take in her allotted hour.

Darya Ahmadi was a twenty-six-year old PhD candidate in astrophysics at the University of Oxford, one of the foremost centers for astronomy research in the world. Her thesis was titled "Frequency of Earth-Sized Planets in the Core of the Milky Way Galaxy." She had been fortunate to have a supervisor with enough influence to secure her a six-month fellowship at the LSST observatory in the Chilean Andes, which was operated by the U.S. National Science Foundation. She had a few weeks left to go before she would have all the data she needed to complete her thesis, but she was already excited by what she had found.

Darya was a British citizen, born to parents whose own families had both fled from Iran at the time that the last Shah was overthrown. From an early age Darya had demonstrated intense interest in and curiosity about the contents of the nighttime sky. Not just the planets of the solar system, but even more so the multitude of other stars in the Milky Way galaxy and the many other galaxies that modern astronomical observations had identified. As she grew older, Darya excelled in mathematics and physics. By the time she came to choosing a specialty, she had a great academic foundation that helped her excel in her field of interest, exoplanets.

The fellowship to the LSST observatory was a tremendous opportunity for Darya. The southern hemisphere was preferable to the northern hemisphere for viewing large numbers of stars within the Milky Way galaxy because the orientation of the solar system, including the Earth, kept the South Pole pointed toward the central core of the galaxy. The location, fairly high in the Andes, had been carefully selected for favorable ambient light levels and low humidity to provide clear viewing conditions without being so high up as to risk altitude illness for the resident scientists and support staff. The LSST itself was an extremely powerful instrument with a twenty-five–foot wide primary mirror and the largest digital camera ever constructed, along with a massive processing and data storage system to record and analyze the pictures of the night sky.

Darya had been using the incredible power of the Big Eye to scan a large number of stars deep within the core of the Milky Way galaxy in the general direction of the constellation Sagittarius, the archer. She was examining a volume of space nearly forty thousand light-years away from Earth, searching for planets in orbit around the many stars packed densely into that region of the galaxy, so-called exoplanets.

As powerful as the LSST instrument was, the young astronomer was unlikely to see many, if any, exoplanets directly in the digital photographs the instrument output. The system would only be able to resolve extremely large planets at that distance and even then, they would need to be at a point in their orbit to one side or the other of their star so as not to be obscured by the glare of the star. In any case, Darya was not interested in large planets. She was interested in planets roughly similar in mass and diameter to Earth. Detecting planets of this size required sophisticated analysis of multiple images taken at different points in time to measure variations in the star's brightness resulting from planets passing in front of it, and small wobbles in its path through the galaxy caused by the gravitational effects of one or more planets. One of Darya's thesis contributions was to be a refined algorithm for imputing the existence of orbiting planets from a star's pathway oscillations.

Darya arrived at the observatory a half hour before her eleven-o'clock time slot. She greeted the senior operator and confirmed that her scan parameters were queued up and ready to execute. She then slipped into an observation room reserved for viewing scans in real time. For a few minutes she watched the large-scale screen mounted on the wall, which was displaying the telescope's current scanning assignment. Then she booted up her laptop and began reviewing the results of her own previous scan.

At eleven o'clock sharp, the large monitor screen went blank and the observatory vibrated briefly as its heavy-duty electric motors repositioned the scope toward the distant section of the galaxy that Darya was interested in. Her first picture began to display a few moments later, followed by another roughly every fifteen seconds thereafter. After fifteen minutes, the scope would adjust slightly to focus on a different area. One of the advantages of the LSST was that its image width was so large that it permitted several different stars to be investigated at the same time.

Darya continued to view the pictures as they formed, somewhat mesmerized by her window into the center of the Milky Way. The pictures were beautiful and awe-inspiring. However, they would not yield their most interesting secrets until further processing by her sophisticated algorithms, which would reveal subtle differences between the pictures undetectable by the human eye. Matters proceeded as expected until about halfway through her time allotment.

Suddenly a soft tone began to sound throughout the observatory — similar to a fire alarm, though not as strident. At the same time a red light began to flash in the upper-left corner of the monitor. After a brief pause the display cycled back to the previous sequence of pictures and a banner popped up along the lower edge of the screen, stating "Transient Object Detected," and a green square outline appeared near the lower-right corner of the screen. The electric motors operated briefly, signaling a repositioning of the telescope, and fifteen seconds later a new picture came up on the monitor, with the same banner but with the green cursor now positioned in the middle of the screen.

Minutes later the senior operator knocked briefly and then stuck his head into the room.

"Sorry Darya," he said, "the rest of your scan has been bumped by a transient object detection override. Maybe you will get an asteroid named after you as a consolation prize."

One of the primary missions of the LSST was to identify any object moving around within the solar system and gather enough data on its successive positions that the orbital mechanics at NASA's Jet Propulsion Laboratory could map out its orbit and assess any risk of collision with Earth. Even though Darya's project had nothing to do with spotting dangerous rocks and was focused far beyond the solar system, the transient object detection program was always running automatically in the background of the observatory's massive processing system. It operated somewhat similarly to Darya's own algorithms, by comparing successive pictures of the same area of the sky and noting any changes — in particular, the vanishing and reemergence of a distant star as a much nearer object moved in between the star and the Earth.

Apparently, Darya's first picture sequence of the night had triggered the alert when compared to an earlier picture of the same area, a picture that could have been one of Darya's or could have been from any other project that had ever looked at the same area. The processing system would have pulled every such picture from its massive data storage banks for comparison, unobtrusively working away in the background.

A detection override was fairly routine for projects that were scanning the solar system itself, since nearly all of the system lies in the same plane, including the asteroid belt. It was much less common for projects such as Darya's, which were scanning down below the plane of the ecliptic, where few objects belonging to the solar system exist. Although near-Earth-object detection was not Darya's specialty, she was aware of all this background as she replied to the operator.

"Yeah, thanks Diego," she replied, "I guess I'll knock off for the night and submit a request for a replacement slot. Based on where it seems to be coming from, I don't think it can be an asteroid though. It must be a comet on a long, tilted orbit out of the Oort cloud, still far enough out that it hasn't started to vaporize and grow a tail yet. Good night."

Although her hypothesis was plausible, Darya was wrong.

Chapter 13

November 10, 2027
Near Clear Lake, Lake County, Northern California

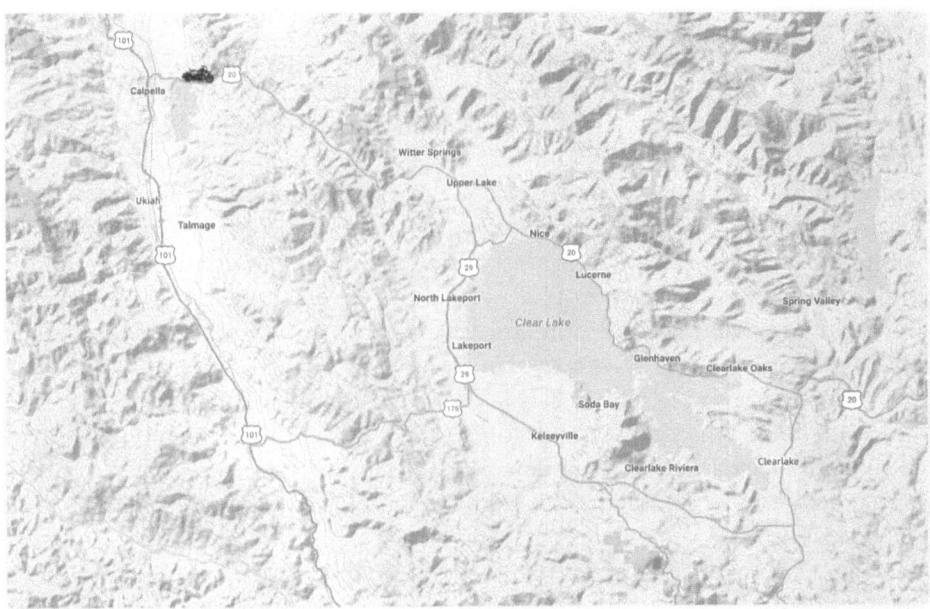

Peter Poplinski was doing what he enjoyed more than most other things apart from beating the crap out of someone foolish enough to get in his way or screwing a young girl unlucky enough to catch his attention. He was cruising his Harley east along the gentle curves of California State Route 20 parallel to the East Fork Russian River in Lake County, California, far from his home base near Twin Falls, Idaho. He was riding by himself, having come from a job he preferred to keep to himself, though he was en route to meet up with a small squad from his club that he had tasked with an important piece of his grand strategy.

As he meandered along the road he continued to reflect on the job he had recently completed and the hundred thousand dollars in cash bulging in his saddlebags. Like any professional, he was playing back the job in his mind, searching for areas of sloppiness or lessons he could use to improve his performance on similar assignments in the future.

***

Peter had been contracted by a capo of the recently established Portland organization to conduct a hit on a resident of the city. It wasn't the first time Peter had been called on for this sort of work, though he knew nothing of the identity of his employer and vice versa. Their entire relationship was conducted through public telephone landline calls arranged through cryptic cell phone contacts.

Peter was not given, nor did he expect, any explanation as to why his employer had chosen to outsource the assignment to a freelancer rather than use his own resources. Likewise, he wasn't informed as to why the target was to be hit, though he expected that it was something beyond just a serious case of delinquency on a gambling or drug debt. Peter had no formal education beyond high school, but he was smart and streetwise. He suspected that the target was either a witness in a case against a member of the organization or a police informant, or he was in some other way a direct threat to the organization or its leadership. He was therefore primed to be on the lookout for private security or police protection or surveillance.

All the details were left entirely to Peter. He was given only a name, picture, and address. He was told what post office box number the payment would be in and where the key would be hidden. The only stipulations were that the corpse had to be found in a public place and be identifiable, and for the death to have clearly not been an accident.

The hired killer had known that the job would involve some risk, though he had planned it carefully and, if anything, the risk and the associated challenges appealed to him. He had left his bike at a local cash-only performance shop to have some engine work done on it and had taken a bus from there. He had bought a nondescript, used Ford sedan from a newspaper ad. He'd paid with cash and picked it up at night in a part of town where minding your own business was the first rule of survival.

He used the car to carefully study the man's house and neighborhood and his comings and goings. At first he kept his distance until he was reasonably sure that no one else was keeping an eye on his target or guarding him. He was careful to park in a number of different observation spots and varied the picture the car presented, sometimes raising either the hood or the trunk. He slept in the car even though the nights were cold. He didn't want to leave any more of a trail than was absolutely necessary.

On the morning of the third day his target left his high-end home in his BMW X2. Peter followed at a discrete distance. He had tailed the man on several previous trips and was still gathering information on his habits and patterns, though Peter knew he was quickly reaching the point where additional information would not be of sufficient worth to justify his continued presence and the risk that his target, or someone else, would notice him. The target, unaware of the following predator, drove to Forest Park and parked on the side of NW 53rd Drive adjacent to one of the many trailheads for the network of walking and biking paths within the park.

Peter was following along NW 53rd at a distance of about a hundred yards, having dropped back once beyond the busier urban roads. When he saw his target pull over he continued cruising along, noting the man exiting his car and heading for the trailhead. He drove on for a half mile and then cut a U-turn and came back, stopping about two hundred yards away, just in time to see another figure emerge from a late model sedan, which had been parked just in front of the X2. The new player had also headed for the trailhead.

Peter had waited a couple of minutes and then left his Ford and walked quickly to the X2. A few seconds later, he had the vehicle open, and he slipped into the back seat. It was a spontaneous and opportunistic strategy that he had known would be both a risky and difficult ploy as he squeezed his large frame down as low into the back seat footwell as possible.

Peter's objective was to blend into the darkness of the car's interior without restricting his ability to move quickly. He was quite sure that his target was meeting someone secretly in the park; he was not just out for a walk. It was possible that the two of them would return together to this car. It was also possible that his target would return alone but for some reason would open a rear door and spot Peter, preempting an attack. Peter considered these risks but found them acceptable. He was confident that if worst came to worst he could either bluff or fight his way clear, though that would harm his chances for a subsequent attack. He settled into the mental discipline required to remain alert despite being able to see very little.

Three quarters of an hour later Peter heard the scuffing of footsteps on pebble-covered gravel. The front door opened, and a person slipped behind the wheel. Peter slipped his garrote, twenty inches of light cord anchored at both ends to wooden handles, around the target's neck. Seconds later, his heels were drumming on the floor in a final convulsion as Peter's crossed arms tightened the cord so forcefully that the windpipe was crushed. As the stench of evacuated bowels filled the car, Peter's attention was already on the outside, checking for anyone nearby who might have seen anything. No one was in sight. The whole process had taken less than two minutes.

Peter quickly confirmed that he had in fact killed the correct person since he'd had no time for a positive identification beforehand. He arranged the body so that it might appear to be resting to a casual observer, locked all the doors, then slipped out the far side rear door, crouching in the ditch beside the car for another scan of the area. Still no one. He didn't dare walk back along the shoulder of the road to his car, so crossed the ditch and made his way thirty yards into the park before turning and paralleling the road back toward his car. Peter froze when he glimpsed the owner of the sedan parked in front of the X2 returning along the foot path to the trailhead and then to his car. The man paused and seemed puzzled to see the X2 still there but got into his car and drove off.

Minutes later Peter was in the Ford, which he drove to a suitable location and abandoned, unlocked and with the keys in the ignition. It was too much of a piece of junk to interest any professional car thief, but the local youth gangs could be counted on to look after it. He took a series of buses back to the cycle shop and collected his bike, then headed to the post box to get the payment. By one o'clock in the afternoon, he was southbound on I-5, which he took only as far as Albany before cutting across to pick up U.S. Route 101, the coastal road, at Newport. He drove carefully, not wanting to be placed in Oregon because of a driving infraction, even though he had solid, clean false ID. By seven o'clock that night, he was across the California border. He checked in at a slightly dilapidated motel in Smith River, had a shower and a shave, grabbed some fast food and then collapsed into his first comfortable sleep in several nights.

***

The hit and subsequent departure from Portland had been just the day before. That morning Peter had slept until seven o'clock in the morning at the motel in Smith River before grabbing a quick breakfast and continuing south on U.S. Route 101. Half an hour before, at noon, he had exited onto California State Route 20 and was enjoying the relaxed pace of the Lake County highway. He was fast approaching his destination, the town of Lucerne on the shores of Clear Lake, one of California's largest bodies of fresh water. Having mulled over his previous day's work he could find nothing that he wished he had done differently. Perhaps if things had turned out less favorably he would have regretted some of his choices, but as it was he was pleased.

The fact that he had snuffed out a human life meant nothing to Peter. He had no idea who the person was, he had very few details about their life and had no interest in knowing. All he was interested in was the cash in his saddlebags, though that would have to be laundered through the cash receipt systems of several legitimate corporations that the club owned. It wasn't that Peter enjoyed killing. For him it was simply a means to an end — either a service to others for payment, as with the Portland job, or the removal of an obstacle to something he wanted. He felt no compunction or remorse, but he didn't enjoy it the way he enjoyed beating a physical challenger into submission, which rarely resulted in death.

Ahead on the shoulder of the road he spotted the half-ton truck he was looking for. He had alerted his crew when he had turned onto Route 20. After exchanging greetings, he followed the truck up a winding side road for twenty minutes, then along a sandy wooded trail for another quarter of a mile. He emerged into a prairie of rolling hills with a pretty little lake nestled in the middle and gentle wooded slopes ranging west back down toward the much larger Clear Lake and up toward the east as far as he could see. There were a few small buildings tucked into one end of the lake. All in all he liked the look of it, with the blue waters of Clear Lake spread out below his vantage point.

For quite some time Peter had been working to disaster-proof the club's financial position. Their considerable wealth was spread around a number of separate investment accounts and bank accounts registered to various dummy corporations that had been established for that purpose.

The representatives of each corporation who were authorized to make transactions on each account always included Peter and one or two other lieutenants, though not the same ones on every account. He kept three separate independent pools. The signing officers all used false IDs, which were well established with the banks. Statements were all handled electronically, as were investment instructions and monetary transfers. Anyone attempting to trace any of those financial affairs back to the club would find very little to go on, and the law firms who hosted the dummy companies were instructed to immediately alert the club if anyone started snooping around.

Peter was pretty confident that if the club's base near Twin Falls, Idaho, was ever taken out by law enforcement, despite his efforts at concealment, the club would retain control over ample financial resources to reestablish itself as long as either he or a few other key leaders escaped. They would have the resources required for high-priced lawyers to represent any club members charged with criminal offenses, and to make life easier for anyone actually convicted. However, he had decided some months ago that in addition to the financial safety net, the club needed a physical disaster recovery site at which members could gradually re-congregate and use as a new base from which to mount whatever defense was called for.

In his travels Peter had gained some familiarity with both the coastal region and Lake County of Northern California. Both areas appealed to him, and he felt either one would be far enough from the Idaho base to allow plenty of space for the club to disburse and break contact with any pursuit but close enough to reach in a reasonable period of time. Earlier in the summer he had dispatched the small team that was gathered around him now, including his senior lieutenant, Angelo Calavechia.

The group's assignment had been to scout the area around Clear Lake for a suitable property. They were authorized to acquire a half-ton truck and a small car for their scouting activities to avoid appearing to be what they were, part of a motorcycle gang. They were meant to remain as inconspicuous as possible in every way, including dressing in civilian clothing. If they were to establish a base in the area they would not want it to be known as a cycle gang hangout to either nearby homeowners, law enforcement, or especially one of the California-based gangs who would likely act to repel an invasion of their territory. Angelo was no angel, but he could clean up enough to pass for a corporate executive with anyone they needed to deal with.

Angelo's first words were, "Boss, I know you wanted a property on the big lake, but in three months of looking this is the place that best fits all of your requirements. You can see Clear Lake, it's a twenty-minute drive away, and this place has its own little private lake, as you can see, which has pretty decent fishing. It's well away from other homeowners with a full section of land for privacy.

"The whole area is covered in horse trails, or ATV trails, both on this property and on adjacent land, so we can ensure we've got multiple escape routes for the bikes. Also, we can access several different roads that lead into the Mendocino National Forest, which is a short hop from here and provides plenty of room to disappear. We just couldn't find a place right on the lake with enough privacy and that couldn't be easily surrounded and cut off. We have a conditional offer on this property, subject to the approval of the senior partner, you. It would take a little more money than what you want to spend, but we could layout another few hundred thousand and also buy another small place right on the lake if you want."

Peter smiled at the team and could see their relief that he wasn't disappointed or angry. "That's fine, guys," he said. "It looks like a great location. The lakeshore was just a personal whim. Privacy, security and emergency egress are much more important. How much is this going to set us back?"

Angelo replied, "The place was up for three and a half million, but it has been on the market for a while and we were able to negotiate them down to two point eight million. I know it's a lot, plus we would have to build a club house and a bedroom wing. There is a small cabin just over there that was once a hunting cabin. It would do for a few of us, but it's not anywhere near big enough for all of us. That'll probably run us another half million or so."

"You're right," Peter replied, "That's more than I thought we'd need to spend, but we've got the money and we do need a backup base. What else can you tell me about the suitability of the area?"

"Boss, it seems like it would work well," Angelo said. "There are the two towns within easy driving distance, Lucerne and Nice, with several grocery stores to spread our business around. We would front this place as a private hunting club and there is lots of hunting here, turkey, wild pigs and deer. So, we would not draw any attention with an occasional large grocery shopping list divided up among the local stores.

"We have also been keeping an eye out for both local law enforcement and other bikers as you asked us to. The Lake County Sheriff's Department is the primary law enforcement. They are definitely around, but they have a lot of ground to cover so we'd have to go out of our way to attract their attention. Of course, they would call in support from the state police, which they call the California Highway Patrol, for anything serious. We've seen very little biker activity, a few solo riders and small groups of six or less, mostly just recreational riders, not hard cases. Again, it seems unlikely we'd attract any action as long as we keep a low profile."

"All right guys, you've done well," said Peter. "I agree, this seems like a good location even if it is pricey. Let's go ahead and close. Angelo, you have access to the funds you'll need. This is now your project, so I am going to have to ask you to stay here and coordinate everything needed to establish a base here for the whole club. Have a proper set of plans drawn up for a clubhouse that can double as a hunting lodge and send them to me. I'd like to move things along as quickly as possible. You never know when we might need it. The rest of you have a choice. If you are tired of being here, then you can ride back home with me tomorrow and we'll rotate some other guys in to support Angelo. Or, you can stay here. I think you'll find the winter here a lot easier to take than back in Idaho. Just let me know.

"Now, I could use some lunch and then, if you have any fishing gear, I'd like to try out our private lake."

Chapter 14

Mid-November, 2027
El Peñón summit, near Vicuña, Chile

Following Darya's discovery of a previously unidentified transient object sitting somewhere between a star in the Sagittarius constellation and the Earth, the ensuing investigation was initially a routine matter. Although the location of the object was unusual, the detection and tracking of such objects was an ongoing activity at the LSST, and in fact was one of the primary reasons it had been constructed.

The tracking process was standardized and largely automated. It began by confirming the detection of the object by immediately recording several fresh pictures with the telescope's viewing field centered on the object, then running these back through the transient object detection program. This had all happened immediately following the initial alert, and it did in fact confirm that a star in Sagittarius, which would normally be completely visible, had disappeared from sight.

The disappearance of the star could mean that it had been engulfed by a massive black hole, but there would typically be evidence of that for some time both before and after. Since there was no evidence of the massive energy flux from the destruction of a star, it was much more likely that the star had simply been temporarily occluded by another object, a dark one, passing between it and the point of view from the observatory. It was important to verify the occlusion fairly quickly. Depending on the velocity of the object, how nearly perpendicular its path of movement lay to the line of sight from the observatory, and how far out along that line of sight the object was situated, it could soon complete its traverse in front of the star and then once again be undetectable against the dark interstellar background.

At this point almost nothing could be known about the object other than that it existed and was moving. No estimate could be made of its diameter, mass, or velocity or even whether it was traveling to the left or right, upward or downward relative to the star, or toward it or away from it.

All of this would require further observation of successive positions of the object. However, such observations could only occur if and when the object occluded additional stars.

Estimating the object's orbit would require at least three observations spaced out over a long enough period for the object to have covered a good distance along its path. However, initially, repeated observations were taken over fairly short intervals of time, starting at minutes and gradually lengthening out to an hour. This was required because, until the next sighting of an occluded star, there was no way to know in which direction the object was moving and therefore it was important to determine that direction before the object moved outside the telescope's viewing field. Once the second observation could be obtained it would be possible to track its direction from there. In the meanwhile, the telescope remained centered on the initial observation. Fortunately the LSST had an extremely wide viewing field and so it was very likely that it would spot the next star occlusion no matter which direction that lay from the initial observation, or how far away.

Two nights later, at the initial hourly scan of the occluded star's location, it was seen to have reappeared, signifying that the transient object had moved on in whatever direction it was moving. Nothing further of note occurred for two weeks, and the observatory settled back into its regular schedule of astronomical research projects. The hourly scans lasted about a minute and were barely noticeable at the end of each scheduled project's allotted hour. Darya had been able to resume her research almost immediately and was quickly approaching the end of the data gathering phase of her thesis. Although she would have no direct role in charting the path of the new object, she still found herself pulling up the pictures from the hourly scans to gaze at and ponder the nature of her discovery.

A couple of weeks later the Big Eye's transient object detection program once again caught sight of the object, or rather it lost sight of another star that the object had passed in front of. One of the advantages of searching in this part of the sky was the huge number of known stars surrounding the background behind the object, leaving it with little scope to disappear for long once first spotted. In this case the second star to be occluded was located in close proximity to the initial observation slightly to the right and above the initial observation, in the telescope's field of view.

Based on the apparent arc in which the object had travelled in the span of two weeks, the observatory's sophisticated software had developed an array of projected potential paths and a search pattern to be initiated the following night at two-hour intervals. The computer's search pattern took into consideration the location of the background stars most likely to be occluded by the transient object on each of its various possible paths.

That morning the senior scientist on site approved the computer-generated search plan after a quick review, knowing that he could never match the computer's effectiveness on such a task. He also e-mailed a heads-up to his counterpart at the Jet Propulsion Laboratory in Pasadena, California, letting him know that they were tracking a fresh transient object and would be forwarding data over in the next few weeks. As a technical matter, the LSST observatory had the ability to map out at least an approximate orbit for the object and extrapolate the risk of it intersecting Earth's orbit at some future date, at a time when the Earth was at the intersection point itself. However, the quants at the JPL were the true experts in orbital mechanics and were mandated by NASA to carry out this analysis.

Nevertheless, with two sightings now in hand as well as the approximate time required for the object to clear away from in front of the initial star, the first clues to the object's path were beginning to emerge. Based on this data, it appeared that the object was either moving relatively slowly or it was quite far out in the distant reaches of the solar system, or a combination of the two. The other possibility was that its orbital path was a close parallel to the line of sight from the observatory to the initial observation point. In that case, its apparent displacement from one observation to the next would still appear to be small from the viewing point of the observatory, but in fact the object could be relatively close to the core of the solar system and moving fairly quickly. Only time would tell.

Chapter 15

December 2, 2027
Boston, Massachusetts/Desert Wadi, near Sirte, Libya

Larry Johnstone was in seventh heaven. After years of scrimping to buy equipment for his research out of his limited grants and often out of his own shallow pockets, he now had a virtually unlimited budget. Better still, his dream of supplying fresh water to an increasingly thirsty world was taking a giant step forward. He looked on as four separate teams of technicians put the finishing touches on four large membrane capacitive deionization cells constructed using the membrane and electrode materials and scaled-up cell geometry from his basic design. This brought the total of completed cells to sixteen.

Each cell was exactly a hundred times the size of his laboratory scale model. Once eight more cells were ready to go, the plant they were designed for would have a target capacity of two million gallons per day, enough to supply the household needs of a 150,000-person city if usage was carefully managed. It would require another two additional such plants to irrigate the agricultural production required to feed such a city, assuming low water intensive crops such as beets, carrots, tomatoes, lettuce, potatoes, and strawberries, and chicken as the primary protein source.

Each plant would require only one hundred and twenty-five kilowatts of power capacity, which could be supplied by a modest three-hundred-kilowatt solar array operating ten hours per day combined with high-efficiency batteries for overnight operation. A low-cost one-megawatt array could supply the needs of all three plants. Alternatively, and even more efficiently, the plants could be tied into a full-sized solar farm serving all the power needs of a district. Solar farms are highly efficient sources of power in the hot, dry middle latitudes where water tends to be the scarcest, and a typical commercial scale farm could have up to one hundred megawatts of capacity, which the desalination plants would hardly put a dent in.

Larry was now employed as the chief engineer of Fresh Water Solutions Inc., a brand-new corporation of which all the shares were registered to a trustee acting on behalf of the Government of the United States of America. The corporation had acquired a perpetual exclusive license to Larry's technology for a large initial payment to MIT plus an annual license fee. It had also acquired the large warehouse in which Larry currently stood, located on the shore of the Boston outer harbor near the Weymouth Fore River mouth. The warehouse had been rapidly renovated, cleaned and fitted out as a high-tech assembly and fabrication facility. It was designed to produce the twenty-four cells required for a two-million-gallon-per-day desalination plant at the rate of four cells every three days. The warehouse included a wharf large enough to berth a full-sized transoceanic container ship, and one was expected to arrive in a few weeks.

The scale-up had gone smoothly. The first unit had required only a few tweaks to achieve the same power usage efficiency as the bench model. Thereafter each unit had tested out within a few percent, plus or minus, of the design efficiency target. Larry was splitting his time between his laboratory and the warehouse, still refining the design parameters in hopes of squeezing out a little greater power usage efficiency.

Larry was amazed and excited by the speed with which his dream was coming true. Of course, he couldn't tell anyone about it, and there was an ample number of very competent-looking security guards stationed around the warehouse to discourage any uninvited visitors. The President of the United States was being kept fully informed of the success of the scale-up and the production rate of the high-efficiency desalination plants.

While Larry mused over how much fresh water would soon be flowing into thirsty lands as a result of his work, another young man was crouched in a shallow wadi in just such a land. A hundred yards from the wadi stood a small compound, the object of the young man's surveillance. The small compound was the home and headquarters of Tarek Maziq, one of Libya's main warlords. Captain Mark Simpson and his team of seven other Delta Force operators had hiked the twenty miles from their drop point to the compound between dusk and eleven o'clock at night. They had travelled in the open desert, away from any roads or villages. They were now resting and observing.

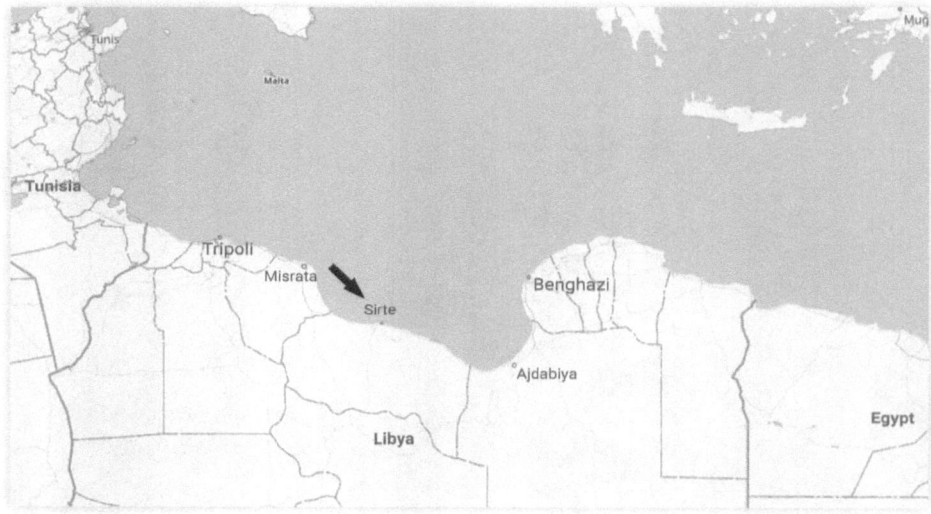

Several days earlier U.S. intelligence sources had determined that a Russian freighter landing at Sirte was carrying, in addition to food and medical supplies, a number of heavy transport trucks loaded with a large quantity of automatic rifles, crew-served machine guns and mortars. This military equipment was thought to be destined for delivery to Maziq, a ruthless and aggressive warlord the Russians had been currying favor with, in contravention of the standing UN resolution prohibiting supply of arms to any of the Libyan factions. The equipment was sufficient in quantity to shift the balance of military power in favor of Maziq in his simmering clashes with adjacent warlords. In particular, Maziq's immediate target was expected to be the territory of Atia al-Obedi, leader of a more moderate faction.

The Delta Force team was tasked with confirming the delivery of the arms to the Russian proxy, assisted by overhead drone photography and then, once confirmed, destroying the equipment. The team had been ordered to avoid any unnecessary loss of life and minimize collateral damage to the compound and its inhabitants, so they were armed with personal weapons only, plus thermite grenades for material destruction. However, the convoy transporting the equipment was expected to be heavily guarded by both Russian covert forces and Maziq's men. The team would be extracted by helicopter from a location only a half-mile back along their ingress route once their mission was completed.

At eleven thirty that night, the team could clearly hear the motors of several heavy-duty trucks approaching. Captain Simpson planned to wait until the convoy was inside the compound, unloading had begun and he had confirmation from the drone operator that the shipment was in fact prohibited military equipment. As the last of six large trucks approached the gate of the compound, eight wraiths slipped up behind the truck to either side of the opening. Minutes later, the overhead drone photographed an impressive array of military hardware being unloaded from the first truck and the Delta captain received the clearance he'd been waiting for.

The gate guards were preoccupied with the arrival of the convoy and its load of toys and took no notice of the arrival of the Delta team. The guards would be found several hours later, still unconscious but with no more injuries than a moderate concussion. The convoy security force was not as fortunate. The Americans moved swiftly through the courtyard of the compound, dispatching all resistance with short two- or three-round bursts from their sound- and flash-suppressed M4A1 carbines. Several of the security force threw down their weapons and begged for mercy as they saw the more aggressive Russian operators meet a violent fate. They were then gagged, bound and moved back to the gate.

Four of the Delta operators took up defensive positions in a crescent between the trucks and the main buildings of the compound. Three snapped additional pictures of the contents of each truck before lobbing several M14 incendiary thermite grenades into each truck plus one under the hood and a half dozen into the well-stocked armory building into which unloading had begun. Captain Simpson stood aside in the shadows, issuing occasional commands into his helmet-mounted speech-actuated tactical radio network microphone and watching closely for any activity from any of the adjacent buildings. He was filling the dual role of team command and tactical overwatch.

For the captain, whose system was now coursing with adrenaline, it seemed to take forever before the incendiary placers reported they had completed their jobs. It was, in fact, less than five minutes from when the team entered the gate until Simpson issued the order for a controlled withdrawal to and then out through the gate. The operation had been conducted in near total silence, partly thanks to the swiftness, surprise and skill of the team operating in a low-light environment, but also partly thanks to luck. It would have been easy to have overlooked just one hostile fighter for long enough for him to have raised an alarm and to have brought fire onto one or more of the team. However, as it was, the captain thought there was a good chance that no one in the interior of the compound was even aware of the assault.

The grenades were fused for two minutes and so most were already starting to cook as the team egressed. Each one would generate a four-thousand-degree furnace for a radius of about five yards. The team had ignited thirty of them. They would melt any nearby metallic objects and ignite any flammable materials. The team had withdrawn to their initial point in the wadi by the time the first of many thousands of rounds of ammunition began to cook off. They paused briefly to watch the fireworks before commencing the eight-minute march to their extraction site. The Blackhawk was flaring in as they reached the site, having been called in by the captain from their offshore station above the USS *Gerald R. Ford*.

News of the successful operation made its way quickly up the military chain of command. President James Rushton disliked having authorized an action that would certainly result in the deaths of several men, even if they were in the service of entities hostile to the United States, and possibly including death or injury to American armed forces personnel. However, he would not shrink from the use of reasonable force to protect the interests of his country and its allies from hostile and unlawful actions by less principled parties. He was very relieved that he would soon be able to provide Libyans with constructive assistance in achieving a better quality of life, rather than just acting as a referee in the squabbles among their leaders.

Chapter 16

December 13, 2027
El Peñón summit, near Vicuña, Chile/Pasadena, California

The third observation of object X/2027U3, the provisional name assigned to Darya's comet, came about three weeks after the second observation. The senior scientist at the LSST observatory, Dr. George Rigby, was pleased to have another data point in hand, though he expected that the observed positions were a little too close together to provide a good orbital solution. The data was downloaded into the observatory's orbital mechanics software and simultaneously transmitted to NASA's Jet Propulsion Laboratory in Pasadena, California. Soon after, the previously routine investigation became decidedly nonroutine.

The data fed into the algorithm in the JPL mainframe computer included the angles of the line of sight between the observatory and the object for each observation, as measured relative to the horizon and relative to true north. It also included the position of the observatory and the time of each observation. The software then estimated the orbital parameters of the object assuming that each of the three lines of sight intersected an elliptical orbit, with the Sun at the focus of the ellipse. The ellipse for long-period comets is necessarily highly eccentric, with the aphelion, or most distant point on the orbit, much farther away than the perihelion, or point nearest to the Sun. The aphelion for a long-period comet would likely be somewhere within the Oort cloud, one hundred AU or more from the Sun, while the perihelion could be less than one AU, that is, inside of the Earth's orbit.

There is typically some measurement error for each observation, so even three widely spaced observations would generate at best an approximate, or most likely orbit. Successive observations would gradually refine the predicted orbit to an eventual degree of precision, at least for the near term, of within a few hundred miles. However, this degree of precision requires multiple observations of the object at different points in its orbit.

High levels of orbit prediction accuracy also require taking into consideration the fact that there are many more gravitational influences on the object than just the Sun. These would include the eight major planets, especially the four outer gas giants, plus the many other bodies orbiting the Sun. How much of an influence all these bodies would have depends on how close the object came to any of them on its various circuits of the solar system. So, the orbital calculations involve projecting the positions of all the major solar system objects in relationship to the initial estimated path of the new object, and then adjusting its predicted orbit to reflect the various tugs that it will experience along the way. This dynamic interaction may need to be extrapolated many years into the future for short-period objects because such an object may experience a different set of gravitational influences each time it passes through the inner solar system, potentially reshaping an initially harmless orbit into a dangerous one. The process involves sophisticated mathematical algorithms and very powerful computer processors. The current version of the orbit prediction software was known as Cruncher IV.

The first sign that something unusual was in play was the extended period of time that Cruncher IV seemed to be taking to spit out its initial estimated orbit before the more complex step of integrating in the influences of the planets. Normally this should have taken a matter of seconds. When the program

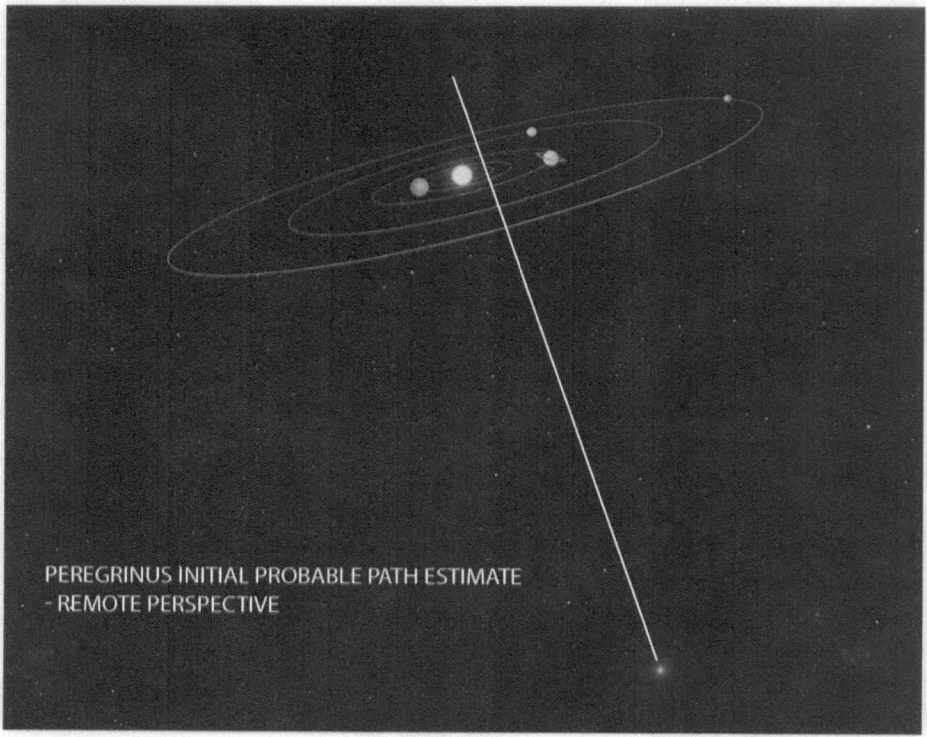

PEREGRINUS INITIAL PROBABLE PATH ESTIMATE
- REMOTE PERSPECTIVE

reported no initial estimate after crunching for over a minute, Tony Galletsia, the applied mathematician who had been assigned to oversee the analysis, suspended the computer run and requested a download of the last few cycles of calculations.

Tony viewed Cruncher's efforts to fit a conventional elliptical orbit to the three data points, including trying more unusual parabolic and hyperbolic paths. He looked at the orbital formula parameters that had been sequentially adjusted to find a rough fit, without success. He also had Cruncher generate a three-dimensional diagram of the solar system with the estimated position of the three observations and then with the closest fit ellipse overlaid into the picture. What he saw was a long, thin, nearly linear path extending back far behind and below the solar system, and then passing up through it. The three observation points didn't line up well enough with the projected ellipse to satisfy Cruncher, which expected to find a near perfect fit, or more likely an array of them.

However, the picture was clear enough to the mathematician to get his adrenaline spiking, especially after expanding the image of the object's path as it transited up through the solar system.

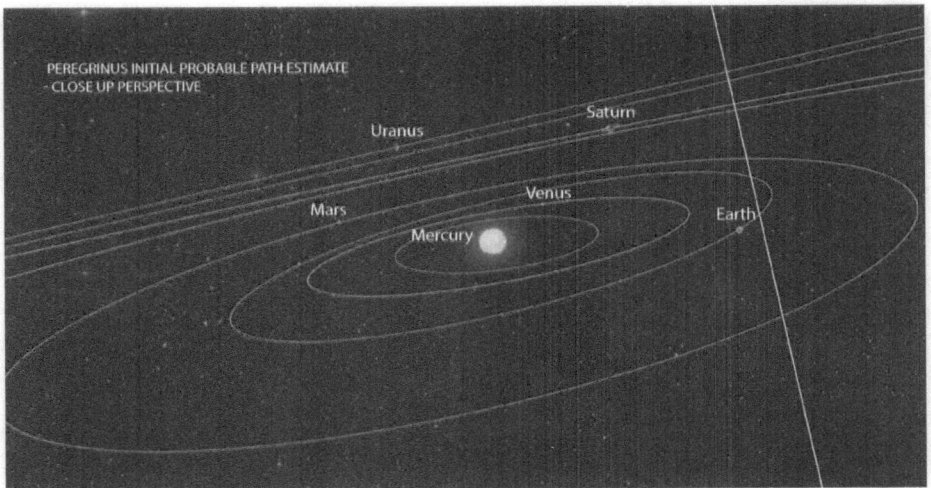

Tony sent off a brief text to the senior scientist at the LSST observatory, to his immediate department head, and to the head of JPL. Then he contacted a doctoral fellow who was under his supervision and asked him to check the information that had been fed into Cruncher against the original astronomical observations, looking for any possible error in the data.

A few hours later Eleanor Appleton, senior manager of the Near-Earth Object Collision Risk Assessment Department at the JPL, joined Tony and the director of the JPL in a small video conference room. Dr. George Rigby, the Senior Scientist at the LSST observatory was linked into the meeting. Once the video link was established, Eleanor got right to business.

"Okay Tony, you've got our undivided attention. Tell us what you know. Do we have a problem?"

Tony replied, "It's really too soon to know if we have a problem or not, but we could, which is why I gave you all the heads-up and suggested that we meet. What we know is this: George's latest object doesn't fit the normal pattern of a long-period comet, the most likely solar system body given where it is coming from, which means it doesn't really fit the pattern for anything we've seen before.

"The path it seems to be on has very little if any curvature, subject to the measurement error inherent in only three closely spaced observations. In other words, it seems to be passing through our solar system in a more or less straight line, not going around the Sun in any kind of orbit, even a highly eccentric one. It is possible that the Sun could capture it on its way through and draw it into an orbit like that of a long-period comet, in which case it might return many years from now. However, its current path seems like this will be both its first pass through the inner system and its last as well. Its path will certainly be bent a little as it passes through, but likely not slowed enough to be captured into a solar orbit. That will depend on how close it comes to the Sun and on how much mass and velocity it has.

"We have no way to estimate mass at present. It isn't near enough to any of the outer planets to perturb their orbits even if it were much larger than a typical comet, and nor will it get close enough for that on its present path. We'll have to wait until it gets close enough to us to reflect sufficient sunlight for a direct observation of its apparent diameter, then use an assumed density."

The department head broke in, "Tony, how long will it be before it is close enough for direct observation and, more important, how close is it going to get to us?"

"Yes boss, I was just coming to that," he replied. "We have a pretty good velocity estimate based on our initial three observations. This thing is moving. It is closing on the inner solar system at two hundred and sixty thousand miles per hour relative to the Sun. That's much faster than a typical comet would travel when that far away from the Sun. So that's another unusual feature of this object. It is currently quite a long way out, about fifty AU, still a lot farther out than the orbit of Neptune, the outermost planet, or even Pluto in the Kuiper belt. However, traveling at that speed it could be within the inner solar system in a little more than two years, sooner if its mass is similar to a typical comet and it accelerates as it gets closer. So, it should actually be visible to a big scope like the LSST in a few months depending on how reflective its surface is.

"As to how near it will come to Earth, well, that's why I thought this is important enough to call a meeting on short notice. With our three observations so tightly spaced together, there is still room for a lot of error in the initial estimates — its current position or distance out, its speed and, especially, its path direction through space. The path direction has the most uncertainty at present because a path uncertainty of only plus or minus one arc degree, which is about what we have at this time, will result in a large cone of possible trajectories when applied over a distance of fifty AU — about eighty million miles in diameter, or nearly the distance from the Sun to the Earth, at the point where the cone of possibilities intersects the solar system plane of the ecliptic.

"The most probable path has the object climbing up through the plane of the ecliptic somewhere in the inner solar system, as indicated in this graphic." Tony activated the large display screen in the video conference room and called up the trajectory he had developed.

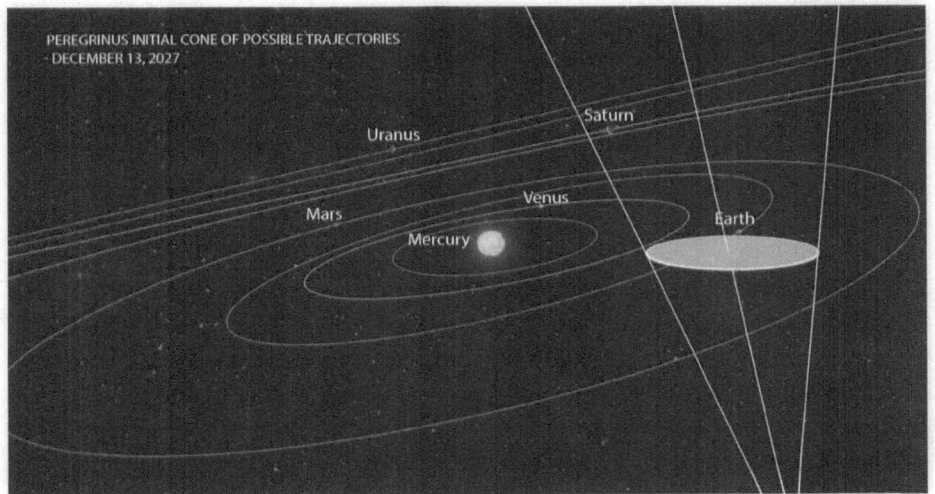

"If we move in for a close-up with the planets positioned where they will be at the time the object intercepts the plane of the ecliptic, it looks like this." He then expanded the apparent magnification of the computer-generated diagram and overlaid the cone of possible trajectories he had developed over the last hour.

A stunned silence ensued as the three leaders reflected on what they were seeing.

Tony continued, "As you can see, the predicted path, as the object passes though the ecliptic, spans a wide range of possibilities until we can refine the data, but it includes a passage anywhere from just outside of Venus's orbit almost

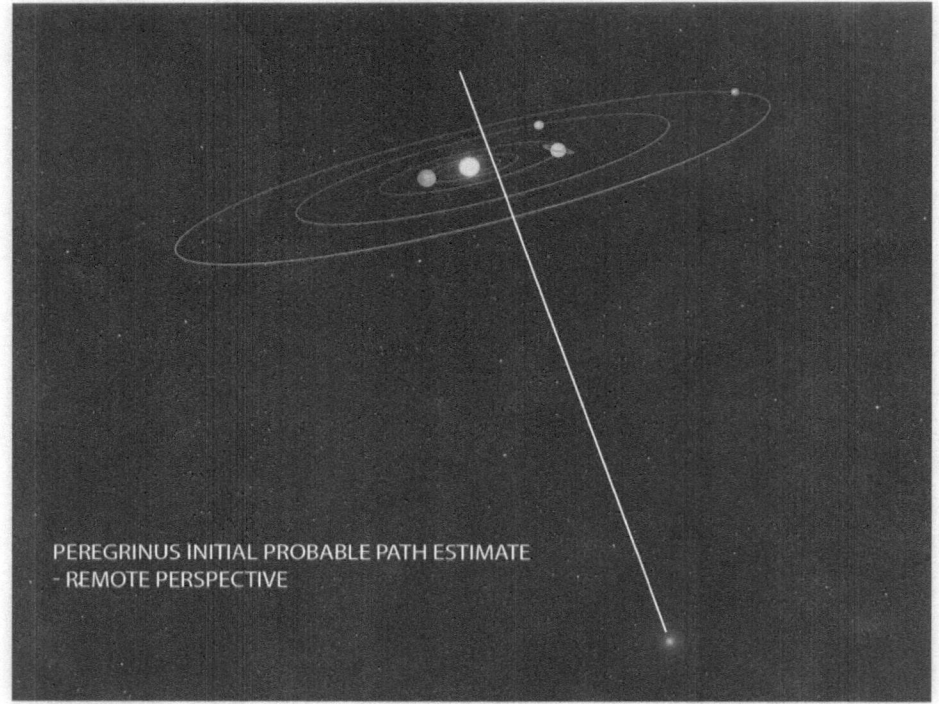

PEREGRINUS INITIAL PROBABLE PATH ESTIMATE
- REMOTE PERSPECTIVE

to Mars's orbit. And it definitely includes an intersection with Earth's orbit as a possibility. That's not a high possibility — there's a lot of space out there — but it is a possibility.

"Of course, even if the object intersects Earth's orbit, it is still unlikely that it would do so at the exact time the Earth is at that exact point in its orbit. However, until we can more accurately pin down the object's current speed, rate of acceleration and distance, we can't pinpoint where the Earth will be in its own orbit as the object passes through the ecliptic, nor where the other inner planets will be. It looks like the Earth will be somewhere on the same side of its orbit as the side that the object will pass through. I don't want to raise the alarm, but there is at least a finite risk of a collision that I can't rule out without additional data."

"Okay, Tony," said Eleanor, "you did the right thing to call us together. Let me sum up what I think you are telling us, but I'll preface by saying I see nothing here that should cause us any great concern. This scenario is similar to many of our initial Near-Earth Object sightings where we have insufficient information at first to rule out a collision. Most of the time it's an asteroid in the plane of the ecliptic and so if it intersects Earth's orbit it does so at least twice and possibly four times each pass, and it will continue to do so on a periodic basis for a long time to come. Here we seem to have a one-pass single-intersection-point risk if there's any orbital intersection at all. So, on that hand we have a much lower risk than a typical NEO initial detection.

"On the other hand, we have some interesting differences. First, Tony, you seem to be suggesting that this is neither an asteroid nor a typical comet. It is coming from an unusual direction, it is coming unusually fast, and it is not following an orbital path. Are you thinking that this object has come from interstellar space rather than from the distant reaches of the solar system? Hold your response for a moment. Regardless of where it originated, we don't yet have any direct observation; therefore, no mass estimate — and it is coming fast. At the speed it is coming it wouldn't take much mass to create a major high-energy impact. That doesn't change the very low risk of a collision, but it does mean a collision could have high consequences.

"So, I think that means this is not a dire situation. Mr. Director, I think we should keep this to just the four of us for now until we have a clearer picture. We all remember the initial scare with Apophis, which eventually proved to be harmless. At the same time, I think we should take this seriously and attach the highest priority to improving our information and the accuracy of our path prediction, timing of approach, and mass estimate. This should be the highest priority tasking of the LSST for the next while. Tony, does that square with your thinking?"

Tony was an applied mathematician, but he was also savvy enough not to disagree with his boss in front of her boss.

"Yes Eleanor, it does seem like this X/2027U3 may come from outside our solar system, and I agree that the risk of a collision is low, and I especially agree that we should make getting more data our top priority. Whether we should be advising anyone further up within NASA is not for me to say."

The director said, "Eleanor and Tony, thanks for this briefing. It is interesting, if at least a little worrisome. How long will it take you to refine your analysis, and can we find a little less cryptic name for this thing, but not one with any scary connotations?"

Tony replied, "Well, any additional observations would help, but we need to see this thing at least another couple of hundred million miles along its path to really cut down the estimate error bands, so about another five weeks, assuming we can spot it at that point. I haven't run its trajectory against the stellar background to know whether it might occlude another star at about that point in time. That's something the LSST folk are best equipped to do."

The director grimaced, "Eleanor, that's a long time for me to sit on this without briefing the top of the house. I'll give you two weeks to refine your risk assessment and then, even if I prove to be Chicken Little, I have to update my boss. George, can you keep this under wraps while still giving it top priority on the Big Eye?"

The senior scientist did not work for the director of the JPL, wasn't a government employee and had his own chain of accountability to consider, but he had a lot of discretion on the operation of the LSST during his tenure on site. He also agreed with the importance of clarifying the collision risk for X/2027U3.

"Yes, Mr. Director, I think I can manage that for the next little while. I am going to need to assign an astronomer to oversee this project, but I think I know just the right person, and she also already knows a lot about X/2027U3 since she's the one who was using the Big Eye when the object was first spotted by the transient detector. I may be able to help you out with a better name too. We will stay in close touch as further information emerges."

The video conference wrapped up and each of the participants went to work on their assigned tasks. Tony Galletsia had an uneasy sense that his boss was a little too optimistic about the risk posed by X/2027U3, but it was gut feeling only and he wasn't about to contradict her unless he had something more concrete to go on.

Chapter 17

Early January, 2028
Sonoma County, Northern California

Brad pulled his Super Stock E-Class 2018 Camaro SS "Red Rocket" out of the staging lanes and lined up in the burnout area of the left lane of the Sonoma Raceway drag strip, as directed by the staging crew. He punched the throttle and spun his eleven-inch slicks in the wetted-down area to clean off any dirt or gravel and let them smoke a bit on the dry pavement at the back of the staging area to warm and soften the tires. He glanced to the right as he inched forward up to the staging line to see where the Shelby GT350 in the next lane was. He moved to the pre-stage line and then the stage line as quickly as possible, knowing his opponent would have to rush just a bit to get staged in time to avoid a race delay disqualification in this, the final Super Stock match of the meet.

SONOMA COUNTY
DRAG STRIP STARTING LINE

Brad's five-hundred-plus-horsepower, 6.2-liter L T1 engine was running strong, and he had the suspension and wheelie bars well-tuned. He had dialed in a time of 9.5 seconds, not quite a second faster than the NHRA index for his class, but his opponent was in the same Super Stock E-Class, so it would be a heads-up race; whoever crossed the finish line first would win with no handicap and no risk of disqualifying on a breakout below dial-in.

The twenty-eight-year-old mechanical engineer knew that the Mustang would be pulling more horsepower than his Camaro. He also knew it was proportionately heavier. He figured he had a modest advantage on torque with his larger displacement, longer stroke engine. It would produce a little more torque at a lower RPM than the hard-working, high-revving, 5.2-liter Shelby power plant. He would need to grab a couple of car lengths out of the hole to avoid being caught by the Shelby at the top end.

The right-hand lane pre-stage and stage lights came on, and a fraction of a second later the three orange lights on both sides of the Christmas tree flashed on, followed 0.4 seconds later by the green "go" light. Brad punched the throttle to the floor the instant the oranges lit. He was relying on his brief reaction time, and the foot or so his car could move before triggering the elapsed-time timer to avoid incurring a red light disqualification if the green light hadn't yet come on.

The big slicks dug in and loaded up, with the soft side walls wrinkling up as they absorbed a portion of the torque energy from the big motor. The Red Rocket launched forward with minimum wheel spin and just a little front-end lift before the wheelie bars counteracted that tendency.

Brad paid no attention to the right-hand lane. He was concentrating entirely on keeping his car straight and centered as the eight-speed programmed automatic transmission kept his motor close to its six thousand RPM horsepower peak, and his car rapidly accelerated down the track. From the stands his girlfriend, Alyssa, and other spectators could see that the Camaro pulled a good two-and-a-half car length holeshot on the Mustang and held it through the first half of the quarter-mile strip. The Mustang began to close the gap, but the Camaro was still a good length-and-a-half in front at the quarter mile.

Brad pulled off into the return lane and was handed his time slip as he passed the timing shack. His elapsed time was 9.46 seconds, so he would have broken out below his 9.5 dial-in and been disqualified if it had been an index race. His top speed was a hundred and thirty-five miles per hour. The Mustang ran a 9.50 elapsed time with a one-hundred-and-forty-mile-per-hour top speed. If the race had been another three hundred feet, or about 23 percent longer, the Mustang would have caught up, but that was irrelevant in the world of drag racing.

From what Alyssa later told him about the length of his holeshot at the starting line and his lead at the finish line, Brad figured he might have launched about a tenth of a second sooner than the Shelby. His 0.04 second lower elapsed time would only account for about nine feet of his car length and a half, or twenty-four foot, finish line lead. Most of the lead must have come from being quicker off the mark. He was happy with the car's performance and his own.

CHEVY HOLE-SHOT

Brad Webber was an analytical thinker by nature. It was a style that fit well with both his job as a design engineer at Energy Systems Inc. in Santa Rosa and his hobby as a race car builder and driver. He was comfortable with the technical aspects and physics behind both heating and cooling systems and high performance motors, but he also enjoyed rolling up his sleeves, grabbing a tool kit and fixing just about anything.

As they drove back from Sonoma to Healdsburg for the weekend, Alyssa thought about their relationship and how far it might go. She knew they had some common interests, but also some differences. Although she was intelligent and educated, her approach to thinking through a problem was more intuitive than analytical. When Brad and Alyssa tackled something together, they had to navigate their different thought styles and work out how their styles could complement each other.

They were both conservation minded, though Alyssa found Brad's love of high horsepower engines and drag racing to be a little inconsistent with minimizing their environmental footprint. Alyssa's price for being Brad's pit monkey and cheerleader for a day of racing was that he would help her out with her morning volunteer shift at the Healdsburg Food Pantry the next day. After that they'd ride up to the power plant to work on her latest extracurricular project. Brad was entirely on board with this agenda, and she didn't really begrudge him his occasional day of tire-smoking, engine-roaring fun. She was looking forward to a romantic dinner and the intimate ecstasy that would follow.

The next day they arrived at the plant at about noon, after an hour and a quarter grunt up the two-thousand-five-hundred-foot altitude gain from Healdsburg. They'd brought bread and cheese and a bottle of wine for lunch, which they set out on a picnic table at the far corner of the plant's parking lot, as far from the humming steam turbine as possible.

After lunch they checked out a few things. First was the makeshift vapor recovery system for pressure spikes releasing through the main pressure relief valve situated just before the pressure regulation manifold outside the plant. One of Alyssa's biggest challenges was managing the amount of makeup water that needed to be injected into the geothermal system to compensate for water losses, both below ground and above. The condenser system inside the plant and downstream of the turbine was designed specifically to recover nearly all the water from the superheated steam spinning the turbine. From there the recycle water was pumped back to the various injection wells to sustain steam pressure in the reservoir rock lying above the magma pool four miles below.

Normally the steam recovery and recycle system worked quite effectively, and it needed to. Western Renewable Power had no local water rights. The water in nearby Little Sulphur Creek was strictly off limits. The company did have a contract to draw water off the Santa Rosa treated wastewater pipeline system, which had been constructed several decades previously to feed the geothermal plants in The Geysers area. However, there were limits to the availability from that source and for several months the Western Renewable Power plant had been pushing up against those limits.

Alyssa had identified the culprit as being her main pressure relief valve. Normally the pressure regulation manifold could control the incoming steam pressure by routing the steam through a variety of expansion chambers or even bleeding a little off into a holding tank. However, when an occasional pressure spike exceeded the manifold's capacity, the main pressure relief valve would be forced open and steam would vent directly to the atmosphere. She liked to keep the setting on the valve fairly low to provide quick relief and minimize the risk of a spike-within-a-spike overpressuring the system and causing a catastrophic turbine failure.

For several months the frequency of relief valve releases had been quite a bit higher than normal. Alyssa had verified that the valve was functioning properly, but and that the subterranean steam reservoir feeding her steam wells seemed to be having an extended case of burps. She had checked with the other large operator in the area, and they were experiencing similar surges. Nobody was seeing anything extreme enough to be dangerous for now, though it was a little troubling, and it was certainly a nuisance.

Alyssa was keeping in close touch with the United States Geological Survey agency, which monitored tremors in much of California, making sure she would be forewarned if anything serious appeared to be developing. In the meanwhile, after discussing her problem with Brad, they had devised a solution of sorts.

The relief valve vented horizontally at a point just after the collection manifold, which routed the pipes from all the steam wells into a single larger pipe, about a hundred feet before the pressure control manifold. The steam plumes would typically jet fifty or a hundred feet out to the side, and the area was enclosed with a chain-link fence well marked with warning signs.

Surrounding the valve and extending almost to the fence line, there was now a large polyethylene tent. Beneath the tent, and extending a couple of feet beyond its edges, was a second, flatter, inverted tent, the bottom of which was about two feet above the ground at its low point in the center, where it fed into a plastic tube.

The steam plumes from the valve rose, expanded, and condensed, with the resulting water vapor particles either drifting down to the lower surface or rising to the upper surface. They dripped from the upper surface down onto the lower surface. Eventually all the condensate would collect at the low point, run down the tubing and be pumped into the main water recovery collection tank. If it happened to rain, which it did in the winter, the system would also collect all the rain that fell onto the upper tent. It wasn't too pretty, but it worked, and it was a cheap solution. Plus, working on it together had been a positive experience for Alyssa and Brad.

After looking over their vapor collection system to make sure it was functioning properly, they moved on to their next project. This was the one that Alyssa was really excited about. It combined several different attributes that were close to her heart. From early on in her job as plant superintendent, she had been struck by how much natural geothermal energy was being wasted because there was no use for the low-grade steam coming off the back end of the turbine, other than to capture it and recycle the resulting hot water back into the reservoir. She had ample heat energy but no good use to put it to.

Then, while volunteering at the Healdsburg Food Pantry, she had learned that much of the fresh produce they distributed to needy families in the area was donated by local farms, except in the winter time when it was too cool to grow vegetables in Northern California. The Pantry would then have to dip into its cash to buy produce wholesale from Southern California. Alyssa had a green thumb and kept a small greenhouse in her backyard for her own vegetables and flowers; so she knew you could grow them year-round with a little supplementary heating and a smart ventilation system to regulate temperature and humidity. Then the penny dropped, and she realized she had found a possible way to put the wasted heat energy from the geothermal plant to good use, though there were still many details to work out.

The final impetus for her project also originated from her volunteer mornings, once a week, at the Pantry. One of her fellow volunteers there was an older man named Jose Ortiz. Jose was also a regular client of the Pantry. He had been a farmworker for most of his life but had reached an age where he was no longer strong enough or productive enough to get much work. He and his wife were scraping by on food from the Pantry, some meager savings, and occasional temporary jobs. Yet Jose was a warm, friendly man who didn't seem to resent his situation. Alyssa felt sorry, and even a little guilty, when she thought about how much she had in her life compared with the Ortiz's. She had wished she could think of some way to help them short of giving them a handout, which she knew they would be uncomfortable with.

Jose had been more than grateful to join Alyssa's greenhouse project, and he was an important and essential addition. He knew a lot about growing produce, and he was plenty hale enough to tend to the operation of a greenhouse. He had a beat-up old truck to go back and forth in, hauling supplies up to the plant and produce back to Healdsburg. Perhaps most important of all, he and his wife had the time to set up a stall at a nearby farmer's market or two each week and to deliver the rest of the produce to the local grocery stores. Once they started harvesting in December, about one third of the weekly production went to the Food Pantry and the rest got sold. About half of the cash revenue was enough to cover wages and gas for Jose and his wife, with the remainder into a bank account for unexpected expenses.

Of course there had been many more details to work through before she was able to put a seed in the dirt. She had needed to get permission from Western Renewable Power. If it had been a bigger company that would probably never have happened, but the company was small and Alyssa was well known and well liked. It also helped that Alyssa had solved the recycle water loss problem at minimal expense to the company. In her pitch, Alyssa pointed out that it couldn't hurt to further strengthen the company's image in the community by covering the Food Pantry's needs. So, the company humored her on the basis that there would be no disruption to the plant or any expense to the plant beyond a small initial donation and part of the water recovered by the vapor collection system.

Then they had to purchase and erect the greenhouse kit, design and install the plumbing for both the hot water heating system and the irrigation system, install electrical for the ventilation system, and set up the control system to manage it all twenty-four seven. Fortunately, although Brad wasn't the gardening type, he was good with systems. They also got a lot of volunteer help from the plant's contract maintenance team, who were fond of Alyssa and keen to help.

The greenhouse now occupied most of a 60-by-120-foot, six-inch-thick reinforced concrete pad. It was constructed of lightweight rigid plastic tubing, covered with double ply polyethylene sealed to a keyway in the slab to keep out insects, rodents and snakes. It also had a gutter system to collect and store rainwater. They'd managed all that for about ten thousand dollars, which Alyssa and Brad had split between them. While they were at it, with space to spare and free labor from the maintenance team, they had poured a second slab for future expansion.

Brad and Alyssa checked the systems to ensure everything was working well, then spent an hour helping Jose pick the week's beans, broccoli, cabbage, carrots, cauliflower, lettuce, onions, parsnips, peas and peppers. There wasn't any weeding to do since they had steam sterilized the soil before planting.

As they mounted their bikes and headed back down Geysers Road toward Healdsburg, Alyssa felt tremendously satisfied. She had a great job, a handsome and caring lover, and she felt she was making a difference for the better in a world that still needed a lot of improving. She was pretty sure that Brad felt much the same. She was excited about their relationship and thought they had more than just a short-term thing.

Chapter 18

Sunday, January 16, 2028
El Peñón summit, near Vicuña, Chile

Darya was delighted with her new role at the LSST facility and the extension of her stay into the Chilean summer, such as it was at nine thousand feet. The new comet tracking project required a relatively small amount of her time, so she was able to dedicate the rest to analyzing her own thesis data. The processing system at the LSST was more than adequate for her needs, especially when downloaded with her own customized special-purpose wobble detection and extrapolation algorithms.

She was making good progress on her thesis, probably better than if she had returned to the family and social distractions of Oxford and nearby London. So, the additional project was nothing but upside, both from a career and a personal curiosity perspective. She had gladly accepted the role offered by the senior scientist after securing the support and encouragement of her thesis supervisor.

Darya had been intrigued by the transient object, currently labelled X/2027U3, since it had first interrupted her exoplanet research. All staff at the facility were subject to a confidentiality agreement with respect to any research they were involved with or became aware of, but apart from that there was no great secrecy surrounding the tracking project and it was a fairly routine task among the variety of other ongoing projects at the facility. So, no one had discouraged her from staying up to date with the progression of the project as she completed the last few weeks of her fieldwork. Consequently, when the senior scientist asked her to take on the leadership of the project, Darya knew as much as anyone on site about the object and its evolving path, which still wasn't much.

Darya was initially puzzled by why George felt that the conduct of the tracking project needed any more oversight than the automated systems designed for that purpose and the facility technicians, though she jumped at the chance to stay involved and postpone her departure. Once George revealed to her the findings at the JPL, which she had not been aware of, she better understood his desire to have another set of eyes and mind involved. Plus, she was familiar with the situation and had at least some relevant technical abilities. She also better understood why he reminded her of her professional and legal confidentiality obligations. Of course, once privy to the JPL's preliminary path projection cone, she was even more attracted to the assignment of gathering additional observations to support the refinement of the projection. The clincher, though none was really needed, was that George told her he was confident that there would be support in high places for any reasonable name that she might wish to give to the object, like perhaps Ahmadil, whether she took on the project or not.

Darya had not tasked the LSST with any additional surveillance patterns in the latter half of December and the first half of January. She knew from her own work in the field that the Sagittarius region of the sky would not be visible above the horizon for that period, which was why she had timed her own research to be completed by then. She was also in close communication with Tony Galletsia at the JPL, and she knew that, while he would welcome any additional observations, he really needed something that showed the amount of position change over a period of several weeks. So, it made sense to wait until mid-January to fire up the surveillance pattern again.

Darya also had a pretty good idea on where to focus the renewed search. With the cone of probable paths from Tony converted into the coordinate system used to program the aiming points of the LSST, she had a relatively small area of the sky to scan. She also had a pretty good velocity estimate helping to narrow down how far along the cone the object was likely to have traveled. She had overlain the search zone on the star map background of that area to identify which locations within the zone she might be able to spot X/2027U3 as it occluded one of the stars. There were several.

All of the search parameters were loaded into the Big Eye's scanning schedule and were ready to go. Darya had secured a number of short scanning windows every night following the resumption of the search. She didn't need much time for each scan because the entire surveillance zone was within the LSST's image width for a single picture. However, she found she had no difficulty requisitioning all the time she could possibly need. Darya also didn't think it would take many days of searching the zone to spot the big rock, but she was allowing a day or two of less-than-optimal viewing because she had set the schedule, with encouragement from Tony and George, to capture the earliest possible redetection of the object.

Darya was on the spot in the observatory at eleven o'clock at night as the Big Eye was automatically tasked to her first one-minute surveillance slot. She planned to stay until one o'clock in the morning to watch a couple more picture sequences. She would review the rest in the morning, but with instructions to be immediately called in her dormitory room if anything notable appeared. She had also promised to touch base with Tony each morning with a video call. The two had developed an easygoing friendship in the short time they had been working together.

The young astronomer sat in the viewing room waiting for her pictures to begin displaying, as she had on so many prior occasions. She couldn't suppress a little shiver of excitement even though she knew that an immediate result was unlikely. The first picture appeared on the large wall screen. A two-dimensional yellow rectangle was superimposed over the target area, taking up about a quarter of the screen so that even if the estimates of the range of possible positions were off by a bit, the LSST could still detect any anomaly over a broader area. Darya could have selected a three-dimensional outline of the target area, but the LSST camera didn't provide a clear three-dimensional perspective on what it was seeing, so that wouldn't have added a useful frame of reference.

As the screen shifted to the second fifteen-second picture of the target area, once again the detection alert sounded, and Darya's pulse rate spiked. Sure enough, the screen cycled back to the initial picture now carrying a "Transient Object Detected" banner and a small green square enclosing a small part of the sky within the yellow rectangle. The difference was that there was also a second banner across the bottom of the screen below the first, which bore the words "Direct Observation." Sure enough, in the center of the green cursor square, she could see a noticeable tiny pale point of light where none belonged.

The transient object detection program continued to sound the alert and to snap pictures every fifteen seconds, overriding the task scheduler. Darya quickly scanned through the next five pictures and could not see any changes perceptible to the eye. She instructed the senior operator, who she knew quite well by now, to silence the alert and resume the regular schedule. She included the proviso that she wanted another minute of pictures every ten minutes for the next hour before reverting to one minute on the hour every hour. She told him she was going to head back to her room to examine the pictures and would be on call if anything came up. He was to turn the alert tone off before each repeat scan to minimize the drama for the rest of the night.

Back in her room Darya examined the six pictures carefully and ran them through a piece of software similar to the transient object detector but set to detect finer variations over very short time intervals. It could even detect the motion of storms in the atmosphere of some of the solar system's planets. She also ran the next four pictures after that. Neither her visual inspection with a special-purpose ten-times magnifier, nor the program, could detect any difference between the photos, using the first one as the base for each comparison.

Every picture showed the same tiny but distinct glow. At first Darya had wondered whether she had captured an energy release in the visible spectrum from the collision of two distant objects, possibly one of them being her comet. However, without even running the calculations on the mass and impact velocity required to generate enough energy to be visible at fifty AU or more, even to the LSST, it soon became clear that the image was both too stable and too regular to be the result of an explosion. Even at that distance the object was large enough for the LSST to resolve the image into a definite disk — a disk where none had been before — even at the relatively low magnification used for transient object searches. Darya knew better than anyone what that must mean. She called over to the senior operator to request a series of four pictures at fifteen-minute intervals but at maximum magnification.

After checking this picture sequence and applying another special-purpose program to the new magnified images, Darya sent a brief note to George. She said only that she had captured another position observation on the transient object, including an unexpected aspect. She suggested that the project team have a video conference at ten o'clock in the morning Pacific time. She could brief him at nine o'clock. She sent a similar message to Tony, suggesting that he give a heads-up to his bosses that the senior scientist would be calling for a conference. She also routed the position data and images from the latest observation to his inbox. She knew that he was well prepared and would have plenty of time before ten o'clock to update the projected path cone and associated visual display. However, she planned to call him at seven o'clock just to make sure he was up and had received the data. Then she tumbled into bed to catch a few hours of sleep before what she expected to be an eventful day.

Chapter 19

Monday, January 17, 2028
Washington, DC

President James Rushton sat at his desk in the Oval Office and took a few minutes to compose his thoughts before a formal call with the President of Mexico. Although there was no prearranged agenda for the call, he was pretty sure he knew what was on the mind of his southern neighbor.

A few days earlier President Rushton had announced both a significant technological breakthrough in the high-efficiency, low-cost conversion of salt water to fresh water, and also the formation of the Libyan Peace and Prosperity Cooperation League. The League's Middle Eastern membership included Egypt and Saudi Arabia, plus both groups who claimed to be the rightful government of Libya, and two other Libyan leaders exercising de facto control over much of the coastal area between Tripoli in the west and Bengasi in the east. The non-Arab members of the League included the United States, Britain, France, Spain and Italy. Membership was open to any other Arab or non-Arab participants willing to agree to the terms of the League.

The League's cooperation agreement stipulated that none of the Libyan members would employ offensive military force to seize territory from any other member, or otherwise attack any other member. Any restoration of centralized government would be by a negotiated consensual and democratic process. The non-Libyan members agreed to abide by the resolutions made by the United Nations prohibiting provision of arms to any party within Libya. They also agreed that they would not participate or assist in a military action taken by one Libyan member of the League against another. The agreement did not require non-Libyan members to come to the assistance of a Libyan member experiencing an attack from some other party but permitted such assistance.

Setting aside the nonaggression provisions of the Cooperation League, which were of considerable importance in stabilizing Libya on their own, the most notable feature of the agreement was the carrot. Each Libyan member of the League was going to receive several water production and distribution systems complete with separate stand-alone solar power plants and pipeline distribution networks, sixteen systems in all.

Each system was capable of supplying the fresh water needs of about one hundred and fifty thousand people, including sufficient water for irrigation for the crops and chickens required to feed them. The result would be to turn a good portion of one of the most arid locations of the world into a largely self-sufficient, agriculturally productive oasis. It would directly substantially enhance the standard of living of nearly half the population of the country, and indirectly benefit most of the rest.

It would have been possible to have a significant favorable impact on Libya's water needs with a less substantial investment, perhaps half or even a third of the sixteen systems committed, but the president had decided to make a dramatic statement about U.S. policy in the region. President Rushton's State Department advisors believed that Libya's resulting improved economic circumstances would greatly stabilize the fractious domestic political situation.

The United States had agreed to supply all the desalination plants to the League at cost, using its latest high-efficiency technology. The United States would also provide overall project management. Other non-Libyan members were supplying various other components and construction and maintenance services. The funding of the total expenses of the fresh water project was being provided by the non-Libyan members, with the largest share from the United States. The president felt it was a small price to pay to improve the lives of many people living an otherwise marginal existence, stabilize a volatile nation, and preempt the establishment of a Russian proxy state in the heart of the Mediterranean while avoiding a military confrontation. His European and Middle Eastern allies shared his satisfaction with the outcome and appreciated the U.S. leadership after a period in which such leadership had been a rarity. Few thought it likely that the situation in Libya would progress anytime soon to a reconsolidation of the country under a single democratic government, but at least the stage had been set.

Not part of the Libyan agreement and not the subject of any public announcement, Egypt and Saudi Arabia were also to receive desalination plants at cost and, in Egypt's case, with a grant from the United States and European members that would cover half the cost.

The phone on his desk rang. He picked it up to hear the White House operator advise that she was connecting the President of Mexico, Luis Lopez. James Rushton knew Lopez fairly well, better than the heads of state of nearly every other country other than Canada. The two respected and liked each other, having worked together on the North American Carbon Tax and Credit Agreement, as well as the reinstituted North American Free Trade Agreement, early in Jim's tenure as vice president and past President Mahally's right-hand confidant.

"Good morning, Mr. President," came across the line in clear, slightly accented English, "I am calling to congratulate you on two counts. First is your recently announced technological breakthrough in the production of fresh water. Although my country has not been made aware of any of the details, I am sure that this could be of tremendous benefit to a thirsty world. Not all countries are blessed with the tremendous fresh water resources that much of your country takes for granted. Congratulations also on your peace initiatives in Libya, including your generous gift of your new fresh water capabilities to that dry country. I am sure that your adversary is no longer a factor in that location. Well struck, as we say in golf and football."

Jim knew that President Lopez wasn't referring to American football but to soccer. More importantly, though, he thought he could also detect that his Mexican counterpart was aware of not only the publically announced carrot component of his peace initiative in Libya, but also of the covert military action. He also detected a soupçon of envy with respect to the desalination technology and perhaps disappointment that more information on it had not been offered to his government. So, he was pretty sure he knew what was coming next, but he kept his reply neutral and open-ended.

"Thank you, Mr. President," Jim responded. "Although I think we know each other well enough to dispense with titles when it is just the two of us talking. I appreciate the recognition of our technology and peace successes by our close friend and neighbor to the south. However, I don't think that you would have initiated this call simply to give me a pat on the back, so do you have any other matters on your mind?"

The Mexican president responded, "Of course, Jim. You are right, and I am proud to know we are on a first-name basis. I assumed that you were alone, but I couldn't be sure. You are also right that there is more on my mind, but please don't feel that my congratulations are any less sincerely meant because they precede another matter I wish to discuss. That matter is simply this: If you are willing to be so generous in supplying fresh water plants to a thirsty country halfway around the world, would you not also be willing to assist your friend and next-door neighbor? We too would benefit greatly from this technology if you'd be prepared to supply us with the plants at your cost, rather than at the large markup that I expect we would face if we tried to buy directly from your business corporations."

President Rushton did not hesitate. He was glad that the gift of the fresh water systems to Libya was recognized by his Mexican counterpart as a multinational effort even if the United States played the largest part and that there were motivations for the gift that included but went beyond simple charity. He also knew that Mexico and its leader would be too proud to request or accept a similar gift and could in fact afford to pay their own way at a reasonable price. It was one of the reasons he had insisted on maintaining government control of the technology. He responded accordingly.

"Luis, of course we would want to share the benefits of this technology with our friends and no we will not be extracting a profit from our friends on such a matter as fresh water, which every human needs to survive. The rights to the technology are fully under the control of our government for the time being. As for supplying you with the plants at our cost, we can do better than that. We will provide you with the technology blueprints at no cost, as well as the engineering and technical support for you to fabricate and install your own plants. You have the fabrication facilities that you will need, plus the technical capability after some initial transition, so I think you can probably make the plants cheaper, save on transportation and keep the jobs in Mexico. We will even loan you the inventor if you'll promise to take good care of him. We will just require a sublicense agreement that prohibits export of the technology or plants without our prior consent."

"Jim, you astound me," responded Luis Lopez, "I remember you as being a fair and pragmatic statesman from our earlier meetings. I see you have remained all of that and more as the new leader of your nation. I am very grateful personally and on behalf of Mexico. You are a true friend. Who shall I have my staff get in touch with to get this underway?"

After they exchanged a few more details and pleasantries, they hung up, and James Rushton was left with a few moments for reflection before his next meeting. All in all, he was feeling pretty good.

The U.S. economy was performing reasonably well despite the increased costs associated with the new carbon tax and credit system. People seemed to appreciate the associated income tax reductions and they didn't greatly resent the higher prices on hydrocarbon-intensive products. In fact, many were adjusting their lifestyles to rely less on such products and were at the same place in terms of the money left in their pockets at month's end, or even slightly ahead. Globally the efforts to cut back on greenhouse gas emissions were beginning to have a favorable effect even if not as rapidly as desirable, and the United States was doing, and was seen to be doing, its fair share. Lastly, for the moment at least, he seemed to have successfully fended off the Russian bear's test of his resolve and gained for the United States widespread international respect for how it was done.

Jim felt satisfied that he had done a reasonably good job of guiding the country for the nine months he had been at the job, though he knew he had been fortunate in not being confronted by any really difficult crises. However, he remained of the view that he wasn't suited for the role on a long-term basis and had advised the leadership of the Democratic National Committee at the end of December of his final decision not to run for election to the presidency, despite their strong encouragement to do so. The New Hampshire primary was now imminent with no announcement yet of the president's intentions so as to give the party leadership some time to encourage one or more other favored candidates to step into the ring. The president and the party leadership had agreed on an announcement now scheduled for the following day.

Jim was looking forward to having his decision public, and thus irreversible. He certainly didn't intend to loaf through the year remaining in his term. In fact, there was still more thought to be given to several files he had worked on but not finished to his satisfaction. He needed to make sure the new fresh water technology was fully exploited; consider the climate change file and if any further action, domestic or international, was needed to step up the pace of greenhouse gas emission curtailment. He also thought he would need to carefully consider the touchy subject of temporary geo-engineering to potentially buy a little more time for longer term emission curtailment programs to take full effect. No, Jim expected to remain as busy as he had been but with his motivation of acting in the long-run best interests of the country made clear. He had no political aspirations or limitations — he planned to make that plain in his announcement.

Chief of Staff Will Templeton knocked and put his head in briefly to advise the president that Dr. Eli Wayman had requested a brief, unscheduled meeting as soon as practical. Eli had not indicated to Will what the subject of the meeting would be.

"Mr. President, I could put him off if you wish," the chief offered. "Or I could insist on him identifying what he wants to talk about and then we could decide. He has had more access to you since you took office than is usually the case for a science advisor."

"No, Will," Jim responded. "You know it is my practice to find time to meet with any senior staffer or cabinet member who requests it, and Dr. Wayman certainly deserves great respect for his stature in the scientific community. Besides, he's interesting and likable. Can you juggle my schedule to fit him in some time tomorrow after my live announcement? It will either be good news, or bad news, but it will be something important. Eli isn't one to waste time on a whim."

Chapter 20

Tuesday, January 18, 2028
Washington, DC

The President of the United States had just announced that, despite only having held that office for nine months, he did not plan to run for a full term in the fall presidential election. He had laid out the key priorities, which he was going to focus on for the remaining year of his mandate. They included climate change mitigation, extensive desalination to reclaim arid regions in the United States and abroad, global security and stability, and encouragement of advanced technology and associated jobs.

James Rushton had endorsed the moderate vision of the last elected president, Tim Mahally, and stated that he would support any candidate from either party who would take up that vision. There were inquiries from the media as to why he himself did not then carry that moderate vision into the election. The president had answered that he did not aspire to the presidency, was more suited to an administrative role than politics, and felt he could make the greatest contribution to the country by avoiding the political fray and focusing on the administrative priorities for the remainder of his appointment.

Following the close of the media session, Jim retired to his private study adjacent to the Oval Office, where he enjoyed a light lunch and a rare luxury of a few quiet moments to himself. It was done. As recently as the evening before, he and his wife had agonized over where his duty to his country lay and had jointly reaffirmed the conclusion he had come to previously. She would have supported him fully if he felt he needed to carry on, but he knew she was relieved by his choice.

He was scheduled next to meet with Dr. Wayman and find out what was on his mind. He had planned to use the more informal setting of the study, but a few minutes before the meeting was to begin, Will Templeton knocked and stuck his head in.

"Sir, excuse me," said the chief of staff, "I have to say that for someone who claims to have no aptitude for politics, you sure have a knack for coming across as a leader. Anyway, I know that's behind us now. What I came in to say is that our learned scientist has an entourage, which he has asked be permitted to join him in his meeting with you, as well as two others he wishes to include by phone. He also wants to be able to tie a laptop computer into a large wall screen. Sir, unless you want to keep it to just the two of you, I think you will need to move into your dining room. You'll have enough room there for the five of them, and I can get a technician to splice a laptop into your TV wall screen."

"Wow, the plot thickens," said the president. "Why am I getting the feeling I am not going to like the story line? Let's go ahead and move the meeting to the dining room, and why don't you join us Will?" A few minutes later the president entered his private dining room, and the four men and one woman rose to greet him, with Will remaining discretely to one side.

"Mr. President, I am very sorry to barge in on you like this," began Eli. "I am sorry today on several counts. I am sorry that you have decided not to run for election. You are the kind of leader this country badly needs, but I listened to your reasons and I respect them. I am sorry to be the bearer of some worrisome news, and I'm especially sorry that I have dragged my heels on this matter. I should have given you a heads-up several weeks ago."

James Rushton was a little taken aback by the torrent of words from the elderly scholar, who was usually a calm and deliberate communicator, but he kept his balance and avoided conveying concern. He interjected before the man went any further, "Eli, I am sure whatever it is, you had good reasons not to bring it to my attention sooner. Please introduce your team and then let's sit down. We'll have drinks brought in presently."

The science advisor introduced General Isaac Montgomery, the lead executive of the Planetary Defense Coordination Office; Dr. Neal Sampson, the director of the Jet Propulsion Laboratory; Dr. Eleanor Appleton, the senior manager of the Near-Earth Object Collision Risk Assessment Department at the JPL; and Dr. Tony Galletsia, mathematician at the JPL. He also introduced the two individuals calling in from the LSST observatory, Senior Scientist Dr. George Rigby and Darya Ahmadi, PhD student of astrophysics. The refreshments arrived and everyone was seated at the table except Will Templeton, who remained standing. The president motioned the science advisor to begin.

"Mr. President, thank you for seeing us on short notice," said Eli. "I think what we have to tell you is significant enough to justify intruding on your schedule. I am going to ask Ms. Ahmadi and Dr. Galletsia to cover the details after I remind you of some of the context that we've discussed previously. The two of them have done all the work.

"Mr. President, when I briefed you several months ago on the potential that an object big enough to do serious damage might strike the Earth, I left you with the impression that the risk of such an event in the next ten years is very low.

I also discussed the Planetary Defense Coordination Office, which is currently led by General Montgomery, and the role it plays in keeping tabs on the solar system so as to warn us of any change in this outlook.

"Mr. President, a little over two weeks ago, General Montgomery advised me that our LSST facility in Chile, which is overseen by Dr. Rigby, had identified a new object in the far reaches of our solar system, and our team at the JPL, who are with us here, had determined that this object is moving relatively quickly in our general direction. Sir, our JPL team was of the view that the likelihood of a collision between the Earth and this object is very low, and they still think so, though it was identified by Dr. Galletsia as a risk. Based on what we knew at that time, I elected not to advise you, sir, of this new development. That was my decision and mine alone, and I now believe it was the wrong decision. I didn't want to bother you unnecessarily, but I allowed myself to be influenced in part by my desire not to appear to you or Mr. Templeton as an old fussbudget trying to claim even more of your time and attention than you have already generously granted me. I didn't want to be the boy crying wolf when none arrives, but I should have at least advised you that one had been sighted."

"Okay Eli," James Rushton said, "I am a little confused. You said our team still views the risk of a collision as low, so what has changed to cause you to second-guess your initial decision and to pull this group of experts into our usual one-on-one discussion?"

"Yes, Mr. President, something has changed," replied Eli. "We know a lot more about this object than we did even forty-eight hours ago. The risk of a collision remains low, but we won't be able to rule it out for another month or so. That's not the main thing that I am worried about. For that I am going to call on Ms. Ahmadi, who has been tracking this object at the LSST observatory. In fact, she is the one who first identified it. Darya, please go ahead."

The president, sensing he was about to receive a lengthy and important briefing spoke quickly to Will Templeton and asked him to clear his schedule for the rest of the day.

The young astrophysicist was glad she was speaking over a communication system rather than being physically present in the president's private dining room. Even so she was more than a little overawed to be addressing the most powerful leader in the world. Still, she was even more awestruck by what she now knew about object X/2027U3 and was about to explain to the president.

"President Rushton," she said, "this object was first spotted on November 6 of last year. At that time, we knew nothing about how far away it was, where it was heading, how fast or what size it was. We just knew that something was there that hadn't been there before. Importantly, we couldn't actually see the object at that time, or at least that is not how it was spotted. It was spotted by what we call the indirect method, when it moved in front of a distant star and blotted out the light from that star. And it was spotted entirely by accident. I was actually examining stars many, many times farther away than we now know this object to be. In any case, we learned more about this object over the following weeks and as of the night before last we now know quite a lot, and it is quite surprising.

"Mr. President, from the beginning one thing we did know was that this object was coming from an unusual direction. I think a few pictures will help you understand, and so I've asked Dr. Galletsia to help out with some graphics, which I believe you will see on your wall screen. The first is one which I understand from Professor Wayman is similar to another that you have seen before. It depicts our solar system as if we were looking at it from one side and slightly above. It isn't to scale with respect to distances, but it does illustrate visually that most of the objects in the solar system lie in approximately the same plane as the Earth as they all orbit around the Sun. In particular, the asteroid belt lies in this plane, which is called the plane of the ecliptic. Th at is where most of the objects that cross Earth's path have come from.

"Our new object is not moving in the plane of the ecliptic. In fact, its path is nearly perpendicular to the plane that most of the solar system occupies. It is

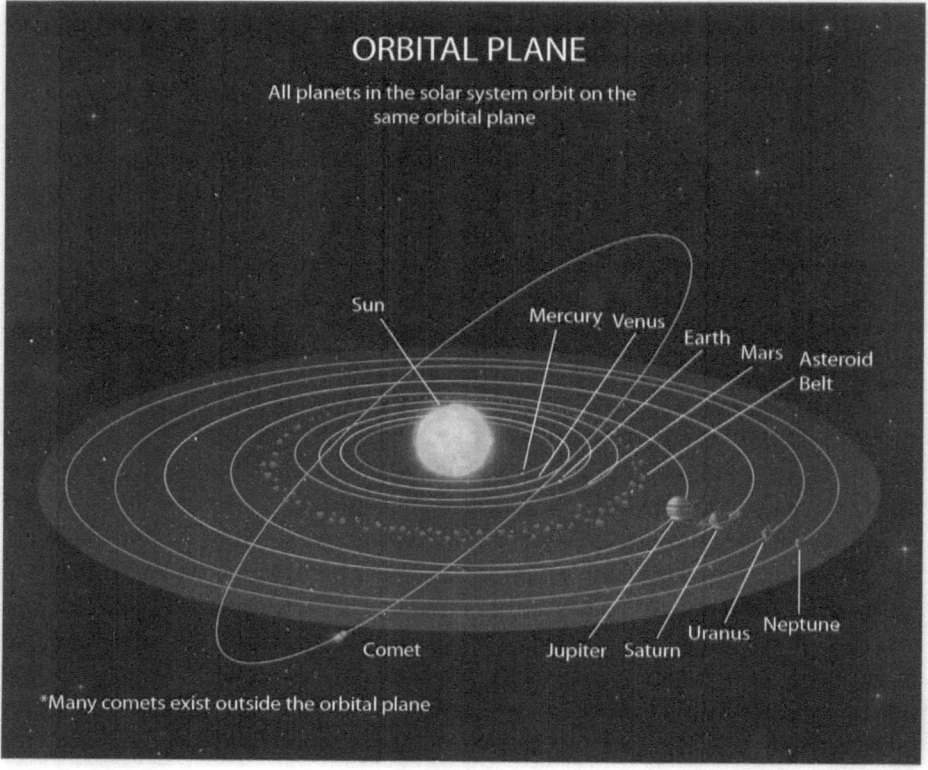

ORBITAL PLANE

All planets in the solar system orbit on the same orbital plane

Sun   Mercury Venus   Earth   Mars   Asteroid Belt

Comet   Jupiter Saturn   Uranus Neptune

*Many comets exist outside the orbital plane

coming toward us from the direction that we might tend to think of as below, given the usual spatial orientation that we visualize for the solar system. The next picture depicts this. For simplicity the path of the new object is shown as a single deterministic most likely path whereas in reality it spans a cone of possible paths, which we will come back to in a little while when Dr. Galletsia takes up his part of this presentation. I should say, however, that he is the one who has calculated the possible paths and has developed all of these graphics.

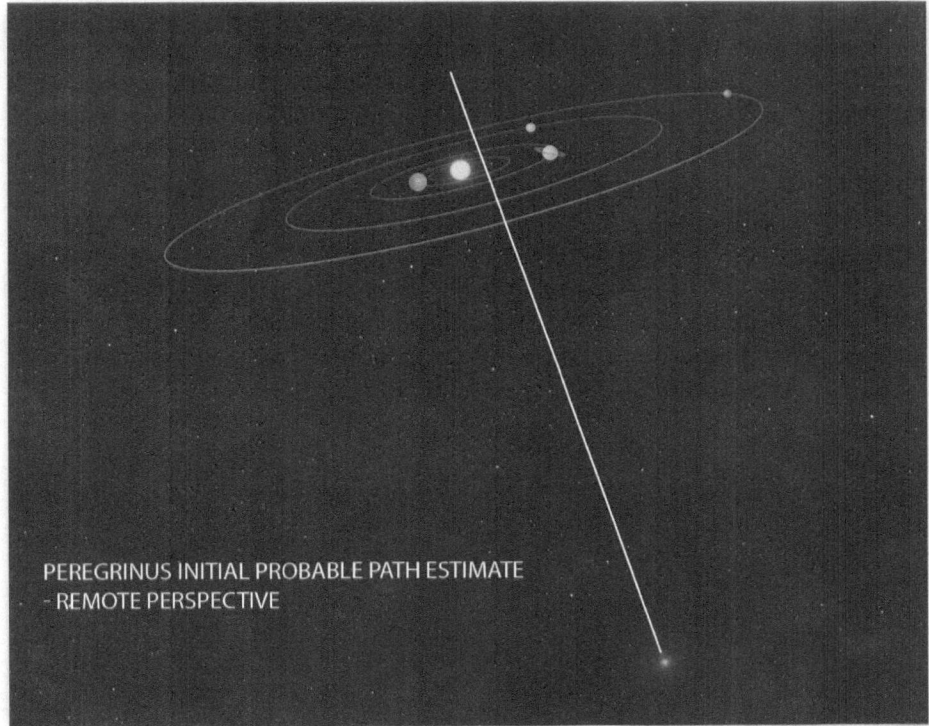

PEREGRINUS INITIAL PROBABLE PATH ESTIMATE
- REMOTE PERSPECTIVE

"In any case, given that this new object rising up through our solar system is coming from such an unusual direction, I expected that we were dealing with a comet originating from the Oort cloud. The Oort cloud surrounds the solar system in a spherical shell at a great distance out and consists of icy bodies that can be disturbed and fall in toward the Sun from any direction, giving rise to a comet, as distinct from the rocky or metallic asteroids that stick to the plane of the ecliptic.

"Mr. President, a comet is a relatively small object. A typical diameter might be six miles long. That's big enough to cause some terrible consequences should one strike the Earth, but still small compared with the eight-thousand-mile diameter of the Earth itself.

"Sir, X/2027U3 is not a comet; it is much, much larger than that. The night before last the LSST was able to see the object directly. In fact, with the benefit of hindsight and going back over the original pictures, a very faint disk was discernible even to begin with despite the low magnification I was using at that time. The LSST missed that because its detection program caught the object first by indirect observation of the loss of light from a star it had passed in front of before the direct observation detector was triggered. We missed it in our visual inspection because it was quite faint and we weren't expecting it.

"Back in November, when the object was first spotted through indirect observation, I wasn't using anywhere near the maximum magnification the LSST is capable of because I was studying a large swath of a much more distant part of the galaxy, and high magnification narrows the telescope's field of view too much at that distance. I was still using relatively low magnification for my search two nights ago as well, until the LSST found this object again, but this time through direct observation; that is, by recognizing an actual object in the night sky in a position where no such object is registered in its memory banks of known objects.

"The next picture shows you on the right side what the LSST saw two nights ago when I adjusted it to maximum magnification. On the left side is another separate picture at the same magnification, which is of the planet Neptune, outermost of the eight planets in our solar system.

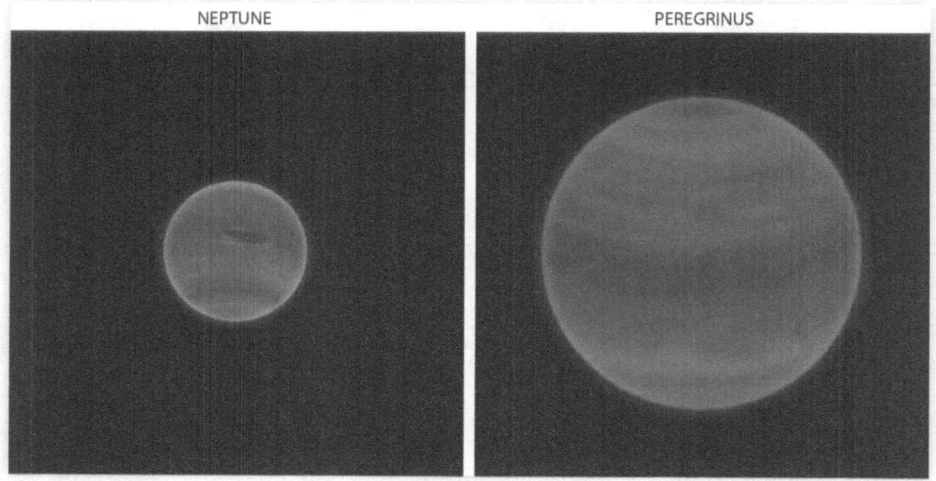

"Neptune is at a distance of about thirty astronomical units from the Sun, versus the Earth, which is at one astronomical unit. It has a diameter of about thirty-two thousand miles, so even at that distance the LSST can easily resolve it into a definite disk. X/2027U3 is quite a bit further out, now at about forty-nine AU, but you can see it already appears to be much bigger than Neptune.

If X/2027U3 was at the same thirty AU distance as Neptune, it would be clear that it is in fact much bigger than Neptune. X/2027U3 is not a comet at all. It is a planet. It is a large planet, not orbiting any sun but off on a romp through our Milky Way galaxy, and apparently paying our solar system a visit along the way. The picture analysis software we have here at the LSST observatory estimates the diameter of this planet at about a hundred and twenty-eight thousand miles across, nearly half again the size of Jupiter, the largest planet in our solar system, which has a diameter of eighty-nine thousand miles. That is toward the larger end of the range of known planets in stellar systems within the Milky Way galaxy, though by no means the largest of them."

The president was deeply shocked by what the young scientist had told them. He was temporarily speechless, with a dozen questions leaping to his mind but none making it to his lips.

Eli sensed the president's bewilderment and said, "Thank you Darya. Mr. President, the rest of us have had from twenty-four to thirty-six hours to absorb this, so I know what a shock it is. May I suggest that we finish up with what we know and then we'll try to answer any questions you have? Dr. Galletsia, it's over to you now."

"Mr. President, my area of specialization is orbital mechanics," began Tony. "That means I figure out what orbits around the Sun the various objects in our solar system are going to follow as they all pull on each other due to their forces of gravity, how those orbits are going to change over time, and whether any such objects are going to collide with each other and especially with Earth. One of the peculiarities we are dealing with here is that object X/2027U3 is not in an orbit around our Sun, which is why Ms. Ahmadi carefully used the term 'path' when she was referring to the object's direction of travel. Nevertheless, we can still calculate the object's most probable path through our solar system. It is largely a straight line as it comes toward us, with a slight bend imparted by the Sun's gravity as it passes us and departs. You saw that straight-line path in one of the pictures a few minutes ago, and I will come back to that.

"From what we can tell, this object comes from elsewhere in our Milky Way galaxy. It is not the first time we've had a transgalactic object pass through the solar system, though it is quite rare, and it is certainly the first time we've seen a transient planet-sized object. Our solar system is orbiting the central core of our galaxy fairly far out, as shown in this depiction of the structure of our galaxy with views from both directly above and off to one side. This object is coming from behind and slightly below our solar system, overtaking it and rising up through it.

"Most bodies in the galaxy tend to lie fairly close to a common plane called the galactic plane, similar to the common plane in which most bodies in our solar system lie, the plane of the ecliptic. The next picture on the screen illustrates this — our solar plane orbiting around the galactic plane. There's a couple of things that might surprise you if you look closely. One is that, unlike the direction of

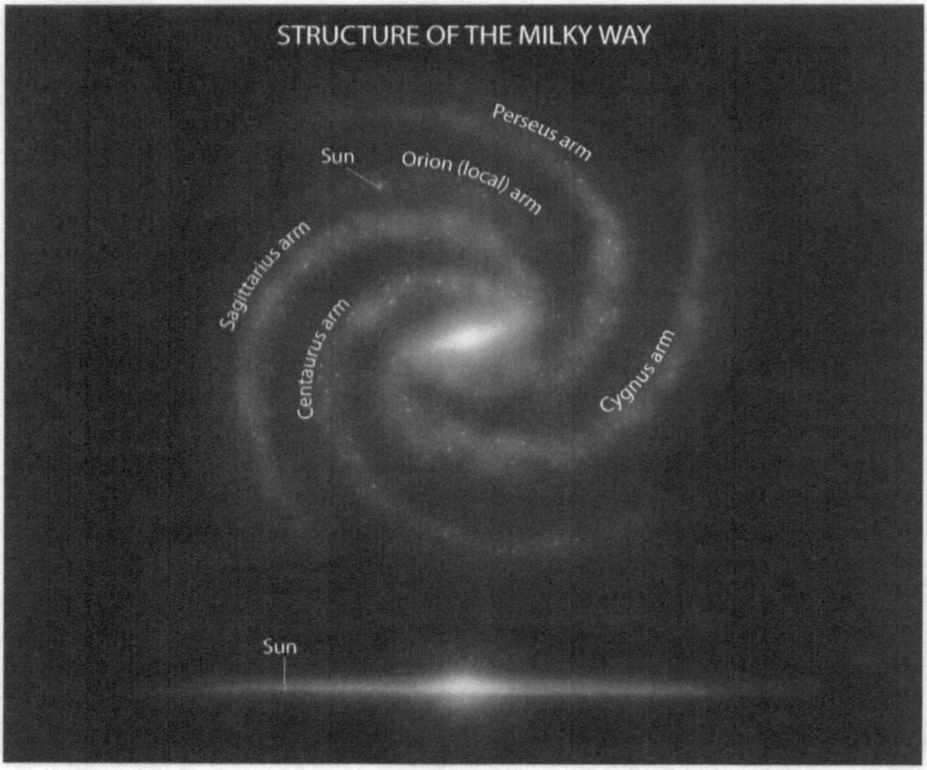

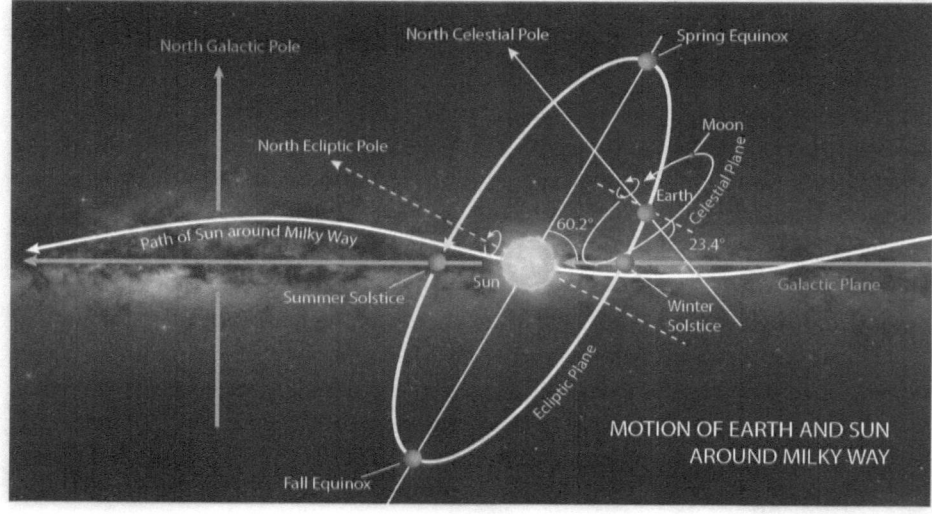

STRUCTURE OF THE MILKY WAY

rotation of nearly everything in our solar system, which is counterclockwise when viewed from above, as we usually think of it, the Milky Way galaxy is

MOTION OF EARTH AND SUN
AROUND MILKY WAY

actually rotating in the clockwise direction about its core. Another interesting feature is that our solar system's plane of the ecliptic is not parallel to the galactic plane but is tipped backward by about sixty degrees relative to our direction of travel, somewhat similar to the way that Earth's axis is tilted relative to its orbit, though the solar system tilt is quite a bit more pronounced.

"This transient object or planet is itself moving at a tangent to the galactic plane, rising from below the plane at an angle of about thirty degrees with the overall result that its path is virtually perpendicular to the plane of the ecliptic, as depicted in this next diagram.

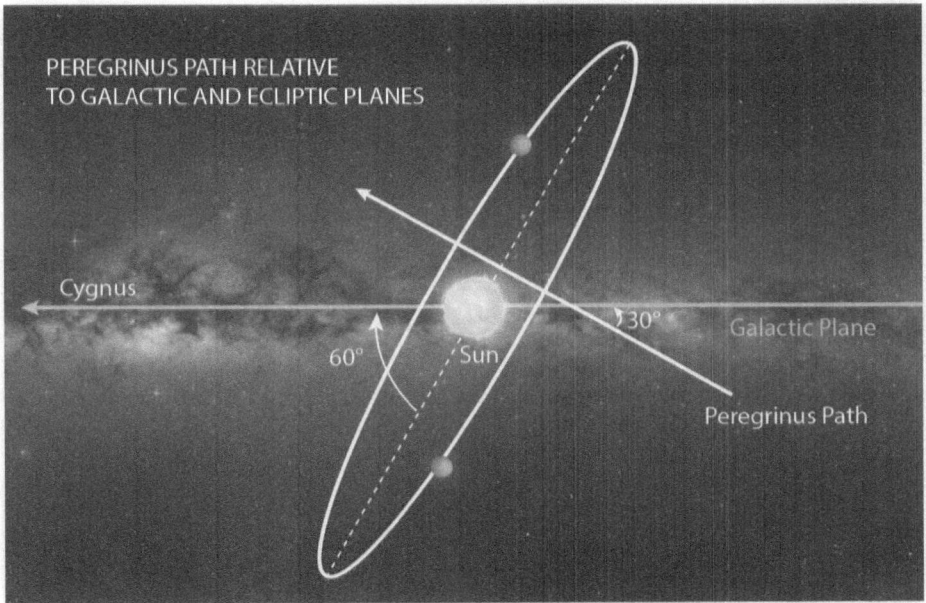

"Since we don't usually orient ourselves with respect to the galactic plane, from the Earth's perspective the planet will just appear to be rising from below us and eventually disappear, continuing to rise above us. This is the perspective adopted in the earlier diagram showing the planet's most probable path, which I am repeating again now, though with the scale expanded to show where that most probable path lies in relation to the inner solar system.

"Mr. President, I want to be clear that, while what you are seeing depicted on this diagram is the most probable path of this planet through the solar system, passing up through the plane of the ecliptic partway between the orbits of Earth and Mars and well away from the Earth, it is not the only possible path.

"Based on the data we have so far, the range of possible paths is depicted by the cone in this last diagram, with the more probable paths lying near the center

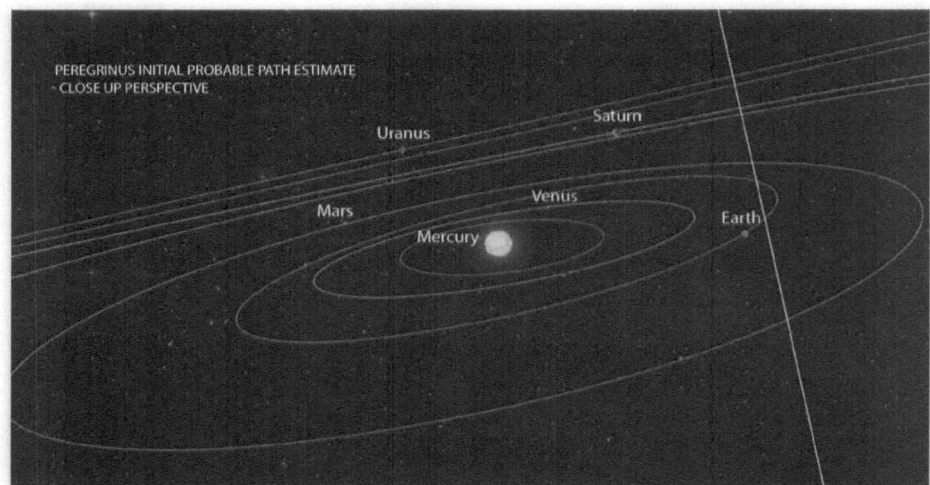

of the cone and the least probable paths lying near its outer perimeter. We have been able to refine this cone of possible paths quite a bit in the last several weeks, and we will be able to pin it down more precisely in another few weeks, but at present, the cone does intersect Earth's orbit at approximately the same time that Earth will be at that point in its orbit. So, there is a possibility, though its likelihood is low, of a collision."

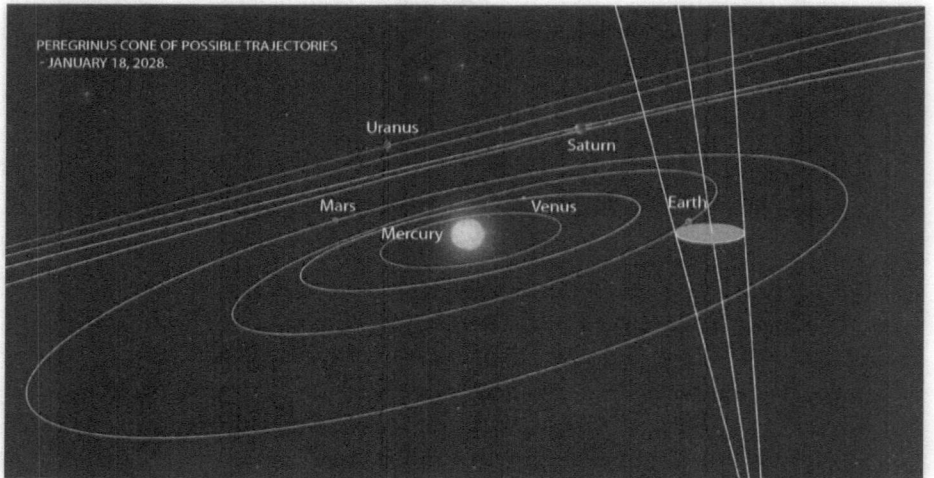

Eli jumped back in before the president could articulate his first question, "Mr. President, there are two things about this situation that are worrisome. One is what you've just heard, that there is a small risk of a collision with this wandering planet. I am really not very concerned about that. It's a small risk and, this may be an indelicate way to put it, but if there is a collision, it will be like a bus running into a bicycle. There will be nothing left of the bicycle and there will be nothing we can do about it. The thing I am worried about is the size of this thing and the potential adverse consequences even if it misses us by several million miles, which it probably will. It may be that there are things we can do to mitigate those consequences, and the sooner we figure that out the better. That is why I regret not warning you sooner."

The president had managed to absorb the news and reestablish his outward-facing calm, even if he was in a state of inner turmoil. He spoke quietly, "Well Eli, time will tell whether a couple of weeks would have made any difference. From what I've heard you didn't know enough to base any action on. I thank you and the rest of this team for this well presented briefing and for all you have done so far to ascertain what we are dealing with here. I do have several questions, though.

"First, how long will it take you to refine your most probable path to the point that we will know one way or the other whether we face a collision? Second, how long before this thing gets here? Third, what kind of near-miss consequences are we talking about? Could we face massive tidal waves, earthquakes and volcanic eruptions? What sort of mitigating actions might we be able to take? Lastly, who knows about this wandering planet?"

The group turned to Tony Galletsia. He was nervous. He knew that the cone of possible paths would narrow steadily with additional position observations over the next few weeks, but he also knew that it could easily narrow in such a way as to still leave the intersection with the Earth's orbit lying within the low probability boundary of the cone. He also knew that the president wanted something to go on, his best guess. He said, "Sir, I believe that in another four weeks we will have sufficient additional data to know whether a collision is in the cards or not. Ms. Ahmadi will be able to gather additional data every night and, if the picture clarifies any sooner, we will advise you immediately.

"As to the estimated arrival time, there I can be quite precise. Our Sun is travelling its orbit of the galaxy at a speed of four hundred and ninety thousand miles per hour. This visiting planet is moving at about seven hundred and fifty thousand miles per hour, so overtaking us at a relative speed of two hundred and sixty thousand miles per hour, which is very fast. None of the natural bodies in our solar system move nearly that fast. Our most recent position measurement placed the planet at forty-nine AU, which is a long way out, well beyond Pluto. However, at that closing speed, it will pass through the plane of Earth's orbit in almost exactly two years — mid-January 2030."

Eli signaled that he would take the rest of the questions. "Sir, I can't yet say exactly what the consequences of a near miss might be. It's not my field and I haven't had time to consult with appropriate earth scientists who could figure out how to predict the effects. I would think that all the things you mention are possibilities, and I am sure it will depend on how near a near miss it is. With your permission, I would like to get one or two specialists working on this based on two or three scenarios. I doubt anyone has tried to simulate anything like this before, so it may take a while to figure out an approach.

"As to mitigating actions, that too is something there hasn't been time to think through. From a protocol perspective, General Montgomery's office would normally — if there is any such thing as normal in this kind of situation — have the responsibility for planning and coordinating our response under your direction. He has all the pre-established links with FEMA, the military, state emergency response and law enforcement, as well as his counterparts in other countries. The current situation is outside anything anyone contemplated when the Planetary Defense Coordination Office was established, however, so you could certainly choose to place someone else in charge of the response and have General Montgomery play a supporting role.

"Lastly, the only ones who know about this at present are the people in this room and the ones on the phone. There are a few other large telescopes in the southern hemisphere that could soon inadvertently spot this thing, but it is quite unlikely that they will be looking in just the right place. Even if it were to be spotted by one of those instruments, in most cases it would be reported confidentially into our system. By September this thing will be approaching a distance from the Earth that is about the same distance as Neptune's orbit, though of course lying in a completely different sector of the sky than Neptune — down below, so to speak, rather than off to one side. By that point the probability that it could be spotted by a high-powered private telescope becomes increasingly high because it will be more visible and because there are so many amateur astronomers. So, we have some time to work on this. Certainly we have more than enough for Dr. Galletsia to refine his probable path and enough to develop some sort of response plan before public awareness develops."

"Okay, I have the picture I think," replied the president. "I don't want to appear heavy-handed, but the first thing I am going to do is declare this matter Top Secret Presidential. That makes it a criminal offense with severe penalties for anyone to inform another person who has not been cleared of any details of this matter, or even of the existence of this matter. It would result in anarchy if word of this got into the public domain before we even know what we are dealing with, or how we are going to deal with it. Will Templeton will maintain the list of persons who are cleared, and names can be added only by him or me. You will receive a written reply to any request to add a name so as to leave no room for misunderstanding. No reply means no permission.

"I will need a little time to think this through but then I'd like to meet with you, Eli, and you, General Montgomery, to cover anything else I haven't yet thought of and to discuss how we are going to predict possible consequences and develop response plans. Let's make that tomorrow afternoon, and bring the names of anyone else you feel should be cleared on this. The rest of the team can continue with your critical responsibilities.

"Finally, we have been calling this thing an object, a planet, a thing, and that alphanumeric code name. Can we give it a name?"

Dr. George Rigby interjected through the speaker phone, "Eli, can I take this please? Mr. President, the tradition on newly discovered transient objects such as this one is that the discoverer selects the common name, usually naming it after themselves. In this case that would be Ms., soon to be Dr., Ahmadi."

"Ms. AIhmadi, have you picked a name for our visitor?" asked the president.

"Yes sir, I have, if I am to be allowed that honor on such an unusual object," she replied. "The name I have chosen is Peregrinus, which is Latin for Wanderer, if no one objects."

"That is certainly fine by me," said the president. "If my schoolboy Latin hasn't deserted me, I think the Latin for something rising from below is *orior*. So, this top-secret file will be called the Peregrinus Orior file — the Wanderer Rises. It looks like our rising wanderer is going to be the main preoccupation for all of us now, and soon enough for the rest of humanity!"

Chapter 21

Thursday, February 3, 2028
Ajdabiya, Libya

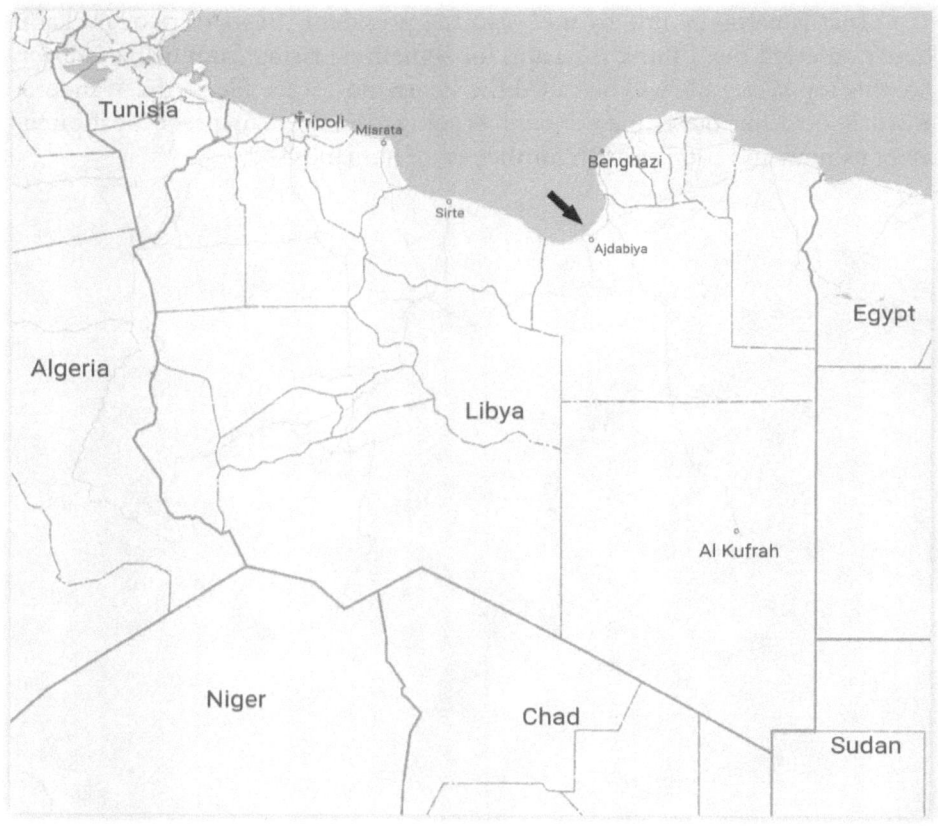

Looking out over the blue waters of the Mediterranean Sea as the Sun began to set, Larry reflected on how pleasant a location he was in. That is, if you ignore the fact that there is no lake, river, pond or even puddle in sight, he thought.

There was virtually nothing green visible in any direction. The occasional tree or shrub was stunted and would remain brown-grey and dormant until invigorated briefly by a rare rainfall. He was in a desert country, one of the driest in the world with about five inches of rain per year, most months having none at all. That compares with Nevada, the driest state in the United States, which would average about ten inches per year.

No form of agriculture is viable in most places within the country. Unlike its slightly smaller neighbor to the east, Egypt, Libya does not have a major river like the Nile that could be tapped for irrigation. In fact, Libya has no rivers to speak of, though Larry knew that even the mighty Nile was quickly approaching the limit of its irrigation capacity.

Then there was the Mediterranean, a vast body of water lying within miles of 90 percent of the Libyan population and connected at Gibraltar to the even vaster Atlantic Ocean, which was too saline for consumption or irrigation. Larry aimed to change that fact to a large degree. He was there to provide technical support and advice on the first of sixteen desalination facilities to be installed on the coast of Libya.

The Ajdabiya facility would have three plants, each with a capacity of two million gallons per day. It would supply enough fresh water to meet the needs of the whole town and irrigate enough of the adjacent arid plains to permit the area to be self-sufficient for basic foodstuff needs. There were to be three more such systems installed along the east central coast, with a similar plan for the two other zones to the west and one to the east.

If everything went according to plan, Larry really wouldn't have a whole lot to do. A team of Italian army engineers and solar contractors had been on site within days of the announcement of the Libyan Peace and Prosperity Cooperation League, so the concrete floor and sheet metal buildings for each of the three plants were well advanced, as was the infrastructure for the one-megawatt mini solar power plant. He had no responsibility for any of that, nor for the physical design of the salt water pumping and piping system to feed each plant, nor the fresh water pumping and distribution system. His capacitive deionization cells were due to arrive in a day or two. Most of the electronics for process monitoring and control were already on site in sealed packages to protect the delicate equipment from grit kicked up from the arid ground by a gust of wind.

Once the first cells arrived by truck from the nearby port of Marsa al-Brega, Larry would begin commissioning them and setting up the supervisory control and data acquisition, or SCADA, system for process monitoring and control. Tanker trucks carrying seawater would be used as the salt water source until the intake system could be completed in the next couple of weeks, and power would be temporarily supplied by portable diesel generators.

The fresh water produced during commissioning would at first just spill out into the desert beside the concrete floor slab of the first plant. Eventually it would be routed through a large collection and distribution manifold to either an on-site storage cistern or to one of the multiple trunk lines being constructed to carry the water into the town or to the irrigation reservoirs. The fresh water from each of the other two plants would also eventually be routed into the distribution manifold and onward from there. Construction of the trunk pipelines and the water distribution system within the town would be the last part of the Ajdabiya project to be completed, though again, that wasn't Larry's responsibility.

The on-site concrete storage cistern was of modest size, twenty million gallons or about three days of production by all three plants. It was designed primarily as a surge tank to absorb fluctuations in both the rate of fresh water production and in the demand of the town. It could also serve as a backup supply if one plant needed to be shut down for maintenance. In the event of any longer-term production shortfall from the design capacity, supply to the town would have first priority, with volumes into the irrigation pipelines being curtailed. Likewise, if more water was being produced than the town could absorb, and if the cistern was full, the excess would be dispatched to the irrigation system, which had its own storage reservoirs. Although Larry's laboratory research had never had to deal with process control for a large complex fresh water distribution system, the technology was well within his area of expertise, and he had been loath to pass that responsibility on to anyone else, preferring to overlay the additional intake and distribution system controls onto the desalination process controls to ensure a single, integrated control system.

Larry's plan was to spend the next few weeks at the Ajdabiya site, overseeing the commissioning of most of the seventy-two cells and tuning the SCADA system. He would also be working with the Fresh Water Solutions expatriate supervisor of the desalination plants and his expat and local Libyan technical staff to train them on the commissioning process and the nuances of the SCADA system. The desalination plant technical staff for the three other east central coast facilities, clustered near Benghazi, were also participating in the training so that they would be able to begin commissioning those facilities without initial assistance from Larry.

Larry would head next to Tripoli, the largest population center in Libya, with the largest number of fresh water facilities to be clustered on the coast nearby. France would be undertaking the solar power plants and building construction for these facilities. In Tripoli, he would repeat the same commissioning and training regime as in Ajdabiya, getting one facility largely commissioned and technical staff for several others also trained up. Then he would head back to Ajdabiya to overlay the SCADA system for the seawater intake pumping, piping and storage system and the fresh water pumping, manifold and cistern system onto the more technical desalination process controls. By that time the overall facility should be complete, and Larry would see his dream come to fruition when copious fresh water gushed into homes and fields in one of the most parched and arid places in the world.

Larry would not linger long in Ajdabiya. He wouldn't be there long enough to actually see the crops that his fresh water was now irrigating begin to be harvested. He would need to return to Tripoli to see how the commissioning of those facilities was doing and provide assistance and advice as required. However, the Tripoli cluster would not be fully operational for another couple of months, so Larry had been shadowed on the SCADA setup for the Ajdabiya facility by several engineers and technicians who could now perform that task in his absence.

His next destination would be the west coast of Mexico, though his role there would be a little different. Rather than supervising the installation and commissioning of cells produced in the United States, he would be providing assistance and support to the startup of a new Mexican plant constructed as a fabrication center for production of capacitive deionization cells. After that he'd be back in the Middle East to work on the Saudi desalination plants. Larry was looking at a very busy schedule with a lot of travel for at least the next year. He didn't object a bit. As he completed the short walk from the Italian mess hall to the small portable dorm unit that housed the few Americans on site, he reveled in the experience of seeing a personal dream starting to come true. Nearby, however, there were others whose immediate objective was to shatter Larry's dream.

***

The six-man Russian Special Operations Forces Command team, better known as the KSSO, crawled out from beneath their camouflage tarp as the last traces of sunlight faded in the west. They prepared for their four-mile approach to the new compound. They had come in from Sudan by truck, a long and boring drive especially since they rarely left the truck at any of the oases that occasionally provided brief relief along the way from the dust and sand of the desert. Only the team leader, who shared the cab with their local driver, had any view of the outside terrain, and there was little to see, even for him.

The team had left the truck and driver the previous evening twelve miles away on the Ajdabiya–Kufra road. From there it had been an easy four-hour march in the cool of the night to their lay-up point. A helicopter insertion would have been a lot easier, quicker and not nearly as boring. However, this close to the coast, there would have been a high risk of detection by an American electronic surveillance aircraft operating from an aircraft carrier in the Mediterranean. In any case, the team was trained at patience and endurance so they felt no real hardship. They were also very highly motivated from two angles.

First, there had been eight Russian covert operators among those killed by Americans at the Maziq compound a couple of months ago. The dead Russians had worked for the Russian clandestine operations group and were not of the same caliber as the KSSO, in terms of physical ability, aggressiveness or tactical offensive and defensive training. Of course, that would be true of nearly any military force in the world compared with the Russian KSSO, whose training and physical requirements matched those of the American Delta Force or SEAL teams or the British Special Air Service.

If the KSSO were not a full match for the Americans in the special operations field, it was only a matter of a small advantage the Americans held on electronic technology, an advantage that the KSSO team leader nevertheless knew could be the death of him, literally, were he facing an aware and prepared position rather than the unsuspecting relatively soft target they had been briefed on.

The KSSO operators didn't consider their countrymen who had been killed not very many miles away as brothers-in-arms, exactly; still, they were cousins and deserved to be avenged. If that hadn't been enough motivation on its own, the KSSO team had been told very clearly that the success of their mission was paramount, and failure was unacceptable. The eyes of their senior officers and of the leaders of their country were on them. The long-serving Russian dictator was not one to accept the thwarting of his ambitions in Libya without retaliation, even if largely symbolic, nor was he one to accept failure by his subordinates either. The team leader understood that his orders were tantamount to "return successful, or die trying." It wasn't the first time he had been tasked in this way and, as with the prior occasions, he didn't believe he would fall short of his superiors' expectations.

The team had spent the rest of the prior night and all of the day in a detailed surveillance of their target, with night-vision scopes at night and high-powered telescopes during the day. The telescopes had specially coated lenses to prevent any reflection back to the target. The imagery from all the optical devices was fed into the team's tactical personal computers so that several of the operators could observe at the same time. They could rerun anything they wanted to examine more closely, expanding and creating freeze-frames as needed.

After nearly eighteen hours of surveillance the team leader was satisfied that the target was just as had been laid out in the team's briefing. It was surrounded by a chain-link fence, topped with barbed wire, with the only gate manned at all times by a detachment of Italian military police. The defenses were certainly sufficient to prevent the local thieves from purloining construction supplies.

They could likely even hold out against a lightly armed militia, of which there were numerous in Libya, until reinforced from elsewhere. However, military police, though armed with automatic rifles, would pose little resistance to a night attack by the KSSO special operators. The team's orders were to dispatch all military resistance, and in particular any American personnel, even non-combatants, then destroy all equipment and buildings.

Although they could have covered the four miles to the compound in an hour or less, they planned to take several hours, moving slowly and cautiously. After two miles they spread out to approach the gate individually from different angles. Their tactical plan was for the team's two snipers to take out the four-man squad on duty at the gate from about two hundred yards out. The leader also had two operators creep slowly up to the fence line about twenty-five yards on either side of the gate to take down any of the duty squad that the snipers couldn't get a clear shot at. All of their weapons were silenced.

If the initial assault went as planned, they would then take the duty officer in a small command post about ten yards inside the gate, followed by the two military police officers patrolling the fence line. They would move next to the portable trailers serving as the barracks for the military police detachment. The KSSO team planned to throw high explosive charges through the barracks doorway, which would likely kill the fifteen sleeping occupants. At that point, with all the military opposition dispatched, the team would split in half with one group assigned to demolishing and the other to identifying and executing any Americans among the remaining construction and technical personnel within the compound.

The KSSO team leader knew that his government would officially deny any involvement in the attack, pointing out the many armed factions active in Libya. However, the world would still know who had counted coup on this project, and the Americans and their president would know for sure. With a grim smile the team leader gave the order over his tactical network for the attack to begin.

About two hundred and fifty yards away, Larry Johnstone slept peacefully, unaware of the nearby team with its lethal intentions. He hadn't even bothered to turn the latch on the door of his small compartment, not that it would save him if he had. He awoke to the sound of a powerful explosion.

The governments of the United States and its allies were fully aware of the risk of an attack on the desalination facility. The president's military and intelligence advisors understood the psychological profile of the Russian leader well enough to anticipate that there would be some form of conspicuous retaliation for the destruction of the Russian arms shipment and its security team, and that it would come soon. The initial desalination plant, in a fairly remote location, was the obvious and most probable target.

The twenty-two supposed Italian military police providing security at the Ajdabiya facility were neither Italian nor were they military police, though several were of Italian heritage and a few could even speak it. Moreover, fifteen of the twenty-two supposed Italian military police were not sleeping peacefully as the attackers anticipated. The twenty two soldiers were, in fact, a full Delta Force platoon under the command of Captain Mark Simpson, plus an attached team of electronics specialists, and they were all awake, in assigned positions, and fully alert. The latter were set up in a compartment within the barracks module with a rooftop antenna that looked similar to the satellite TV antennas on all of the habitat modules but which provided both satellite and line-of-sight communication with an overhead unmanned aerial vehicle and an offshore surveillance aircraft.

The unmanned aerial vehicle, a state-of-the-art ScanEagle 4, was an unarmed long-endurance miniature aircraft equipped with synthetic aperture radar, a high-resolution camera operating in both the visible light and infrared spectra and an integrated optical detection system. The system could spot a rabbit running through the desert either by day or by night at a range of up to ten miles when on station at its optimum altitude of sixteen thousand feet. From four thousand feet it could spot a moving mouse at a range of about two miles. The ScanEagle could remain stationed for a full twenty-four hours. Two ScanEagles were tasked to the Delta platoon to provide continuous coverage.

The electronics team had been alerted to the incursion of the group of six men soon after they left their truck. Such a group moving at a steady pace through sparsely inhabited desert terrain matched a primary threat profile within the electronic database of the system. The KSSO operators had been continuously monitored ever since.

Captain Simpson had his command fully briefed as the attackers approached. His defense plan was carefully prepared, and he had rehearsed it with the soldiers in a walk/talk-through within the confines of the barracks module. He had used the time the enemy was in motion, and not likely to detect movement within the compound, to deploy all his men to their assigned positions. Two men would provide security for the electronics team and another four would protect the civilian habitat module. That left sixteen of them to intercept the attackers.

The four Americans stationed in the gatehouse would be at greatest risk. The half walls of the structure were heavily reinforced with plate steel but were open from the waist up except for the corner posts. At least two of these men would need to be visible within the gatehouse to present a credible picture to the attackers. While their flak jackets would provide some protection, a head shot would be fatal. Captain Simpson had no intention of allowing his opponents to take the first shot.

Six members of the Delta platoon were fully qualified snipers with sophisticated electronic sniper rifles tied into the battlefield management system from which Captain Simpson would direct the fight. Each of these had moved into position on the roofs of the buildings in the compound nearest the gate. Each was zeroed in on a primary target whose precise location was established by a combination of the rifle's independent infrared scope and the position data from the ScanEagle. Each marksman also had a secondary target they would shift to immediately following elimination of their initial target to provide redundancy in the event one of them missed a primary target. However, with a clear sight picture from eight feet above ground, a miss was unlikely at a range of only two hundred yards.

Four Delta Force operators were positioned out of sight behind the command post and would serve as a reaction force to support the team in the gatehouse. Captain Simpson sat in the command post. A single rifleman guarded him as he peered into the screen of his battle management laptop, watching the cautious hostile force move into position. He noticed four of the attackers come to a stop about two hundred yards out while two continued on toward the fence. He knew that the four who were now motionless would include snipers who could bring fire on his gatehouse men within seconds, but he reasoned that the leader would almost certainly undertake a few minutes of final surveillance before initiating the attack. Mark Simpson then made a tough judgment call and withheld his command to open fire while the last two attackers continued to move into position.

The battle played out something like a shoot-out from the American Wild West days, with gunslingers drawing and firing on each other in the same split second. Captain Simpson gave the command to open fire almost simultaneously with the command from the KSSO leader to commence the attack. The outcome could have been quite different in terms of American casualties if the two commands had been separated by a few seconds in either direction.

As it was, the gatehouse soldiers had been ordered to immediately drop behind the reinforced walls when the shoot command was given to the Delta snipers, and their reactions were quick enough that the KSSO sniper rounds passed harmlessly slightly above them. If the Captain's command had come a second later, they likely would have been added to the casualty list. In fact, if Captain Simpson had delayed another second he likely would have been unable to issue the open fire command, and the battle would have slid into a melee of independent actions.

The KSSO leader had barely issued his order to commence the attack when a .308 caliber high-velocity steel-jacketed round struck his prone body just behind the shoulders, destroying his spine and lungs. A similar fate befell the remaining members of his team within the same second. However, the sixth member of the team had just enough time to fire his weapon before being struck, as had the two KSSO snipers. His weapon was not a rifle aimed at the gatehouse. It was an RPG-35 anti-bunker rocket launcher aimed at the stationary target of the command post just beyond the gatehouse. The armor-piercing high explosive shell ripped through the corrugated steel of the command post and the Captain never had the satisfaction of seeing his plan culminate in victory.

Larry and the other civilians, both American and Italian, were restrained by the security team from leaving the habitat module and were told that the explosion was caused by local criminals attempting to breach the fence and pilfer construction materials. Larry continued on with his plans completely unaware that his death had been carefully planned by a ruthless bully leading the world's second most powerful nation and that the plan had been thwarted by a professional American military leader who had given his life in the process.

The battle of the Ajdabiya compound was never publicized or acknowledged to have taken place. The KSSO operatives were buried in unmarked graves without ceremony. The two deceased Americans were buried with full military honors but without fanfare. The President of the United States privately extended his personal condolences and appreciation to their families.

The Russian leader was furious at having been thwarted yet again. Although the setback to his plans to bring Libya into his sphere of control was known to only a few senior political and military leaders, he knew it had cost him loss of credibility with his subordinates. He now regarded the amateur American president not with dismissiveness and disrespect, but with deep enmity. It would not be the last time that the two would cross swords.

Chapter 22

Wednesday, February 16, 2028
Washington, DC

President Rushton sat pensively in his study beside the Oval Office. He'd just finished a long-distance call with Larry Johnstone and was pleased by the progress of the fresh water program and cheered by the young man's enthusiasm. The Boston cell fabrication plant would complete production for the Middle East program in another month or so and would then begin on the U.S. domestic program.

The president had signed agreements with California, Arizona and New Mexico covering the scope and funding for large scale fresh water projects for each. The federal contribution in each case was making the technology available at no cost and providing loan guarantees to permit each state to debt finance the capital costs at low rates. For the Arizona and New Mexico projects, salt water would be piped in from the Sea of Cortez, which had required an agreement with Mexico. The agreement was readily achieved thanks to President Rushton's close relationship with the President of Mexico.

There were requests for fresh water programs from several other North African and Middle Eastern countries. However, while he was more than willing to supply the desalination plants, the president knew that in most cases new facilities would need to be financially self-sufficient rather than gifts from his Treasury and his allies. He also knew that Americans would need to see some direct domestic benefits themselves in addition to the international humanitarian and foreign policy benefits of disseminating the application of the new technology.

The president was also worried about his next meeting, which was with Dr. Wayman and several others. Eli had sent an e-mail the day before with a preview to the meeting. Jim was happy to read that Peregrinus would very surely not collide with the Earth and that they could now focus on plans to manage the secondary consequences of its flyby. It was the latter part of that message that worried the president.

A short while later his chief of staff stuck his head into the study to advise the president that the group was ready. The president followed Will Templeton into the adjoining dining room, which had once again been set up to display diagrams from a personal computer. James Rushton recognized several of the group, including his science advisor; General Montgomery, the chief of the Planetary Defense Coordination Office; and the young mathematician from the JPL, Dr. Tony Galletsia. He was also advised that Darya Ahmadi and Dr. Rigby from the LSST observatory were on the phone. Eli Wayman introduced two new participants whose names and backgrounds were familiar to the president because he had cleared them for the Peregrinus file a month earlier.

One of the newcomers was Dr. Sarah Wellington, the chair of Geology and Geophysics at Yale University, with a research focus on geophysics. The other was a younger woman named Rachel Holms. She was doing doctoral research in the area of climatology under the supervision of Dr. Wellington.

The president greeted each of the participants, reminded them of the top-secret status of the Peregrinus file, and asked Dr. Wayman to begin.

"Mr. President," Eli began, "I am going to ask our various experts to cover most of the briefing. We promised a month ago that by now we would have better answers to your questions than we did at that time. We now do have those answers, which isn't to say that there's no further testing and refinement still left to do. I am pleased and relieved to confirm, as I mentioned in my recent note, that it appears mankind does not face a catastrophic event, though we will face some major challenges. I'd like to begin today's discussion by having Ms. Ahmadi and Dr. Galletsia give an update on Peregrinus's expected path and the resulting astrophysical picture."

Darya Ahmadi began, "President Rushton, Dr. Rigby and I have been keeping a close eye on Peregrinus as it rises up through the bottom of the solar system. It's not hard to do with the LSST observatory when you know where to look. As expected, during the last four weeks Peregrinus has moved about two astronomical units along its path, getting closer to the plane of the ecliptic, so now it is about forty-seven AU away, still well beyond the orbit of Pluto. We have confirmed our estimate of the Peregrinus's diameter to be one hundred and twenty-eight thousand miles, which is 1.44 times larger than Jupiter. That means a volume, which is proportional to the cube of the diameter, of three times that of Jupiter. We still can't measure its density because it hasn't come close enough to another known object for us to be able to measure gravitational effects. However, it has a fairly high albedo, or light reflectivity, like Jupiter. So, it is likely a gas giant with a similar low density to that of Jupiter. That's good news because a denser planet would have a higher mass and greater potential to wreak havoc on its way through the solar system. Three times the mass of Jupiter is already plenty big enough. However, we're just the data gathering part of the team. The data all goes to Dr. Galletsia for analysis."

Tony Galletsia was pleased to be the only spokesperson present from the JPL. His boss, Eleanor Appleton, had requested administrative leave as it became increasingly obvious that she had downplayed the risk from an unknown transient object with several sorts of unusual characteristics, initially overruling Tony's concerns. "Sir, as we advised last time, what we clearly have here is a wandering or rogue planet. There are thought to be many millions of these knocking about in our galaxy, but this is the first we know of that has passed through our solar system.

"When I last spoke with you there was a distinct risk of a direct collision with the Earth, or a near miss that would have been just about as bad as a collision given the size of Peregrinus. However, with the new data provided by Ms. Ahmadi, we have been able to refine our estimate of Peregrinus's path as it intersects the plane of the ecliptic and continues on into the upward or northern reaches of our solar system. It is going to come a little closer to us than it first looked like it might, but we have also been able to tighten up our error bands around the most probable path. In combination, I am confident in saying that there is no risk of a collision or even a close call. Peregrinus's nearest approach to Earth's orbit will be about ten million miles, plus or minus about two million miles. That's about one-fifth of the way from Earth's orbit to that of Mars. The error band of two million miles may seem like a lot, but it's actually less than one twentieth of one percent of the distance Peregrinus is away from us. We'll be able to tighten up the accuracy even further in another month. The diagram on the screen depicts this, though, as before, it is not to scale.

"So, we will escape the complete doom of a direct collision, as expected, though Peregrinus will be quite a spectacular sight as it sails by, initially appearing to be about the size of a peppercorn held at arm's length at about two

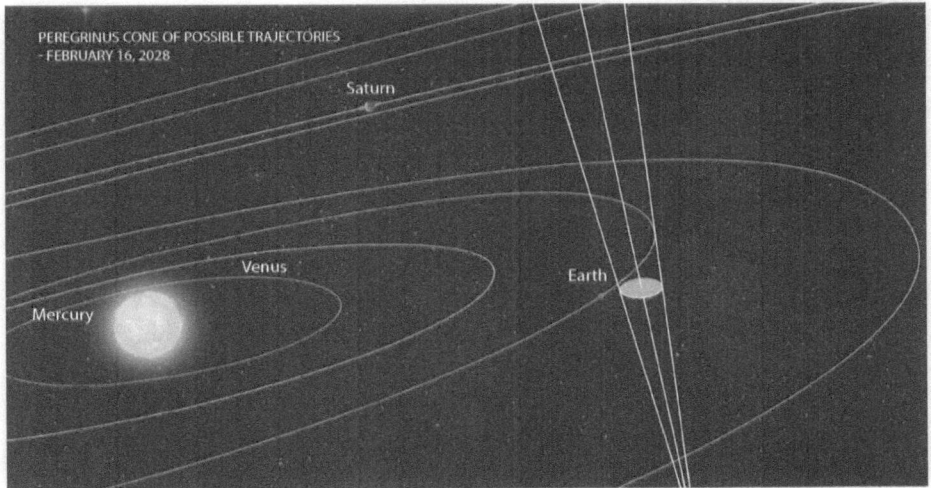

and a half weeks before its closest approach, then growing rapidly to appear to be bigger than the Moon even though it will be forty times farther away than the Moon at that point. Next is the question you posed about tidal waves, eruptions and earthquakes. Your intuition that those could result from a near miss was correct. In this case, ten million miles of separation is not really a near miss. It is more than enough spacing to avoid any such secondary consequences. It would be a different story if Peregrinus was going to go hurtling by at five million miles. That is still a good clean miss, but the resulting tidal forces would be very significant.

"The tidal forces we are familiar with are those exerted by the Sun and the Moon. They are the result of the fact that the gravitational attraction between each of these and the Earth is stronger on the side of Earth closest to each of them, and weakest on the opposite side. This differential in gravity stretches the Earth's crust, but especially the oceans, toward the Sun and the Moon causing the tides and also causing small movements of the Earth's crust as the Sun and the Moon move relative to the Earth.

"Fortunately, at ten million miles of spacing no catastrophic tidal effects are in store. Tidal forces actually diminish in proportion to the cube of the distance of separation — so despite the much greater mass of Peregrinus, we are looking at a tidal force about equal to that of the Moon for the few days surrounding the point of closest approach. That could result in some local flooding in places where the Peregrinus tidal effect and the lunar tidal effect occur at the same time on top of each other, but it is unlikely to be very serious. Likewise, the slight additional rolling distortion of the Earth's crust could possibly be the trigger for a significant earthquake or volcanic eruption but only if one was already imminent and likely to occur within a few years anyway.

"Sir, that brings me to the last matter that I, as the orbital mechanic on the team, can address. While the tidal forces Peregrinus will impose on us will be small, the direct gravitational forces will be substantial for a period of time, even from ten million miles away. Gravitational force is proportional to the product of the masses of the two bodies, the same as tidal forces, and it is inversely proportional to the square of the distance between the two, whereas the tidal force is inversely proportional to the cube of the distance. So while the tidal force is minor at ten million miles, the gravitational attraction of a body as large as Peregrinus is still powerful even at that distance — about one quarter of that of the Sun, albeit for a fairly short interval of time.

"This will result in a tug-of-war between Peregrinus and the Sun. The result of this tug-of-war is that the Earth's orbit will expand somewhat outward away from the Sun, with its current circumference of five hundred and eighty-five million miles expanding by about 2.3 percent to a circumference of about six hundred million miles. Our average distance from the Sun will likewise increase from ninety-three million miles to ninety-five million miles. Our orbit will be drawn into a more elliptical shape than the current almost perfect circle. Our year will be longer by nearly thirteen full days. We will need to establish a new calendar with an extra day in each month, and leap years with a thirtieth day in February in two years out of three, rather than our current one leap year in four.

"To wrap up, Mr. President, as Professor Wayman said to begin with, we will escape a catastrophic collision with Peregrinus and we won't be devastated by tidal waves, earthquakes or eruptions, but we aren't going to escape totally scot-free. There will be some significant consequences from the new orbit; however, the assessment of those consequences is beyond my area of expertise."

The president turned to Dr. Wellington. "Dr. Wellington, I think you are going to explain the consequences of this new orbit. It doesn't seem like all that much of a change."

"Yes, sir," began the Yale professor, "Rachel and I will lay out what we see, but I am afraid that the change in Earth's orbit that Dr. Galletsia is predicting will be far from benign for our global climate, despite the seemingly minor magnitude of that change. Mr. President, it is a cold universe out there, an extremely cold universe. Out in the far reaches of our solar system, several billion miles out and beyond the reach of the Sun's warming rays, the temperature is nearly four hundred and sixty degrees Fahrenheit below zero. Even at the much closer distance that the Earth is to the Sun, only ninety-three million miles, the Sun doesn't radiate enough energy to the Earth to warm it to a habitable temperature absent the greenhouse gas effect, which traps and holds much of that energy in our lower atmosphere."

"Based on Dr. Galletsia's work, the Earth's average distance from the Sun will increase by about 2.3 percent. The warmth that any object gets from the Sun is inversely proportional to the square root of its distance from the Sun, when temperatures are measured on the Kelvin scale. So, a 2.3 percent increase in distance will result in about a 1.1 percent reduction in average temperature. This may seem like a small decrease, but it is 1.1 percent of the Earth's temperature as measured on the Kelvin scale, not the more familiar Fahrenheit scale. So that will mean a decrease in our current effective average temperature of 288 degrees Kelvin down to about 284.7 degrees. On the Fahrenheit scale that we use in everyday life, this means our global average will drop from its current 59 degrees, which is a couple of degrees warmer than fifty years ago, down to about 53 degrees. A decrease of even that amount will have a profound effect on the Earth.

"Sir, when it gets that much colder, the other factor we have to consider is the Earth's albedo, which is the term for how much of the Sun's radiant energy gets reflected back from the Earth's surface. Apart from that which is captured by our greenhouse effect, the solar energy that is reflected from the Earth's surface escapes back out into space and doesn't help protect us from the cold. Our current albedo is 0.30, which means 30 percent of the Sun's energy is reflected back by the Earth. This is due to the effect of clouds and polar ice. However, at the colder temperatures resulting from our more distant orbit, the polar ice caps will expand. We will have lots of ice and snow lasting year-round in the northern latitudes beyond the sixtieth parallel, which will increase the Earth's albedo. If we lose only another 3 percent of the Sun's warmth, this will drop the average temperature down by another six degrees Fahrenheit to 47 degrees. Sir, I am afraid that is likely a best-case scenario without some sort of intervention.

"Mr. President, I am sorry that we geoscientists are the bearers of this bad news, but we have a little more to put on the table. Rachel, it's your turn."

The young doctoral student felt a little intimidated, but she sat up straighter and spoke with confidence. "Mr. President, we are sure that you would want as complete a picture as possible. The global average temperature impacts that Professor Wellington has described are fairly straightforward to estimate, but they are global averages. Different parts of the world are going to be affected differently.

"For one thing, the southern hemisphere has a lot more ocean-covered surface than the northern hemisphere, which has much more land-covered surface. Land heats up more quickly than oceans do, but it also cools down more quickly. So, the northern hemisphere temperature decline resulting from the new orbit will be much quicker than in the south, especially the inland areas of the north. At the same time, the more elliptical shape of the new orbit means that we will experience a much more pronounced drop in temperature in our summer season than in winter, the converse in the southern hemisphere. In the parts of the north where we have always had a winter season with snow, the usual spring melting will occur later and later. Because of the combination of these two effects, the increase in albedo caused by ice formation with be more pronounced in the north.

"Mr. President, I am unhappy to have to tell you that the northern hemisphere is going to experience temperature declines even somewhat greater than what we've estimated for the decline in the global average. The southern hemisphere will be colder than at present during the peak of its winter, but summer will be about the same as it is now, and will melt the winter snow accumulation and prevent much increase in local albedo, except in the very southernmost latitudes. There is some fairly complex modeling to determine these location-specific temperature impacts, which is under way, but directionally that's what we can expect."

"Sir, a drop in the global average temperature of twelve degrees but with the albedo component of that decline more pronounced in the northern hemisphere means a significant ice age in the north with ice eventually covering all of Canada and the northern United States as well as Russia and northern Europe. The southern hemisphere will fare much better. Even as far down as the south island of New Zealand and the southern coast of Australia will remain relatively hospitable."

Most of the group were hearing the details of the climate impacts for the first time. They were all absorbing the information, including the president who mused out loud, "I feel a little like a yo-yo. At first, I feared maybe we would be totally obliterated by a collision, and the difficulties posed by any other outcome seemed to pale in comparison. Once you took the collision risk off the table I was only relieved for a moment before I started to worry about the potential destruction and desolation from what you described as the tidal forces resulting from a close pass, but then you ruled that out as well. Then it sounded like maybe the Sun would lose the tug-of-war with Peregrinus and we would be dragged along in the thing's wake, but once again I felt like we dodged the bullet when you explained the minor change to the Earth's orbit, which is all that would result from the tug-of-war. Now I am told that even what seems to be a small change in Earth's orbit will have unfavorable climate effects that will make much of the world unlivable. It is still an enormously better outcome than some of the alternatives, but that's little consolation."

Eli responded, "Sir, your mixed emotions are completely understandable. I think we are all feeling much the same. I don't want to downplay the seriousness of the climate effects at all. They will be the greatest challenge man will have ever faced, at least since the Great Flood. However, Sir, like Noah, we are getting some time to prepare.

"We have two years before the temperature will start to drop. Then it will take quite a while for the atmosphere to cool off, maybe another year — we are working on this. At first there will be no change to the albedo so we will not face the full cooling impact. It will take many years, possibly thousands of years, for the polar ice cap to cover the northern third of the globe. During the early part of that period, it will still be livable in much of the north and, importantly, it will still be possible to grow crops. It will be a colder existence, with winters even more bitter than those experienced by the early Icelandic settlers on the shores of Lake Winnipeg in Canada. However, we have much better technology for coping with the cold than back in that day. So, we will have time to plan how we are going to respond and time to execute that plan. It is a challenging outlook for sure, but not an insurmountable one if we rise to the challenge.

"Mr. President, I think we should brief a few of General Montgomery's staff on the Peregrinus file to at least map out the broad outline of a response plan, including options for your consideration. That may include additional energy infrastructure. It may include long-term relocation plans, though that can likely wait for many years and be undertaken on a phased basis. Mr. President, I think we will also need to consider the geoengineering possibilities. I touched on that subject when we discussed options to curtail global warming, but there are also strategies that would act in the opposite direction, to reinforce the greenhouse effect and curtail global cooling."

"Eli, of course you are right," replied the president, "I was just feeling sorry for myself, or maybe for mankind, for a moment. We need to turn all our ingenuity and effort toward mitigating this galactic event and preserving the quality of life on Earth as best we can. Yes, let's start to develop the response plan and options. I'll want a preliminary look at that within a week. We should identify which departments within our government are best suited to refining the plan and implementing the actions.

"Eli and Will, I would like to have this team brief the full cabinet on the Peregrinus file in a couple of weeks and to have the response plan far enough progressed that it will provide some comfort and a point for us all to rally around. I am also going to invite the congressional leadership to sit in on that briefing, still all under the top-secret strictures. The following day I will communicate privately with the leaders of our key allies and two days later I will address the American people. Can the two of you organize all this, please?

"Thanks to all of you for your work on this file. Because of you we know what we are facing and we have time to prepare for it. Please continue your efforts on every scientific front."

Chapter 23

Saturday, March 11, 2028
Washington, DC

President James Rushton sat with his wife, Julia, and children in the family room of the White House, watching CNN. The president had returned moments ago from the White House studio where he had announced to the American public, and the world at large, the news of Peregrinus. He had then participated for about half an hour in the media scrum that followed, leaving Eli Wayman and General Isaac Montgomery to field the remaining questions. CNN was carrying a live feed of the question and answer session.

Both Eli and the general were responding calmly, objectively and reassuringly, as Jim knew they would. Eli was a well-known, respected and trusted face of science, having participated in numerous public education discussions. General Montgomery was a new face, though one that would be increasingly familiar in the years to come, but he was solid, pragmatic and optimistic. Both had been thoroughly scripted over the last few days on a range of probable questions and the agreed upon responses, approved by the president.

The media questions were somewhat moderated by a written media briefing that had been made available two hours before the president's announcement on an embargoed basis. Nevertheless, the questions ranged from insightful to amusing. For example, one reporter asked, "Is there a risk that people could be swept off into the sky by Peregrinus?" All questions were treated with the same respect and logical response. It was too soon to know how Americans were going to react, much less people in other parts of the world, many of whom would be affected even more profoundly than most Americans.

It had been a busy three weeks since the consequences of Peregrinus's passage through the solar system had been first laid out. Jim had been tempted to delay for a few more weeks to allow a little more time for the preliminary response plan to be developed. However, as the severity of the global cooling became clearer, he came to feel that the American people had a right to know what lay before them as soon as possible. So, as soon as a rough outline of the response plan was in hand, he set the date for a presidential address, though initially the date was not publicized.

Jim had changed one thing in the sequence of notifications he had originally laid out. As the global cooling picture became clearer, he decided that he had to give the leaders of the most drastically affected countries more lead time to grasp the situation and at least sketch out their own response plans. Even before that he took a few selected cabinet members into his confidence, including the secretaries of state, energy, homeland security and defense.

He was going to need the secretary of state and her department to coordinate the dissemination of whatever information could be provided to the governments of the rest of the world to assist them in their own planning. The Department of Energy would likewise need some forewarning to plan how best to secure the United States' access to energy, the resource that had always been — but which was about to become even more — the world's most precious commodity. The president hoped that the roles of the departments of homeland security and defense would not need to change appreciably, at least to begin with, but he wasn't entirely sure what sort of havoc Peregrinus was going to wreak on global political stability. All of these and their key staff members were drawn behind the top-secret veil of the Peregrinus file.

One week before his planned public address, having already gotten his own country's preparations underway behind the veil of secrecy, James Rushton began to contact the leaders of the world's major northerly countries. The list included American's northern neighbor and staunch ally, Canada, the United Kingdom, Germany, France, the Scandinavian countries, Italy and Japan. The president had even contacted the president of Russia and the premier of the People's Republic of China, though the former had responded pugnaciously as if suspecting some sort of ploy. However, before contacting any of these, in fact within a few days of learning of Peregrinus's climate change consequences, Jim had spoken with his southern neighbor and friend, Luis Lopez, president of Mexico. It was a conversation that spanned several subsequent calls, some secret work by the attorneys general of the two countries, and a brief visit to Washington by President Lopez, ostensibly for further discussions on their joint fresh water project, which was in fact part — but not all — of what they discussed.

The morning after the briefing with the full cabinet and congressional leadership, James Rushton addressed the nation. He advised Americans that a large planet was approaching the inner solar system from the far reaches of outer space and would pass by Earth about ten million miles away in a little less than two years. He made it clear that there was absolutely no risk of a collision. He further explained that there would be no sudden or cataclysmic effects on the Earth, in fact no noticeable initial effects at all, even though this planet will appear visibly larger than the Moon when it reaches its closest distance to Earth. However, the Earth would gradually and smoothly be drawn very slightly farther away from the Sun, to an average distance of about ninety-five million miles compared to the present ninety-three million miles. He didn't get into the nuances of the other orbital changes, though that information was to be made available.

The president calmly advised that even such a minor change in the Earth's distance from the Sun was going to have a cooling effect of several degrees on the Earth's average temperature, with an even more pronounced effect on the northern hemisphere. He went on to say that in time the cooler temperatures would result in a gradual build-up of ice and snow in northern latitudes, unless counteracted by human intervention, with year-round ice coverage eventually extending as far south as the forty-second parallel, though not for many decades.

President Rushton went on to say that the federal government was developing extensive plans to cope with the changes in the environment and would be coordinating closely with state and municipal governments. He emphasized that there would be two years in which to marshal the nation's energy resources and make other preparations before the temperatures began to fall, and probably several decades if not centuries before permanent ice extended down as far as the country's northern border. However, he did say that eventually most of the population of Alaska and the northern tier of the contiguous states would likely wish to move to warmer climes in Hawaii and the southern United States. Fortunately, the climates of Florida, Texas, New Mexico, Arizona and southern California would, if anything, become more pleasant on a year-round basis, and several of these states had large swaths of undeveloped land available for new cities and industries.

The president closed his remarks with the statement that Americans, working together, had the technology, resources, ingenuity and determination required to surmount this challenge. He called for calm, cooperation and patience as plans and preparations were developed and communicated. Lastly, he called for sympathy and support for the many northern countries that would be more seriously affected than the United States. It would be an overstatement and a poorly chosen figure of speech to say that all hell was breaking loose at that moment in many of those other countries, as their peoples began realizing what a grim future they faced.

Jim knew he had to focus primarily on readying his own country for global cooling. However, he was not a person to turn his back on a neighbor in need, and he believed most Americans weren't either. His northern neighbor, Canada, was among those facing a grim future. Canada had not been just a neighbor, but an ally and friend. The two countries were closely interwoven economically, by language, culture and shared democratic beliefs.

There were pragmatic reasons not to let the Canadians freeze in the dark. Canada had vast energy resources, which a cooperative effort, including U.S. capital, could tap in time to benefit both countries, supplementing the ample but not inexhaustible U.S. domestic supplies. Jim had spoken at length with the Canadian prime minister over the last week about how the two countries could work together. He had even confided with the prime minister on the ace he was holding up his sleeve, while insisting on absolute secrecy.

As Jim relaxed with his family after an intense morning and mused on the initiatives he had set in progress, the irony of it all was not lost on him. Many of the new programs he was initiating were largely counter to the direction that he and his predecessor had been following during his tenure in public office to date. However, James Rushton was a pragmatist, not an ideologist. He knew by historical precedent that species that failed to adapt their ways in the face of climate change were at risk of extinction.

Chapter 24

Friday, April 15, 2028
Lakeview, Oregon

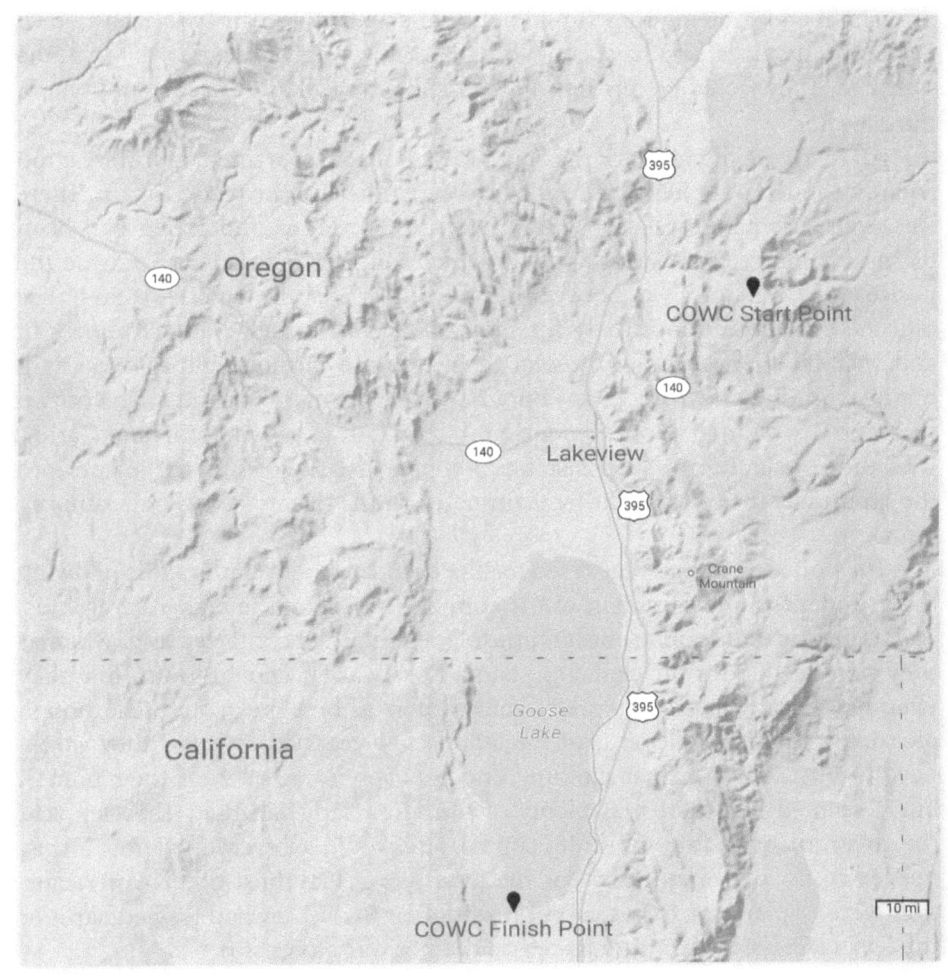

It was seven thirty at night. John Kirk was relaxing on one of the twin beds of the small motel room he and Carlos were checked in to. He had unfastened his shoulder holster and placed the sidearm within easy reach on the bedside table. Carlos, who was working on maps and compass headings at a small desk, still wore his. They had just registered and picked up their race packages and then had a light dinner with their teammates, Fiona, Helen and Kevin; had appointed Carlos as team navigator; and agreed to reconvene in the women's adjacent room for a route briefing in two hours, at nine thirty. Kevin would be their van man and had elected to sleep in the team van rather than pay for a room. The other four needed a comfortable sleep if they could manage it.

At six o'clock the next morning they would launch into the 125-mile California/Oregon Spring Classic Adventure Race, a thirty-hour test of endurance, navigation and strategy. They would need to be up by three thirty to grab a quick but hearty breakfast and have enough time for the long winding drive out to the start line. They would be carrying all the food and drink they needed until noon the day after.

All five were members of the Santa Rosa Police Department and were good friends, though only John and Carlos were members of the tactical team. There was even a romantic relationship between them. Fiona and Helen had been dating for four years. Carlos and Kevin had long-term girlfriends outside the police circle, and John was between relationships. The women were solid police officers, but more importantly for present purposes, they were extremely fit and well experienced in all three of the adventure race disciplines, mountain biking, running and tandem kayaking. The race format required teams of two men and two women. Fiona and Helen were marathoners and John and Carlos, who didn't usually run such distances, hoped that they wouldn't be run into the ground by their lighter, lither teammates on the twenty-seven mile running segment.

The police team had registered for the event several months ago. Following the president's announcement of the coming passage of the planet Peregrinus, and its anticipated cooling effect on the planet, they had conferred as to whether they were still up for the challenge. Santa Rosa was far enough north that they would eventually face some pretty cold winters as best they could tell, though it should remain livable, at least for quite a few years. They knew they would have to buy some warmer clothing and probably weatherproof their homes, but it seemed like there was plenty of time to arrange all that. They felt that the government had things under control and would let everyone know if they needed to do anything more. For the time being, like most other Americans, they were all planning to just carry on with their lives. They had trained hard for the Spring Classic Adventure Race and did not want to miss it.

The route planning decisions that Carlos put in front of the group were pretty straightforward. The initial seventy-five-mile mountain bike course started on the Oregon Timber Trail near Morgan Butte and followed that trail south until it connected with Crane Mountain National Recreation Trail #161. The route continued south on either of the two trails, which paralleled and crisscrossed each other nearly all the way to the transition point to the run segment, just over the state border and into California. There was little to choose between the two trails and many places to switch from one to the other.

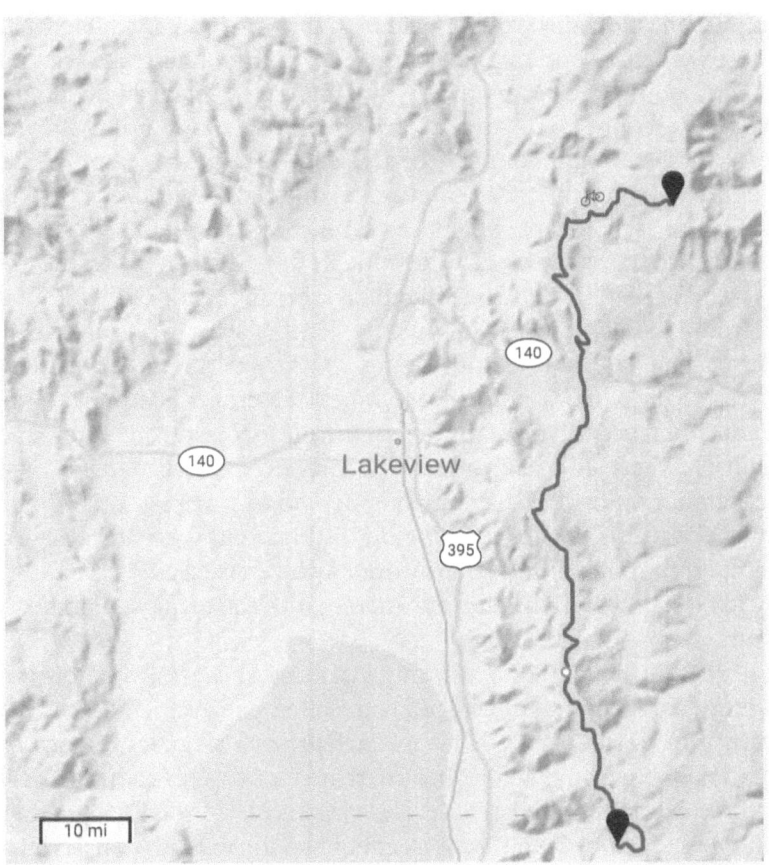

The elevation at the start line would be about 7,200 feet with ups and downs but generally descending down to 5,000 feet over the first twenty miles, then ups and downs with no real trend for another fifteen miles before climbing steeply back up to 7,000 feet over the next five miles to the connection with the Crane Mountain Trail. From there the trail would descend to as low as

5,500 feet before the brutal climb to the peak of Crane Mountain at 8,450 feet, which was accessed only from the Crane Mountain Trail and which included a mandatory checkpoint. The last ten miles to the running segment transition point was an easy descent, which would allow a little recovery of cardiovascular and leg muscle systems.

These trails were well-traveled and would be easy to follow in the daylight, which meant they didn't require any difficult navigation. The team simply needed to keep track of their progress. Carlos had marked his map with various landmarks and distances, so he would be able to keep the team informed. Of course, no electronic navigation aids were permitted in the adventure racing format.

There were three optional checkpoints on the mountain bike segment. These added extra points to a team's time score. They each involved dismounting and climbing a short but steep slope to a readily visible high point above the trail where a marshal would confirm the presence of all four teammates and sign their logbook. Altogether, they might total one thousand three hundred feet of vertical ascent and descent, which wasn't much by themselves, but they added a little extra challenge to an already formidable day. Some of the teams would skip these scrambles, but it would be difficult to score in the top ten without the extra points from the optional checkpoints.

Carlos had laid a rough route up to each of the three, and the team concurred that the extra points were worth the effort. But they all knew they could adjust this plan. One of the key factors in successful adventure racing was the ability to react to circumstances as you encountered them, including the physical condition of all the teammates, and adjust the plan accordingly. Fiona would be the team's checker and would lead any plan revision discussions for this competition, though decisions would be by consensus.

By ten thirty that night, the four members of the team were in bed with the lights out.

It seemed to John that he had only just closed his eyes when his wristwatch alarm sounded. Kevin was already up with coffee, pancakes and sliced ham ready to go on a propane stove behind the van. Each person's backpack had been prepared and checked the evening before and contained a two-liter camelback filled with water, three extra liters of Gatorade, and various high-protein, high-energy food bars and gels. Each of them had a sleeping bag for warmth conservation in the event of a problem, as well as a rain jacket and a medium jacket, which they were wearing for now, and warm gloves. It was right on the freezing mark in the parking lot and would be a good eight degrees Fahrenheit colder at the start line. They would shed the jackets at the first planned break at the low point of the route, about an hour into the race. By ten after four in the morning, they were in the van and heading out for the hour-and-a-half drive to the start point. All side arms were chain-locked to an anchor point in the floor of the van.

At shortly after six thirty, the starter waved them onto the trail. For safety and sanity, the starter was releasing teams at three-minute intervals, starting with those with the fastest predicted times based on a combination of past performance and self-evaluation. This was the police team's first thirty-hour event, so they were released twelfth of the twenty conforming teams. Nonconforming teams, with fewer than four members or which lacked the specified male to female mix would be released last. Race rules required an overtaken team to pull off the trail and allow an overtaking team to go past. It would not be uncommon during the first couple of hours for teams to trade places back and forth several times before reaching a steady state riding order.

The police team was planning to push the pace hard to begin with, risking a fall in order to try to gain some open space. It seemed that most other teams had the same strategy. During the first two hours, they were able to overtake three teams and move up to ninth. They were overtaken themselves by one two-man nonconforming team that pounded down the trail as if intending to test the medical aid stations positioned along the route at several access points.

Throughout the morning the team stuck to their planned steady pace, working hard but maintaining reserves. They took the breaks they had agreed on at the map points that Carlos had suggested. They made sure they stayed hydrated. With the cool temperatures they weren't losing much to perspiration, but they were exhaling a significant volume of water vapor. They also made sure to eat small amounts at each break. Fiona kept a close watch on everyone's condition, but they were also all keeping an eye on each other.

As they tackled the long ascent up Crane Mountain some fifty-two miles into the race, they were feeling pretty good. Their pace dropped to an average of four miles per hour, about the same as what they could sustain if they were running up the grade. During the three-hour climb, they stopped for five minutes on the half-hour and ten on the hour. The climb was taxing, especially after nearly six hours of strenuous activity, including the forays to the optional checkpoints, all three of which they had signed off in their logbook. It was not a race that just anyone could take on. In fact, they had all had to qualify at shorter events in order to register for the Spring Classic. They were, however, exceptionally fit, both physically, but, even more importantly, mentally. They also benefited from being a close and mutually supportive group.

On the uphill stretch they overtook three more teams, each of them stopped and off their bikes. Two of the teams were ministering to one of their members who had collapsed. In each case the downed team member was wrapped in a sleeping bag and was eating and hydrating. One was having his calves and thighs massaged to work out cramps. A team was required to stay together, which was why it was so important to keep an eye on each other to make sure a weaker member wasn't inadvertently run into the ground by stronger teammates.

There was always one member who was the weakest or slowest on any given day, but it wasn't always the same person. Anyone could have an off day. The police team was well balanced to begin with and made sure to watch each other for early signs of exhaustion. They briefly hailed each team as they passed and inquired if they should send back medical aid, which was refused in all cases.

The third team they overtook looked almost entirely blown. They may not have had a weak member, but they had committed the classic error in a long-distance event of adopting too aggressive a pace at the beginning, using up all their reserves and burning themselves out. They might have had one of the fastest paces as far as they got, but with an hour or more required to recuperate, they would now be near the back of the pack, if they could finish at all. The police team pushed on, hoping they could hold their sixth place spot, or maybe even improve on it.

By five thirty-five in the afternoon, the team was jogging their way out of the transition point. They had dropped their bikes for Kevin to load back into the van, taken a quick rest and calorie break, had their logbook signed off and were on their way. They had planned on twelve hours for the mountain bike segment and were pleased to have completed it in slightly under eleven hours. In some ways the twenty-seven-mile running segment they now faced would be easier, but in some ways it would be tougher.

On the easier side, it would be more downhill than up, descending from 7,900 feet down to the shoreline of Goose Lake at about 4,700 feet, though there would be one stretch where they would have to regain about 2,000 feet before continuing down. However, a long downhill run can be harder on muscles and joints than the same distance on a flat, or even slightly uphill stretch. It was also only a third of the distance of the mountain bike segment.

On the tougher side, it was running, not riding. Their full weight, including backpacks, would be on their feet and legs, not split up between legs, arms and seat. This would be an especially significant factor for the men whose greater upper body musculature was an advantage on a downhill bike ride but was just extra weight on the running segment. Lastly, it would be night in a few hours and the latter half of this segment would be run in the dark. Darkness has no effect on energy consumption or muscle fatigue, but it definitely has a psychological dampening effect. It also makes navigational decisions much more difficult.

The topographical maps that had been issued to all teams had the start point and finish point of the running segment clearly marked. However, there were several different possible paths they could take through the network of unpaved county roads and trails spanning the first three-quarters of the descent, and route selection was up to each team. Given that part of the twenty-seven miles would be covered in darkness, there would be one mandatory checkpoint and aid station shortly after the point where all the feasible routes converged on the Fandango Pass Road for the last quarter of the run. Several SUVs would be available to track down any teams not passing through the checkpoints within their predicted window.

Carlos had studied the alternative paths the prior evening and had marked what appeared to be the shortest, straightest route. He had also tried to identify prominent landmarks near each junction point where they would need to turn. He had measured and noted the number of paces between each landmark and each junction, and the compass heading they should be on after passing each such point. They each had clickers for pace-counting, one click for every ten paces, and at least two of them would independently count the paces on each section of the route. In daylight it would be relatively straightforward to follow the chosen route. Once darkness fell the risk significantly increased that a team would turn at a junction prior to the correct one or continue on past the correct turn, either because they didn't realize it was time for a turn, or they just missed seeing it in the dark.

The team planned to alternate between jogging and walking, making sure to reserve some strength for the final kayak segment, though that would involve upper body, not leg, work. Carlos had roughly planned where they would run and where they would walk, starting with a long run to make the most of the remaining daylight to get past some of the more complex navigation points near the beginning of the segment. That would also bank up some extra run time to allow for more walking on the uphill section of the route.

They were soon approaching the point where they would turn off the Oregon Trail onto the road network, and all four were feeling pretty good. That's when they began to catch sight of another team in front of them. At first they would only catch a glimpse as the other team rounded the next bend in the trail, but it was soon apparent that they were gaining. There was a temptation to close the distance more rapidly and overtake the other team, but Helen, who was setting the pace, cautioned against doing that this early in the run. She kept the pace steady and easy. For a while, as the other team became aware of them and picked up their own pace, the separation between the two teams increased. This continued for about five minutes until the team in front was no longer visible while Helen continued to set the same steady pace. Another five minutes later the other team once again came into sight and, if anything, the gap closed more quickly than before.

As the police team closed up behind the other team near the turn from the trail onto the road network, the other team again picked up their pace and began to draw away. A few minutes later they came to an abrupt stop and moved to the side, with one member heaving on all fours. The police team also halted briefly to confirm that the other team were in control of their situation but soon resumed their steady jog. In fact, it was not just a single team that they had caught up to.

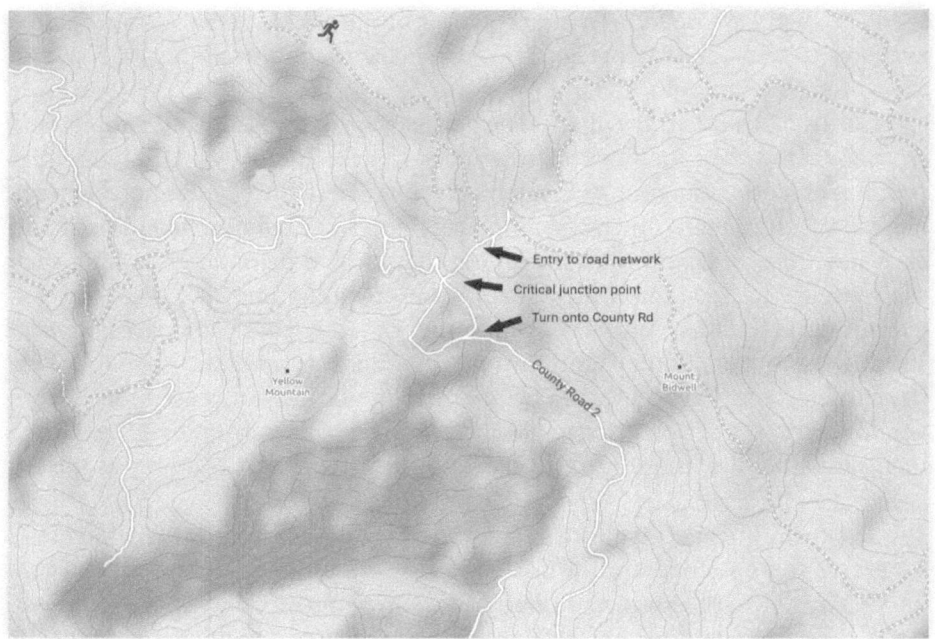

and the front team had also been bouncing their pace up and down to stay in front as the police team closed in from behind. The cycle repeated itself and soon the police were nipping at the heels of their next competitors, although this time the other team seemed determined to sustain a position about thirty yards in front. After another few minutes of this, Carlos quietly called a halt.

John, Fiona and Helen gathered around Carlos, slightly puzzled. It was true that he was responsible for planning their walking breaks but they were less than twenty minutes into the run, with a good stretch of daylight still before them, so it seemed much too soon to slow to a walk. Carlos quietly advised them that they had just run past what he believed was a turn required to follow the shortest route. If they continued to follow the other team, then both of them were going to at least add an extra half mile to the route, with increased risk of further navigational confusion in identifying the correct junction to turn back onto the shortest route.

Carlos led them off the road to the edge of the adjacent forest and backtracked parallel to the road for about fifty yards and then turned off onto another road where it intersected the one they had been on. The intersection would have been easy to overlook in the dark. It was reasonably visible in the soft light of the late afternoon, especially if you knew where you were and were therefore on the lookout for it, as Carlos had been. Clearly with the pressure of pursuit, all members of the team ahead of them had missed it, including their navigator.

Navigation skills were an important competitive aspect of the adventure race, and Carlos basked in the glow of his teammates praise as they hydrated and resumed their jog down the mountain road. However, they kept their celebration brief. Assuming that no other team had missed the turn, they were now in fourth place but knew that they had yet to face the more elite competitors. For some, holding onto fourth spot in their first long race might have been enough. For John Kirk and his teammates, they wouldn't be satisfied with less than the front of the pack. As it turned out, the only other front running team that had missed the cut-off was the nonconforming duo.

The sun was low in the western sky a little over an hour later as the team turned right off the well-graded county road onto a smaller, rougher road, and began the uphill section. Carlos soon confirmed that they were on the right route. They were pleased to have made that turn with some light still left to guide them. It wasn't difficult to spot, but any team missing it would go a long way out of their way. Soon thereafter Carlos called a break for calories, hydration and other biological necessities. They had maintained their steady jog for nearly all of the nine miles of the run segment covered so far, so they would drop back to a brisk walk for the uphill grind. Four miles later, in twilight, after pushing up the 10 percent grade for a little over an hour, they had reached the top of the climb. Shortly thereafter they resumed a running pace. The next seven miles to the mandatory checkpoint on Fandango Pass Road were uneventful.

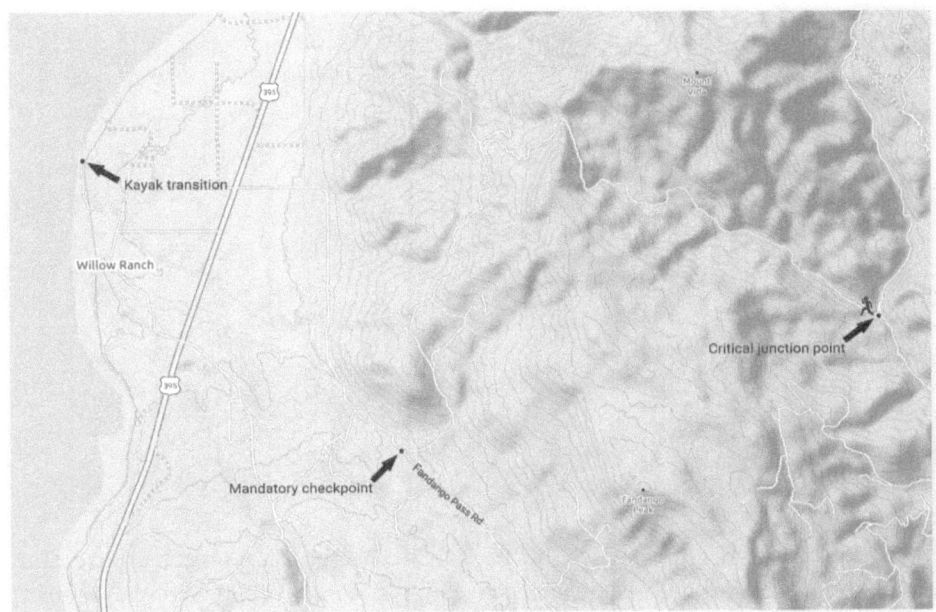

At the checkpoint, with only seven relatively fl at m iles t o go t o t he k ayak segment transition point, they were pleased to learn that their remaining three competitor teams were only minutes apart from each other and that the lattermost had only left the checkpoint a few minutes before. Th is meant that the police team had gained on them, having started the race that morning with a time roughly half an hour aft er the departure time of the fi rst three teams, assuming that's who was still at the front. Although John and his teammates now knew how close they were to the other teams, the lead teams were unaware that a new competitor was hot on their heels. Once again, the temptation to pick up the pace and go sprinting past the competition was strong. And once again, Helen held them to the same steady, endurance pace. An hour later, a little aft er t en o'clock, t hey were at t he boats, having held pretty close to the four and a half hours they had allowed for the running segment and still close to an hour ahead of their overall schedule.

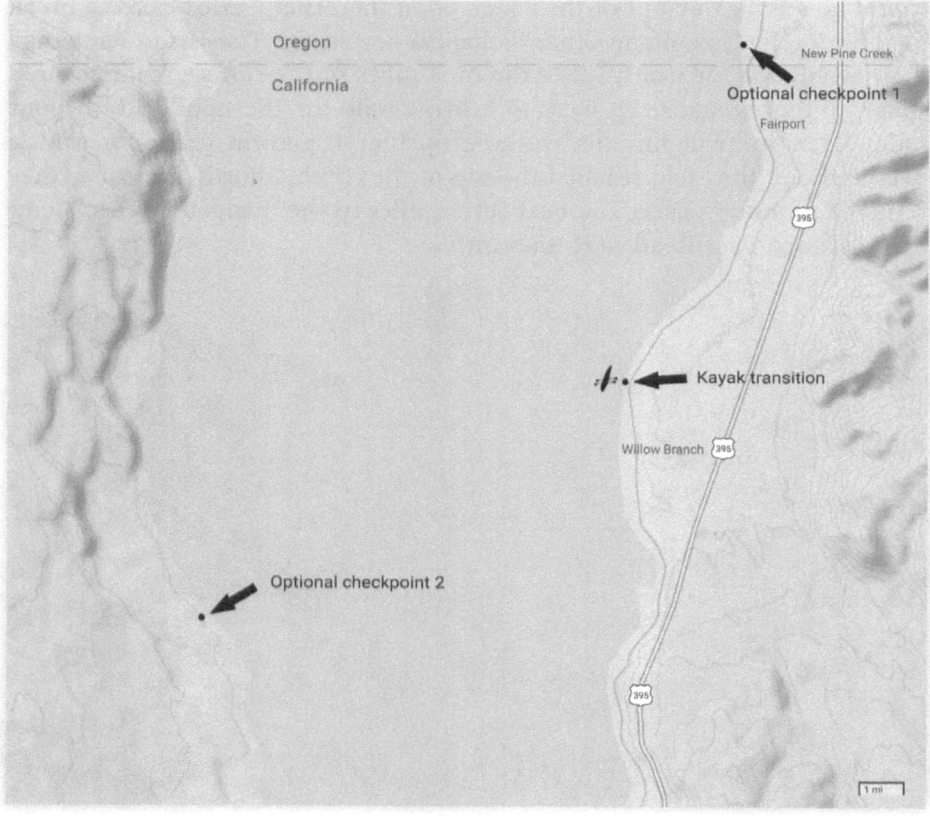

The transition area was well lit by lights powered by a portable generator. Tandem kayaks and life vests were provided by the race organizers and all team members needed to check in with life vests fully fastened. The kayak segment had been planned by the organizers to be at night when winds would tend to be lightest. They had also reserved the right to cancel the kayak segment, or to shorten it, if conditions were judged to be a risk to safety. There was in fact a light breeze from the north kicking up four-inch wavelets as the marshals cleared the police team onto the water. They had seen another team departing the shoreline a few minutes ahead of them, but it was now invisible on the dark lake.

John was paired with Fiona, Carlos with Helen. There were two optional checkpoints on the kayak segment, in addition to the finish line at the eastern end of the Westside Road Bridge at the bottom of the lake. Many of the teams, especially the slower ones or those having endurance difficulties, would skip one or both of the optional checkpoints to avoid exceeding the thirty-hour time limit and incurring overtime penalties. If they chose to skip both they could head straight south close to shore with the wind — a relatively short, low-risk twelve miles. John and the team had once again planned to roll up the extra points for both the optional checkpoints. They were in good time and still feeling strong after sixteen hours of strenuous activity. Carlos took a reading from his compass and led them forth, into the wind and waves, toward the lakeside town of New Pine Creek straddling the Oregon–California state border, six miles away.

As the team paddled their kayaks through the dark, the wind began to freshen and the light chop began to strengthen, sending occasional waves over their bows and into their cockpits. The going was tough, but John and Carlos were in their element, digging deep with each power stroke. Although they were only making two miles per hour, within the first hour they caught the next team, which appeared exhausted and were floating and being blown backward. The next team they overtook had actually put to shore. One crew was carrying their kayak along the shore and the other were thigh-deep dragging their boat. Both were having a difficult time. Their strategy was within the rules, but didn't appear to be helping them much.

The team reached the checkpoint at State Line Park Road after three hours of determined paddling. They beached their boats and tumbled out of them, numb with cold and fatigue. The lead team was just putting back out into the lake as the police team came ashore, but they knew that they needed to warm up and rest before pursuing. The marshals gave them a few minutes to recuperate before checking them out. The next optional checkpoint was across the lake on an angle to the southwest, a fifteen-mile crossing on the shortest path. The marshals would check their physical condition, looking for any indication of incoherence or other signs of hypothermia. They had the authority to require them to skip the crossing and the second optional checkpoint or even to withdraw completely from the race. There was a safety boat, but it wouldn't necessarily be able to spot and assist anyone having trouble.

After a brief break, some calories and some extra cloths, the team caucused, checked each other and presented themselves to the marshals. Minutes later they were back out on the lake. All four had high-intensity headlamps to ensure the two boats did not get separated from each other, all the more important because they would no longer have the shoreline as a reference point. Here was where Carlos's navigation skills would be put to the test. Not only would he need to keep them on a constant heading in the dark and with no external reference points other than his trusty Suunto compass, he also would need to adjust that heading from their course line to allow for leeway drift caused by wind and waves on their starboard stern quarter.

At first the going was easier than when they were heading straight into the north wind. They had both wind and waves pushing them along and were making double the speed of the first leg. However, the wind then began to pick up strength. The bows of the kayaks were riding slightly higher than the sterns with the lighter women in the front, and soon the kayakers were having to paddle almost entirely on the port, downwind side to keep the wind from forcing their bows around to the south. At the same time, they were having to point more and more to the west in order to maintain a southwest course line. With waves running over a foot high and now striking the kayaks almost full on the beam, they were increasingly unstable. A change of plan was needed.

John brought the two boats alongside each other. They grasped gunnels, held two paddles across their decks as braces, and allowed the wind to blow them around until they were stern-on to the waves. This was a much more stable arrangement. They floated for several minutes to rest, accepting the fact that they were being blown straight south. Then John had his two bowmen take one of the bowlines and tie the two boats tightly together at the bow while he and Carlos continued to hold the sterns together and to stabilize with a paddle held across the deck. They then tied the sterns together, and last they removed one stern line and used it to lash a paddle tightly across all four gunnels as a cross brace.

The team could now take the waves nearly broadside without danger of capsizing. They were down by one paddle, but most of the paddling was still required on the downwind side of the makeshift catamaran, which John had taken. Carlos, on the upwind side, could help by prying the stern downwind and then taking a few strokes before prying again. The craft was actually stable enough that Fiona and Helen could crawl over the gunnels and spell each other off. They were back in the race.

After four hours of fighting the lake, the darkness began to recede and the wind began to abate. The four police officers began to peer hopefully toward the western shoreline. It had been a long night, and each of them was approaching the limit of their endurance. They then heard a faint cry for help. Looking toward the sound, about a quarter mile to the south, they could just make out an object on the water. They immediately turned to the south and picked up their stroke rate.

The lead team had decided to cut straight across to the west side of the lake and then straight south along the shoreline. The strategy had worked well for the first two hours but they hadn't adjusted quickly enough to the strengthening wind and mounting waves. First one kayak had capsized, then, in trying to assist, so did the other. They had eventually righted one of the boats and, with the two men stabilizing the boat from the water, the two women had been able to slide onboard and bail most of the water out. However, the men had grown too clumsy with fatigue and cold to successfully climb aboard the second kayak. In the calmer waters of the early dawn, the women were doing their best to tow the other kayak to shore with the men holding onto the side, having tied themselves on with the last of their strength. They were making very slow progress.

As the police team came alongside, they quickly assessed the situation and realized that they needed to get the men out of the water immediately as a first priority. Fortunately, their lashed-together twin hulls provided a stable enough platform that they were able to haul both men out of the water and lay them across the decks. They got the wet clothes off the men and covered them with sleeping bags. Everyone knew, though, that they needed to get these guys to a warm place as soon as possible. They could now see the shoreline clearly in the distance, but they still had at least an hour of hard paddling to get there, even if they cast loose the unmanned kayak.

The small flotilla had not gone very far when a motor launch arrived. Marshals and a paramedic team were onboard. The two shivering men and their female teammates were quickly taken aboard the launch and given warm drinks and thermal blankets. Not so for the police team, which would be disqualified if they accepted any assistance, including directions. The team judged that they had swung at least a half mile south of their course line during their assistance to the other crew and probably had added a good hour to their time. They decided to strike straight west to the shoreline and then work their way back north until they could spot the checkpoint.

The rest of the race was anticlimactic. They reached the second checkpoint at seven thirty in the morning, having been on the water continuously for six hours. Once again, they could barely climb out of their cockpits and needed several minutes of stretching out their cramped legs before they could venture the few steps to the sign-in post. They took a good break to recuperate but were back on the water by eight o'clock. The last seven miles south to the finish line was an easy two-hour paddle.

They got a good cheer as they beached their kayaks and carried them to the drop point. Many of the teams were there already, having started the paddle section later in the evening but then choosing, or being directed, to either skip both optional checkpoints, or to return straight south along the eastern shoreline after the first checkpoint.

They had their logbook time-stamped and signed-off at the marshal station and were told that they were the unofficial winners with the second fastest time into the paddling segment and the only team to complete both discretionary checkpoints. They were pleased with that outcome but were more concerned to learn of the status of the team that had capsized.

One of the marshals took them aside and said, "The team you rescued are all fine. They are at the hospital in Lakeview being monitored, but they seem fully recovered. They are asking to be taken back out on the lake so that they can finish the course, even though they realize they are disqualified. You know, it could have been a much less happy outcome if you guys hadn't come to their assistance."

The police team perfectly understood their fellow adventure racers' desire to complete the race even though technically they were no longer in it. They connected with Kevin, enjoyed a light brunch put on by volunteers from Lakeview and New Pine Creek, and headed off for the drive back to Santa Rosa. On the drive back there was much reliving of the high points of the race, and a shared sense of mutual accomplishment. Although no one put it into exact words, while they were all very satisfied with their individual and team performance in the race, their greatest sense of accomplishment stemmed from having helped out their peers in difficulty. That was just the way they were all wired.

Chapter 25

Late April, 2028
Washington, DC

James Rushton sat behind his desk in the Oval Office awaiting the arrival of the chairman of the Democratic National Committee with mixed emotions. A week earlier he had met with the chairman plus a group of ranking Democrats from both the House and the Senate, as well as the governors of several of the states. It was a group that had been carefully selected to command respect for their views and to be able persuaders. They had a sole objective. They had not come seeking favors for particular constituencies, or to try to influence policy in any way. They had come to persuade the president to change his decision and to accept a nomination from the floor of the Democratic National Convention to stand as its candidate for election to the presidency of the United States of America. He would not need to run in the primary process, and all other contenders for the nomination would withdraw.

There had been lots of speculation in the media about the direction the upcoming presidential election would take. The scenarios had included the extreme of an indefinite suspension of the constitution and the election, which Jim had quickly quashed. He had appeared again before the national media to convey that the situation did not call for such extreme measures. Though Peregrinus was a serious matter that would require hard work, sacrifices, some hardships and a lot of cooperation among Americans and all the peoples of the world, it would not require any lessening of America's democratic traditions. The country had survived other crises with its democracy intact and would do so again. As to another speculative scenario that he would reverse his decision and run for another term of leadership, the president would only say that he was fully occupied with overseeing the nation's preparations for the arrival of Peregrinus and did not have time or inclination to engage in the political process.

Speculation continued, so it was no surprise when Will Templeton advised him of the meeting request, attendees and purpose. In fact, he had been called upon individually by several of the individuals the week before, so he was already well versed in the topic. He and Julie had talked it over extensively the evening before that meeting.

After hearing out the principal spokesmen of the group and exploring their thinking for a while, James had offered a counterproposal. He had advised them that he was planning within a matter of days to announce several new policies and programs that had been developed by the various federal government departments. Some would be controversial. Most he could effect by presidential order under existing legislation, though some would require new legislation for which he would expect their unreserved support. If they provided that support, and if they still wanted him to run once they had gauged the public reaction to his Peregrinus measures, then he would agree to do so. The group of leaders had recognized the wisdom of the president's approach and had pledged their support without even insisting on knowing the details of the new programs.

A few days later James Rushton had returned once again to national television to lay out his plans as to how the United States and its neighbors would adapt to the new climate challenge Mother Nature had thrust upon them. Jim began by congratulating his countrymen, as well as their neighbors to the north and south, on the progress they had achieved in mitigating man-made global warming, in part through cooperative efforts among the three nations. He went on to recapitulate the facts of the new scenario that would result from the brief visit by Peregrinus, including a decline in global average temperature within a year or two after it passed of about six degrees Fahrenheit. The result would be that eventually all of Canada and the northern tier of the United States would face year-round ice. Apart from a few key centers of strategic importance, most northern communities would need to be relocated eventually, though likely not for several decades. Likewise, on the same timescale, alternative arrangements would be made for the agricultural production from this huge area that currently met much of the needs of the two countries and a good part of the world.

President Rushton went on to enumerate the measures he had authorized. There would be an immediate cap on all energy prices with increases of more than 10 percent above preannouncement prices prohibited subject to exemptions, which would be considered by a new administrative division within the Department of Energy. Of all the measures, Jim had the greatest qualms with this one. It ran contrary to his belief in free markets as the most effective long-run system of production and consumption. However, he had been convinced that soon the world was going to realize how precious every bit of energy was about to become. Chaos would result in energy markets. Jim accepted the reality that the accompanying exemption process would be bureaucratic, slow and clumsy.

Along with price caps there would be tax incentives for increased production of any form of energy. The government would also provide selected direct subsidies for the development of more expensive sources of energy, including, by agreement with the government of Canada, the accelerated development of the vast reserves of the Canadian oil sands.

The government would begin to fill the capacity of the existing national strategic petroleum reserve from its current stock of six hundred and fifty million barrels to its capacity of seven hundred and fifty million barrels. At the same time the Department of Energy and the Army Corps of Engineers were tasked with developing additional storage reservoirs for both crude oil and natural gas as well as propane and butane. Any additional pipeline infrastructure required to accommodate increased production and storage of these products would be expedited under presidential emergency orders. Modifications to existing production and transportation infrastructure to permit continued operation at below-design ambient temperatures would receive additional tax incentives.

The government would initiate a federally owned and operated nuclear power program. It was expected to take five years to produce any additional power from this program even with an executive order preempting any state or local regulatory processes.

The Fresh Water Production Accord between the United States and Mexico would be substantially expanded and large tracts of land in Northern Mexico, California, Arizona, New Mexico and Texas would be set aside for irrigation and agricultural production.

President Rushton revealed a new agreement with the governments of Mexico and Canada providing for three ninety-nine-year leases of fifty thousand square miles each of land in the states of Sonora, Chihuahua and Coahuila in Northern Mexico, adjacent to the U.S. border.

In combination, these three 250-mile long by 200-mile deep tracts of land would equal more than half the size of the state of Texas. Two would be administered under the laws of the United States and one by Canada. The boundaries had been carefully drawn to exclude the few major urban centers in Northern Mexico and were otherwise sparsely populated. Any Mexican citizens remaining in the leased territories would retain their citizenship but would also be granted all rights and benefits of a U.S. or Canadian permanent resident while being exempt from filing U.S. or Canadian tax returns and from military service.

New planned communities would be gradually developed in the new Mexican territories, and in the adjacent U.S. border states, over the next couple of decades with sufficient housing and infrastructure to eventually accommodate up to two hundred million relocated people, when that became necessary.

The president knew that similar arrangements were being made between the northern European countries and those of southern Europe and North Africa, including, in the case of the latter, an extensive fresh water production program. Like Mexico, the countries of North Africa were going to receive significant economic benefits as a result.

The last component of the Peregrinus response measures the president announced was a homeowner subsidy program for increased insulation, weatherproofing and heating system upgrades.

The only other possible measure that President Rushton and his cabinet had reviewed but set aside for the time being was a geoengineering program to amplify the atmospheric greenhouse effect. This was too much for even the broad-minded president to get his head around after so recently and for so long having considered greenhouse gases to be the bane of the world. President Rushton directed that the research on the methods, costs, effectiveness and risks of such a program could continue, but he wanted to concentrate on the execution of the rest of the measures to start with and to see how cold it would really get before considering geoengineering any further.

The president stood as Will Templeton ushered the chairman of the Democratic Party into the Oval Office. Jim was of mixed mind because he didn't relish committing himself to another four years in office, yet he had concluded in discussion with his wife that it was now a duty he could not avoid, if asked. He knew that the public response to his announced measures had been largely favorable. There were harsh outcries by the more extreme anti-fossil fuel groups and likewise the anti-nuclear energy groups. However, the population at large seemed mostly relieved at the concrete actions being taken so far in advance. Even most environmentalists, which an increasingly large segment of the population were to some degree, seemed to recognize that the game had changed and that preparing for global cooling had become the new priority.

The president shook hands with the chairman of the Democratic Party and asked him to be seated. Jim sat opposite and motioned for the chairman to begin.

"Mr. President," said the chairman, "thank you for this meeting, and congratulations on your thorough plan for protecting our country from the effects of Peregrinus. Mr. President, my message to you today reflects our discussion of a few days ago. I am here to say that the leadership of our party continues to hold you in the greatest respect and endorses you to run as the party's candidate in the presidential election to be held later this year. The people of our country trust both your character and your leadership skills. You are the man best suited to lead this country through the coming challenges. The party will organize the nomination process so as to minimize your involvement in the preelection process. You will have no opposition to your nomination at our national convention in August. We would like you to be present for a nationally televised acceptance speech, and you will need to invest a moderate amount of time in public appearances during your run for election. Do you accept this invitation?"

"I accept your invitation as you have explained it," said James Rushton.

The next day all the major newspapers carried an announcement from the Democratic Party the main content of which was, in summary:

"The Democratic National Committee of the United States of America is pleased to announce that in view of recent developments, President James Rushton has changed his previously announced intention not to run for an elected term as president. President Rushton has now agreed to accept the Democratic Party's nomination as its candidate for the presidency. The nomination will be formally confirmed at the party's convention on August 19, 2028. All existing Democratic Party nomination contenders have agreed to withdraw from consideration. James Rushton will also be eligible for a second elected term in the 2032 election, enabling continuity of leadership as our great country meets the challenges of the future."

Jim was mildly peeved at the final sentence of the announcement, which, though inarguably factually accurate, was not a message that had been discussed with him and was, he felt, getting rather further ahead of the game than necessary. However, he had much bigger matters to deal with.

Chapter 26

June 2029
Near Brest, Belarus

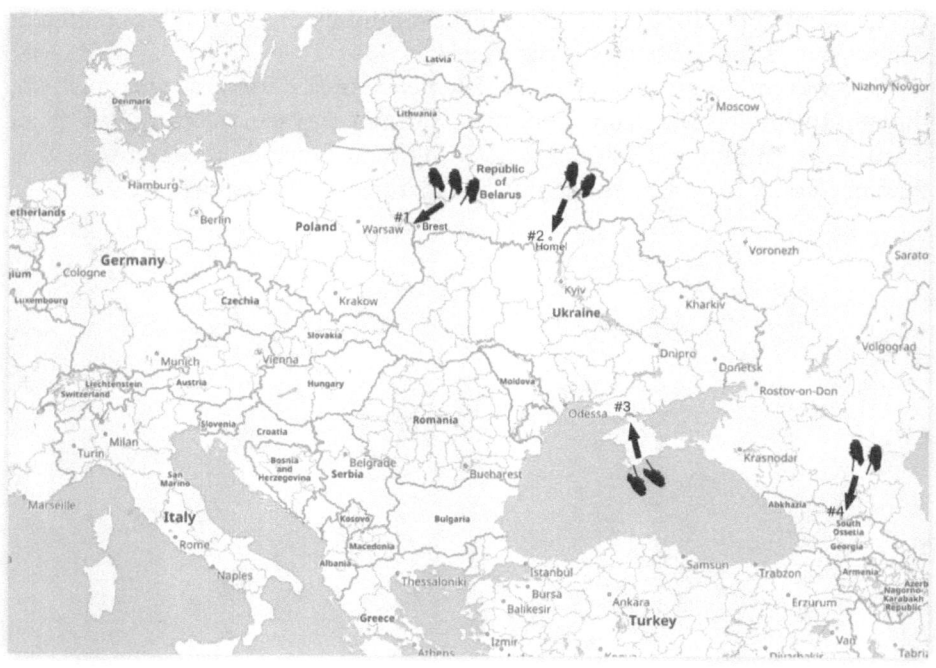

Lieutenant Gregor Aleksevich sat on the edge of the turret of his T-14 Armata tank at nine o'clock in the morning. From this position, he could just see above the crest of the lightly wooded minor ridge to his front, though his main gun, a 152-millimeter cannon, would not be able to engage targets on the other side of the ridge without moving forward about fifty yards, which he had been ordered not to do. It mattered little, he thought, because there were no targets to engage, other than a small Polish border post about five hundred yards forward. At least there were no targets visible to his binoculars over the two thousand yards of open meadows and fields between him and the next small ridge now that the early morning mist had lifted.

What might lie beyond the next ridge inside Polish territory remained to be seen. Gregor's was one of eleven tanks assigned to the 2nd Company, 1st battalion, 1st Guards Tank Regiment, 2nd Guards Tamanskaya Motor Rifle Division. The other ten tanks in the company were spaced about fifty yards apart, roughly the distance they would maintain as they raced into Poland on the attack. The 1st Company of the battalion was spaced out on a similar line to his left and the 3rd was to his right, with the 4th and 5th a hundred yards behind in reserve. He could see the soldiers of the supporting infantry company hunkered down behind his company's tanks.

The battalion had moved into position the night before during a violent storm, which muffled the noise of their engines if anyone was listening. The other three battalions of the regiment, and their supporting infantry, had likewise taken advantage of the weather to move into position, having awaited such a stealth opportunity for a week. One was on each of his battalion's flanks and the fourth was immediately to their rear. Now all were well camouflaged with a random assortment of netting and foliage just short of the border between Belarus and Poland on the eastern flank of the NATO alliance.

Although Belarus was officially independent of Russia, the last pretense of that status had blown away in the face of the arrival of Peregrinus. Belarus had always leaned more toward Moscow than its fellow eastern European members of the former Union of Soviet Socialist Republics when the latter was dissolved in 1991. It had fallen quickly into the arms of Russia following the announcement of Peregrinus. As a relatively poor country, it would need support to weather the coming cold, and to have chosen NATO would have precipitated its own early destruction as the battlefield for an immediate war. Consequently, the Russian military command had been able to position their primary offensive start line on the western border of Belarus within relatively short striking distance of Berlin, Brussels, Paris and eventually Madrid.

A similar though smaller offensive would also use Belarus as a springboard, launching from Gomel in southern Belarus into northern Ukraine, through Hungary and Austria into Italy. A third army would launch from the Crimean peninsula through southern Ukraine, Romania, Bulgaria and into Greece, while a fourth would launch from the Caucasus through Georgia and into Turkey. It was a bold military strategy but, if successful, it would gain Russia the industrial capability and wealth of Europe as well as several Mediterranean refuges from the cold.

Gregor was positioned at the apex of the three-battalion-wide regimental front of the primary and strongest assault force. He would have been proud to lead the attack, but he knew that role had been assigned to the 4th Battalion, which would advance rapidly through his line, following path marker ribboning, once the command had been given. The rest of the regiment would follow immediately behind the spearhead 4th Battalion. Behind him he knew lay another two full heavy armor regiments, another four hundred and forty tanks, plus an attached artillery regiment of two hundred self-propelled cannons, comprising the armored strength of the rest of the division. Altogether, including three regiments of integrated infantry, the division fielded more than eleven thousand men under arms, a formidable force set to punch through NATO's thin outer shell of border defense and subdue its targets before enemy reinforcements could be brought to bear.

Aligned behind the 2nd Guards Tamanskaya Motor Rifle Division were another four of Russia's twenty-two active divisions, likewise heavily armored given Russian military doctrine, which favored massive armored formations. In fact, Russian land forces, which were mostly based in western and central Russia, could field nearly twenty-five thousand main battle tanks compared with the United States at about one third that number across all of its theaters of operation. The follow-on divisions would consist mainly of the previous generation T-90 main battle tanks, which were still potent.

Each of the other three offensive thrusts were likewise led by a spearhead division built around the state-of-the-art T-14 Armata tanks, with another two or three follow-on armored divisions. The follow-on divisions, including their integrated infantry regiments were, in every case, tasked with occupation and suppression roles following behind the spearhead divisions. The overall attack would be a formidable sledgehammer blow, unstoppable by the reckoning of Russia's president and his military advisors, and beyond any effective retaliation or counterattack by NATO's superior strategic air power once in occupation of Europe's key urban and industrial centers.

The young Russian tank commander was excited at the prospect of combat, even if it was only a lightly armored mechanized brigade they were facing. The officers in the company had been briefed to expect resistance and casualties but not much of either. Their greatest threat would be air-to-ground missile attacks and cannon fire from U.S. Thunderbolt ground-attack aircraft and from Apache, SuperCobra and Tiger attack helicopters. However, the division was equipped with extensive antiaircraft support weaponry, both surface-to-air missiles and next generation ZSU autocannon mobile batteries firing four thousand 23-millimeter armor-piercing incendiary rounds per minute. The NATO ground attack aircraft were expected to have little opportunity to engage the Russian heavy armored division before being ripped out of the sky.

The Russian military leadership was hopeful that the trans-Poland attack, the strongest of four across the European continent, would catch their NATO opponents at least partly by surprise. They had deployed the attack divisions carefully over a period of six months, avoiding any readily observable large scale movements. In many cases, the Russian military deployed the attack divisions to replace other forces they supposedly recalled for rest and training. However, the trucks and trains intended to return north with the withdrawing troops had actually returned empty. All the while, their political leadership and the president himself played a carefully orchestrated game of deception, pretending to negotiate with their European neighbors to provide increased shipments of oil and natural gas to stave off the coming cold.

The surprise attack was poised to explode across the frontier. The Russians had concentrated their forces at four strategic axes of attack with multiple divisions stacked in echelons behind the spearhead of each axis. Once the spearhead division on each axis had pierced the border defenses, the following divisions would fan out and race toward their assigned objectives. No manpower would be wasted on flank protection or defending supply lines. Each division was expected to be self-sufficient for two weeks of combat, after which they should control their objectives and commandeer all of their supply requirements.

The Russian military expected to have overwhelming firepower superiority for their ground forces and had focused on expanding the numbers and capabilities of their air defense forces to counter the NATO air superiority. Russian military doctrine revolved around heavy armor packing a massive punch both in strength and speed of advance. They expected to occupy the capitals of all the major NATO countries of continental Europe, including Turkey, within a month.

These countries would be reluctant to authorize strategic defensive bombings of their own lands and would be vulnerable to the Russian threat to lay waste to their industries and cities if they didn't capitulate. Of course, the Russians had no intention of destroying the industrial base of western and central Europe. They intended only to expropriate it for their own purposes — to build a redoubt against the ice fields that would otherwise soon encroach on their own country. If the populations of their vanquished neighbors were left with few resources of their own to combat the coming cold, that was unfortunate but unavoidable.

Like most young Russians of his age, especially those in the military forces, Gregor viewed his president as a great hero, one who had been preparing for many years to reestablish Russia as a world power, the equal or the better of the United States. He had been schooled to believe that NATO existed only to see Russia reduced to the status of an impoverished third-rate power. He felt deep anger toward the perpetrators of this scheme. He felt no fear, only great pride and excitement, at the prospect of the powerful high-explosive shells from his 152-millimeter main gun tearing into the enemy before him. Any potential for remorse over or pity for those he was about to destroy had been thoroughly schooled out of him by the long-standing education and propaganda system of Russia's unscrupulous president.

The Russian lieutenant, and thousands of other junior officers like him, received the order to commence the attack. The mayhem was about to begin. It wasn't expected to last long, and Gregor, intending to have a clear view of the opening act, commanded his tank to advance to the top of the ridge to act as overwatch for the lead attack battalion, which had just passed through his ranks.

The Russian military planners were correct in several of their assumptions, though catastrophically wrong in others. They were correct that the NATO heavy armor forces opposing them were greatly outnumbered, and they were correct that mayhem was about to be let loose.

Back in Washington it was three o'clock in the morning. President Rushton had risen a half hour earlier, after a few hours of sleep, and descended to the White House Situation Room. The Russian military leaders had failed to achieve their intended element of surprise. President Rushton had been advised late the preceding day that the Russian attack likely would be underway soon after midnight Washington time. He had decided to rise early to get the first reports and ready himself for a critical call to the Russian president.

President Rushton had considered carefully and discussed thoroughly with his national intelligence advisors, his military advisors and the leaders of his European allies, the likely reaction of the Russian bear to the arrival of Peregrinus. These discussions and the resulting preparations had begun immediately following the original public announcement, so, among other things, American satellites had been closely monitoring the expected Russian military preparations. The satellites were equipped with infrared capability and terahertz synthetic aperture radar. They had detected the movements and heat signatures of thousands of main battle tanks maneuvering into forward positions the previous night on several fronts, despite heavy clouds and precipitation.

Being forewarned would certainly give the NATO defensive forces a fighting chance, but would that be enough given the massive amount of Russian heavy armor compared to the relatively light armor and mechanized infantry constituting the bulk of the NATO forces? That is where another aspect of the preparations of the United States and its allies came into play.

American military doctrine had been evolving away from heavy armor for several years, well before Jim unexpectedly stepped into the role of commander-in-chief. The recent previous presidents had been convinced by their advisors of the need for changes to America's war-fighting capabilities in the evolving global political environment. Ironically, though Jim was likely better able to grasp the military reasoning behind those required changes than his predecessors had been, it would have been too late if the changes hadn't been initiated until he took office. He had certainly been quick to support those changes, and to encourage their acceleration, and so they were well underway by the dawning of Peregrinus.

The changes to America's military forces were twofold — two separate but complementary changes — and they had been mirrored to a greater or lesser degree by most of the other NATO members. The changes were firstly a modest but meaningful expansion in army combat personnel after many decades of decreases in combat strength following the Vietnamese war and even after the Iraq conflicts. By the middle of the last decade the army had shrunk to half a million, of which roughly 40 percent were combat personnel deployed across thirty-two combat brigade teams, plus various independent regiment-sized units, including special operations forces. The army reserve and army National Guard could field about another half as many combat brigade teams. The Marine Corps could field another hundred thousand combat personnel allocated among four autonomous divisions, three special operations battalions and four aircraft wings.

Over the following decade, four additional independent combat brigade teams fielding about 4,500 personnel each had been gradually added to the army's strength with little fanfare or profile. This represented about a 10 percent growth in army combat personnel, not by itself a very intimidating increase.

What was even less known about the new units than their existence and strength, was their weaponry and tactical mission. They were designated as mechanized infantry, which in fact they were, but they were designed first and foremost to be defensive tank killers. Every four-man fire team in all four brigades consisted of two conventional infantry men armed with rifles, or possibly one of them carrying an M249 belt-fed 5.56 millimeter squad automatic weapon and charged with defending the other two squad members who wielded the latest generation FGM-148H Javelin fire-and-forget rocket-propelled guided missile.

The missile of the Javelin carries a tandem warhead with two high explosive sequential shaped charges focused by metallic cylinders to concentrate the resulting stream of high-velocity molten metal into a narrow diameter armor piercing lance. The first charge is intended to defeat any composite or reactive armor protecting the target. The second charge is then able to penetrate the target's primary armor. The Javelin is designed to destroy enemy main battle tanks and, though not yet proved, is believed to be able to penetrate the thick frontal armor of even the Armata. However, the weapon's primary attack mode against a tank is not a direct frontal trajectory; rather, it will climb immediately to five hundred feet and then scream down from above to strike the thinner topside armor of the tank.

Once launched the Javelin will home on an infrared designated target at two thousand miles per hour. The missile, with its seeker head, is fully independent, leaving the crew free to take cover, change position, or prepare another shot. Its flight time is less than two seconds out to an effective range of a mile. There were over a thousand such weapons in each of the new brigades. Now one such brigade was positioned across each of the four Russian axes of attack.

Supporting each of the new tank killer mechanized infantry brigades was a full regiment of one hundred tank killer helicopters, AH-1Z Vipers or AH-64 Apaches. Each of these was armed with an automatic cannon firing five hundred armor-piercing shells per minute and an air-to-ground missile system using a fire-and-forget laser target designation system. The helicopters were existing units previously attached to other more conventional ground forces but in a similar tank killing role to that with which they were currently tasked. The main difference was a new attack doctrine. Previously they would fly extended missions in a high overwatch position, attacking enemy armored units when called in to support U.S. infantry or armored units encountering enemy armor, or if they could spot enemy armor themselves.

In their new role, the tank killer helicopters were strictly limited to pop-up fire, drop-down tactics. Their air-to-ground tandem warhead high-explosive Hellfire missiles could be fired while the helicopter was rising or descending with equal accuracy as if standing still or moving forward. In this attack mode they would rarely be visible to enemy forces for more than a couple of seconds, not long enough to be targeted by counterfire from surface-to-air missiles. Their combat survival rate using the pop-up tactic was expected to be much greater. The pop-up tactic was only suitable for defense of a fixed position or line, not for a forward moving offensive, but in that anti-armor defense role, the new tactic was very effective indeed.

The NATO defense was of course not wholly dependent on the four new anti-tank brigades, though they were the primary shield against Russia's overwhelming main battle tank advantage. There were also extensive conventional divisions from the many NATO countries but especially Germany, France, Italy and Great Britain, as well as the remainder of the United States Army Europe headquartered in Wiesbaden, Germany. These forces had all been augmented over the last decade as Russian belligerence increased. They comprise NATO's own main battle tanks, including the formidable though aging U.S. M1A2 Abrams tanks. The remainder of the NATO defense was positioned either to support the frontline anti-tank brigades or to defend other key locations. Multiple regiments of deadly 155 millimeter howitzers were positioned well behind the anti-tank brigades but close enough to reach several miles beyond the front lines of the four attack axes. However, among the senior NATO commanders, there was no illusion. If the four new and little-known frontline brigades could not stop or at least seriously cripple the armored spearheads aimed at the European capitals, it was unlikely that the remaining forces could repel the Russians.

By the time Lieutenant Aleksevich's tank reached the top of the low ridge along with the other ten tanks of the 2nd company and the other two lead companies of the 1st battalion, the 4th battalion lead tanks were just crossing the Polish border, five hundred yards in front, having accelerated to their top speed of fifty miles per hour as soon as they had reached the bottom of the ridge. On both flanks the fifty-five tanks each of the 2nd and 3rd battalions were beginning to pour over the ridge and surge toward the border slightly behind the fourth battalion. It was an impressive sight — 165 T-14 Armata main battle tanks on a tight thousand-yard-wide front pounding across the two thousand yards separating the two ridgelines. Gregor's heart swelled with pride. The assault appeared to be unopposed. Then all hell abruptly broke loose.

From his position, the lieutenant observed multiple discharge flares from the top of the opposing ridge all along the battalion wide front — more than he could count. He also noted several dozen helicopters come briefly into view from behind the ridge, spouting missiles and cannon fire briefly before disappearing back behind the ridge, and he could hear the shriek of heavy artillery rounds in the hundreds screaming overhead at the same time. Russian antiaircraft batteries positioned adjacent to his tank punched missiles and cannon fire at the helicopters, but none could establish a lock on their target before the helicopters ducked behind cover. Several surface-to-air missiles and a few thousand rounds of thirty-millimeter cannon fire flashed over the opposing ridge to fall harmlessly in NATO's rear area.

Before Gregor could make sense of the scene in front of him, he, along with the other fifty-five tanks of the 1st battalion were ordered to attack, providing covering fire for the 4th battalion and then passing through to the point of the spearhead. As he ordered his tank down the ridge and onto the battlefield, the helicopters reappeared and the lieutenant suspected that the multiple large explosions on both flanks immediately to his rear meant the end of most of the air defense units supporting the regiment. Apart from that, the helicopters appeared to be ignoring the regiment of tanks racing toward their ridge. In fact, the Apaches and Vipers, with the long range of their Hellfire missiles, were concentrating their fire on the regiments to the rear of Lieutenant Aleksevich, while the NATO artillery fire bases, as well as cruise missiles from several submarines stationed in the Baltic Sea, were hammering the divisions lined up behind the 2nd Guards Tamanskaya Motor Rifle Division.

The U.S. brigade, with its supporting helicopter regiment, was spread out across a ten-thousand-yard front spanning a couple of miles on either side of the anticipated axis of the Russian attack, with additional conventional armored regiments extending the flanks yet further. This was to guard against a rapid flanking maneuver by the Russian armor, either prior to the initial engagement or as a response to the strength of the defense. Consequently, only about a tenth of the brigade was positioned directly in front of the thousand-yard-wide initial thrust by the Russian 1st Guards Regiment. This meant that only one hundred of the brigade's one thousand anti-tank squads were on the ridgeline directly opposing the two hundred and twenty tanks of the 1st Guards Regiment. However, another one hundred squads on either flank were close enough to the Russian line of advance to bring their Javelins to bear on the tanks, especially once they closed to within a thousand yards of the ridge.

As Lieutenant Aleksevich raced toward the opposite ridge, he searched desperately for a target for his main gun to bring counterfire against the NATO forces that were wreaking havoc on his regiment. He sought a tank or any armored vehicle, but could find no such target either with his periscope set to a maximum magnification optical view or on the infrared receiver. He could occasionally glimpse a few dismounted infantry moving out of sight immediately after the bloom of a missile launch, but they were gone by the time he could traverse the 152-millimeter cannon the necessary degree or two. He took to discharging the main gun at the top of the ridge even without a clear target and hosing the ridgeline with his 7.62 millimeter coaxial machine gun. Though he couldn't tell himself, this tactic was actually quite effective. It kept the anti-tank Javelin squads hunkered down with much reduced opportunity to set up a shot on the rapidly approaching tanks. Had it been adopted by more of the Armata crews it would have made for a substantially more even outcome to the battle.

As it was, most of the young Russian tankers had their hearts set on knocking out one or two of the M1A2 Abrams tanks, or maybe a few of the U.S. Stryker – A1 light armored fighting vehicles. By the time the tank commanders and their company and battalion commanders recognized the need to suppress the U.S. anti-tank squads, it was too late.

The nearly three hundred Javelin squads within range of the 1st Guards regiment line of advance generally got off three or four Javelins each before the tanks closed to within five hundred yards of the NATO line of defense. It was a sophisticated weapon with very few misses and a high kill rate, even against the heavily armored Armatas. With roughly one thousand Javelins targeted at the two hundred and twenty tanks, the result was an almost complete decimation of the Russian tank regiment. Nearly all the Armatas took at least one hit and many took three or four. Even one hit was usually sufficient to disable an Armata, though a few that took a single glancing shot off the frontal armor were able to continue, and a very few, by the fortunes of war, managed to make it to the opposing ridgeline unscathed. Gregor Aleksevich's tank was one of those. In no small measure, he was the author of his own salvation, having significantly reduced the rate of Javelin fire from his front.

As the young lieutenant threaded his way through the smoking remains of the regiment and crested the ridge marking NATO's forward defense line, he realized that he had not seen a NATO handheld missile launch for the last several minutes, though the Hellfire missiles from the support helicopters had continued to devastate the few remaining Russian tanks. All that Gregor could see was a rapidly retreating line of personnel carrier and support vehicles making toward the next ridgeline a couple of miles away. He was tempted to fire a few main gun rounds at the retreating NATO forces that were still within range. The result would have been an immediate return of fire from the many attack helicopters hovering protectively a few dozen feet above the retreating anti-tank brigade. Gregor chose to live.

Quiet descended on the battlefield, but for the continued shriek of 155 mm howitzer rounds passing overhead to pound the Russian divisions assembled in the rear. The 1st Guards regiment had achieved its objective and nearly on time. NATO had been driven from its line of defense and the Russian army was in Poland. However, there were not many left of the regiment to celebrate this success, and it wasn't really much of a success from a practical point of view. The NATO retreat was entirely strategic. NATO casualties and equipment losses had been very light and they were well positioned tactically to repeat the damage to the Russians. A full tank regiment was nothing but tatters. The armored spearhead had been blunted.

The Russian chain of command was hugely distressed at the outcome of the initial Poland attack. However, one battle does not win or lose a war. The two remaining regiments of the Division were ordered to sweep right and left to test the NATO flanks. Although they had been held in reserve, these two regiments had been close enough to the front line to be pretty badly beaten up by the Hellfires from the NATO helicopters. Nevertheless, those flanking attacks were not as completely one-sided, with more attention now being given to suppression of the Javelin squads. Yet, neither was there any decisive victory for the Russian division, and casualties of men and destruction of equipment continued to mount with little corresponding damage to the NATO defensive forces. By late afternoon, the Tamanskaya division had made no further progress and had been reduced to the equivalent of less than one full regiment. The remaining four divisions of the Russian battle group had also been significantly degraded by continuous artillery and cruise missile fire. Much the same pattern had been repeated at two of the other three Russian axes of attack.

In the fourth case the Russian battle group commander had, at the last minute, discarded his preapproved attack plan and had executed a long flanking attack, trying to outflank the NATO defenders. However, the Javelin brigades were highly mobile, and the one facing this tactic had simply shifted its front line orientation to match the flanking attack. There was less direct engagement on this front, and therefore less destruction to the spearhead Armata division, but at the end of the day no significant penetration of the NATO defense had been achieved, and the tightly packed follow-on divisions in the rear had still been fish in a barrel for NATO artillery and cruise missiles from a U.S. Black Sea flotilla.

At eleven o'clock in the morning Washington time — six o'clock at night in Moscow — President Rushton had initiated a call to his Russian counterpart. The American president had not chastised the Russian, though he had to maintain a tight rein on his emotions to avoid conveying the intense dislike he felt for the man. He had simply proposed that in the interest of avoiding further bloodshed an immediate cease-fire be declared following which Russian forces would have twenty-four hours to move back behind their initial line of attack and to remove all armed forces from Belarus. NATO forces would not pursue the withdrawing Russian forces, and artillery and cruise missile strikes would cease.

The Russian president responded with his usual belligerence, proposing that NATO surrender or Russia was prepared to unleash chemical, biological and even tactical nuclear weapons if necessary. The American president responded calmly and coolly that NATO troops were trained to withstand nuclear, biological and chemical warfare and that NATO would not resort to such weapons itself, but if so attacked, the U.S. Air Force would commence high altitude strategic bombing of the rear areas of the current offensive, completely destroying the remaining Russian ground forces. The American president also added that if Russia was prepared to accept the cease-fire and certain other conditions, NATO might be prepared to return to normal economic relations with Russia and work cooperatively toward managing global cooling, which had seemed to be the direction Russia had been pursuing prior to commencing hostilities. This cooperation would include nonopposition to Russian emigration to an agreed list of Russian client states in southern latitudes.

A short scuffle could be heard on the Russian end of the line. The Russian translator requested the American president to await a call back in a few moments. History may never know exactly what transpired in the Kremlin that evening, though it isn't difficult to guess at the gist of it given the result.

A few minutes later the hotline was activated again from Moscow's end. The translator, who seemed slightly ruffled, announced that the president had resigned, and he was now speaking on behalf of the prime minister of Russia together with the commanding general of all Russian ground forces. These two individuals had been temporarily appointed as co-presidents pending further deliberations of the Council of Ministers. The Russian co-presidents had asked the translator to inquire of the American president as to what additional conditions, beyond immediate cease-fire and withdrawal, would have to be met by Russia in order to reestablish normal relationships with NATO and its member countries. James Rushton had calmly replied that they had already met the first condition, removal of the previous Russian president.

Chapter 27

January 17, 2030
Near Pasadena, CA

Darya shivered in the cool mountain air as she stood gazing up at the night sky a little before midnight. Although she'd spent so many nights staring up into the vast universe — as a child, as an undergraduate student, a graduate student and now as a full-fledged astrophysicist — this night was different from all those other nights; it had never happened before and would never happen again. Her planet, Peregrinus, hung in the sky above her at its closest approach to Earth. It was a huge, radiant ball reflecting back light from the Sun, which was now shining brightly on the other side of the Earth, but fully illuminating Peregrinus. On certain nights as Peregrinus climbed up through the plane of the ecliptic, the Earth's shadow could be seen falling on the face of Peregrinus, though the huge planet was now slightly above the plane and beyond the Earth's shadow.

It was also a full Moon tonight, with no part of the Moon obscured by the Earth's shadow. The Moon was still high in the western sky and the two celestial bodies hung near each other, lighting the night with their combined glow. Peregrinus appeared to be more than twice the size of the more familiar orb despite its much greater distance away. It was a spectacular view — beautiful and awesome beyond description.

Darya had spent many evenings in the last two years observing the approach of Peregrinus, the Wanderer, as it rose steadily in the southern sky. Much of that time during the first year, she had been looking at the monitor of the Big Eye at the LSST observatory in the Andes, and the focus had been purely scientific. She had continued to monitor the Wanderer closely since her initial discovery of it, gathering as much data as possible and supporting her colleague and teammate, Tony Galletsia, as he continually refined the path of the planet. Of course, after the initial announcement and revelation of the visitor, she had been far from alone among astronomers, professional and amateur, observing the rise of Peregrinus. Nevertheless, she still had the best vantage point and the best tool for the job, and she was the primary astronomer on the president's Peregrinus advisory committee. So, she took her role very seriously.

After the initial big surprise, there had, thankfully, been no further surprises. Peregrinus's diameter and mass had been confirmed at values close to the initial estimates, nearly one and a half times larger than Jupiter and three times more massive. Most importantly, the planet's projected path had remained at a comfortable distance from Earth, with a point of closest approach of ten million miles, which was occurring this very night, a few days after rising through the plane of the ecliptic. Unfortunately, a comfortable separation distance from a collision risk perspective was not, as Darya well knew, going to be all that comfortable from a climate perspective.

While she continued to monitor the approach of Peregrinus, Darya had ample time to complete her thesis on exoplanets. Though a valuable contribution to her subject area, the thesis itself was somewhat anticlimactic relative to her discovery and study of Peregrinus. In fact, she had since submitted for publication a couple of papers on the transient planet, exploring its possible origins. These would be more extensively read than her thesis ever would be.

Darya's oral thesis defense had occurred in the ivied halls of Oxford University in the summer of 2028. Ivy is generally tolerant of cold temperatures, so there was optimism that it would continue to dress the campus in year-round green for many years to come. Darya was surprised and delighted to discover that her examination committee included both Dr. George Rigby and Dr. Eli Wayman. The defense had gone well, in this case a forgone conclusion. She had received her doctorate at the university's fall convocation, at which the prime minister had delivered the keynote speech with none other than the president of the United States of America in attendance. Darya had also been awarded a two-year post-doctoral fellowship to continue her studies of Peregrinus.

During the last several months, Darya had been spending fewer hours in the antiseptic confines of the Big Eye and more in direct visual observation. She had watched as Peregrinus grew from a bright pinpoint of light, not distinguishable from the resident planets by visual impression, to the size of a coriander seed, to a pea, a marble, golf ball and, dramatically in the last weeks, to a softball and finally a beach ball.

As on many of those prior evenings, the young astronomer was standing outside on the top of a mountain with a clear view of the western horizon where Peregrinus hung, a little further to the north each night, before it set into the Pacific Ocean. The mountain she was on tonight was not in the Andes. She stood on Mount Wilson in the San Gabriels just east of Pasadena, California, in the staff parking lot of the Mount Wilson Observatory. It had been many decades since Mount Wilson had been at its prime as a center of astronomical research and it now primarily served as a public education and engagement facility. Nevertheless, it contains the one-hundred-inch Hooker telescope, which had been the largest in the world from 1917 to 1949, as well as its predecessor, a sixty-inch telescope, which also held the size record in its time. It was the site of many great strides in astronomical research, including Edwin Hubble's discovery that the universe extends far beyond our Milky Way galaxy, which is really just our immediate neighborhood, and that the universe is constantly expanding away from a central point.

At 5,715 feet above sea level, the Mount Wilson Observatory lay well below the altitude of the LSST facility in the distant south, though it was still cold at this time of year, with a blanket of snow covering the nearby meadows and woods in white. Darya was warmly dressed, and she was not alone. Tony Galletsia was standing with his arms around her gazing at the two orbs. The two young scientists, with differing but complementary fields of expertise, had grown very close over the last two years. What had begun as a friendly and mutually cooperative professional relationship had progressed to a personal friendship and then a full romance.

The two members of the president's Peregrinus scientific advisory committee had some time ago, even before their relationship had progressed to romance, agreed to observe together on the night of Peregrinus's closest approach. It had seemed a fitting thing to do together, even then, for the person whose research had first led to the identification of the wandering planet, and the person whose expertise had quickly alerted humanity to the coming close passage of the visitor. Now that the time had arrived, they wouldn't have been apart on this unique and spectacular night no matter what.

The couple had carefully thought through their life plans in a post-Peregrinus world. Pasadena seemed the obvious choice of place to live. With a relatively southerly location and less than one thousand feet above sea level, it would retain a hospitable climate in the years to come, possibly even more pleasant than at present in the peak of summer, and at worst an occasional snowfall in midwinter. Tony would keep his job at the JPL and on the faculty of the California Institute of Technology, and the university had been delighted to offer the now famous discoverer of Peregrinus a faculty position as well. They remained in touch with Eli Wayman, but their part of the drama was now largely behind them.

For many people the rise of Peregrinus would lead to great stress and dislocation, if not a threat to their very survival. Darya and Tony were among the fortunate few to benefit from the galactic event, its discovery leading to their discovery of each other. They were aware of, grateful for, and humbled by this reality. Would they be able to live happily ever afterward despite the travails of much of the rest of the world, they both wondered. It appeared that would depend on them and not on the broader global and galactic happenings they had forewarned mankind about.

Chapter 28

December 2030

Boston, Massachusetts

Larry Johnstone sat gazing out the window of his small apartment in Tang Hall. He still served as the president of Fresh Water Solutions Inc., which required less and less of his time as the desalination technology matured and the commissioning of new desalination plants and new fabrication plants around the world became routine. He was now relatively well-off, at least by the standards of a young researcher, with a generous salary and a parsimonious lifestyle. He could easily have afforded a larger, more upscale apartment off campus, or even a fancy home in one of the more exclusive neighborhoods of Boston or Cambridge. He preferred the familiar surroundings of the MIT campus and had been grateful when the university administration had agreed to extend his research fellowship and allow him to retain his apartment.

One reason Larry was fond of his apartment was its proximity to the Charles River and the extended pathway system along both banks of the river. Over his years at MIT he had often generated new ideas while out running along those paths, arriving back at the apartment eager to record the idea and begin fleshing it out. Both the physical location and the proximity to several great academic institutions contributed to a creative environment. However, today was not a running day. Outside was a cold and blustery winter day and the running path was spotted with patches of snow and treacherous ice.

As Larry peered toward the morning sun, it seemed a feeble and shrunken thing, even though he knew that the reduction in its apparent size was actually too small to detect by eye. The northern hemisphere was experiencing its first full post-Peregrinus winter. It was, as expected, shaping up as a cold winter with average temperatures in November and December running about two degrees Fahrenheit cooler than the five-year average. It was by no means the coldest winter in recent decades, but knowing that it presaged even colder times to come made it seem bleaker than it actually was. Yet Larry was determined to stick it out for the time being. He still had his small desalination laboratory to tend to with potential for further efficiency gains or cheaper materials to be found. He still had the first fabrication plant down at the Weymouth Fore River mouth to oversee. He also had another little project he had begun to think about.

Larry's mental state was a conflicting combination of fulfillment and restlessness. The fulfillment came from having established a clear path toward achieving what had been his life's ambition for many years. He had done so by the age of thirty. Recently he had attended a celebration of the Weymouth plant's production of the hundredth two-million-gallons-a-day desalination plant. The original fabrication plant had tripled in capacity shortly after the first facilities in Libya had been commissioned and was now producing four cells every day, so six days to complete a twenty-four cell plant, which could supply the needs of a town of one hundred and fifty thousand people.

A typical complete desalination facility consisted of three plants supplying together sufficient fresh water for irrigation as well as drinking, cooking and bathing. There were now sixteen such facilities on the coast of Libya, which had been producing nearly one hundred million gallons per day for almost two years. Satellite imagery revealed a distinct green fringe along the coastline where none had existed in written history. Libya was still a politically fragmented country, but progress was being made toward reestablishing a democratically elected federal government. With increased stability, tourism and other commercial development were on the rise.

Beyond Libya, additional large-scale desalination facilities were now in place in many other Middle Eastern and North African countries, and some in southern Europe as well as Northern Mexico and the southern United States. Some of these had been fabricated at the Boston Fresh Water Solutions Fabrication Center, but there were now two more such centers in Italy, two in Mexico and two in New Mexico. Before the advent of Peregrinus, it would have been a financial challenge for some parched underdeveloped countries to afford much desalination investment, even with Larry's low-cost technological breakthrough. The developed countries now had ample motivation, beyond philanthropy, to develop ties with their southern neighbors. Terrorism, war, genocide, starvation and disease did not vanish instantly from the troubled regions of the world. However, global cooling was providing an even greater and more urgent impetus for global cooperation than global warming had, reinforced by a stable and broad-minded American leadership, and with fresh water as an important tool and incentive.

Larry was well aware of the beneficial impact that low-cost fresh water was having on the people of many impoverished places in the world. He was also aware that his home country would reap significant benefits in its arid areas as well. He was less cognizant of the catalyzing role of Peregrinus, and the spin-off benefits of increased global stability, which fresh water and a common climate challenge were, in combination, giving rise to. Yet, based on what he did know, he had very good reason to be proud of his success, which resulted from his hard work.

Yet Larry was also restless, and not just because the winter weather was preempting his running program. For most of his adult life, his time had been fully absorbed in his studies, his desalination research and then more recently by overseeing the commissioning of the desalination plants based on his research, and the setup of the fabrication facilities to produce the cells. There was still further work remaining on optimizing the design of the capacitive deionization cells, but the main breakthroughs were already in hand and the remaining refinements were not all that exciting in terms of the difference they could make in the world. Likewise, there was still some of his time required to support the dissemination of his technology, but others were now largely well trained enough to look after most of that work.

Larry needed a new project, a new challenge, a difficult problem with potential world-shaping impacts. He had been thinking about just such a challenge for a few days. Actually, the idea had been popping into his head on occasion for quite a few years, but there had previously been enough else on his mind that he'd been able to put it aside. Now it wasn't so easy to ignore, though he almost wished that he could.

During his work on desalination he had always known that there was a risk he wouldn't achieve much, though he was pretty confident that he would at least make some contribution to the advancement of the science. As he considered this new challenge, he was hesitant. The basic electrochemical theory behind his desalination technology was well established. He had no such theoretical underpinning to support his latest conjectures. He also was aware of the notorious failures of others who had tackled the same challenge, whereas such negative precedents had not been a factor in his desalination research.

Despite being hesitant, the size of the prize attracted him and lately had been coming to mind more frequently. What if a brand-new renewable and plentiful energy source could be tapped by mankind, at low cost, requiring only a simple apparatus, and posing no significant risk to public safety or the environment? Such an achievement could have been an antidote to both global poverty and global warming back when the latter was a concern. It could now be a more environmentally and health-friendly alternative to the massive combustion of fossil fuels, which was otherwise going to be required to combat global cooling. It would overshadow his development of low-cost desalination technology, though the two would complement each other.

Larry knew something of the physics of nuclear fusion, involving extreme temperatures and pressures to recreate the conditions found in the interior of the sun so as to drive hydrogen nuclei together to form helium, with a concomitant massive release of energy. He knew that despite enormous time, effort and expense, no commercially practical fusion reactor had been developed. However, conventional nuclear fusion was far outside his area of expertise and he had nothing to contribute to the development of that potential source of energy.

What Larry felt he could claim some expertise in was the manipulation of ionic solutions, and the related materials technology. He knew a lot about the effects of anode–cathode geometry and composition, and about the geometry of an electrochemical cell. He knew that the main difficulty in getting two hydrogen nuclei to spontaneously join together was energizing them sufficiently to overcome the Coulomb repulsion barrier resulting from the positive charge of each one of them. What if this could be done without reproducing the temperature and pressure of the core of the Sun? What if it could be accomplished within an ionic solution? What if the hydrogen nuclei could be stampeded into a concentrated space adjacent to a cathode with enough velocity to penetrate the Coulomb barrier? Would a spherical reaction chamber with the cathode at its center be the best geometry? Would a high-grade vacuum within the cell support rapid acceleration of the hydrogen cations?

These and other questions were plaguing Larry as he sat in his small apartment looking out at a cold Boston winter, with much colder still yet to come. He had reached his decision. Others had tried to produce nuclear fusion without using high-energy plasma and had failed miserably. He might also be destined to fail, but he was going to risk it. He was going to find the answers to all his questions, and he was going to explore every configuration of a fusion cell that he could imagine, to see if any permutation would work.

Larry didn't intend to expose himself unnecessarily to skepticism or ridicule. He would conduct his work in secret, which he thought was easily accomplished in his circumstances. He had already identified an available laboratory of suitable size, and he had confirmed a promise made to him by the president's science advisor — that funding would be available for any new projects Larry wanted to undertake, no questions asked. He had even identified potential suppliers of components and had begun to sketch some out.

Larry realized that he had made the decision to take up the fusion power challenge several days previously. It had just taken a little longer for his conscious mind to catch up with his subconscious. Now that it had, he was eager to get started.

Chapter 29

January 2032
Near Healdsburg, California

Alyssa Morgan buttoned up her heavy jacket and donned her gloves before climbing out of the pick-up truck to check another wellhead. It had always been cold on a January morning when doing her circuit of steam wells and injection wells supporting the Western Power Inc. forty-megawatt geothermal plant she was responsible for. Now it was even colder than ever.

At her home down in Healdsburg, the overnight lows had been consistently below freezing since early December, frequently with a blanket of snow to greet her in the morning, December and January being the wettest months of the year. Most days the snow would melt by early afternoon. Up here in the Mayacamas Mountains, 2,500 feet above Healdsburg, it was colder still by about nine degrees Fahrenheit, with the snow not melting until late afternoon, if at all, and only then on southwest-facing slopes. On northern- and eastern-facing slopes, and any shaded areas, there was a steady accumulation, with drifts as high as three feet.

She and Brad had married the previous May. They had discussed the idea of moving further south, possibly to Southern California or even one of the new refugee communities being developed along the Mexican border. They had quickly come to the conclusion that they would stay put. Healdsburg was well south of the zone where federal government relocation assistance was available. They would take a beating on selling their homes in Healdsburg and Santa Rose, and at the same time Southern California real estate had become very expensive. They knew that even now Healdsburg was not as cold in winter as many places to the north had always been. Even up at the plant the average low in December of twenty degrees Fahrenheit was no colder than Twin Falls up in Idaho had been before Peregrinus, and not nearly as cold as Bismarck, North Dakota, never mind Fairbanks, Alaska. So, they knew, at least at an intellectual level, that the new Northern California winters were certainly livable, maybe even in time they would be enjoyable. They had begun to try out cross-country skiing as a winter pastime instead of road biking.

The factor that ultimately weighed most heavily into the couple's decision was their work. Brad's expertise with heating systems was in high demand, with the company he worked for struggling to dig out from under a huge backlog as everyone sought to add supplementary heating to their homes. They were trying desperately to recruit additional engineers and technicians with little success. He didn't feel right about leaving them now, stretching them even thinner. He felt accountable not just to the company and his coworkers, but especially for all the customers, ordinary Americans trying to stay warm.

For Alyssa it was even more of a nonstarter. With the increased electric baseboard heating load, her power plant was now critical to meeting the energy needs of Northern California. In fact, Western Power Inc. had taken advantage of the new incentives to refit the steam turbine with an updated blade and vane design, and to increase the turbine inlet pressure. The plant was now making a steady forty-six megawatts, and Alyssa could never bring herself to leave her power plant behind. Compelling her to stay even more than the plant itself was the greenhouse operation. Food had become even more expensive, with a shorter growing season throughout the state, and the Healdsburg Food Pantry was even more dependent on Alyssa. She and Brad had expanded their cottage agriculture operation. The second concrete pad was now shared by a smaller greenhouse, a small chicken barn and a small three-bedroom cottage.

One of the bedrooms within the cottage was for a new helper they had recruited to assist the Ortizes with the increased workload of the expanded operation. Lourdes had also been a client and volunteer at the Food Pantry and welcomed the opportunity to tend to the chickens and the laying hens, as well as pick and pack vegetables in exchange for room and board and a little extra cash. The young woman had chosen to stay behind in Healdsburg when the rest of her family decided to go south to a home they owned in Manzanillo. She was living in the family's Healdsburg home and subsisting on a little money they had left for her and whatever odd jobs she could pick up, but was finding it hard going. She now lived on site seven days a week, which meant that the chickens would be fed and the eggs gathered even on the occasional day neither Alyssa nor the Ortizes visited the place. Lourdes, at eighteen years old, was slim with straight black hair and looked a lot like Seychelle Gabriel, the actress whose character in the sci-fi series Falling Skies Lourdes had been named after. She proved to be a great addition to the team — hardworking and a source of constant optimism and cheerfulness.

At first Alyssa and Brad had worried a little about leaving Lourdes alone overnight on the site. She had telephone and Internet contact but, with Alyssa using the truck during the winter, there was no vehicle on site if she needed to get down to town. They considered buying a used Jeep, but after a week it seemed unnecessary. Lourdes was perfectly comfortable being by herself. The little cottage was warm and cozy and well stocked. She was working on a science degree offered online through the California Community Colleges system so her evenings were mostly taken up with studying.

Lourdes also enjoyed running. Her days usually began with a one- or two-hour run up and down Geysers Road, even on most winter days. She had promised Alyssa and Brad that she would stick to the main road and not run on the side roads linking the steam and injection wells to the plant. There was very little traffic on Geysers Road, but the resident mountain lion population tended to keep back in the hills, away from the road. They also bought her a small can of bear spray in a waist belt holster, which she promised to take with her any time she went outside the cottage, including on her runs.

A couple of times a month Lourdes would catch a ride back to Healdsburg and spend a day or two with some friends, always checking first with Alyssa on what days would work best. She also kept in touch with friends and family through video chat, but as best Brad and Alyssa could tell, she had no romantic attachments. Once they'd all been together for a while, Alyssa broached the subject with Lourdes, who explained that she had dated a few guys in high school but hadn't yet found anyone she really cared for. She found the boys her age had only one thing on their minds and it was a thing she wasn't ready to give to anyone yet. Alyssa had said she would keep her eyes open for any good prospects she might come across. So far, she hadn't found any.

Brad had built the little cottage, with lots of volunteer help from the crew of the contract maintenance company that performed most of the heavy work on the wells and the plant. Brad had taken an off-the-shelf cottage design and beefed up the windows to the lowest low-energy glass available in California, and also both the R-value and depth of the wall and attic insulation. The cottage had a high-efficiency heat pump, which doubled as an air-conditioner on the now rare summer day that got above eighty-five degrees Fahrenheit, plus a 2,400-watt baseboard system for supplementary heating. Brad was confident that the cottage would remain toasty warm on the coldest foreseeable winter night.

The second bedroom was available if the Ortizes wanted to stay overnight, which they often did. Likewise, Alyssa often stayed in the third bedroom, and both Alyssa and Brad stayed there some weekends. If she was by herself, Alyssa had the option of a cot in the back of her office within the plant itself, but the cottage was certainly a lot homier and far quieter. On these evenings, Alyssa and Lourdes got to know each other well and became good friends. Alyssa had no siblings but came to feel much like an older sister to Lourdes. She even helped her with some of her coursework.

Alyssa opened the door of the truck and stepped out into the snow, pulling her Browning 308 from the gun rack mounted on the rear of the cab. She cracked the lever action down just enough to open the breech and confirm that she had one in the spout, ready to go. As she closed the action she also double-checked that the hammer was down in the uncocked position. There was no safety on the rifle. All she would need to do to make it ready to fire was apply a little pressure with her thumb to the wide, grooved top of the hammer to pull it back to the cocked position. She practised cocking, aiming and firing on a regular basis and could get a round off and in the bullseye of a target fifty yards away in less than a second, followed by five more as she cranked the lever action and emptied the clip.

Alyssa had made her own promise, in her case to Brad, that whenever away from the immediate area of the plant she would always carry the rifle outside of the truck. She had spotted mountain lions frequently, so needed little encouragement to keep the rifle ready, but so far she had not had occasion to need to fire it.

It was becoming a different, colder world than the one Alyssa had once thought to be a permanent state of affairs. She knew it would get colder still in the years to come but felt confident that she and Brad had taken sufficient precautions to be able to continue to enjoy a pleasant and satisfying life.

Chapter 30

January 2033
Canadian Rocky Mountains, near Golden, British Columbia

It was the third full winter since the passage of Peregrinus. The oceans of the world still retained a portion of the energy they had previously absorbed, moderating the temperatures of the coastal regions for a few more years. For most inland locations, the last vestiges of the warmer climate were now long gone, especially in the northern hemisphere. The entire world was in the grips of an ice age, the Quaternary Ice Age, the fifth such ice age in the 4.5-billion-year geological history of the world. That was nothing new. It has long been known that all of man's recorded history has occurred during a temporary warm interglacial interlude within what is in fact a long-term multi-million-year ice age. What was new was that the interglacial interlude was over, ending prematurely by several tens of thousands of years. The glaciers of the world were once again thickening and beginning to retrace the paths of their previous retreat, though that advance was still a matter of less than fifty feet.

Tom Svenson knelt and retrieved a plump rabbit from the snare beside his path through the thick forest of fir surrounding his cabin. He kept a five-mile circuit broken through the ever-deepening winter snow cover, with small snares set every hundred yards or so. Mainly he was on the lookout for the local turkey flock, of which he only planned to take one. He was a bit worried whether they would be able to make it through the winter with most of their food source on the forest floor now beneath six feet of snow, and more still to come.

Tom pulled off his outer mitts to remove the rabbit and reset the snare. At twenty degrees Fahrenheit below zero, he needed to be quick. Even with his inner gloves on, his hands would rapidly become too numb to work effectively. He was particularly careful to ensure that he kept his right hand warm enough to work the action of the deer rifle slung across his back. It wasn't that he expected to see a deer, though that was certainly a possibility he would take advantage of if it occurred. He was more concerned about being able to react quickly if one of the local cougars became emboldened enough to take him on. Normally that wasn't something he would consider to be much of a risk, but lately there were more of the stealthy cats around as they descended from higher elevations in search of food, and with few humans now contesting with them for the benchlands.

He knew there was at least one such predator in his immediate vicinity. He had seen the paw prints in the deep snow converging with his trail and then following it. There had been little left of another rabbit caught in one of his snares a quarter mile back along the trail, just a bloody patch in the snow and a few pieces of fur. He was happy to get to this catch before the cat took it too, but he sensed that the animal was not far away, probably watching from the shadows of a big deadfall, of which there were many near his trail.

Some of these cats were a good three hundred pounds of tooth, claw and outright ferocity. Tom knew that if a big one could take him unawares he would be hard-pressed to defend himself, even with the large Bowie knife he was using to do a quick field cleaning of the rabbit. He also knew that a charge, if one came, would be swift and silent, from a place of concealment, and likely coming from behind to spring onto his back, knock him down and deliver a fatal bite to his neck. Tom was glad he had left his son Arthur back at the cabin protecting the family and with instructions to both Arthur and his wife, Trish, to keep the whole family inside the cabin until his return. Arthur was a brave and competent woodsman himself, nearly seventeen years old, but still lacking the size and strength of his father just yet. The young man would be an even easier target for a desperate cougar than Tom would.

The experienced woodsman kept a careful watch as he quickly finished with the rabbit, focusing mainly on the direction he had last seen the tracks heading. He knew, however, that if an attack came it was much more likely that he would be alerted by his companion, Beast, than that he would be the first to notice. Beast was now a fully grown 150-pound Tibetan Mastiff with a superb sense of smell and hearing, and he was a fearless protector of the entire family. While a cougar would need to be highly motivated to take on Tom by himself, it was almost impossible that one would be bold enough to brave the dog. In fact, it had been a difficult decision whether to bring him or leave him on guard back at the cabin. He was glad now to have him along. Nothing could harm the family as long as they stuck to his instructions to stay inside.

Tom placed the rabbit in a game bag tied onto the toboggan he was pulling along the trail. The toboggan wouldn't be needed unless they got a deer, but then it would be essential. Normally Beast supplied the motive power, but once they saw the cougar tracks it was safer to have the canine warrior unhampered in any skirmish. They reached the outer limit of the trapline and headed back toward the lake, with Beast guarding the rear and Tom focusing on potential ambush locations in front. It looked like the haul for the day was going to be just the one rabbit.

Tom had little concern that his family would run out of food anytime soon. He had been able to drive the Suburban down to Golden last summer and restock all their staples with a comfortable three-year supply. There were fewer people in the town but the Save-on-Foods grocery store remained well stocked. However, he thought it was unlikely that the road back to town would be passable again this next summer, or even if it was, there might be limited supplies available. He preferred to think of their store-bought supplies as a reserve and to rely on fishing, hunting and trapping to provide their primary source of food. Tom had learned that the plan was to evacuate Golden but likely not for another couple of years. The railyard was to be kept open and so a skeleton staff would remain. The trains had been equipped with special snow-clearing equipment and ice-melting steam lances. They expected to be able to operate trains year-round for the indefinite future.

The family had thought a lot about their plans for the future. The winter of Peregrinus's passage in 2030 was not very remarkable. They had firm snow at the popular Kicking Horse ski hill above Golden until early April, and good spring skiing until early May, an extra couple of weeks. The following winter was a little cooler and a little longer with snow still on the ground in town until mid-May, and later up on the bench. Neither Tom nor Trish wanted to leave their outdoor mountain lifestyle behind. Tom was confident that they could handle the cold and was keen to stay. They had decided it would be easier to hunker down in the cabin than in their Golden home. It was a smaller area to heat, with ample no-cost fuel for the woodstove, and ready access to hunting and fishing for food. So, the next winter they stayed up at the cabin, coming down once a month for supplies, social occasions and church. Tom had installed a satellite antenna and a twelve-volt battery with a stationary bicycle charging system in the basement. They now had the Internet for homeschooling, which Trish firmly enforced. By late winter the road down to Golden had become too snow-clogged and icy to attempt a drive into town until late June.

The couple expected that they would eventually have to pull up stakes and move either to Calgary or to the south. They had taken the precaution of filing an application to immigrate to New Zealand, and with their skill sets had been granted deferred entry visas for 2038. They hoped to be able to stay put until then and avoid uprooting the family twice. With overnight temperatures now plummeting to thirty degrees Fahrenheit or colder, Tom was beginning to have second thoughts. The cabin was certainly warm enough, though he was rising twice in the night to stoke the stove. They were consuming firewood at a rapid pace, but there was lots more waiting to be sawed and split, with Art a willing helper. Yet how much colder could it get? Of greater concern, what would they do if one of them got hurt?

Tom was mulling over this dilemma as he reached the lakeshore and turned onto the last short leg of the trail, looking forward to a warm cup of tea, or maybe something a little stronger. Although his mind had wandered a bit, he remained alert to his surroundings. Suddenly Beast let out a series of growls and short barks and bounded out in front of him on the trail, peering through the firs down toward the lake. A moment later Tom spotted a small group about a quarter mile out on the frozen lake and coming toward the cabin. He gave Beast the "go home" command and sprinted after him as quickly as his snowshoes and the snowy trail would permit.

The visitors they were about to have were likely harmless. There were a few other cabins on the lake and occasionally one of the other owners would skidoo in from Golden for the weekend, though it had been quite a while this winter since any of them had. He knew there was one other family wintering in a cabin on the far side of the lake and they had occasionally hailed each other in the distance, but there hadn't been a convenient opportunity for any social interaction. Maybe this was a social visit, but it was late in the day for such, and Tom wanted to be prepared for other possibilities.

Tom reached the cabin with a few minutes to spare. Beast was down on the dock, barking constantly at the approaching group. The rest of the family were up on the deck outside the main room of the cabin, and Trish had a pair of binoculars out.

"Tom," she said, "it looks like two adults and two children."

"All right," he replied, "I think it would be best if you all went inside while I find out what this is about. Let's have some hot tea ready to go."

The group of four reached the shoreline in front of Tom and stopped. The two adults removed their parka hoods and balaclavas while the children remained behind them. One adult was an older man and the other a young woman, probably close to Trish's age.

The man spoke. "Hello," he said, "I apologize for dropping in unannounced like this late in the day, but we are in a difficult spot and we need help."

Tom replied "Is it an emergency? Is someone injured or ill?"

"No," the man said, "it is not that immediately dire, but we are backed into a corner. My name is George McCormack and this is my daughter-in-law, Melissa, and those are Melissa's two daughters."

"If it isn't an urgent matter, then why don't we all go inside and warm up a bit while you explain your difficulty? My name is Tom Svenson and my wife Trish is inside with our three children. I think I recognize you, George, from around town."

Soon the adults were all seated comfortably in the snug living room of the small cabin, and the five children were up in the loft sipping hot chocolate and chattering away. Melissa's two daughters were aged sixteen and twelve. The twelve-year-old was between the ages of the Svenson's two girls. The sixteen-year-old, named Nancy, was an attractive girl with long blond hair and elfin facial features. Tom couldn't help but note Arthur's sharp intake of breath as her parka and toque came off. Trish had surreptitiously slipped another pound of venison stewing meat into the pot bubbling on the woodstove, along with four more potatoes and a couple of onions. George began to explain their situation.

The McCormacks were in serious trouble. George's son had passed away in a car accident several years ago and his wife even before that. He and Melissa were making a go of it in Golden and doing their best to raise the two girls. Melissa was a school teacher with a steady income, George a retired locomotive maintenance foreman with a good pension. For similar reasons to the Svensons they had decided to den up for the winter at George's cottage at the far end of the lake. Things had been going reasonably well until about three weeks ago. Then calamity struck. First, their skidoo, which George had been relying on to make occasional runs down to Golden, had broken down, followed not long after by his chainsaw seizing up.

George had tried to replenish their food supply by spending more time hunting, but he hadn't been able to take a deer and they were nearing the end of their supplies, even with tight rationing. He had also tried to keep up with their consumption of stovewood using a Swede saw, often working well into the night. With the increasingly cold days and even colder nights, he had not been able to do it.

For the last few days they had been burning just enough wood to keep their cabin above the freezing point and wearing their parkas and mitts inside. Even so, George was exhausted and they were down to burning small branches that Melissa and the girls could scrounge from under the deep snow. George finished the story and slumped down, a beaten man.

"I realize now how foolish I was to bring my family here. I look at all the firewood that I saw stacked up around your place as we walked up, and curse myself for how poorly prepared I was. I have tried to deny it for the last week, my pride insisting that I could find a way, but there isn't a way. My pride is gone. My family will freeze or starve to death unless you can help us. Could I buy some food from you? Do you have a skidoo? We could pay you for some stovewood if we could haul it across the lake?" As he finished, Melissa consoled her weeping father-in-law.

"He did the best he could for us," she said.

Tom looked across at Trish. He knew they had ample food, but sharing it with this family would cut their safety margin nearly in half, potentially risking the safety of his own family. Yet there was no doubt in his mind what they should do, and he knew Trish would feel the same, as her slight nod confirmed. They were firm followers of Christ's teaching and knew his clear message of charity, as recounted in the Gospel of Matthew, chapter twenty-five, verses thirty-four to forty, but they had never expected their beliefs to be put to the test in such a way.

Tom swallowed to get his own emotions under control and then said, "George, you have been a hero and a pillar of strength for your family. You've had some bad luck and that can happen to anyone. You've done absolutely the right thing to come here this afternoon. I have a better idea than selling you food and wood, which I would gladly do if we had an effective way to get it across the lake, but we don't. I could really use another man with your kind of drive and toughness around here; and Melissa, if we'd known there was a teacher in the neighborhood, we'd have sought you out much sooner. So, what we're going to do is move you all in here with us. You will be warm and well-fed, starting with dinner in a few minutes, and you'll all contribute your own skills and efforts to our little community."

It would be a tight fit for nine of them in the cabin, but it was workable. The four young girls would easily all fit in the loft, which had three double beds. Arthur would move out of the second bedroom and he and George would sleep in the living room, which had two couches. Melissa would have a room to herself.

Tears of relief and thankfulness ran down both George's and Melissa's faces. Life came back into George's eyes and posture. He said, "I'll do anything you need to earn our keep."

From up above they heard, "So is it true, Grandpa? Are we really going to have a sleepover like Nancy and Arthur say we are?"

The adults all began to laugh, having realized firstly that the background chatter from the loft had been absent for several minutes as the children eavesdropped on the living room conversation. Secondly, the children had figured out where this was all going well before the adults had.

Tom had no doubts about his decision to open his home to this family in need. If he had, they would have been quashed by the smile that shone on his wife's face when their eyes met as the nine of them sung grace around the dinner table minutes later.

Outside the cabin it was now fully dark and the reading on the thermometer visible from the kitchen window was falling steadily. Inside, the three propane gas lights were lit, the curtains closed on the two large picture windows overlooking the lake, and Arthur was demonstrating to Nancy the proper technique for feeding another log into the woodstove as Trish began ladling out large steaming bowls of venison stew.

Chapter 31

May 2033
Lake and Sonoma Counties, Northern California

Peter Poplinski was cruising south on State Route 175, just past Cobb, with four other members of the club behind him. They were dressed in casual clothes rather than club uniforms, in keeping with Peter's strategy of maintaining a low profile. It was nearly eight thirty on a sunny but cool May morning, about fifty-five degrees Fahrenheit, which was still chilly enough on a cycle to need a heavy jacket and gloves. The bikers had been on the road for almost an hour.

Peter was feeling good about the club's situation. Although they were under no particular law enforcement pressure, he had decided to relocate their main base from their Idaho farmhouse to their backup base, in the hills above Clear Lake, California, the summer before. Central Idaho was still livable but tending toward the cold side, and the California base, though definitely also experiencing colder winters, was a more comfortable location. The majority of the club's members were now housed in a newly constructed hunting lodge on six hundred acres of bush and trails, including a small private lake. Peter had left a small garrison and one of his lieutenants back in Idaho to handle their drug distribution business. He would rotate a new crew in over the summer.

Today's mission was a combination of reconnaissance and recreation. Peter liked to have a thorough understanding of the general area around their base, and he liked to see it for himself. It was also good sense to give some of the guys an opportunity to spread their wings a little. Peter was planning a 120-mile circuit today, which he had laid out on a state road map. He had no particular objective. They would just keep their eyes open and stay out of trouble, though he was confident that five of them were more than enough to handle any trouble they might encounter short of a patrol from the local club on whose territory they were encroaching.

The boys were all seasoned and hardened players and all were well armed with untraceable handguns and, in some cases including Peter himself, a backup gun; plus they had a couple of buckshot-loaded, sawed-off twelve-gauge automatic shotguns hidden in saddlebags.

The group turned off the highway onto the Socrates Mine Road, heading now roughly west, though it was a hilly, twisty road threading its way through the Mayacamas Mountains, and not paved. They slowed down considerably to keep their bikes under control. Peter thought it would take them a good half an hour to cover the eight miles over to Geysers Road via Mine Road, Dillingham Road and then Big Sulphur Creek Road and Geysers Resort Road. Then they would decide whether to continue west on Geysers Road and pick up U.S. Route 101 at Cloverdale, or turn south and pick it up at Geyserville, making for a little longer circuit.

Another group of four were heading north from Santa Rosa, nearing Cloverdale on U.S. Route 101, in a two-vehicle convoy. Carlos and Helen were in front in Carlos's half-ton truck with four stubby white-water kayaks lashed down in the truck bed. John Kirk was riding behind with Fiona in her Jeep. Following their victory in the California/Oregon Spring Classic Adventure Race five years before, the four had become even closer friends than before.

Not much had changed in the lives of the four Santa Rosa police officers since the passage of Peregrinus. Winters were colder and longer, summers cooler and shorter, but there was still lots of opportunity for their favorite outdoor fitness pursuits, which they more often than not did together. They continued to compete in the occasional adventure race and were pretty well established as the team to beat in Northern California. The two women had talked the men into taking on marathoning. In turn John and Carlos had introduced Helen and Fiona to white-water creeking. The women had taken to the wet and wild sport with interest and enthusiasm. After mastering a series of progressively more challenging routes, they were now a close match for the men in guiding their maneuverable little boats down the wild creeks of Northern California. The same could not be said of the level of proficiency achieved by the men at marathoning.

John and Carlos had been planning today's white-water run in Little Sulphur Creek for several years. It was the most difficult in Northern California at eleven miles of mostly Class V white water. It was a steep, technical course with eight portages around unrunnable sections, taking a good ten hours and requiring a high level of skill and stamina. There was only one possible intermediate take-out point along the route as the creek runs far away from any roads most of the time from put-in at a little bridge on Geysers Road to take-out where the Little Sulphur Creek runs into Big Sulphur Creek, adjacent to another section of Geysers Road.

John and Carlos had considered taking on Little Sulphur Creek together several years ago, but, even though they were risk-takers, they decided that they needed four boats to have sufficient backup if something went wrong. Then, when Helen and Fiona began challenging the sport, the two tactical team officers decided to postpone the Little Sulphur until their teammates were sufficiently skilled. Today was the day. All four were extremely fit and well-polished on their technical skills. They were all either in the gym or doing roadwork six days out of seven, and the men also continued to hone their karate skills, always striving to advance to a higher level of dan black belt.

The plan for the day was to drop off the jeep at their take-out point on Geysers Road about five miles east of Cloverdale. Then the four of them would all continue in Carlos's truck further east and then south on Geysers Road to the Little Sulphur Creek south branch bridge. There they would park the truck on the shoulder and unload the kayaks, hoping to be on the water by nine o'clock in the morning and finished by seven o'clock at night. Things were on plan and on schedule as they crossed the north branch of Little Sulphur Creek heading south.

Just before the abandoned hamlet of Mercuryville, they passed a lithe young woman running along the side of the road headed in the same direction, ponytail bouncing up and down in time with her stride. Carlos slowed the truck and gave her a wide berth. John, riding in the back behind Carlos couldn't help but look closely at the shapely girl as they passed her. She was concentrating on foot placement and didn't even glance at the truck.

"She looks like she is hitting a pretty good pace," commented Fiona, who was certainly qualified to judge such a thing.

"Yes," agreed John, as if that is what he had been studying too, "but I wonder what she is doing all the way out here by herself."

A few minutes later they pulled up to the south fork bridge and began to unload the truck and make ready. As they did, another half-ton truck heading north came up, pulled over and rolled down the driver's side window. Inside were a fit looking young couple about the same age as the police team. They all gathered around the truck briefly to exchange greetings. The couple were fascinated by the group's plan to tackle Little Sulphur Creek in white-water kayaks. The woman explained that she was the plant engineer for the geothermal plant that the group had passed about a half-mile back up the road, and she and her husband were just heading in to check that it was all operating properly.

John queried, "Is there a dark-haired young woman that is part of your operation? We just passed her running on the road about ten minutes ago."

"Yes, that would have been Lourdes," responded the woman driver. "She is quite the runner." John was inclined to agree with that description at several levels, though he did not say so. After a few more minutes of chatting, the couple continued on their way and the kayakers got back to work organizing their departure. They were just completing the final step of securing their sidearms alongside Carlos's Remington 700 rifle in the truck's gun locker when they heard the unmistakable report of a nearby high-powered rifle. They all stopped and stood dead still listening for anything further.

John was the first to comment, "I don't like the sounds of that. We're not in season for deer or boar, and it seems like it came from near the plant that couple was headed for. I think we better check it out."

"Do you want to drive back up the road?" asked Carlos.

"No," said John, "I think a quieter approach might be better since there is gunfire involved." The four police officers quickly rearmed themselves and Carlos also took his rifle. In minutes they were jogging back up the road, taking less than five minutes to come within sight of the plant gate. At that point they moved off the road to the east side and continued in the shadows of the ditch until they could see into the plant parking area. They could tell immediately that they were looking at serious trouble.

As Lourdes continued to run south on Geysers Road, picking up her pace for the last mile back to the plant, she was relieved that the half-ton truck had not tried to engage her. She didn't want to take the risk of being grabbed and, even if the occupants were harmless, she didn't want to break the rhythm of her run to help someone with directions or make small talk. The truck had just disappeared around the next bend when she began to hear another vehicle coming from behind. She was only five minutes from the plant but was pretty sure the second vehicle would catch up to her before she could get there. It was quite unusual for her to encounter any vehicles during her hour-long, eight-mile run, never mind two. She was glad to have the little can of bear spray close at hand.

Peter Poplinski was surprised as he came around the sharp bend in Geysers Road to see a girl sprinting along the side of the road a couple of hundred yards ahead, and he was immediately intrigued. As he closed the gap and came up behind the girl, he was even more intrigued. She was wearing a pair of skimpy running shorts that displayed her slim well-muscled legs from ankle to upper thigh and did little to camouflage a trim, well-rounded little butt, swaying slightly as she strode from leg to leg. He maneuvered his way up on her left-hand side, forcing her to move away from the shoulder toward the middle of the road as he waved his boys up to flank her on the other side and box her in from behind. She increased her pace and the gang leader could see the shape of her nipples moving beneath her tunic and sports bra. He felt his need rising swiftly within him, wild and uncontrollable as always.

After enjoying the show for a minute, Peter was just about to reach out with his right arm and sweep her up onto his bike saddle, which he easily had the power to do, when she caught him off guard with a rapid sprint ahead, crossing in front of him to the left, into a driveway and skirted to the other side of a locked gate.

Peter drove his bike down into the ditch and also skirted the end of the gate, his four followers close behind. He caught up with the girl halfway across a parking lot, headed for a small house. She tried to dodge past him as he dropped the bike and cut her off, but he was quick enough, with a long enough reach to catch her on the way by. He held her tightly to his chest as the other four rode up, his left arm encircling her chest and trapping both of her arms. Her wild struggles and bucking, with her breasts rubbing against his arm and her butt thrusting backwards into his crotch, did nothing to calm the fever burning in his loins.

He told two of his boys to check out the house and find him a bed as he used his right arm to strip Lourdes's top and bra over her head and off, her bare breasts now squeezed under his left arm, as he called after them, "I am going to give this little filly a ride she won't ever forget or find the better of."

He was about to strip her shorts down when a half-ton truck screeched to a stop outside the gate, a man jumped out and quickly unlocked the gate, and the truck roared in and toward him with the man running behind. The truck stopped twenty yards away and another young woman came scrambling out, pulling a rifle from the back of the cab as she did.

Peter was moving before the truck came to a complete stop. His quick reactions had assisted victory in many skirmishes over the years. He tossed the topless girl toward one of his boys and charged the truck as the woman swung the gun in an arc toward him. He was able to knock the barrel up just as she pulled the trigger and cranked another round into the chamber, but by then he was on her, and the gun was ripped from her hands and thrown back to his boys. There would be no second shot.

The massive biker was looking over the latest arrival — young, though not as young as the first one, blond, trim and also very attractive. Just as he was thinking about what a lucky day he was having, her passenger came blasting around the back of the truck and rammed into him at full speed. Peter had a moment to brace before the collision and dropped his shoulder down to take his attacker in the chest. The other man was not small, but he was no match for Peter's two hundred and fifty pounds. Peter was driven back a step, but the man bounced back several steps and dropped to the ground. Before he could get up Peter stepped forward and delivered a solid kick to his groin and another to his stomach. The man groaned painfully and began to vomit. Next the driver attacked him but he readily restrained her, groping her thoroughly in the process and thinking that this was really getting to be fun.

The heartless gang leader had no scruples about carrying on with his plans for both women and his excitement of anticipation was almost beyond his control. He would happily kill the man if that would serve any purpose, but he didn't think it would. The man would be incapacitated by his injuries for a good while. There were more eyes here that had seen his face than was a good idea, but he would follow his usual routine of recording their IDs and addresses and threatening extreme retaliation if they went to the police. No one knew where his base was and they would vanish into the countryside long before anyone could raise an alarm. They might have to lay even lower for a while at the base, but all things considered, there was little risk to permitting himself to indulge his needs. He had just concluded this when he noticed yet another man approaching. Where the hell had he come from? If he planned to interfere, he was going to soon be very sorry.

As John and his three teammates surveyed the scene in the parking area, they knew they had to take immediate action. They could see a man on the ground and another holding a rifle while the woman they had chatted with only moments ago struggled to escape the clutches of a large brute of a man. The runner with the dark hair and ponytail was being restrained by a third rough-looking character and two others were standing nearby. From the presence and make of the five motorcycles and the appearance of the dismounted riders they could tell the type of men they were facing and doubted they would back off without a fight, being willing to absorb injuries and even fatalities to avoid arrest. They also knew they were likely well armed. John issued instructions in clipped sentences. There was no time for consultation or planning, they would have to wing it, as risky as that would be.

Carlos backed down the road a few yards and started to scramble up the small hill flanking the road and from the crest of which he would overlook the parking lot. John sent the two women a little further back to try to work their way around the lot and come in from behind the small house. It would take them longer to get into position, but they could get into effective range with their sidearms without being exposed to rifle fire. John walked toward the confrontation, his mind racing as he thought through how to buy enough time for his teammates to be ready if a gun battle was to ensue.

With one rifle already out and pointed in his general direction, able to knock him down before he could get into range for his sidearm, he elected to leave it stuck in the back of his neoprene wetsuit shorts. As he approached the bikers, they all faced him, waiting for him to make a move. The only motion came from Alyssa as she continued to struggle with the big guy, kicking and swearing, none of which seemed to bother him even a little. John sized him up as the leader of the gang, or at least the most dangerous of them, and decided that was the best place to start.

John spoke to the man, "What kind of a coward are you? Let that girl go. You're a poor excuse for a man to be taking advantage of someone half your size." John suspected that this guy was unaccustomed to being challenged and would react emotionally without thinking through any strategy, and he was right on the mark.

Peter Poplinski flushed with anger at being called a coward. He could see that his accuser was a well-proportioned guy, younger, fitter, maybe even quicker, but he was confident that he lacked the power and ruthlessness that

Peter himself could bring to bear. He would destroy the guy, leave him with injuries he'd never fully recover from, and then get back to enjoying the two women. He flung the blond toward one of his guys and responded, "We'll see who the coward is here."

The two men squared off. John feigned a bit of surprise and consternation at the size of the guy as he closed in, and back-pedaled several steps saying, "Okay, maybe I misspoke a moment ago. Let's see if we can talk this out." In fact, John had fought with big men in the past, some as big as this guy, though perhaps not as heavily muscled. His experience was that such brutes usually relied more on their size and strength than on technique. He knew he would need to avoid taking a punch or a kick because one solid connection from this guy would deck nearly anyone, but he had enough full-body contact tournament matches behind him to be ready for this one, even if the stakes were a little higher. The only purpose for his gambit was to gain a few more seconds, and to make sure he was well clear of Carlos's line of sight to the guy with the rifle. John was pleased to see that of the other four men, two were occupied restraining the girls and the one with the rifle was surely zeroed in on Carlos's scope, leaving only one other who could easily bring another weapon to bear.

Peter Poplinski responded to John's peace offering with a sneer. This was more the kind of behavior he was accustomed to from his inferiors. However, he was much too wrought up to even consider a nonviolent resolution to the situation, though in fact nothing had yet actually happened in reality that would make such a result impossible, even if it had already happened in the dark abyss of his mind. He replied, "Too late for that now, big mouth. Nobody talks to me like that and walks away, some can't even crawl after I'm done. Let's have your best."

First things happened fast, then they happened even faster. Peter lowered his head and charged straight at John, building up unstoppable momentum in three quick steps. As he reached John, he raised his arms, intending to grapple him about the upper body as he took him down, and then to pinion him on the ground and punch his lights out. John stepped aside at the last moment, landing a full 360-degree spinning flat-handed chop to the front side of the brute's neck, over the carotid artery, as he thundered by. The aim was perfect, and the spin, combined with the snap extension of John's powerful arm, delivered a tremendous blow to one of the most vulnerable spots on the human body, even one as big as this. Peter Poplinski sprawled on the ground, dazed and barely conscious. It was a short but decisive fight.

John sensed movement behind him and turned just as the one with the rifle began to bring it to the aim and then dropped to the ground like a sack of potatoes as a .308 175-grain bullet from Carlos's Remington 700 punched through his sternum. Then the man with the free hands grabbed his gun from out of his jacket pocket, but John drew quicker and nailed him before he could bring it to bear. At the same time Helen and Fiona stepped up behind the remaining two bikers still standing and ordered them assertively to release the women, raise their hands straight up and lie face down.

John turned back to his big opponent, surprised to see him back up on his knees with a small handgun pointed right at John. The guy was tough, that was for sure. Then the rifle on the hill spoke once again, the bullet passing downward through the spine and destroying the heart and lungs with lead and bone splinter shrapnel. That was the end of big Peter Poplinski, the world a better place now by at least a little.

There was a moment of frozen silence, then Alyssa and Lourdes ran to each other and embraced briefly as Alyssa gave Lourdes her jacket, then they both helped Brad up and supported him as he staggered into the house. John borrowed Alyssa's cell phone and took several pictures of the parking lot from different angles while Fiona tended to the seriously wounded biker as best she could and Helen stood guard over the last two uninjured bikers who were then securely tied and thrown in the back of Alyssa's half-ton for the time being. Carlos was then waved down from his position and assigned to stand guard over the two in the truck.

John used the landline in the house to make three quick calls. The first was for an immediate ambulance even though he thought that the injured biker was unlikely to live until medical assistance arrived. The second was to the California Highway Patrol detachment in Healdsburg, alerting them to the situation and requesting assistance. The third was to the Santa Rosa Police Department's tactical team supervising lieutenant asking him to notify the chief and have a good word put in for them with the highway patrol.

The police officers did what they could for the injured biker, but their first aid was insufficient to the task given the extent of damage from the .45 ACP bullet wound, and the man gradually bled out internally. Before the end, and while still lucid though in considerable pain, the man grew remorseful for the life he'd led, apologized and asked forgiveness, and disclosed the location of the Satan's Wheels base near Lucerne.

Two ambulances and three Highway Patrol cruisers arrived soon thereafter. The two uninjured bikers and all weapons were taken into custody, and the patrolmen asked that everyone come into their base within the next couple of days to make a statement. A truck would be sent out to remove the motorcycles to the pound. Then the patrolmen left and the rest of them gradually began to come down from the horrific and high-stress events of the morning. Alyssa spoke up first, in a quavering voice and thanked the four police officers for coming to their aid, for reacting so quickly and placing their own lives at risk for some people they knew nothing about. The police team accepted the gratitude graciously, the unspoken feeling among them being tremendous satisfaction with having fulfilled their duty to protect people.

Then Lourdes ran forward and threw her arms around John, weeping with relief and stammering out her feelings, "Oh, thank you, thank you, thank you. I was so terrified of what that monster was going to do to me. I could feel his evil radiating out like the flames of hell, and then I was even more frightened when Alyssa and Brad got caught up in it."

The young woman's highly emotional outpouring broke the dam of restraint and soon everyone was hugging everyone else and crying and laughing at the same time. Some noted without comment that the hugging between John and Lourdes seemed a little more intense than any of the other embraces.

It seemed like a whole day had gone by even though it wasn't even noon yet. Taking on Little Sulphur Creek this late in the morning was out of the question though, especially given the fatigue beginning to set in after the stress of the battle. The police team agreed to stay on for lunch, no one being eager to end the group bond just yet.

They all prepared to head back to Santa Rosa in the early afternoon. Brad seemed to be mostly recovered from his injuries but Alyssa was anxious to get him fully checked out at the Santa Rosa Memorial Hospital. As preparations for departure got underway, it dawned on everyone that they were all leaving except Lourdes. Alyssa suggested that the chickens could get by for a day or two, and Lourdes should just come down and hang out with her and Brad. However, the plucky young lady insisted that it was her job to look after the chickens. She had already done enough harm by attracting the attention of the bikers, and she would be just fine by herself for the rest of the day and overnight, as usual.

Before John's brain could intercede, before he could consider the fact that this brave and stunningly beautiful young woman was a good deal younger than he was, before the rational part of his mind could point out that the immediate aftermath of a traumatic experience was not a wise time to make a quick personal decision, the words popped out of his mouth, "If Lourdes has to stay, I'd be happy to stick around and help out with the chickens if she'd be comfortable with that." His mouth slammed shut and his ears burned and cheeks flushed as he registered how patently obvious he must sound.

Lourdes took his hands in hers, her eyes beaming up at his, her smile glowing brightly and said, "John, would you do that for me? How could I be uncomfortable around the man who just saved me from a horrible experience? I will cook you up a special dinner to show you how grateful I really am."

Knowing glances were exchanged among the rest of the group as Alyssa concluded "Well, that settles it then, we'll check in with you two tomorrow morning." Soon after there were just the two of them left at the power plant, though they wouldn't have taken much notice of anyone else anyway as they strolled hand in hand toward the chicken barn.

Chapter 32

January 2036
Washington, DC

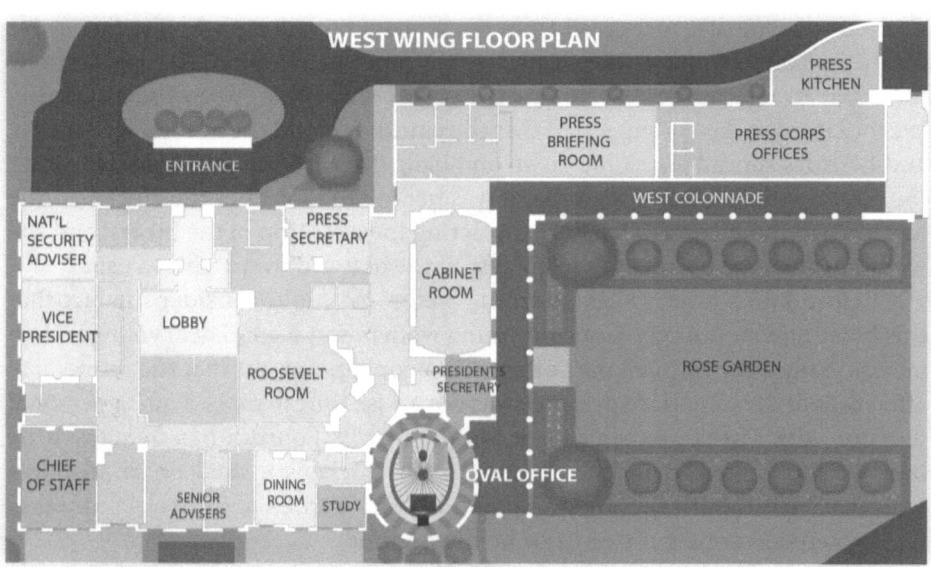

WEST WING FLOOR PLAN

PRESS
KITCHEN

PRESS
BRIEFING
ROOM

PRESS CORPS
OFFICES

ENTRANCE

WEST COLONNADE

NAT'L
SECURITY
ADVISER

PRESS
SECRETARY

CABINET
ROOM

VICE
PRESIDENT

LOBBY

ROOSEVELT
ROOM

PRESIDENT'S
SECRETARY

ROSE GARDEN

CHIEF
OF STAFF

SENIOR
ADVISERS

DINING
ROOM

STUDY

OVAL OFFICE

James Rushton was enjoying a few minutes of quiet reflection before his next meeting. He was seated at his working desk in his private study beside the Oval Office and connected to it by a small interior hallway. It was a place that he had grown very comfortable with over his many years of occupancy.

Jim had easily won the presidential election in 2028, having yielded to the persuasive arguments of the leadership of the Democratic Party that he was best suited to lead America's preparations for the arrival of Peregrinus. The country certainly had thought so, finding comfort in the face of a frightening future in the plans that he had initiated, and in a known, soft-spoken and businesslike leader. Having crossed that bridge, and grown increasingly comfortable in the role, it was an easy decision to agree to seek a second term, which had again been favored by the electorate, including continuation of Democratic majorities in both houses of congress. For a change, America was led by an individual who was well-liked and well-respected by people of most political persuasions, and who was often praised by other global leaders. America had a president to be proud of.

James Rushton was not a man to beat his own drum and proclaim his many accomplishments. For one thing, he relied heavily on teamwork both to make decisions and to implement them, knew that credit for success was due to the efforts of many others and always acknowledged those contributions. It was partly why many government staff so willingly did their utmost to support him. Apart from that, it was just not his nature to be boastful. Nevertheless, he was mostly satisfied and privately proud of what had been accomplished during his presidency.

The Russian bear had been declawed. Its military capability was greatly degraded, and its political leadership had passed into more moderate hands, now focused on the survival of its populace through peaceful and cooperative means. Elsewhere around the world the standard of living in many developing nations was significantly improving as their warmer climates became sought-after places for investment and immigration. Terrorism and civil war were much on the wane. With both Russia and China in a more cooperative posture in the face of rapid global cooling, the United States had succeeded in having the mandate of the International Court of Justice expanded to explicitly include prosecution of all crimes against humanity.

On American soil matters were generally proceeding favorably, despite the cold. The economy was strong, largely because of heavy infrastructure investments in both energy and transportation by business and governments, but also with widespread stocking-up of consumer goods. Inflation was an inevitable result, but most needs were being met. Preparations were well advanced to maintain access to sufficient energy to keep Americans alive and, for the most part, warm, comfortable and well-fed. This included the development of new communities, industrial facilities and large-scale farms in preparation for the abandonment of much of the northern tier of the country. Some of these communities were already occupied, but the bulk of the relocations were yet to come. The new farms, generally drawing on the new national irrigation network, were already in full production, though, as crop production in Canada and the northern United States was rapidly shrinking. Not much more could be done to protect the country, and Jim felt he would be turning over a house in good order to his successor in a year. However, he knew he still had a few crucial decisions to make before he could pass on the baton of responsibility — decisions that likely couldn't wait a year. He expected he would face some of these in the meeting he was about to join.

The president's Peregrinus advisory group stood as he entered the dining room beside his study. It was a small enough group that the dining room was big enough and Jim felt it was a little more relaxed and informal than the larger Roosevelt Room across the corridor, or the even more formal Cabinet Room. The group included the president's chief of staff and science advisor, the chief of the Planetary Defense Coordination Office, the secretary of the Department of Energy, the secretary of state and the vice president. This group met periodically with the president to update him on the status of preparations for global cooling and to put forward any decisions requiring his approval. Participation flexed up and down as required, coordinated by the chief of staff. The group was informally referred to as the Peregrinus advisory group, though Peregrinus had long since disappeared from the solar system. Jim motioned them all to be seated.

The secretary of Energy spoke first, "Sir, I have been asked to start with a summary of the nation's energy position if that is all right with you?" The president motioned him to continue.

"Sir, we remain in good shape on all fronts. Our consumption of all forms of energy has significantly increased, of course. However, industry has continued to expand energy supplies supported by your tax incentives. We have had no need, yet, to draw on any of our strategic reserves and in fact we are continuing to construct and fill new storage reservoirs for crude oil, natural gas and propane. We are holding off for now on closing some of our most efficient coal plants. Production of fossil fuels from Canada and our northern states has held up reasonably well so far, though we are starting to see some climate-related curtailments. Production from the oil sands has increased considerably with the additional investment in facilities and pipelines that you encouraged. In fact, without that we'd be looking at running out of transportation fuels and heating oil much sooner.

"We are unfortunately seeing much reduced availability of hydroelectric power from Quebec and Manitoba as more and more of the typical spring run-off that fills their reservoirs is now remaining frozen in the far reaches of their catchment basins. Keeping the coal plants on line will help bridge us to the start-up of our own new nuclear fleet, which remains on track for a couple of years from now. Mr. President, eventually we are going to start to lose the oil sands and other northern sources of production, including the production of both oil and natural gas from Prudhoe Bay on the Alaska north slope. I don't know how much longer we still have, maybe another five to ten years. With the preparations we have made we should be able to support the current level of energy consumption well beyond that time."

James Rushton replied, "Thanks for that update. I am glad to hear that we have a good margin of safety. Your report does appear to confirm our working hypothesis, though, that we are not going to be able to indefinitely sustain large population centers in the northern part of the country, especially if it continues to get colder. Who is up next?"

General Isaac Montgomery spoke up, "Sir, that would be me I think, and my subject follows directly from your last observation. We are now in our seventh winter following Peregrinus. I don't want to steal Eli's thunder, but it is very cold in our northern states and appears to be getting still colder. December and January have been averaging about ten degrees Fahrenheit colder than before Peregrinus, and we are told this differential will continue through the spring and summer, before widening further next winter. In places like Bismarck, North Dakota, and Helena, Montana, it won't start to thaw until the end of April and won't be snow-free until late May, then they'll see snow again by early October. That's already barely long enough for winter wheat. Fairbanks, Alaska, is experiencing an even greater decline in average temperature and will likely be snow-free for only July and August this summer. Midwest cities like Chicago and Detroit are warmer but will still be marginal in a few more years if the current trend persists.

"Sir, it's not that people can't survive in these temperatures. With modern clothing and homes, no one is going to freeze unless their car breaks down on a back road. It's more a question of logistics and of the local economy. On the logistics side it becomes more and more difficult and expensive to keep urban roads, as well as state and interstate highways, open. In the end, this always comes back to energy. Then, as you've already noted, there is the increased direct consumption of energy for heating homes and workplaces. Next is the local economy with many of these communities dependent on farming, which is withering in the face of shorter and shorter growing seasons for food crops and silage. Last is the psychological impact of cold temperatures and long winters. It wears on people's morale.

"The bottom line is that we are going to need to start evacuating the north before too much longer, which is of course why we have been busy developing new communities in the south. We have a number of those communities ready to go and, with a gradually phased relocation, if we get started soon, we will be able to handle the logistics of it all. We have already had a fair bit of voluntary relocation from smaller towns and villages and from a segment of the population of the larger urban centers, and these early movers are settling in well. From what we are seeing, about 20 percent of the population will relocate with just a little encouragement, about 70 percent will go if they are told that they must, and about 10 percent will strongly resist.

"We don't intend to drag anyone out of their homes, but they will be told that all services, including garbage, police, fire, schools and hospitals, will be shut down. We are planning to maintain skeleton utility crews to keep the power and natural gas infrastructure operating, but the water will be turned off. We'll give people lots of opportunity to change their minds, and most eventually will. Sir, with your permission we plan to issue the evacuation order for Fairbanks presently, to be implemented over the summer.

"The Canadian government has already pulled in the majority of the population of its northernmost hamlets and towns and will be evacuating the capitals of its northern territories this summer – Whitehorse, Yellowknife and Iqaluit. Next year they will shift the bulk of the population of their western provinces. We can likely wait another year or two before having to evacuate our state capitals in the northwestern states, and then a couple of years after that it will be Chicago and Detroit, unless the cooling trend abates. Sir, I believe we are ready."

"Thank you, Isaac," the president said, "I think we have known since the beginning that it would likely come to this, the only question being how much of the north we will have to abandon. I am glad we are ready for it. We would lose a lot of people and maybe even face a civil war if we had an unplanned sudden exodus from the north. Now, I understand that you are last on the agenda this morning, Eli, and I have this feeling that the strategy here is to save the bad news until the end. I hope I am wrong."

"Mr. President, I don't think you are wrong very often and I am afraid that this isn't one of those times. Your intuition is correct for the most part," answered the president's science advisor. "I have been working closely with Dr. Wellington and Dr. Holmes in studying our global temperatures as they trend post-Peregrinus. I have also been consulting with climate experts in Canada and the United Kingdom. I could tie our own experts in to this meeting if you wish, sir, or I can summarize for now and arrange a separate, more detailed briefing for you."

"Let's stick with the summary for now," the president directed.

"Yes, sir," Eli Wayman responded. "Here's the picture as it now appears. You probably recall from your first briefing on the climatic effects of Peregrinus that we estimated an eventual decline of twelve degrees Fahrenheit in global average temperatures over a long period of time. That was based on a 10 percent increase in the Earth's albedo, from 30 percent reflection of the Sun's energy to 33 percent, as a result of more snow and ice in northern latitudes. That was an educated guess because we have mostly theory and not much actual data on variations in wide-area albedo from which to establish a more reliable figure. It was described then as a best-case scenario, absent intervention, and it is becoming increasingly evident that such a best case is unlikely.

"As expected, global average inland temperatures dropped relatively quickly by about six degrees Fahrenheit but colder than that in the northern hemisphere with our now-longer winters occurring when the Earth is at its most distant from the Sun within its new orbit. The average has continued to slide downward every year since, again as expected, as ice and snow build up in the north. The slide was quite gradual at first, 2033 only very slightly colder than 2032, but the curve has since steadily steepened. This year is nearly a full degree colder than last year, bringing us to a global average which is about eight degrees colder than before Peregrinus.

"The decline has been even more rapid the further north you go. So, at the equator it is still not much more than the initial decline of six degrees, whereas at the forty-fifth parallel, which runs through our northwestern states, it is a full ten degrees, and at the sixtieth parallel and further north it is at least twelve degrees colder. There's less and less surface area contributing to the global average in these higher latitudes, so below-freezing temperatures lasting into late spring and beginning in the early fall don't cause the global average temperature to drop as dramatically, but those are the latitudes where snow and ice are persisting for a longer and longer portion of the year.

"Sir, you may recall from when I first briefed you on global warming that the Earth has experienced considerable variations in temperature in both directions from what we now think of as normal. In particular, there have been several ice ages in which our northern states would have been covered in glaciers, thousands of feet deep. Many climatologists think that during at least one of these ice ages, either the Sturtian or the Marinoan glaciations of the Cryogenian period, these glaciers extended most and possibly all the way to the equator, the so-called Snowball Earth scenario.

"The mechanism that is thought to have brought about a snowball Earth, starting from a more benign initial temperature drop, is called the ice-albedo feedback loop. The initial drop results in more snow and ice in the northernmost and southernmost latitudes, which increases the local albedo and reduces the temperature even more, causing the ice to last longer and spread further from the poles. With more extensive ice, the albedo rises more, and the cold intensifies and spreads even further. This sequence continues in a vicious cycle until an equilibrium is reached at a latitude where the angle of insolation and corresponding solar heating balances the cooling. Depending on how substantial the initial cooling is, this equilibrium might not be reached until ice has encroached on the equator from both the north and the south.

"Mr. President, we do not yet completely understand what it would take to kickstart a Snowball Earth scenario, how long it would take and what it would initially look like. However, the temperature declines that we are seeing in the northern latitudes are more pronounced than we originally expected, and the rate of decline in the global average is higher than we thought it would be. The temperature decline appears to be resulting from persistent and expanding ice cover in the north and the resulting local albedo increases. This is mainly a northern hemisphere issue. The southern hemisphere is experiencing a cooler but longer summer with only a moderate increase in ice cover and albedo surviving each summer.

"Sir, even if we aren't facing a northern hemisphere Snowball Earth scenario, and we probably are not, it wouldn't take a much greater southern extension of our original forty-second parallel permafrost line estimate to make our current challenges much more severe. Just a couple of degrees further south would put New York City into year-round ice. If the ice extended as far south as the thirty-fifth parallel, we would be left with only the Deep South, and even that would be pretty cold. We'd also lose all of Europe and even the Mediterranean coast of North Africa, as well as Japan. We might have a couple of decades before things would reach that point but probably not much more. The modeling that's been done suggests that the ice-albedo feedback cycle evolves quite rapidly compared with other climatic trends."

James Rushton absorbed this latest information and thought, *so much for the orderly house I was going to turn over to the next president.* However, as bad as it sounded, he doubted his science advisor would just drop a problem this big in his lap without also bringing some sort of solution. He said, "Eli, I am sure it has been hard on you and our climate experts to have to abandon the previous best-case scenario and now be bringing this message. However, you mentioned that this is the picture unless humans intervene. I am pretty sure you have something in your back pocket, so let me off the hook. How can we preempt having our country freeze over?"

"Thank you, sir. Yes, it hasn't been easy to accept what the data is starting to tell us and then to have to lay it on you. After everything you've done to preserve our way of life, you deserve a better outcome. We all do. You are right, there are some possible options to halt the spread of ice, or at least slow it down, though they all have some hair on them.

"All of the options we've thought of so far could possibly serve as a long-term counter to global cooling, but they are more likely to be successful as a temporary bridge. They may be able to hold back the ice-albedo feedback loop until our carbon dioxide emissions reinforce our greenhouse effect to the point where it offsets the reduction in solar energy from our slightly increased distance from the Sun. At our present rate of carbon dioxide emissions, this will eventually happen as long as we can last long enough before our global population, economies and emissions begin to falter. We are currently at an atmospheric carbon dioxide concentration of about four hundred parts per million and, despite the Paris Agreement, still rising.

"To strengthen our greenhouse effect sufficiently to reverse the ice-albedo feedback loop, it looks like we will need to get to about eight hundred parts per million — almost double our current level. That would eventually warm us back up by about five degrees Fahrenheit and, as long as the ice hadn't advanced too far south, would reverse the ice-albedo loop and leave us overall about one degree Fahrenheit cooler than before Peregrinus, only slightly warmer than preindustrial temperatures, which I think we'd all be very happy with. At our current rate of carbon dioxide emissions, with increased fossil fuel consumption because of the cold, and retaining coal plants, it will take us about thirty years to reach that level, if we last that long. Fortunately there will be enough greenhouse warming within about fifteen years to at least halt the feedback loop and the continued expansion of the ice. So, how do we buy fifteen years of time while holding the ice to the forty-second parallel in the meanwhile?

"One option might be to substantially expand the nuclear program we already have underway and just pump vast amounts of heat out along the forty-second parallel. However, unless there's a breakthrough with nuclear fusion, it would be nearly impossible to generate enough energy to halt the ice with our current fission technology, and there is no sign of such a breakthrough. In any case, we probably couldn't build more plants fast enough at this point, even if we relaxed some of the safeguards for survival's sake. If this was the only option available, it would be worth pursuing as a last-ditch effort, but there are some that we think are better.

"From there we move to less direct geoengineering strategies. We have looked closely at two categories. One of those is to artificially reduce the albedo of the snow and ice in the north. The other is to temporarily but more quickly reinforce the greenhouse effect using more powerful greenhouse ingredients than carbon dioxide. Manipulating the albedo has been studied for quite some time, though most of the work has focused on raising the albedo to offset the greenhouse effect. Here we are looking at the exact opposite. There are longer-term nature-based strategies for reducing the albedo such as increased forestation, but that is impractical once the ice is already present and would take far too long in any case. The only way to drop the albedo quickly once the surface is already ice covered is to cover much of the ice with a less reflective substance.

"Sir, it is possible to raise the albedo of ice by encouraging the growth of a naturally occurring pink algae which thrives on icy surfaces, but not at the very low temperatures now occurring in the north. We are left with a less elegant and more intrusive approach — spreading or spraying a dark-colored liquid or powder across wide swaths of the ice. The best candidate seems to be powdered charcoal in an aqueous emulsion. Charcoal is a nontoxic and largely inert compound, so covering a large surface area with a thin film of it will probably not have significant adverse future environmental effects if the ice eventually melts and the residue washes into riverbeds and lakes, though we don't know that for sure. On the other hand, there won't be much of an environment to worry about if the surface is deep below the ice for a long period. A charcoal emulsion could be economically and efficiently spread over large areas in Canada and our northern states using existing crop dusting aircraft. All in all we think this approach will work, is feasible to implement, and the benefits would far outweigh the risks."

The president relaxed a little and said, "Eli, I knew you would have a rabbit up your sleeve. What's the catch?"

Eli chuckled, "Yes, sir, that's what science advisors are for, and we don't see any obvious catch. The only real question is whether it would work quickly enough, but we think so. We also have a second rabbit for you to consider though. The other approach, rather than trying to lower the Earth's albedo, is to quickly but temporarily strengthen its greenhouse effect beyond the gradual but long-lasting effects of increased carbon dioxide concentration. There are a number of gases that are much more potent than carbon dioxide. The best candidate is difluoromethane. A molecule of this gas will absorb about seven hundred times as much infrared radiation from the Earth's surface as will a molecule of carbon dioxide. We'd only need a few parts per million, to substitute temporarily for higher carbon dioxide concentrations while those build up.

"Difluoromethane is a common refrigerant. It is also used as the pressurizing agent in the canned air products that are used for dusting keyboards and the like. It does not have any adverse impact on the ozone layer, unlike the chlorofluorocarbons once used for these purposes; and it has an atmospheric lifetime of half a decade so will automatically go away. In the amounts required it could be effectively dispersed through the upper atmosphere with minor modifications to the existing fleet of freight airliners. Like the charcoal dusting it is hard to see what could go wrong with this approach though it is possible that something unforeseen could. That seems like a small chance to take compared with the high risk of extensive glaciation which otherwise exists, though there would likely still be complaints from some.

"Mr. President, either of these two approaches will likely work. Both involve the once-controversial subject of geoengineering, though I think the time for such sensitivities is past. I personally prefer strengthening the greenhouse effect, which is, in its origin, a natural phenomenon, rather than painting the north black. Strengthening the greenhouse effect will tend to warm the entire globe right from the start, whereas reversing the ice-albedo feedback will initially just warm the northern latitudes, taking longer before this improves the temperatures to the south. It was the greenhouse strengthening that I had in mind back when we first briefed you on the climatic effects of Peregrinus, and

I mentioned that we might need to resort to geoengineering. Sir, I recommend that we start dispersing a very low concentration of difluoromethane into the atmosphere as soon as possible and then monitor the effects. If we don't see the rate of global cooling and ice propagation stabilize very quickly, we still have the charcoal approach in reserve."

"Thank you, Eli," said Jim, "I don't see that I can do anything other than accept your recommendation. I am just very glad that there's something we can do about this less-than-ideal scenario that seems to be emerging. I will want to have this as a multinational plan rather than just a U.S. initiative, so your work isn't over. You will need to help me convince the rest of the main national leaders. Madam Secretary, would you please set up private meetings with each of them over the next couple of weeks and ask them to include their principal climate advisors. General Montgomery, could you work with Dr. Wayman to be ready to activate the difluoromethane dispersal as soon as I give the word?"

Chapter 33

Early June, 2039
Canadian Rocky Mountains, near Golden, British Columbia

Arthur Svenson lay in his sleeping bag enjoying a last few moments of warmth and relaxation before tackling the day's activities. It was five o'clock in the morning with good daylight, though the twenty-three-year-old knew it would be chilly outside his small tent, especially in the early morning mountain shadow for which the lake beside him had been named. He was camped, as he had many times before, about 4,500 feet above the town of Golden in the Purcell Range. This time was different. He was by himself, except for his devoted dog, Beast, whereas in past it had always been with his dad and occasionally the whole family.

The prior summer the Svenson family and the McCormack family had walked the six miles from the cabin where they had been living down to Golden, which was now largely deserted. The adults had collectively decided that they needed to abandon the increasingly frigid climate of the mountains and move their children to a warmer place. Tom and Trish Svenson had been able to have their New Zealand immigration permits expanded to include the McCormack family as part of their household, which they certainly had become. In fact, they were all in-laws now. Arthur Svenson and Nancy McCormack had fallen deeply in love pretty much at first sight and their parents had given them permission to marry after two years of supervised chastity. The two newlyweds had been young by usual standards, Arthur at nineteen and Nancy at eighteen, but the old standards didn't really apply in the aftermath of Peregrinus. It had been a small ceremony in June 2035 — just the two families in the living room of the cabin, with a priest presiding by video call. Melissa McCormack had vacated the second bedroom of the cabin and moved up to the loft with the three younger girls.

A year after their wedding, Nancy had given birth to a healthy baby boy, carefully tended to by her mother and mother-in-law who had extensively researched and rehearsed the art of midwifery. Little Tom had been nearly two by the time they all walked down to Golden, riding most of the way on his father's shoulders. Once in the town, Arthur and Nancy had finalized a tough decision, but one they had been contemplating for some time. They decided that they and little Tom were going to stay behind. They knew it might get colder still, but they were accustomed to living in a cold climate and were prepared to accept the risks. Arthur had completed a science degree online and could likely have found a good job to support his family in New Zealand, but his heart yearned for the mountains and the outdoors of his home. He was his father's son, and Nancy would be happy anywhere she could be with him.

The decision had hung on what they could scrounge down in Golden. Tom had insisted that if they were going to return to the cabin, they would need to restock the staples, propane and chainsaw fuel, and they would need a reliable snowmobile and trailer to haul it all back with, and as a getaway vehicle if something ever went wrong. Arthur had agreed to that condition to gain his father's consent and blessing. They had been able to arrange to have their consumables brought in on the same train that would take the rest of the family to Calgary, and the local skidoo dealer had happily agreed by telephone from northern Mexico to give them one of the brand-new snow machines still sitting in his abandoned showroom.

It had been a tearful parting at the Golden train station. Tom and Trish would have made the same decision to stay, but for the young girls, all three of whom needed a chance for more social interaction and a gentler lifestyle than a backwoods cabin could provide. They all embraced and promised to stay in close touch by video chat. Little Tom was keen to visit his grandpas and grammas on the 'puter as the three of them headed back to the Svenson's Golden home, which the three men of the combined family had previously dug access to through the roof-high snow cover. There they would wait a few weeks for the three feet of slushy summer melt snow, laying on top of twelve feet of permanent snow, to firm back up enough for the uphill ride.

Arthur extracted himself from the small tent. It was sitting on top of a canvas tarp with a layer of spruce bows underneath as insulation from the twenty-five feet of snow sitting on the shoreline and the lake. He greeted Beast and got to work building up a decent fire of dead branches he had been able to scrounge from the part of the surrounding forest still reaching above the snow. The once plentiful deadfalls on the ground were buried too deeply to get at. Art had melted snow the prior evening to have water for coffee and he soon had the pot warmed up enough to melt the overnight ice accumulation. Venison patties and bushcakes were next. Even Beast seemed to welcome the warmth of the fire, though his shaggy coat had kept him comfortable outside despite an overnight low of twenty degrees Fahrenheit.

While savoring his breakfast, Arthur gazed up at the snow-cloaked mountains to the southeast across the lake. He was looking forward to his little campsite coming out of the shadow when the Sun rose in the notch between two adjacent peaks, as it always had when visiting the lake as a boy with his dad. He finished his meal, making sure Beast was fed and had enough water, then began packing up his tent and gear. He strapped the gear to the toboggan and began to tie his snowshoes. These were old-fashioned shoes designed for deep snow, wood frames with catgut mesh. They were five feet long and fourteen inches wide with up-turned tips, designed to keep from digging into the snow, and fastened to Art's boots with traditional lampwick harnesses.

Art shouldered his deer rifle and grabbed the tow rope of the toboggan but paused sensing something was out of place. Then it came to him. Although the morning was noticeably brighter and the sky above was a deep blue, he was still in shadow. The Sun was just beginning to glimmer behind the western edge of the easternmost of the two peaks forming the vee, and it was about to rise over that ridgeline well above the bottom of the notch. Arthur thought back humorously to the words of his father on another cold morning many years ago.

He said to himself alone, "Dad, I guess you were only half right. The Sun did rise right up through the bottom of the vee, as you predicted that day, but you weren't right about that being the way it would always be. I really wish you were here with me to see it." Then he took up the slack in the rope and headed back along the trail he had broken the day before.

The reasons for his overnight journey were partly nostalgic but mostly pragmatic. He had chosen Shadow Lake as his destination and turnaround point in part to visit this favorite spot he and his dad had frequented before Peregrinus. However, his main purpose was to move a good distance beyond his usual hunting grounds in the area surrounding the cabin, which was offering fewer and fewer opportunities to him. He hoped to take either a deer or a mountain goat. A deer would be better eating, but a goat would have a nice thick white coat that could be tanned and made into a warm jacket for little Tom. Either one would meet their protein needs for about six months. In the current climate, there was no difficulty in preserving the meat that long, well frozen and stored in an ice shed surrounded on all sides by thick slabs of ice cut from the lake by chainsaw.

Art had set out the previous morning. Once he had departed from the already broken trail of his usual hunting circuit it had been slow, heavy going, as he knew it would be. The snow was so deep that the lower layers were compacted and solid, and with a crust from last summer's melt about five feet below the surface, but five feet of loose snow was still challenging to move through, especially with a toboggan to pull and Beast bringing up the rear. His snowshoes were designed to compress a large volume of snow and keep him from sinking more than about eighteen inches, and they performed quite well as long as he didn't lose his balance and fall to one side or the other. If he did fall it was quite an acrobatic exercise to get his feet with their awkward snowshoes back underneath him before becoming smothered upside down in the deep soft snow.

The greatest danger from the deep snow was falling into a tree well. This was a deep hole in the snow where the branches of an evergreen tree kept the surrounding loose snow from compacting, leaving a gap of several feet around the tree, which might be covered with a foot or two of firm snow on top but dropping down ten or twenty feet below that through loose snow and air space. If a person strayed too close, the snow would collapse underneath and could leave that person suspended a dozen feet or more down, possibly upside down, while a small-scale avalanche poured down on top of them. Art was careful to keep well clear of the tops of the trees.

For the most part Beast was able to walk on Art's trail with his big paws spreading out wide enough to keep him from breaking through the layer of compressed snow. Sometimes the big dog did sink in the snow and then would have to be helped to fight his way back onto the trail. When this happened, the dog was trained to lie still until Art could break a solid platform of compressed snow alongside the trail to heave the dog up onto. Beast was now fourteen years old and nearing the end of his life. The big dog wasn't as fast or as strong as he had been in his youth, but he was still smart, courageous, loyal and as fierce as ever when it came to protecting the Svenson family. Art had considered leaving him behind but knew it would break the animal's heart, and his partner's hearing and sense of smell were still far better than his. Then too, even though Beast was old, the huge canine was still a major cougar deterrent.

Their uphill journey was slow as they covered the six-mile distance and three thousand feet of elevation gain. Art was conserving his own strength, using the slow shuffling pace best suited to keeping the tips of the snowshoes on top of the snow and the wide parts of the edges from clashing against each other. He was pausing regularly to look for game sign and to listen while Beast rested and processed the scents of the forest. It took them nearly eight hours to cover the distance, arriving late in the afternoon. They had not spotted a deer or a goat, but for the last mile of their journey Art had noticed that the budding tips of the upper branches of many of the aspen groves had been stripped off, as well as the tender new-growth bark. Art worried that in another three years or so the trees would be entirely buried and game would have nothing left to eat. For now, there were also occasional spots where visible tracks and droppings indicated the presence of game since the last snow a couple of days previously. The hunter was optimistic that on the way back, with more time to follow leads, they would encounter some game.

Moving downhill on the broken trail was much easier, though Art kept their pace slow to be as quiet as possible, and to allow them both time to carefully examine their surroundings. Within half an hour they came across the tracks of five or six goats, cutting across their trail and heading east and slightly downhill. They left the toboggan and followed the tracks as quickly as they could, keeping silent and wary, and taking advantage of the trail broken by the small herd. An hour later Beast had begun chuffing quietly but insistently. Art had shouldered the rifle and scanned an arc of thirty degrees on each side of the trail with the scope set to eight times magnification. Sure enough, two hundred yards ahead he spotted the goats in a grove of aspen, feasting on tender spring buds that they normally wouldn't have been able to reach.

Art considered taking the shot from there. It was certainly feasible, but there was some light brush in between and a risk that a twig might deflect his bullet and spoil his only shot. Although there was also a risk he might be detected if he tried to move closer, he decided to take that chance. He signaled Beast to lay down and stay. Then he slid slowly and silently forward, checking the scope every twenty yards to see if the goats were showing any sign of nervousness. When he was a hundred yards away he stopped, rested the rifle on a convenient branch, picked a large ram and centered it in the crosshairs. One of the ewes would be tenderer, but Art preferred to keep the herd breeding capacity intact. He stilled his breathing and gradually loaded up the trigger. The rifle fired, the ram dropped and the rest of the herd scattered. Beast bounded up from behind and went on to claim the kill.

The dog was excited and happy to be part of a successful hunting team with a master he adored, as he had been so many times before in his long life. Art was pleased and relieved that he would have meat for his family for another year without having to resort to canned chicken or ham. He removed his pack and retrieved a short piece of rope, placing his rifle atop the pack before cinching the ram's front legs together and suspending it from a branch of a tree a few feet away, with its abdomen at his waist and hind legs just off the ground. The animal was a good two hundred and fifty pounds and he had to tie the loose end of the rope to Beast's harness to help drag the ram the last couple of feet up.

The day was now warming up nicely under the early June mid-morning sun. Beast was content to lie down in the snow, with his chin resting on his paws, and watch as Art began to clean their kill. In a few minutes the big dog closed his eyes. The two-legged member of the team used his razor-sharp Bowie knife to make a circular cut around the animal's anus, pulling all the intestines out through that hole and throwing them onto the snow. Even this elicited no response from the slumbering dog. Art's knife was bigger than most would want for the purpose, but it had belonged to his dad, and both liked the firm grip of the large wooden handle in their own big right hands.

Art continued on cutting up through the belly and chest cavity, removing the internal organs and tossing them on top of the intestines except for the liver and kidneys, which he packed with snow in a separate pile. They would be coming home, with the liver destined for tonight's dinner. The twenty-three-year-old was in his physical prime with the strength and stamina that comes not from exercise but from days filled with physical activity, shoveling snow, chopping ice, splitting wood and snowshoeing up and down mountainous terrain.

As he prepared to lower the carcass down to the ground, the first that Art was aware anything was wrong was a deep chuff from his partner, Beast, followed by a series of growls and barks as the big dog threw himself to his feet. Art followed the direction of Beast's intense gaze to see a massive grizzly bear break into a full charge from not more than forty feet away, straight at him. The bear had undoubtedly just come out of hibernation a week or two before as temperatures had begun to warm up. It was a longer-than-normal hibernation, and the bear was very hungry and in need of large quantities of food to rebuild his reserves. The bear would normally have difficulty catching one of the fleet-footed goats. He nevertheless viewed the carcass that Art was standing beside as his own personal property, and Art as a trespasser and poacher at best, a threat to survival and maybe, under current difficult conditions, as a supplementary source of protein and fat.

All of this flowed through Art's mind in an instant as time seemed to slow to a crawl. He could see the bear charging down a shallow incline toward him, snow flying everywhere as it launched off its powerful hind legs and then skidded down the slope on its chest and forelegs before gathering for another leap. He could see Beast begin his own intercepting charge as he turned to take the four steps to his pack and rifle, knowing he would not have enough time to reach the gun, never mind to get it up, before the bear was on him. He assessed his chances of surviving an attack with nothing for defense except the big Bowie as low, but he would give it everything he had, knowing Nancy and little Tom depended on him.

As Art reached the pack and swept up the rifle, he saw Beast collide with the bear less than ten feet away, temporarily halting the carnivore's charge, but only for an instant as the bear stood and raked its powerful and sharp-clawed foreleg across the dog's chest, sending Beast reeling backward. The instant was just enough to give Art a fighting chance. He brought the rifle up, cranked the empty shell case out and a fresh cartridge into the breech and fired point-blank as the bear resumed its charge, then twice more before the bear reached him and lunged down to take his head in its powerful jaws. The bear leapt on top of him, but as Art fell back, it continued to roll over him and into the grove behind.

Art struggled to his feet, slightly dazed by the bear's impact, and cranked the last round from the magazine into the breech, noting the Bowie knife he had dropped on the pack as he brought the rifle up to take a final shot. The bear did not get up to resume the attack. It didn't move then, or ever again. After watching closely for another minute, Art ejected the magazine from the rifle and replaced it with a fresh one, then turned to check his dog.

Beast lay unmoving on a layer of bright red snow. As Art gently rolled the faithful animal over to examine the wound, he immediately knew that Beast had paid the ultimate price for saving his master, with his chest slashed wide open and blood welling out in a steady stream. He held his companion and gazed into his eyes as they gradually dimmed and then closed. Art wept freely over the great shaggy head.

Art sat still for a time, immersed in thoughts of all the times before when he or his father had teamed with Beast on a successful hunt, the dog always insisting on a full share of the credit for every kill. "You sure earned it this time, old boy," he said as he rose to carry on with the life he had been given back.

The sorrowful hunter took the time to skin the bear. The large bear skin would serve his little family well and would be a lasting tribute to their long-time friend and protector. Then he retraced his steps back up the mountain to retrieve the toboggan. By the time he returned and lashed both the ram and Beast onto the toboggan it was midafternoon, and almost warm. He shed his parka, adding it to the load on the toboggan, and headed back downhill, breaking a fresh trail but angling to the west to intercept his broken trail from yesterday's trip in.

Art reached the last leg of the trail home in the late afternoon, having had several hours to reflect on the day's events, and was at peace. He knew in his heart that Beast had at most another year or so before he would grow too old to go out on the hunt anymore. The dog had died doing what he lived for, hunting and protecting. It was a good ending even if he would be greatly missed.

Art ploughed down the steep slope beside the cabin, being careful not to upset the toboggan or let it get away. The cabin and its surrounding outbuildings now sat at the bottom of a twenty-foot-deep crater in the snow which extended about one hundred feet out in every direction. One of his most time-consuming tasks was to shovel the snow back away from their dwelling after every snowfall. Little Tom, now four years old, thought that the resulting toboggan slide, down one side of the crater and up the other, then back, was well worth his father's efforts. Art placed both the ram carcass and Beast in his work shed. He would rest and have dinner before digging a grave and butchering the carcass.

Inside the cabin, Nancy threw herself into his arms while little Tom tackled his knees. It was Tom who first noticed the absence of the big dog who would normally follow his master in for some patting before retiring to the landing to the basement where it was cooler. Art fetched himself a dark rum and Coke Zero before relating the whole story, doing his best to put it in a way that was not too frightening to his little guy. He could fill in the details for Nancy later that evening.

They were all sad but took their lead from Art, who explained that Beast would live on, always happy, for as long as they all were happy when they thought of him. After dinner Art went back out and dug into the snow slope behind the work shed, bringing an eight-foot-wide section right down through the fairly solid lower layers of snow to the frozen ground below. There he placed his long-time companion and covered him back up, entombing him in the snowy grave.

Later that evening, after the boy was put to bed and they had both had time to wind down themselves, Nancy suddenly piped up, "Oh, I have some news, two pieces of news actually. I had almost forgotten with everything else. Maybe I should save it for a better time though."

"Is it good news or not so good news?" Tom inquired.

"I think it is all good news," she replied.

Art beckoned a come-here gesture as he said, "Well, there can't be anything better than getting back to my beloved wife and child, but I'll happily listen to anything more in the good news category."

Nancy cuddled up beside the big woodsman and looked up into his eyes as she continued, "First, I am pretty sure that we are going to have another baby."

Considerable embracing and murmuring followed, but eventually Art released his wife and said, "Was there more good news? That first one will be hard to top."

"Yes," replied Nancy, "there is more, and I am pretty sure it is nearly as good as the first. Art, yesterday it warmed up enough by midafternoon that we got some meltwater running off the roof and I could see the snow starting to melt along the southwest walls of the cabin and all the other buildings. Today it happened again, with even more melting, and it was warm enough that Tom and I could make the dash from the front deck to the biffy just in our shirts. Art, we haven't had melting this early in June since three years ago. Last year it was nearly the middle of the month before we had our first melt and it had just been getting later and later each year until I was starting to think maybe there would eventually be no melting at all, a year-round deep freeze.

"I know I shouldn't leap to any conclusions too quickly, but I really have the feeling that the worst is behind us now and little Tom and baby two will one day get to see the world that we once knew before Peregrinus, and get to enjoy what a true summer in the Canadian Rockies should be like. Oh Arthur, I know that won't be anytime soon, but I think that we now have reason to be hopeful for a better world for our children. Before today I never dared to even hope for such a thing."

Technical Information and References

In the writing of *The Wanderer Rises*, I have spent a great deal of time on the internet researching various subjects to ensure all the details in the book are as accurate as possible. Google has been my primary research tool, Wikipedia my most common source. It would have been a much longer and more laborious process to dig out all the details without this modern capability. We now have instant access to virtually any information, from the size of the most powerful telescopes to the long-term history of climate change –with cycles of extremes from snowball earth to tropical poles – to the impact of asteroid strikes of various sizes.

I am not going to list every article that I read, but some of those I found especially useful or interesting are as follows:

1. Orientation of the Earth, Sun and Solar System in the Milky Way (author's name not indicated)

    www.physicsforums.com/threads/orientation-of-the-earth-sun-and-solar-system-in-the-milky-way.888643/

    This forum is a great source to help visualize how our home planet and its motions fit into the bigger picture.

2. Astronoo Simulator

    www.astronoo.com/en/articles/positions-of-the-planets.html

    This is a program with animated 3D graphics, showing the correct relative position of the planets as they orbit the Sun and running out decades into the future.

3. Moonrise, Moonset, and Moon Phases

    https://www.timeanddate.com/moon/

This provides data on the Moon's position in the sky, as seen from any place on any date.

4. Earth Impacts Effects Program – Robert Marcus, H.J. Melash, Gareth Colins

    teachspatial.org/earth-impacts-effects-program/

    A program that predicts the severity of the effects of an impact from an asteroid of specified size, speed and angle of impact.

5. Temperature and Radiation – Mike Luciuk

    www.asterism.org/tutorials/tut40RadiationTutorial.pdf

    An article that sets out the formulas for calculating the approximate temperature of an object orbiting the Sun at a specified distance, albedo and greenhouse atmospheric factor.

6. Methods of Detecting Exoplanets

    en.wikipedia.org/wiki/Methods_of_detecting_exoplanets

    An interesting Wikipedia article on how astronomers can detect planets as small as Earth, and even measure a number of their characteristics, when orbiting stars many hundreds of light years away. An amazing number of planets of varying sizes have been detected.

7. Climate Action Tracker

    climateactiontracker.org

    A website that sets out the nationally determined contributions (NDCs) of the various Paris Accord signatories and compares them on a gigatonne per capita basis.

    Various formulae have been used to ensure the scenario described in the story is scientifically sound. The main ones are as follows:

8. Python program was developed by Dr. Colin Bantin to calculate the gravitational interactions of Peregrinus with the Earth, Moon and Sun, incorporating Newton's law of gravitational attraction and Kepler's laws of orbital characteristics.

The inputs to the program include the basic mass of the Sun, Earth and Moon; the orbital parameters of the latter two; and Peregrinus's mass, position and velocity on November 6, 2027, when first identified as follows:

Mass = 3 Jupiters or 5.7 x 10^{27} kg

Initial position P(x,y,z) = (-.509, .966, 53.7) AU (helio-ecliptic coordinate system with X axis pointing to the first point in Aries. This position is about 53.7 AU below the plane of the ecliptic.)

Initial velocity V(x,y,z) = (0,0, 259,870) mph (about 260,000 mph straight up, orthogonal to the plane of the ecliptic)

The program calculates a closest approach of 10.07 million miles on January 13, 2030, with Peregrinus passing through the plane of the ecliptic just outside of Earth's orbit. The resulting impact on Earth's orbit is an increase in the semi major axis of 2.3% and a new period of 377.65 days.

9. Newton's law of gravity is expressed by the formula:

$$F = G \, M_1 \times M_2 \over D^2$$

Where F is the strength of the force of gravitational attraction measured in newtons between two bodies of masses, M1 and M2, measured in kilograms positioned at a distance (D) from each other, measured in metres (m). G is the gravitational constant and equals 6.67 x 10 -11.

The masses of the four bodies are:

$$M_{sun} = 2.0 \times 10^{30} \text{ kg}$$

$$M_{perigrinus} = 5.7 \times 10^{27} \text{ kg}$$

$$M_{earth} = 6.0 \times 10^{24} \text{ kg}$$

$$M_{moon} = 7.3 \times 10^{22} \text{ kg}$$

Average distance between Sun and Earth = 149.6 x 10^9 m

Distance of closest approach between Earth and Peregrinus = 10.07 x 10^6

miles = 16.2 x 10⁹ m

Average distance between Earth and Moon = 0.393 x 10⁹ m

Substitution of the appropriate masses and distances into the formula indicates that the force of attraction between Peregrinus and Earth at closest approach is about 25% of that between the Sun and the Earth.

10. The formula for the strength of the tidal effect of one mass on another is the difference in the force of gravity between the point on the surface of the mass being considered, which is nearest to the other mass, and the point which is farthest away.

$$F = (2 \times G \times M_1 \times M_2 \times r)/D^3$$

Where r is the radius of the mass being considered.

Substitution of the appropriate masses and distances into this formula indicates that the tidal force exerted on Earth by Peregrinus at closest approach is approximately equal to the tidal force exerted on Earth by the Moon.

It turns out that for a mass travelling at the speed of Peregrinus there was a fairly fine balance between how close it would need to come to Earth to induce the requisite change in Earth's orbit without coming so close as to cause substantial tidal effects. Much closer than 10 million miles of separation would result in quite destructive tides and probably trigger earthquakes and volcanoes, all of which I wanted to avoid in order to limit Peregrinus's damage to seemingly modest orbital effects with concomitant climate impacts. Much farther than 10 million miles of separation would result in orbital effects too subtle to have a rapid enough impact on the climate to fit the story's timeline.

11. The formula for the amount of solar energy received by the Earth from the Sun is:

$$E = \frac{r^2 B}{D^2}$$

Where r is the radius of the Sun in metres, B is the Stefan – Boltzman constant, 6.32 x 107 watts/m2, and D is the distance from the Sun in metres.

Substitution of the appropriate amounts into the formula indicates that an increase in the Earth's distance from the Sun by 2.3% from 149.6 million kilometres to 153.0 million kilometres would result in a 4.4% reduction in the amount of solar energy received by the Earth.

12. A formula that can be used to directly calculate the impact on the temperature of a solar system body due to changes in distance from the Sun, in albedo and in greenhouse gas energy recapture is (See Mike Luciuk's article, referenced above.):

$$T = ((1-A)/(1-G))^{.25} \times (280K/D^5)$$

Where temperature is measured in Kelvin, A is the Albedo factor (or fraction of the Sun's energy reflected back by the gases and clouds in the body's atmosphere and by its surface, currently about 0.30 for earth); G is the greenhouse effect factor, currently about 0.40 for Earth; and D is the distance between the Sun and the body, measured in AU.

Substituting the values for A and G into the formula indicates that an expansion of the Earth's average distance from the Sun from 1 AU to 1.023 AU would result in a decline in average global temperature of 3.3° K or C and 5.9°F. A 10% increase in albedo from 0.30 to 0.33 would result in a further decrease of 3.1° K or C and 5.6°F, or 11.5°F in total. A 5°C drop in temperature was associated with the last glaciation period within the current Quaternary ice age, the latest of five ice ages the Earth has experienced.

IN MEMORY OF MY GRANDMOTHER

AND TO MY AMAZING MOTHER AND SISTER

I want to thank everyone

who has played a part in making my dreams a reality,
anyone who has inspired and empowered me and
those who taught me a lesson or two
about life, art, and love.
God bless!

Part One

Funeral pomp is more for the vanity of the living than
for the honor of the dead.
- Francois de La Rochefoucauld

Gory Glory

Sunday, January 4, 2009
Emergency Room
Houston, Texas
2 am

Twenty-four-year old, boho chic hipster, Autumn

White, had blood stains on her tribal print cocktail dress. The juggler of three part-time jobs was used to stress, but she looked like she had been in a hurricane of emotions; she tried to get centered but it was too chaotic in the cramped emergency room. She found herself a corner in the small area, plopped down Indian-style and closed her eyes. In a yoga pose, she couldn't even imagine what Deon, her aunt, was going through at the moment. She believed that people should put themselves in other people's shoes. She had to silence herself for a moment in order to not break down. Family would be there soon, but it wasn't fast enough.

Twenty-six year old, preacher's wife, Kyla Withers, was silent but in prayer. Her twin, local TV producer, Kennedy James, was talking a mile a minute, frantically stating, "I...I...can't wrap my head around how this came about. We can't lose Deon!"

Kyla interjected, "She is going to make it out of this. We must pray, not panic." She held out her hand to her sister, who reluctantly placed hers inside it.

By the window, a man in a salty tear-stained business shirt sat huddled with his head in his hands. Twenty-nine year old, Quincy McKnight, who had invisible blood on his hands, was crying like he had lost his best friend. He kept shaking his head in disbelief and ignoring his vibrating phone. Black Widow, Nadia Masters, at home alone in Missouri City was leaving back-to-back texts and voicemails on Quincy's cell, as she could not get the sirens of last night out of her head.

Hair Stylist, Sister Snow, saw Quincy there in distress and wanted to tend to the handsome man, one who happened to be one of Houston's most eligible and notorious bachelors.

Once away from the prayer circle, Kennedy, a former investigative reporter, found herself busy, reading while thinking about the circus of events that led up to this moment. The closed-circuit information on the waiting room screens was alarming: *It is estimated that a head injury occurs every seven seconds...hospital emergency rooms treat 1 million people for brain injuries every year.* She couldn't help but feel there was more to Deon's fall. She just couldn't imagine it being an accident. She felt Deon was pushed, but by whom? She had seen so many people that night while promoting her latest project, *Dating Deon*, a reality show that was in pre-production. It was slated to feature the bachelorette and Kennedy's new company, *Ambitious Bitch Productions,* was producing the project. Kennedy felt like she owed Deon. Who was upstairs with Deon that night was the question? She had an eerie feeling that she had crossed paths with the person who wanted Deon dead! They could possibly be in the waiting room right now. Although she appeared busy reading, she was all ears.

There were hair stylists around. Ruby, Celestina and Snow were all twenty-somethings from Deon's salon. They were talking and carrying on when suddenly, a short, round nurse with a patchy birthmark under her left cheek, approached the growing crowd – one forming out of moral support and carnal curiosity.

"Hi, I'm nurse Georgia. Who was with...," the nurse quickly glanced at the clipboard, "Ms. DeVaulle at the time of the accident?"

Everyone looked around guiltily.

"Did anyone witness the accident...or was anyone with Ms. DeVaulle before, during, and after the injury?"

What happened was anything but apparent, but all of the women who were a part of the b-day planning stepped forward. Autumn responded immediately.

"Deon was at the club, laughing, dancing. She was in a great mood for the most part. She had a couple of drinks throughout the night, but nothing too heavy for her. It was her celebration. We were all dancing; she needed to go to the ladies room. She was gone for a couple of minutes longer than expected. I went to check on her, but didn't see her in the restroom or downstairs. I was about to text her, but that is when I saw...her falling."

All of a sudden, Autumn was overcome with emotion. Kyla and Kennedy held her up and signaled her to the

11

nearest chair a couple of steps away. Autumn, while sitting, tried to gain her strength before continuing.

The nurse was getting a little impatient. "I know it is hard, but it'll help us to treat her."

Autumn nodded and swallowed before continuing.

"She tumbled, she seemed to have been trying to break her fall of course, but she still hit...fell really hard, so much force. It was really unbelievable. I saw it, but it was so unreal to me. I just remember that my instincts kicked in and I was over there by her, trying to call 9-1-1. She wasn't responding to me."

"Did any of the rest of you see the fall as well?" the nurse inquired while looking around. There were a lot of *nos*. Mostly everyone saw and rushed over after it happened.

"Nurse, is she..." Autumn attempted, but Autumn didn't want to finish asking her question.

"How is she doing Miss Georgia? What is going to happen?" Kennedy asked.

"Are you kin to the patient?"

Kennedy shook her head no.

"I'm her niece. I called for paramedics," Autumn continued and seconds later, politely, the others stepped away to give the two some privacy.

"She is not conscious. We are running radiological tests and CT scans checking for any skull fractures, bleeding, swelling or lesions on the brain. It's still early. Her vital functions are stabilized, we are still doing a thorough evaluation.

The sound of a middle-aged woman screaming hysterically alarmed everyone in the room. Instantly, Autumn knew whose voice it was, her Aunt Josie, Deon's mom. Autumn braced herself. Aggressively, Deon's Houston family burst through the doors to the emergency area and into the even smaller lobby...Deon's father and a pack of cousins, nieces and nephews all embraced Autumn shortly after, but her mother was hysterical and she tackled nurse Georgia without thought. "Where's my baby!?"

Georgia wasn't speaking fast enough. Josie, on a hunt for her daughter, brushed past them. The family was used to tragedy, but this one was not going to be easy to bare. Deon was different.

***

Word travels fast.

Across town, in Sunnyside, Houston, low profile hair stylist, Sheila was at home, listening to Pandora radio, humming to the Kirk Franklin's gospel song, "Melodies from Heaven". Desperately trying to drown out the crackling sound of bill envelopes being opened, she kept going. On the kitchen table, one pink invoice after the next piled up. Many monetary options had run out and she was in deeper than the Gulf of Mexico. She was going to have to pick up another job since she didn't get the job at Deon's Hair Divas.

It was time for her to check on her babies. The kids were doing well. *Thank God!,* she thought. Then she proceeded to check her boyfriend's accounts, *her routine. Gotta keep my eye on him.*

His inbox was filled with the usual females asking if they could be in the next music video...*in Dallas. In Austin. In SanAnton. In NOLA*...she would joke that *he had hoes in different area codes* and she had grown accustomed to *blocking bitches,* as she called it.

Then she checked her own online Facebook status and gasped at what was in the news feed...Sheila's eyes bulged...in black and white, there it was, her *up* was *down:*

> HOUSTON, TEXAS Hair stylist is in critical condition this weekend. Authorities say she had a steep fall down a staircase during a birthday celebration at Club Sentinel in Downtown Houston. DeVaulle was celebrating her 30th birthday.
> *Houston Chronicle* reports.

Before she could read another word, she was hearing the local news carry the story on the tv that sat in the den. Sheila knew it wasn't a hoax, but she still couldn't grasp that her idol had fallen. Scratching her neon Mohawk while watching the reporter in front of Club Sentinel, an uppity club on Main Street, Sheila thought her mind was playing tricks on her.

She looked back at her timeline, one flooded with local news stories about the incident:

> Local star stylist, Deon DeVaulle is in ICU at a local hospital. A statement issued by her family is, "This is a very devastating time. We hope and pray this freak accident is not a tragic one."
> *Bayou City News* contributed to this report.
> Share your comments.
> *This can't be true. I can't believe this is happening. I hope everything works out for Deon. She is a brilliant artist and person.- Candi F.*
>
> *Oh no!!!! I'll be praying for Deon. This is very sad to hear. - Br. Kelton*
>
> *Please pray, that if she dies, she will go to heaven. - Anonymous*

Sheila was speechless. Then she was at fault for her next thoughts...*what goes around, comes around. What goes up, must come down*. She remembered that day in September, like it was yesterday. Based on a favor for her hair school teacher, Romeo, a former classmate to Deon,

Deon agreed to interview her for a job, but some unforeseen events took place that day and Deon changed Sheila's life forever.

Sheila, in zombie state, sat with her eyes and mouth open. She needed to talk to someone. She called a woman who had helped her get through a tough period in her life.

***

In her apartment in Cypress, college drop-out, "Gift of Gab" columnist, Gabrielle Villa swallowed hard. Coffee was not helping her after her sleepless night. This morning was tough for one who was always watching and always had a mouthful to say but what she saw last night, she wished she hadn't. Millions awaited her latest words. Especially what happened with the infamous Deon this week. Her blog was the hottest gossip site out there. But chilled to the bone, this was the first time Gabby felt silent, hesitant about writing. She never had writer's block - this was different. What she knew, she couldn't quite put into words. It was dangerous to let emotions get in the way. How would she handle such a story? But she knew time was ticking and she needed to say something before people started to speculate.

***

Back at the hospital, everyone's sense of consternation continued to heighten with every passing second, especially when more of the family started to emerge. Now, they were coming all the way from Louisiana. More and more of them started to pile up in the small lobby, looking for answers and ready to give marching orders.

***

On the other end of the line, in her River Oaks office, all Dr. Lynne could do was shake her head while listening to Sheila's news. She had heard a lot about the woman with the golden scissors. *Could a hair stylist be that good* or was it just the aerosol can's fumes skewing the mind? Were the eyes tricked while watching the fluffy ego floating around in all the viral videos?

Lynne always said beauty is a funny thing...*it can get ugly*. It opens doors outside of yourself, but it also closes doors within.

She knew a thing or two about women in general. She was hoping that the horrible event was not because of a man, but since many women's problems revolve around the male species, she figured it was.

Dr. Lynne was a relationship therapist with a Muslim background. She held many women's secrets; one happened to talk about Deon over the course of four years. She tried to not form opinions, but she was human. She was not comfortable using profanity; it was her personal preference, but she had heard Deon was *no saint* and she

17

was called out of her name on a number of occasions by all types of women she counseled. So as one quick to coin terms, Lynne found one double entrendre fit for this type of Queen. *Botch*. Her next book was slated to talk about this *type* of woman and would uncover the harsh reality of how some girls don't outgrow *mean*, but instead grow into a new-age materialistic, barbaric Barbie style, Queen Bees that need to be recalled because of harmful defects.

Toxic City

2009 US Census report that 53.5 million women are single.
(divorced/ never married/ widowed)

In my book, there are three types of people: *faces, voices* and *doers*. At the "Divas" salon, reading people is a big part of what Deon does, but categorizing people came from an early training ground. A dehumanizing truth resurfaces - data *did* it. Data played a huge part in her demise. *Data did a number on her, and especially her dating life.* Categories were more than just boxes on a page; they were places WE all fit into, whether we like them or not.

One of her first jobs had been working at a small lab as a data clerk; importing demographics for experiments and for tests became routine.

The company also used her computer competency for other things; she did work as a site developer for them. Coding was her favorite part, but the main data job proved that *life* is never enough, numbers are.

The more she dated, the more she realized, as she quickly summed people up, her love life was flat-lining. But she continued to import data as if her job became her and her life depended on the money. Over the years, it became more and more apparent that something still wasn't clicking: *Even if she stayed on top of deadlines, even if she got the corner office at each company, even if she become the boss, even if flowers were delivered to her every other day.*

Human touch - she never knew the beauty, the power, the importance of her own. She was product oriented. She defined life by design, but she was a natural healer. Her miracle hands touched lives. They allowed growth to take place where damage was done. They helped give a new attitude just from mastering a fresh cut, a refined color. Yes, she had an eye, a sharp one, but she had a magical touch that did all the work. It responded to her mind's creativity, her eye's catch.

People may assume Deon is a *face*, but she doesn't sit and look pretty; she just appears to be the part. The *faces* actually aim to please. What they say and do may be rehearsed. Up close and personally, they are not original, but far away, they make everyone feel better because they look like it's all A-okay. They are the face of a company, a movement, an organization. They are the *Social Media* kings and queens. They put on great shows; their persona sells dreams and even pyramid schemes. They make awesome spokespeople you can feed lines to. Their demeanor and their performance is their bread and butter and they operate to appease the *seeing is believing* types.

Now the *voices* on the other hand may not be seen, but boy are they heard. And when they speak, people are sitting on the edge of their seats, or at a standstill, savoring the language they spill. You could sit through every YouTube audio-video they have ever made and never get enough because they have a wealth of knowledge and you are just hoping to get a drop. They don't have to have beauty or charisma; *sometimes it is better if they don't* - they actually have something to say. No distractions. With every syllable, they grow more and more striking each day. Some may even think, after leaving "Diva's" salon, Deon is a voice because she's always in their head. But since talk is cheap, she does very little of it. These people with voices don't get paid what they are worth. Instead, Deon did what a lot of people avoid. *Do.* This category is the smallest in size. Doers, like NASA Spaceships, keep everyone on their toes as they lift off. They are the experimental wildcards, the dare devils, the gamblers who can rise higher than you'd think was humanly possible and in one split second, could fall lower than six feet under. All this could happen in the blink of an eye - it is the most risky category to be in, but for these die-hard types, it is the only way to live.

Deon wanted to live.

But someone had a problem with her doing that.

The now thirty year-old dichotomy, Deondria DeVaulle, even in her artificial world, was as real as they come. Her blunt*isms* earned her many *hate hers* or *love hers* but no in-betweens. In spite of all the love, she had a passionate affair with *hate*. It seemed to push her to success, a word tattooed on her thigh. And far from modest, unapologetically, Deon did everything in a Texas-size way, capitalizing on her talent, her shrewdness and her ever-growing

21

hair business bank account. Business was pleasure and she was known for being on top of her game.

Her high-profile salon, *Deon's Hair Divas*, a hot spot, a day party in Houston, was a beautiful place, full of beautiful people who aspired to look more beautiful than when they came. The salon's décor was a marriage of two styles: traditional and contemporary, an extension of the owner.

It was the *place to be,* for many narcissists and a safe haven for the clueless diamonds-in-the-rough who needed make-overs, pronto. The salon was also a satirical soiree: a fusion of love tales sashaying around and a mélange of faces and voices to match. Ironically, there was an unsightly side to it all; the method to Deon's madness was not always appreciated. She was mechanical, systematic, a control freak of the week, a bit of a OCD machine operating in a manner that kept her staff on their toes as they walked on eggshells. For Deon, this salon was her baby, her cradled love, her everything. She counted clients, employees, vendors and walk-ins, the way she counted coins. The more the merrier, for she was on to the next level in the beauty biz.

Deon's salon was at a crucial point and she was finding it hard to trust her workers. But even in life, she was at a crossroads and she found it hard to trust herself. It didn't help that she was...single.

Why is this lovely lady single? Good question and it was posed in many gossip blogs. She wasn't like the many women in the salon who *never* had a *male figure* in her life. *Daddy* issues run high in this day, but that wasn't Deon's deal...As for this playette, serial-dater...it's her family secret, or better yet, *curse*. Deon was not the woman she *appeared* to be. Her mother, Josephine, warned her as a little girl that there would be some things she would never understand about herself, especially when it came to her love life. Boy, was she right. Josie's gibberish was always right and it was starting to unfold and come full circle as she got older. But Josie's unorthodox voice of reason, every season, felt like a curse more than a gift. Her family was in the business of spells. Some are hard to break if the root is not known. So she loved privately and hated publicly. There were only a few people who could actually help her get to the root of her issue...but Deon must self-reflect...in love; otherwise, she would self-destruct in hate.

But in a city that can be cold one minute and hot the next, it's hard to figure out one's *true* temperature.

Yes, the Bayou City is three-dimensional, full of paradoxes and one-of-a-kinds. It's a tempting town that is busy, but it gets plenty of sleep. Deon could attest that Houston is a very hypnotic place that has a hold on you. At a glance, it's comfortable, flat and uncomplicated, but honey, *don't mess with Texas!* Yes, it's the home of sweet warm, southern hospitality, but also quite a few ice-cold, heartless killers.

Compliantly split into two halves: the *North*side and *South*side, residents sing their happy claims. Then there are the many little worlds in and surrounding it, such as the high-browed, the low-browed, the working, the looking for work and a whole lot of in-betweens. *In between:* You can get lost in *The Wards, South Park, Sunnyside, Acres Homes, River Oaks, Bellaire, Memorial, Cypress, Pearland, Sugar Land, and The Woodlands.*

Indisputably, and in a nutshell, the vast area is great for several endeavors, but the most popular aim would be, "settling down". Here, many men and women's goals are to start families of their own and live the *American Dream*, even the status quo kind. Yes, cookie-cutter success was welcomed and encouraged; the steps are laid out for women: get the degree(s). The ring. The house. The kids. *Their* kids. That's THE life. That's success, or at least what the women of the village teach. *Then, live happily ever after.*

Houston was home and Deon's heart beat for it. Hey, and the price of land and housing is *very* attractive. It's so striking that one can easily ignore the icky smell of gas, the inevitable allergy-seasoned-smog and bi-polar weather just fine...but the road rage, and the distance from one place to another, that is another story. But...patience *is* a virtue that can get a person pretty far here. Now, if love *in close driving distance* is found, that's a miracle and who knows where that could take you *since you save on gas*!

Overall, H-Town is where the fairy tale can come true for many hopeful and *even* skeptic romantics, like Deondria DeVaulle, an asocial beauty genius.

There was a plethora of tastemakers that flirted with the energy in *The Heights, Montrose* and *Midtown*. Deon loved, lived, worked and shopped in *Rice Village* and she couldn't stay away from *Uptown and Downtown*. There she did more shopping and had lunch meetings and it was where all of the movers and shakers congregated.

It was also where her life changed one fateful night.

On the Other Side

Humanity has advanced,
when it has advanced, not because it has been sober,
responsible, and cautious, but because it has been playful,
rebellious and immature. - Tom Robbins

A lot can happen in one night. Deon's eyes popped open. She was a light-sleeper for many reasons. Her mind started racing. *Time out!* she thought. She couldn't see faces, couldn't hear voices, couldn't do anything; loneliness surrounded her even though she had some company. *Where is everybody?* she thought and tried to say. Locked in her own suspended state, she couldn't move anything but her eyes. In front of her was a stranger, her mirror. Face-to-face, in close parameters, they both were monuments...statues, but from totally different theme parks.

Although her eye-sight was shadowy, she managed to fix her focus on the man. *It actually happened to me.* She blinked in disbelief. His face was still blurred. They were about the same height and build. He was pretty tall; she had on heels. In the flesh, she could not search anything therefore, she relied on the other skill that got her through years of business: women's intuition. Her body reacted to the external cold. Other senses kicked in and she could smell him, an ailing scent it was. Without her consent, she could feel the heat from his body, entering her own. The two spirits shared this unsettling indifference that resonated in their stillness.

While Deon's mind wandered, her morale sank, but didn't settle. Like a miracle, she exhaled.

She felt she had been to hell and back, and Deon didn't care if the detached visitor could smell it on her breath or from her pores. She was inhaling a nightmare: a heap of scum, screams, sinister laughter stacked on ambitious lies and lazy ones too. The poisonous grit seeped into her crevices, she knew the stones and gravel that scarred her weren't invisible. *I should have seen them coming since they were thrown all my life. Yeah, you would think I would know when to duck. Well, as they say...every Diva has her off-day.*

The stranger stood motionless for moments in his all-white attire. He was so close that she couldn't see a name tag and getting the name was the furthest thing from her mind. She wanted answers.

Suddenly his face started to come into focus, and it was not at all easy for Deon to look at; for it had no sensation or beat. The gray eyes were eerily familiar; she couldn't help revisiting them after realizing they didn't even blink. The stiff, but not stoic face was grayish, and plastic-looking.

Her heavy hands felt stuck to her sides. She wanted to tap him on his shoulder to see if he'd react because she was convinced he was a mannequin, a cute one, like the ones displayed at Old Navy, but a doll.

Oh my God, Deon's heart pounded. *My hands feel uncovered.*

That would mean her scars were as well. But he didn't seem to notice.

Deon looked away out of nervousness. Although she saw white clouds, maybe smoke, she knew at this moment, she wasn't at Club Sentinel anymore.

Speaking of smoke, boy, could I use a cigarette right now, she thought. Deon was convinced she did her best thinking then.

Where exactly am I? Deon had no clue; she just knew this wasn't home. With muffled ears, she struggled to make out the stranger's gibberish. She heard him say something about trees...*Was he offering?* She perked up. Never one to hold her tongue, she grinded her teeth. Grunting, she even tried to make conversation...but she could only produce an anguished-filled moan. She swallowed...Her throat felt as rough as coarse new growth hair that needed a relaxer. Attempt number two garnered the same unsatisfactory result. She huffed.

Her prized possessions, her hefty double Ds, were crying out for a high quality Victoria Secret support bra; her back was screaming for a comfortable bed to lie her sorrows down and smother with a pillow. Although her body ached, her heart was contaminated and damaged and the leakage was rapidly forming gunk around her.

She closed her eyes shut to keep the tears from burning. The burning question haphazardly floated in her mind, a twilight zone. Trying desperately to separate the truth from deception and fill in the gaps, her home-sick and tongue-tied self was physically and emotionally impaired. She stood frozen in time, paralyzed.

***

Kennedy was on a mission. Since Deon was not pronounced dead, no one looked at the club as a crime scene. She needed to move fast, before anyone caught on.

She convinced Quincy to let her into the club after hours. She slipped away from the hospital and was back at Club Sentinel where the horrible fall occurred, hoping to find answers.

Surveillance cameras were installed throughout the club. She was determined to get a good look. But what she got was far from that. None of them were set at an angle to see Deon upstairs that night.

So the next best thing was actually to comb through the minutes and hours of footage leading up to the fall. She needed to see the party-goers with her own eyes, from her angle.

She was soon to be on the clock at the television station. She had to work fast.

***

Standing in the same place, words were on the tip of Deon's tongue, but if only the net would catch. She wanted to ask

- presently, indoors or outdoors? She still couldn't move her head enough to see, so she just stared ahead. *Why was I here? How did I get here?* And then, she heard these words:

"A tree can grow to be very lofty, but the falling leaves always return to their root," said the stranger. His soothing voice ruffled her feathers because she was struggling to speak, but it was as if he read her mind.

She frowned. As a child she had heard that same proverb, and of course, avoided it happening at all costs. Who actually wants to see the day when they descend, especially after all the reaching? she mused. Growing defensive, she thought, yes, I fell, but I am trying to stay above it all. In a split moment, she convinced herself that down was the "new" up and she would be back up again.

When can I leave this place? She still couldn't get her words out. It sounded like *wen orso snk racs?* instead. Even though this guy looked like a hip rocker Lenny Kravitz wannabe, the kind she used to like, he was creeping her out big-time! The fact that he smelled like her uncle's funeral home and how he was looking at her in the weirdest way added to the feeling.

She didn't even want to see her own face because imagining the crud acquired along the way was enough for her. Was that what he saw? The underhanded journey prior to this puzzling encounter was so beneath her, she could cry of embarrassment. *They saw me fall. Now I just needed to get over falling in love by falling in hate.* Deon felt she could do that easily. *Time to take the easy route here on out. Romantic love was overrated anyway.*

Work was all she needed in order to get money - her one true love.

"You don't really believe that, do you?" the guy asked.

Suddenly, her blinks were producing very vivid images in her head.

Nightmare on Main Street

Her life may not have flashed before her eyes in the

cliché sort of way, like what they say on TV, but her day did. In her head, the vignette started playing her now infamous birthday.

It started early Saturday at *The Breakfast Klub* in midtown.

"Hey doll! You look juicy as always!"

Deon was embraced by her former co-host for an ambush make-over show that had pretty much helped propel both of their viral careers. Romeo LaSalle, a teacher at a beauty school in the hood, held her tightly. "Hey boo!" She felt some *new* accessories on his upper body; she was about to speak on it, but he beat her to it.

"Order what you want boo. I just want my usual. Be right back," Romeo said before sashaying off to the mens' room. He had offered to take her to breakfast and Deon insisted he didn't have to.

While she waited for him to return, she started checking her messages on social media; most were flirty, some were platonic. Dating was a sport and online dating was a trip. With both, she was burned out with having the same conversation with different guys.

Romeo finally returned.

"Girl these hormones are driving me crazy."

"I knew I felt some boobage. So I see you are actually going for it now." Romeo had told her about taking hormones in order to change genders years ago, but his family was having a hard time with him coming out.

Working in hair and make-up, Deon knew many men who were sexually ambiguous. She had so many gay guy friends, people used to call her fag hag. She didn't care what anyone called her as long as she made her money in the salon. She was loyal to those who were loyal to her. She had helped Romeo, in high school, come out to his mother. This was the hardest thing he had ever had to do. But Deon stressed that the truth always sets one free. She knew he was living a lie and she knew that was the worst way to live.

"How is your mom?"

He rolled his eyes, but was eager to share.

"Girl, mad as hell. Dad too. But I got to do this for me. But enough about me. Give me the tea girl."

"Oh man, things are...interesting."

"Who is the new man of the hour."

"That's the thing. I am thinking about taking a year off from this dating thing."

Romeo threw his head back with laughter.

"It takes a lot out of you. Not every connection is divine. Some are just random wastes of time. You need stamina and strategy in order to stay in the game. I'm so tired of playing with these little boys."

"Bitch please. You know how hungry these women are out here. You take a break and that is it for you. You are out of the game. You just need a real man. Once you find that, that's it."

"It's just a gamble I feel I need to take before it's too late." Deon knew when to walk away from the slot machine. "Because you can't hit the jackpot warming the seat."

Ironically, Romeo was the only person Deon talked to about guys. She habitually made record of past dudes and dates so that it wouldn't be revisited. She had a rule - don't go back. If it didn't work the first time, let it go.

She was getting tired of letting go.

"Well I heard about this show you are about to do and was wondering..."

Deon shook her head before he could finish. "I am all dated out - I haven't signed anything." This *Dating Deon* show was in the works and Deon was tired of the topic. Even though she was rooting for natural meetings versus online and blind dating, they weren't any better.

"What happened to Henry?"

"Oh, Henry. That was so long ago. Henry, who almost made it to the pros. Let's just say, he *almost* proposed."

"What about the NASA engineer? Big bucks."

Deon's eyes bulged. "Grant, oh he was great on paper, but no chemistry whatsoever."

"What about the young tender?"

Deon chuckled. "Jerome, Jerome, Jerome." She shook her head. "He has no clue what to do."

They talked about Fabian, the wannabe comedian; Ethan, the fling from Vegas; Dylan, the nice guy who claimed lack of chivalry was due to being daddyless; Clyde, the sweet guy who sends holiday cards every month NOW, but back in the day, had her in a love triangle she didn't even sign up for; and Ricardo...the recluse.

"He off in the mountain somewhere writing a book and growing his own fruit."

They both laughed.

"See, maybe those guidance counselors in high school knew what they were talking about after all, huh? *Forget the BS, or the MBA...graduate with a MRS.*"

Deon laughed. "Right, my honor roll ass didn't listen."

"He mocked her high school self. "Um, I want to live my life, *then* become somebody's wife."

"Right, I did say that. Without that face though."

They both cracked up.

"You gotta get hitched bitch. You know that being single is a sin in this town AND being content with being an independent woman is a crime. You are so beautiful; I can't believe you go through this. It's a shame really."

"Romeo, I never factored into the equation that the selection gets worse with time. What can I say? Society thinks that I have been a bad girl."

"So you're finally conforming in your 30s?"

"That was always the plan. Being off the market by 30. Plus, I am tired of being asked, *why a woman like me hasn't been swept off my feet yet?* I just want to respond, because so many doofuses waste time asking bonehead questions like that instead of actually doing it."

"You are killing me over here!" Romeo tried to control his laughter. "Well, when it rains, it pours."

"So my 30th birthday is here; it's just something about those two digits and what happens when you put them together." Deon clutched her napkin in her hand.

"Well, when you look at what the average single woman faces while dating (weeding out the jail birds, the gaybirds, the bi-birds,) - *no offense, Romeo...*"

"None taken. My mates know what they are getting when they get me."

"...*True, but as I was saying,* the mama's boys, etc it is easy to believe dating is some type of cruel and unusual punishment. It's not fun."

At the time, Deon held her tongue. She was not going to admit to Romeo the whole idea of coming up short was driving her to drink a little more, smoke a little longer. She had a reputation to consider. Luckily, she had a back-up plan, a win-win situation. A serious proposition back in her college days was made by fellow business major, Quincy McKnight. A man, the only man (after her daddy, her king) that she ever loved. He was once jazz music to her ears, now haunting silence.

After Romeo's gourmet omelet and French toast and Deon's homestyle pancakes, eggs and sausage arrived, the two were quiet for the first time at the table as they gobbled down their food.

"Baby, that hit the spot!" Romeo announced to what seemed like the world.

37

"Yes, that was good, as always. I could just go to sleep now, but I am going to the salon to do a few heads. Thanks for breakfast. That was sweet."

"I hate you are not doing anything big for your 30th. That is totally unreal. You of all people should celebrate."

Deon sipped the popular homemade lemonade and slowly shook her head. "I know right. I just have not been feeling it. Turning 30 and all."

The two kissed and said goodbye and Deon was back at work, on her birthday.

As Autumn, Deon's niece, her receptionist, sat in the styling chair, Deon couldn't help but feel awkward; lately Autumn seemed to give her the cold shoulder. She felt it wouldn't be the first time someone close to her, rather abruptly did so without any manifested reason. Wouldn't be the first time either that it was blood. She expected water to thin, but blood was supposed to be thick.

Although Autumn was unusually quiet lately, she slipped and spilled the beans before Deon even started on her hair at the salon, an innate water cooler in itself. The conversation went a little something like this.

"So what are we doing today A?" she asked as they both looked forward at each other's reflection in the mirror. Deon was hoping to do more than her usual. She wished Autumn would change it up a little, straighten it out a lot.

"I want to keep it crinkly and natural, but just styled cute for your party tonight."

"Party? I'm not having a party; I mean, Ruby and I were going to meet some of the..."

You should have seen both of their faces in the mirror that very second.

Well, I'll be damned, Deon thought. She didn't have too much time to give it thought because like clock work, her 8' o clock arrived. After she finished shampooing, defusing and diffusing Autumn's wild hair, Kennedy was in Deon's chair.

Kennedy James was texting furiously the whole time. Kennedy is a "doer" and a lot of the ideas that came from this sharp, passionate local news producer who had light bulb moments by the millisecond were highly profitable. That is why Deon listened to her and respected her fellow *alpha chick*. Deon bet that the explicit fire inside of Kennedy would eventually run her out of town if she wanted to float like helium. Deon always felt Kennedy was in the wrong town for her "I don't need a man" persona which really gets in the way of her finding Mr. Right, a BLACK Mr. Right, because she was sleeping with Conner, a fine white man last time her and Deon talked. And although he seemed to be a great guy for her, her unhealthy dose of Black pride kept her feeling ashamed and eventually they broke it off. But he still tries her. Deon told her on a number of occasions, "luckily you are married to your mission; I wish you the best because Oprah can't be the only one." Deon could tell by the look on Kennedy's face she was talking to Conner on text; Deon wished she would give the cutie pie a real chance and stop brushing him off because of his race.

"So what you got going on tonight, Kennedy?"

"My same ole same ole," she said shaking her head. "Networking on a Saturday night."

Kennedy's hair cut was as blunt as she was, and under strict orders, Deon kept it that length for years because if her hair grew past her chin, she would have a fit and have her remove it expeditiously as if it was a cancerous growth. Deon laughed at how Kennedy, this feminist, was always in some deep shit; she would re-write history if she could. Yes, Deon agreed with some of the causes she stood for, but she thought Kennedy a bit self-righteous when it came down to being Black. She joked with her that all she needed to complete her agenda was a Davis fro, and a clenched fist pumped high in the sky. But they agreed, as far as hair, that would be too much in her work environment; so she kept her hair straight to downplay her militancy.

In no time, Autumn was ready for her style. The smile on her face let Deon know she had achieved what the client desired.

Soon, the ladies were getting cozy on the topic of 2009.

"For some reason men seem to know a heck of a lot about angry black women but they don't seem to know a thing about angry black men. The kind that turn on their own just like the old slave masters wanted them to do," Kennedy said. "There needs to be more self-reflection within the black race."

As Deon trimmed Little X's bob, she refused to buy into the "single ladies epidemic" no matter how much news covered the topic. Kennedy was one media pro who helped it gain exposure in the southern news market. Deon felt she couldn't break away from Kennedy's real radical escapades even if she tried. Deon remembered how Kennedy's slick self didn't let on that she knew about the surprise party, but she did let her know about her latest idea that involved her, the dating show.

Kennedy, after hearing about Deon's unproductive online-dating experience, persuaded Deon to sign up for *Dating Deon*. This was a project Deon was still not 100% sold on, especially after hearing that she wanted to have a shrink, Dr. Lynne, be a part of it. Though successful as an author, psychologist, and a relationship therapist, that lady irked Deon for a plethora of reasons. "One, she needs a relaxer," Deon said on more than one occasion. *The natural do is not good for everyone.* "Two, she is 40, single and too calm about it, *I certainly don't want her to rub off on me.*" Lynne was a "voice" Deon wanted silenced and a "face" she wanted erased from her life.

"I am still not sure, Kennedy. Living and dating in a technological era is a Catch 22 and I don't want to get that caught on tape," Deon said.

"What about on digital?" Kennedy asked.

Deon just looked at her. Although Deon was a business woman, she wasn't like Kennedy, a modern-day careerist with a strong sex drive, *well not anymore*. She wasn't sure about going on a series of dates just for show. She really wanted just one man in her private life. Deon found a need for a man other than sex and she didn't trust Kennedy playing cupid – quality versus quantity was Deon's objective. Deon wanted to have the traditional family life, like her own childhood example.

Deon was glad to hear another voice in the conversation.

"Oh my gosh, my sister and I were just talking about that. How back in the day, mommy and daddy, and grandmommie and granddaddy had courtship and trust; digital distractions is what we have now," Ruby, Deon's right hand woman, added.

"Yep, don't you just love how these Smartphones outsmart even the most crisp players?" Deon said.

"Lord knows what's next," Ruby agreed. "My nieces and nephews are showing me something new every weekend." Ruby and Deon worked mostly with the African-American sisters. The other ladies, Snow and Celestina, were a part of the talented team. All three stylists got their start in Deon's salon and she took pride in seeing them grow to be top stylists due to so many things they had been exposed to under her tutelage. They brought a lot of great energy to the salon and when she says energy, she means currency.

There was a lot of playing going on in the salon. Snow, a comedic relief, was always cracking jokes and Celestina played Devil's Advocate far too many times for Deon's taste. Deon couldn't deny their skill. She could tolerate anyone if they are profitable. As Snow took on her Caucasian sisters and some Black women that loved her braiding skills, Celestina's clientele consisted of her Latina and Asian sisters. So the Divas had a lot of heads covered. Because Deon had been doing this so long, she could pick and choose. The salon runs itself; Deon rents out booths, she really didn't have to do hair, she just did it because she loved it. A lot of high fashion, drama, and edgy projects came her way since the basics were taken care of on a daily basis. There was plenty of tension in the all-women salon. Deon normally worked in her own secluded studio in the back and the ladies worked in the open space in the front. Ruby was always in and out of Deon's salon when they didn't have clients in their styling chairs.

Deon continued with the forbidden conversation about love in the 21st century in her private studio. "Yes, all these gadgets have a mind of their own. They have all these traps for you or your latest boo. With love, I guess I am a bit old-fashioned. So not only is the chivalry dead, but the mystery is too...which sucks. I swear social media is Pandora's box. No one has to work to get to know anyone. I miss that sacred conversation."

"I still think you should do the show," Kennedy pleaded as she was handed a mirror. "Date your way, not society's."

Kennedy looked in the mirror at the back of her hair and started dancing. "Girrrrllllll, you did that! Thanks boo!" Deon smiled. "You welcome, hun". She was never so happy to see who was walking in. With her bible, notebook and knitting materials, her 9'o clock interrupted *all that nonsense* – at least for a second. I cannot tell a lie, Kyla Withers, came in ten minutes before time. She was a "face," and she had one of the most adorable ones ever seen.

Although Kyla and Kennedy share the same face, the twins grew up in different households after their parents' bitter divorce. Kyla lived with the mom and Kennedy lived with the dad. These sisters, too, had their fair share of fall-outs throughout the years, especially after Kyla's wedding in 2005. But after some push from Deon and the ladies at the salon, they repaired their relationship recently and it was great to see them both in the same room again, acknowledging each other.

Kyla was always on some religious stuff and was the polar opposite of Kennedy. The uber-feminine, stocking-wearing, virgin-bride, Proverbs 31, down for her "can't do no wrong man" type of woman took a seat, almost curtsied as she did it. Now Kyla was a housewife. Although Deon respected this First Lady, especially her being a virgin until marriage, she couldn't really relate to her. Deon's mother could have been a housewife, but she had to do something outside of the house to keep the rest of her sanity.

Soon she was shampooing Kyla's long, feathery locs, her pride and joy. Deon couldn't do too much with the length without her hubby's consent. Kyla never questioned her faith in her man;

44

to Deon, this was a nasty type of allegiance. Her man seemed sweet and sound, but he had a hold on her that must be understood behind closed doors. Even when Deon did her do, she felt she may as well ask what he wants done. "Bless your heart," Deon says to Kyla every time. Sometimes Deon wondered if Kyla worshiped hubby more than God. She hoped not because word is hubby is creeping, *but you didn't hear that from me*. Hopefully, God's protection whispers that she needs to start using protection.

"I am still waiting on you to come," Kyla said to Deon in a half-joking manner. Kyla was always trying to get somebody, anybody to her husband's new church, and her antics work because their church is growing like wildfire. Deon promised that she would visit, but with business cards, not a bible.

Loyal was Kyla's middle name. Anyone in need of a friend is lucky to know her. To Deon, she still wasn't off the hook. After a quick consultation and smalltalk, Deon went right to it.

"So, what are you doing tonight Mrs. Withers?" Deon asked with a sly smile. "Going to church?"

Kyla looked like she had seen a ghost. Finally, she gathered her thoughts.

"Getting out of the house for a minute," Kyla managed.

Deon laughed at the thought of the preacher's wife surrounded by all the smoke and skin-tight dresses floating around. Telling a preacher's wife to go to a secular party is like telling Kyla to go to hell.

Kyla said she loved her blowout. She always gave the biggest tips. They hugged. Soon she was off to her wifey duties. This Saturday morning, these ladies acted as though Deon's wishes were going to be carried out. She deliberately wanted to keep her 30th as low key as possible. Dinner was even a bit more than she desired. She was grateful for Autumn's slip; it gave her enough time to get herself together for the semi-surprise party. She did want to rise to the occasion.

After working on two more heads, Deon replied to a text from her cousin, Noelle. She was hoping she wasn't making a mistake with another favor after going through details with the bride-to-be. Deon, then Ruby, stood on the back stoop for their usual smoke break.

Noelle's wedding happened to be next week...one in which Deon had agreed to be the maid-of-honor and one that she had agreed to let take place at her elegant estate, the one the family dubbed, Queen D's Castle. To Deon, weddings AND funerals were saunas, bringing out all the toxins, through salty tears. She avoided them as much as she could, but her line of work made it nearly impossible.

As the smell of embers filled Deon's insides, she stood...exposed to recycled havoc, over and over again. Fumes seeped in, causing Deon's spirits to suffocate, positivity to be polluted and soon dissipated. Deon was hung up on the idea and shackled to it too. In her mind, she managed to loosen the toxic noose. Soon her hands would follow, she hoped. Soon she'll step away from the gallows. But until that day, puff puff. She was so caught up, she forgot to ask Ruby about the party. She wasn't in the mood to see anyone else squirm with lies.

"So are you going to do Kennedy's dating show?" Ruby squealed. "From what I gathered, Kennedy's show is like *The Bachelorette*, but you actually *see* Black people. I heard Dr. Lynne is on board. I love her books."

"Is that the question of the day? All I did was agree to check out Kennedy's proposal, to see if it's worth it, money-wise."

"Business expansion?" Ruby asked.

"Right. Now, if she wants to capture my professional life, yeah, great. You know? That is what I truly love. But since she wants me outside of my comfort zone, the money has to be right. I don't know if she has it on that level yet."

"Some opportunities can open doors to others," Ruby shared.

"Right, although I am skeptical, any check is better than no check. I still want to add a spa to the salon and it may be good timing since the other shows I was working with for years ended when the producer decided to move to the Bay Area," Deon shared.

Deon and fellow licensed aesthetician, Romeo, had met in high school and kept in touch years after, which led to them joining forces for the make-over show. He delved more into the

47

fashion side while she stuck to the hair and make-up. They made good TV and the videos went viral and both were offered a deal, but the show would be filmed in LA. Deon only like being featured as a correspondent on local shows. Romeo thought it was a great idea, but he wasn't offered the part as a solo act.

"Jetta moved?" Ruby asked.

"Yes ma'am. Girlfriend actually wants me to fly out to LA to do her make-up and hair for some event photos."

"She knows you're the best at what you do, but, if it's not her wedding, I think that is extreme."

"You and me both. I mean, when I say, J offered to take care of all traveling expenses, I couldn't help but laugh. She doesn't know me too well. I've been all over the world; I just *hate* traveling."

"I can't believe she left on a whim," Ruby said, still looking surprised.

"I can. *No husband. No kids.* Just dreams. Why not? It was only so much she could do here with her company and her way of thinking. Silicon Valley is a good fit. If Kennedy knows what's best for her, she'll move too. Maybe to LA or DC. Luckily, this pace and space works for me," Deon said.

"Might as well since drama can't be escaped," Ruby added.

"I know when I did some work in LA, there was buzz about me opening a salon there. I was like, I'm good. Plus, I got so much that has accumulated over the years I don't feel like packing! Especially not to fit it all in no little bitty high-priced apartment. Girl, please."

"You are too much! Well, I have a favor to ask. I know someone who needs your services and she's closer to home, Madison, my dear friend for eighteen years, wants her make-up done for her wedding that is in two months. And she just adores you."

"Does she not know, after wedding 300, I retired from the bridal party game, *period?* I refuse Ruby, I don't even know why you entertained that! Noelle's is the last of these things. Just can't take it anymore."

"Yes, we have seen a lot of Bridezillas in our day and in the salon, but she is super-sweet," Ruby claimed. "I still think you should reconsider."

"Doing her make-up?"

"Well, yeah, but I also feel you need to not turn down the dating show either. Why would you not venture out? I think it will be good for you."

"No, to the wedding. And as far as the show, I don't know about that. Being over-exposed has never been my thing."

"Really?" Ruby looked shocked.

"Bitch, don't play me," Deon laughed. Ruby chuckled. "I guess. I just wonder how you are going to break the news."

Deon let out her deepest breath. "By just telling *her* like it is. Just not today." Making hard decisions was the story of many business women. Deon wanted one night off from all that. Just one night and then she'd gladly be back to business. Besides, she'd be a fool to not celebrate such a monumental year in one's life, even though she felt there was something missing, or better yet, someone.

Mannerisms

Traffic moved in a sluggish manner on

the Houston highway. On the road home, Deon was realizing that forgetting her iPod at home was a true mistake. *How did she put it?* - loud, old ass, young acting deejays really got on her last nerves so she had to *play deejay* in her Mercedes to avoid them.

Miss Independent by Neyo was on a station. The last time she heard this song, she was riding in the car with bold-face lying/jobless, "God told me not work" invited her to dinner, then got mad when the bill came, Isaac. When this guy popped in her head, the tune turned her stomach, so she turned the station.

She smiled when the voice of hometown girl, Beyonce entered her speakers. She sung along to *Diva*. What a relief, but after a couple of seconds, it suddenly struck a chord when she remembered dating Patrick, now Patricia. Ugh. That was his song too, now she knew why.

Okay, let's try this again. She turned the station. As big as the city is, there weren't too many stations.

Neyo's *She Got her Own* was playing. That can't do any harm, right? she thought. It was alright until she remembered the video playing as her ex Renaldo felt okay eating the last Twinkie left in her pantry. Deon loved her Twinkies. But the killer part is not that; when they went to his place, he acted like he couldn't share his. *Stingy Ninja!* she said, as she shook her head while pressing the button for another station.

She snapped out of it as *Superwoman* by Alicia Keys almost pacified her until she remembered Morgan. Morgan said this was his theme song alright. Deon figured she should have known since he later wanted her to save him from foreclosure. The nerve, she shook her head. "Do I look like a bank?"

The man montage that just went through her mind panicked Deon. This wasn't like her - being sentimental and all. Her twenties were dead and delayed reactions plus no satisfaction, made it make sense to look ahead to the one who promised her love at 30. He was great in bed, he was financially stable and he walked like a god. She lightened up.

Her hands were tired and she settled on a Leela James' cover of *It's a Man's World*.

She rolled her eyes. "I concur," she said while throwing her free hand up in the air. She ignored the man in the car to her left who was trying to flirt while driving.

She let her ears listen to the truest thing on the radio. *Talk about mind-control.*

Once home by 6 pm, she was scrolling down birthday blessings from family in New Orleans, bday wishes from acquaintances on her Facebook timeline and messages from strangers who flooded her inbox with flirty advances.

She had so many people to thank...so she decided she would respond the next day...*so she thought.* In the hour left, she made time to do what any cosmetic junkie would - she beat her face, the way any straight girl drag queen would. She was MACed out, femme fatale style. Once she planted her occasional mole, she put away her cosmetics and she pulled up her opera length gloves, adding that touch of drama to the ensemble. In the mirror, she posed in a Burlesque pin-up meets Rockstar look for the evening and posted a selfie on Twitter, Facebook and Instagram.

Ruby arrived at 9:00 that night. Ruby insisted on chauffeuring the birthday girl around, but driving luxury was not Ruby's priority like it was Deon's. When the rubber hit the road, Deon swore she could feel every little element outside of her economic sedan and vowed never to sit in her car again. She also added how Ruby didn't have XM or an iPod or even good CDs. She had radio and a tape deck. So riding with her was far from a treat. Deon insisted on driving, and they both headed to Deon's garage. They were almost out the door when Deon stopped by the mirror.

"Alright Diva, what more can you do?" Ruby chuckled. Deon knew that Ruby did her make-up but without all the works, so it figured. *Oh Baby* was the only lip gloss Ruby owned. And her basic black dress was probably from Ross, her favorite store. *You can't tell her anything,* thought Deon. That's cool. Deon felt they could always agree to disagree, especially since Ruby was different from the "die-easy" fair or foul weathered friends Deon had acquired over the years. She was faithful, so Deon knew if she celebrated with anyone, it had to be her. She was starting to see the importance of quality versus quantity when it came to folks in the circle.

As she smiled, something she rarely did, her pearly whites were free of colorful residue. Next, she checked lashes and the smoky-eye; they were still on point. She quickly combed her vampy nails through her bangs, tousled the straight jet black strands and her layers fell into place. She had been rocking the Egyptian for a decade, *maybe I'd change after tonight...maybe not,* she thought to herself. The lips were perfectly stained with MAC Russian Red but she applied a bit of clear gloss while reluctantly humming Lady Gaga's *Just Dance.*

"You're flawless. I don't even know why you double check," Ruby continued.

"You know seeing is believing, girl." Another selfie was taken and posted to Instagram. She tweeted the pic before putting her phone in her clutch purse.

Deon pressed the button for the garage door and both were getting in the car but as the garage door lifted, Deon couldn't believe her eyes. To her surprise, a sleek limo was waiting outside.

"You have really outdone yourself!" Deon said as she strutted to the limo. Seconds later, she was seeing Kennedy, Autumn and KYLA inside!

"You ain't seen nothing yet," Kennedy promised.

The ladies were letting the music take over in the limo. The ride was smoother than silk. In her Gucci dress, one that fit like a glove, Deon was trying to hold tight, since she was sitting on secrets. While sliding around on the leather seats, what was *really* surprising...she was *actually* excited about the night.

Occasionally, she looked out at the city's beautiful skyline. For January, it was warm for winter, not much of a surprise for Houston, but she brought her black fur just in case the temperature dropped. The night was clear and the roads were packed. The limo inched along the highway; they got closer to their Downtown exit. Deon grew antsy, dying to know where the party was. Once on Main, sitting at one light after the next, one could see the out-and-about, artsy, dressed-in their-finest, cultured elitists who subscribed to events of the Museum and Theatre District. Then there were the *easy-to-entertain* subscribers of Red Box, who could be seen outside of any drug store all hours of the day.

It was ten o'clock. All of a sudden, the ladies wanted to blindfold Deon.

"Is this necessary?" Deon asked laughing. As they carefully got her out of the car, Ruby tried out all her little white lies to explain why they were at a different place than where she had said they'd go. Deon played along.

As the ladies walked down Main, there were several long lines of people waiting to get inside different clubs. The girls showed their invisible *too-fine-for-the-line* card and strutted past.

All the Belles and Whistles

It costs everything to win and everything to lose. In my mind, you might as well at least try to give it your all.
– Maya Angelou

"**S**urprise!!!" Amongst a sea of people, Deon's blindfold was removed and she was embraced by her other salon girls: Sista Snow and Celestina stood with at least twenty current clients.

Overwhelmed, Deon walked into the club and the lights from the cameras flashed her blind. When her eyes adjusted, her little black book came alive right before her. Familiar faces greeted her with shouts, smiles and grins that you could hide daggers behind. Embraced with more hugs and showered with compliments by too many to count, she could barely take a step further. Luckily she was great with names. *Becoming 30 may not be that bad by the looks of things.* It was time to celebrate! That is until she saw an infamous blogger. Gabby, from *Gift of Gab,* with her Canon Rebel was snapping away. She feeds 2.0 million cult followers gossip every month. Girlfriend is a college drop-out from Deon's alma mater too. *You would think she'd lay off of me, certainly not,* Deon said to herself. Deon didn't consider herself a celebrity, but Gabby did and boy did she feature Queen D a lot.

57

And Deon hated that she kept catching her bad side. *A little to the left please.* Deon was pissed that Gabby didn't even say happy birthday. *Bitch, why you here?* Deon frowned thinking to herself and pushed her mind back to the bright side. Plenty of her people from the salon were present, from workers to clients to corporate sponsors and she was actually delighted to see them.

Larry and Tami Gunt, who supplied Deon's first business loan eight years ago, handed her fresh flowers. "Aww, thank you guys so much!" Deon always stated that they are good, good people. She'd always say, *they just don't make 'em like that anymore.* She appreciated how they really gave her a chance, before the others did, a chance to build a dream. They were all smiles tonight.

Soon, Deon's mouth was The Sahara and her cheek muscles were starting to twitch after awhile. So many compliments continued, but they were losing their initial effect, their shock value, their surprise. Deon hated feeling like a real brat for thinking that. But words weren't as important as actions to her. Quality time counted. That was something money couldn't buy or shape. When they, words and actions, align, that's even better. But she acted appropriately; she kept a pleasant demeanor. Ruby, Sista Snow, and Celestina seemed to be enjoying themselves and Deon admitted they did a decent job surprising her.

"Where am I?"

"Club Sentinel."

Deon's mouth dropped and she could feel her heart pounding as many emotions washed over her. She had never been. This was...Q's club...Maybe this was fate...their destiny awaited. The pact that they had made years ago...maybe the stars were aligned?

As TI's *Live Your Life* pumped through the speakers, the girls sung Rihanna's part. Deon was led to the reserved VIP booth, a luxurious spot that they fit into perfectly.

"Wow, I had no idea!" Deon told her niece, making her laugh. Autumn had to have played a huge part in getting some of these people together, being that she was the only person who had access to that many of Deon's personal and professional contacts.

"We have been keeping it a secret for two months now!" Snow squealed as she gave the ladies high fives!

"That was the longest ride ever," Ruby laughed. Deon agreed.

"At least you didn't have blindfolds on. That was the longest walk ever," Deon said.

"This place is packed!" said Kennedy, ready to hand out promo print materials.

"Yes, it is," Kyla said sheepishly.

Deon felt like she had seen one third of Houston, but Quincy McKnight, the owner of the club, was *still* not in sight. Both the club and he were the talk of the town, and of course, Houston was massive. Q was what she called him. Double D, then later DeeDee is what he called her. These weren't exclusive pet names, but rather busy business folk IDs. Where was he? She swallowed her disappointment as she continued to sit on the comfy-cushioned seats shaped in a semi-circle. In her seat, she danced to one jam after the other. The deejay was on point and she guessed he knew she was enjoying the music. Until she got some drinks, the music would save her.

The biggest shocker of the night was Kyla. She was present, but uneasy in the smoky club. She probably had an early curfew as well as an invisible, unsigned permission slip hanging over her head, Deon thought.

"I can't believe you were able to make it," Deon squealed. Kyla kept nervously playing with the ends of her long, soft cascade curls; she probably was silently reciting just about every appropriate scripture she knew in regards to *living in, but not being of the world* Deon thought as she asked her was she okay. She shook her head no and answered yes.

"That just goes to show how important you are to me," Kyla said to the stylist.

"Aww, that makes my night, Kyla," Deon smiled. "But let me know if you need to go."

"Will do. Now I know I will be seeing you in church soon, right?"

Deon smiled and turned her attention to Autumn's thick, auburn, unruly tresses. They were as natural as she was. Her crinkly curls were getting in her drink as she sipped.

"I knew you were going to mess your hair up somehow!" Deon laughed. Autumn looked down and tried to dry her tips.

Deon was grateful that her clients along with stylists, didn't know of her history with Q. They were two discreet people, *maybe too much when it came to one another* Deon started to think as she came to terms with some things. Deon thought about New Year's; her resolution list was pretty intense, even for her. Butterflies in her stomach reminded her of her college days. What was that moment going to be like when their eyes reunited, especially knowing what they had planned for this era?

"Shout out to our Birthday Girl. The Queen is officially in the building!" said the deejay.

Deon gave a smile and a pageant wave as cheers echoed in the building. Deon didn't see the 50's style cake that was brought over to the table or the pile of gifts and card envelopes.

"Happy Birthday Mama! Drinks on us!" he continued.

"That's all I needed to hear!" Deon said.

No shying away, just straight-up staring, creepy Gabby kept her eye on Deon like true stalkers do. Deon got Ruby's attention. "Lately, she has been following my every move, J. Edgar Hoover style." Ruby laughed while Deon remembered that even the day that she conjured up a meeting with Q. She checked the gossip site afterwards, hoping to not see the disaster in disguise. So far, she was relieved to have not seen anything salacious, *yet*. The look in Gabby's eyes tonight said something spicy was brewing. Deon was certain to not let this baby shark take a bite out of her.

"That's her?" Ruby asked for clarity. "I heard she was making a career out of that...blogging thing." Deon laughed. "Blogging thing. You sound so old right now. But yeah, she is doing something called riding off her own hype. And I'm not hating either. If she wrote some credible stuff then I could respect her hustle, but the chick is breaking up married couples and hooking up mistresses. I know I am officially old-er but I have never been one that was anti-new. With all these social media gigs, like the old-heads who looked down on hip-hop and said it wouldn't last, I do think that this medium very well may be here to stay, forever plus reposts. But when all you produce is sensational versus substance, is it really worth it? So she just has a lot to learn, that's all," Deon stated.

Under her breath, Deon added. "And anyone who takes pics of your every move needs to be shot...eye for an eye."

Reality Check

*Love doesn't hide. It stays and fights. It goes the distance.
That's why love is so strong. So it can carry you all the way home.
– Pietro Aretino*

On the dance floor, in the elaborate club, Deon's heart continued to pound louder than the speakers playing her favorite jams. Being the life of the surprise party felt Herculean. After hearing a thousand *Happy birthday Deons* at every twist and turn, she was feeling heavy...drained...and school-girl giddy. She continued to party in the heart of Downtown, the place to be, ignoring the feeling that Club Sentinel felt like the biggest no-no of all. This was THE night. *At midnight, the clock will strike and I, Deon DeVaulle will be officially grown and sexy,* she laughed at the thought.

Dancing with the salon girls, Deon's eyes jumped from subject to subject. Photographic memory kicked out names and experiences she would rather forget.

Heavy-hitters were present making it easy to ignore the wannabes who stood out like a sore thumb, holding on to the event fliers like memorabilia, desperately looking around trying to be found or *find*.

Then there was one ex after the next...There was Butch, who tattooed Deon up in '99; Tracey, the Chef who could make a *mean* lasagna from scratch but scratched himself when he made it; Biker boy, Marlon was generous with rides on the back of his red Harley; Amy, the HotYoga instructor, and Juan, the former Drug Dealer, "*I thought he was in jail,*" she frowned. One uncanny thought went through the birthday girl's mind as she saw a montage of men and women scattered in the club: Deon thought to herself, *after so many no's, I just can't wait to say yes.* Saying "no" was easy. She had said "no" to Frank, the Atheist; Casper, thinks he's the new Millennium Disciple; Bob, the Bedazzler; DeAngelo, thinks his smile replaces hard work; Van, thinks everyone works for the Feds; Steve, the Seat Filler; Nat, the Anti-Dreamer and Taylor, thinks we have all day. Seemed like all her exes *did* live in Texas and she was far from happy with the *past-packed* present. She had a rule in love...do not go back. But she was finding out the hard way that no new faces made it hard to move on.

An array of former dates and a calendar full of weddings to attend was never a good combination. It was hard to escape the idea of love. Deon shut the formers out of her mind. Moving forward was all that mattered to her and she'd be 30 in due time. Not one for self analysis, she was more into self exploration. *I know who I am. I am a Queen waiting for her King.* She tried to convince herself, for she had never had to look before and besides, they had history.

She stopped herself from *looking* for Q, the former buddy, who was also reaching the big 3 0 later in the month. Two

Capricorns. Two head honchos. Two University of Houston Cougars Alumnus. Two Business Management Majors. Two peas in a pod.

Seems like just yesterday, but it was actually their junior year in college when the two exhibitionists were underneath the bleachers. At that very moment, Deon's back itched as she remembered the stinging blades of grass that rubbed up against her body as the man who wore that number 10 Coog jersey, did as well.

Football practice was over and all the other players were long gone. Till this day, how she ended up underneath Quincy was still a mystery to Deon. Nothing else mattered at the time - not even the dewy, humid air that stuck her freshly-relaxed hair to her face. At moments like this, which were routine for them then, all she valued was how perfectly their bodies stuck together in the moisture of it all, considering that the perfect fit is hard to find.

Suddenly, Deon felt her stomach drop. Her face burned when a tall, dark, beautiful woman with an exotic presence, walked toward the ladies room.

Deon's eyes squinted as she watched the woman with her hair slicked back in a Sade chic ponytail, waltz through the club, like it was her party. Her tropical print, light-as-a-feather maxi dress flowed gracefully, effortlessly. She was the woman that Q let ruin their meet-up. This was the woman she despised with all her heart. Never had Deon felt so inadequate in another woman's presence. She was not the jealous type, but this woman made her angry. Trying desperately not to let Nadia Masters ruin anything else was hard. Yes, she was a jaw-dropping goddess, but the stuff Deon found out about her was appalling and *downright criminal*. Deon was sure that Q did not know of the Black Widow's past. So she, armed with plenty ammunition, was about to share some info, but was caught off guard with an outburst from the talk of the town, Kennedy James.

Beaming, while swaying her hips to the island beat, Kennedy looked up from her iPhone, here and there. She yelled over the music, "Girl, you should see all the responses to your comment on the *Dating Deon* blog!" She called herself screening potential cast for her reality show pilot, on the dance floor.

Omg! Here she goes with this Houston's Most Eligible Bachelorette show again; Deon cringed. Beyond annoyed, especially because a pet peeve of hers was guys who had "internet courage", but in person were more mice than men, Deon kept dancing. She had even seen a couple of these types of suitors in the club that night.

"Kennedy, let me show you why I don't give a damn about what they say online." Deon placed her hands on Kennedy's shoulders and maneuvered her to see whoever she was talking about.

"Some guys who talk all day on social media, have no social skills. Look." Deon turned Kennedy to face a man who looked like he was caught off guard by the women's stares. "Over there, look at the wallflower, Berlin, an art festival director. From my

Facebook profile, he wanted me to be a board member, just like that. He didn't know me from jump, and when we met up, I realized that he didn't know how to run a meeting even if they had put a gun to his head. It was painful sitting there, being respectful as I watched paint dry. But there he is over there. Even in this setting, he was rather quiet. Hadn't heard a single peep out of Mr. Boss man all night. But he sure has a lot to say online."

Deon looked around, then Kennedy turned to the next guy.

"Exhibit B - this one, Jack, a hustling self-published author who wants me on his panel for his next book launch. I have read his opinions and boy does he make me mad, blaming everything on Eve. I doubt he knows anything about the opinions I have. I doubt more that he actually wants to know. He seems like the type that just looks versus listens. He's asked me just about the same three questions over and over again. But tonight, he's rather quiet too."

Kennedy was turned a little to the left.

"Oh, and if it ain't Rapheal. I want to go over and ask him how in the hell he made it to the club. Homeboy is pictured in a different homeboy's wedding like every other weekend. I'm sure he just wanted a date when he got in touch with me those different times. On Instagram he asked me why I wasn't married yet, right under my selfie. Then proceeded with, 'Didn't I know how old I was?' I said, yes, the same age as you, fool. Are you married yet? But the main thing with him is that he is always going out of town, but brother's car is always in the shop when he wants us to go somewhere. I am not sure how he thinks we are going to get there...but I never liked perpetrators and I certainly won't be driving a bum around town. Certainly not. So I have stopped answering all of his calls, texts, and inbox messages. He's fly online...Purely disgusting offline."

"Let's see, who else do I recognize from The World Wide Web." Deon's eyes opened wider when she spotted another guilty bystander.

"And there goes Simeon, a distinguished documentary filmmaker, wants me in his next project for women who are too pretty to be...truly loved. Since he doesn't seem as bold in person, I'm not taking bold chances on him attaching my face to that project. Call me superstitious, but that sounds like what I won't be doing."

Kennedy was getting dizzy.

"Then there is Froy."

"I get the point." Kennedy pleaded, but Deon was on a roll.

"Oh, no, you don't. Oh, Froy, can't forget him. I rarely go out with Facebook people, but he was a childhood friend of one of my closet friends from college. She shared how he loved my pics but once we actually talked, he never said why he wanted to get to know me, no wooing me whatsoever, just straight up wanted me to visit his home in Katy. Girl, I played trifling, ghetto, you name it. Told him I didn't have any gas then he felt the need to treat me like a chicken-head over the phone in front of his boys. I am so glad I saw his true colors beforehand. I sure wish he would talk all that mess tonight. He'd get clocked. But he sure had some balls over the phone."

"There is Norm. He has a radio show, late at night, playing oldies and goodies. But I wasn't hearing him. He lacked guts to be new and bold and ask a girl out for real, for real. 'Maybe we can do lunch,'" Deon blurted out mocking him. "Boy please. Maybe we can do nothing."

"I see, I see," Kennedy said smelling the liquor on Deon's breath.

"I am not finished yet. I see Bo over there. He's a lawyer who wants to do good in the hood. Indirectly, he told me I am too high and mighty, not realizing...that I just don't want to help those who don't want to help themselves. Yep, I said it. I have a thing against community service projects and social work for lazy ass folk. That is someone else's job and I don't think it's a bad thing if I leave the missionary work to those who signed up for it and are called to do it.

Deon turned Kennedy all the way around to face her. "Just because you like someone's picture doesn't mean you like them, or worse, they like you...looks can be deceiving."

Kennedy started, "I know Facebook is the po man's dating site. *Shucks,* I don't even entertain any of those lusty inboxers either. This *is* a legit dating site. I can assure you will have a quality dating experience."

"Internet-induced relationships are unnatural to me and I prefer bumping into potential loves in real life. At least we know what we are *really* getting. Period. Kennedy, why...are you looking at that mess right now anyway?"

Never had Deon taken the online dating experience to heart, although she flirted with the idea in the past. The idea of putting out in black and white what she was about, seemed like the best route, but it still played out poorly.

"Deon, you just don't understand how this is the real deal. I really interviewed some really good guys. They are ready for the real deal. These many men applaud you for who you are and your reason for being single. So yes, they are of course attracted, but not only physically." Kennedy updated Deon on her stats.

Damn, why am I always hit with that subject everywhere I go? The last thing the birthday girl wanted to see was something so trivial. *Was I the last solo act standing? Certainly not!*

"They all want me to hook them up on a date with you so *they* can show you a good man, no games. The demand alone is there. So girl, I don't know why you are not supplying yet."

Deon couldn't find the words, well she could, but she didn't want to cuss. She was desperately trying to make the night a good one. A great one.

Popping the Question

Man proposes, God disposes – proverb

Still yelling over the music, the ladies continued.

"You are perfect for this and you know it. Plus, I have been known to be quite the matchmaker."

"Really? That is news to me!" Deon said.

At one time, she did let people, good people, hook her up. But one hook-up from hell after the other, and far too many *wish you really were blind* blind dates, she saw this as a no-no. Lancelot and Toby came to mind.

Even outside of hook ups, Deon was starting to not trust her own judgment when it came down to it.

Maximillian had swag. He worked in retail most of his college days and knew how to dress his butt off, but his man'boobs couldn't be ignored. Deon tried to not react loudly in the movies when he tried to feel her up. She was super grossed out. "Hey dude, help yourself to your own cleavage." She said when she got up and walked out the theatre.

Even Roland was cool, but rarely in town because of his job. When sober, he saw how great she was. If home, he wanted her to compete with Jack Daniels.

Approaching a new decade, she was ready for real love, not flings and things. Focused on the one that set such a high bar that no other man has come close to, not even the two after him that pulled out all the stops, she had tunnel vision and would rather tie up loose ends with an old crony, than meet random half-hearted guys.

Deon's savvy stylists, Celestina, Sista Snow and Ruby were starting to get in on the convo.

"If she won't, I will," Sista Snow interjected. "Who you got for the guys?" Snow moved over to check out pictures on Kennedy's phone.

"Look here, we so need Bachelorette in Black!" Ruby chimed in. "So back off!"

Snow looked a bit upset and then amused at another challenge awaiting.

"Snow, stop being horny for a minute and think; have you seen any women of color on these type of shows?" Ruby continued.

Kennedy's smile indicated she is hearing exactly what she wanted, but Deon could care less about being a spokesperson for something outside of her control especially considering all the complexion complexities she had grown up dealing with. She was not here to change the world. Anything she did, she did because she really just wanted to make money. She ignored the PSAs on the dance floor and started to get back in the groove she was losing.

"I love you Snow, but she is right. You know the message that is sending, right? That we, as Black women are undateable...out of sight, out of mind. Then the trashy train wreck shows that are featuring women of color are close to being jokes with no punchline," Kennedy validated. "We need more diverse representation in reality TV."

Celestina and Sista Snow didn't look as offended.

Celestina chuckled. "But Deon doesn't even look like the average Black woman. People don't even know what she is. So you still are sending out a message that doesn't really matter."

Both Ruby and Deon met eyes before looking away.

"Girl. She don' opened up a can of worms tonight," Ruby said to Deon.

"Or whoop ass," Deon said, pissed to be interrupted again. New Year's resolutions were hard to keep. After clearing her throat, she gave a strong pout. "All my life I had to fight. I had to fight Blacks. I had to fight Mexicans. I had to fight Whites. I had to fight Straights. I had to fight Dikes. Girl child ain't safe in a place full of color-struck haters. I never ever thought I would have to fight my own stylists," she said in her best Sofia impersonation. She started to make boxing fists and squared herself to the women.

The ladies all burst into laughter. Even Deon.

"Shit, these aren't boxing gloves, but they will work," Deon said.

Kennedy took back the wheel. "Stereotypes kill too many people. There is no one way to be black you guys. That is the problem in modern media and in Black culture. Deon is someone who knows who she is. That is what we need. Plus, it's an opportunity to keep this convo going and opportunity for the city. Hey, this may even be Autumn's big break writing for television."

Autumn looked more assertive than ever and Deon was happy for her, but was tired of being the nucleus of so many dreams. Suddenly Kyla was seen frantically trying to carry all of the ladies' clutches without dropping them in the packed club as she came toward them. Kyla looked like she was beyond ready to go. They all took their bags, thanking her for watching them for the time being.

"I get the whole race void being filled, but personally, I just don't know about me being right for that type of show, considering I am undateable. At least, that is what e-harmony.com said, of course, ever so nicely."

The ladies laughed. Deon was glad they thought she was joking.

"Then it's that Dr. Lynne." Deon frowned a bit, sickened at how so many ladies kissed this lady's butt, as if she were God's gift to women. "What can she tell me? She does not have a man. And plus, a beautician is the doctor women can afford. There have been so many women in my chair day after day, clearing their heads and asking and getting advice they need. I need to start charging for fixing two heads instead of one," Deon argued.

Kennedy continued. "I really want you to read the proposal."

Deon laughed. "Not quite the type I was hoping for tonight."

Kennedy continued, "I already have four major sponsors interested in backing the project. You don't have to be "perfect" literally to be perfect for a show. You just need to be you, Deon. The guys want you. The women want to be like you." She eyed Sista Snow and Celestina before they could attack. "You just have to be open, honest and responsive...plus, I can get you a fat check!"

"Now we're talking." Deon was finally understanding where she fit in.

Kyla shook her head and began her sermon to who she thought were the sad and single. "Ladies, a man is supposed to find you."

"Right Kyla, the man who is interested in the woman signs up," Kennedy refuted. "The woman determines whether or not she

76

wants him. She looks at her options and selects the best candidate. That is something some married women don't understand, don't do, but need to. Just because a man asks for your hand in marriage, you should have a say in who is the best hand to hold...unless you don't have choices."

Kyla's eyes bucked.

"Wow, IS this an electoral process too?" Snow asked. "You ladies are so complicated."

All this talk was starting to be too much and too upsetting for the private Deon. Lately, mixing work with pleasure was not working. *If only love was that simple,* she thought. So many thoughts were occupying her mind. What happened to having a good time? *Why couldn't I do this?* Looking too cute to be looking stressed, she knew she had to get away from this dialectic nonsense. Plus, after all those drinks and all that twerking, she had to go to the ladies room. Fast!

After excusing herself from the girls, Deon made a run to the restroom, barely seeing the brothers making a beeline to her.

The Proposal

Philosophical habits of mind do not come quicker through fiber optics. Clear thinking is not aided by better dot resolutions. Understanding ourselves and feelings of others does not come with a software upgrade.
– Linda Ray Pratt

I *need to make it in time; otherwise, urine is about to be*

streaming down my leg, Deon thought...then, it happened. A suave man appeared. Her eyes delightfully explored him...Who knew a man could be *beautiful, still...*His body looked like it was made of precious stone and dipped in delicious milk chocolate. The three piece suit never made him, he did it a *huge* favor. And the fedora added to his mystique. He was still the poster child for charisma. It wasn't one particular thing, but an overabundance of details that drove her crazy. Like a symphony, all the drama, the sensuality, the mellow undertones came together so effortlessly and in the most alluring way. Even in discomfort, his presence made Deon forget why she was squirming and wiggling seconds before. A smile spread across her face. She had been waiting to feel like this again, for what seemed like a lifetime. Determined to win the battle of mind over matter for the hundredth time, the panic inside quieted. Stopping in her tracks, all she could think was *Please don't pee on yourself.* Not a good look.

Since the last meet up, he had grown a goatee that was very becoming. Trying not to get lost in his dreamy face was pretty hard. He had the smoothest skin she had ever seen or felt, the kind that tons of clients wished they had, a complexion so clear.

So much went through her mind. *Where do I start?* So she just stood there for a second. So did he, like an *idiot,* she thought.

"Hey stranger," she said.

"Happy Birthday Deon!" Quincy McKnight managed to say. All she could do was look at his sexy lips, the ones she couldn't wait to be reacquainted with, then it hit, *my goodness, he got formal with me*. Couldn't remember him ever saying *Deon*. Could not imagine him ever being so...distant.

"I hope you enjoy yourself," he said generically and gave a limp hug. Sensing uneasiness in someone she was more than familiar with made him a sudden foreigner, without real conviction.

Deon pushed aside the disheartening feeling forming inside of her because she wanted a word with the man who owed her a conversation and now an apology; he seemed to not hold up his end of their pact. Not sure what came over her, but against her better judgment, she batted her eyes. "Can I talk to you for a moment, in private?"

Reluctantly, Quincy signaled for her to follow him upstairs. To get away from the noise was a gift in itself. As they walked upstairs to one of the offices, she followed, wondering why she was being treated like the many women she heard venting in the salon chair. It broke her heart with every step. She wondered, *Am I supposed to ignore the pact that we made?*

While trying to keep it lady-like walking up the steep, carpeted stairs that were far from heel-friendly, she relished in the thought that she knew Nadia's dark past. She held onto the rail tightly and clinched her v-muscles while looking to see how many steps were left. Finally leveled, the two passed a restroom on the way to the office. *Great.*

"What is going on?" he asked, once in one of the vacant offices. Quincy looked confused but he gave his undivided attention.

"You know, I went to great lengths for us to come together and chat for a little," she recalled the meet-up a while back at the coffee shop where Q first saw Nadia and became infatuated with her right then and there.

Quincy stood, as if he had nothing to add. Could it be that the scandalous beauty had stripped him of all his common sense? Could the cat really have his tongue? Was he still under that spell? She didn't know. All she knew was that she was tired of being denied access. His lukewarm attitude was disgusting to her and she wanted more from him. She was going to get to the bottom of the arrangement because she just could not take it anymore. The pace was slower than she ever imagined. This woman that had come into his life recently created this paradigm shift, this memory-loss monster. *Oh hell no,* she thought. Did he forget the *verbal contract?* Her blood pressure started increasing. *The internal investment?* Her blood started to boil. *The potential profit?* Now she was fuming like a car with a bad radiator. Was she making an absolute fool of herself in the name of...*love?* She had barked and now she was getting ready to bite. She was done with the teasing. Lies. False advertising. A breach of trust. The decency had left his body. Hopefully the truth hadn't.

Deon snapped.

"What in the hell is wrong with you? Don't you have something to say...You know what today represents? Your big idea..."

Her heart was pounding. *Who did he think he was, rejecting me for some loony-tune outsider?* And it seemed that since she could not release her bladder, her glass eyes melted right before Quincy's. Shieldless she stood. He appeared worried. She never cried. She felt sicker. She never cried.

"Didn't have to be this way...but you asked for it," Deon said.

"I know you have been celebrating your birthday and I know you enough to know when you have some drinks in your system." Quincy started. Deon rolled her eyes; she hated when guys acted paternal. *I have a damn guardian. I know my limit and I hadn't come close to reaching it. I just want you to be honest asshole!*

She was seeing red, then green..."So what is it about her pussy that has you so strung out, huh!?" Deon shouted loud enough for the great state of Texas to hear.

Quincy just shook his head, offended, disappointed.

"You can't have everything you want, Deon," he said firmly.

Was he serious? Deon had deleted her electronic black book months ago and was willing to turn in her card for *him*! Shaking uncontrollably, she continued to shout whatever came to mind.

"Look who's talking! Who the fuck are you right now? Acting like that doesn't apply to you!" Deon couldn't believe this was the conversation they were having, especially on *her* night.

"Look, what we had, we don't have anymore. Don't try to make something out of nothing, please, not now," Q said.

The music was still blasting downstairs and Deon wanted him to hear. "I know what this is. You couldn't even handle me!" she continued to scream carelessly.

Quincy gave her a blank stare. He then...tried to hold back laughter. Then he turned his back on her and began to walk away. But he stopped in his tracks and turned to face her once more. "I knew I could have you any which way, any day," Quincy said calmly. "I didn't want to."

As the words entered, Deon wanted to run and hide. This is not the same man. She wondered who performed his lobotomy. Deon could not believe what she was hearing, nor did she want to listen any further. As he walked out of her life, she wanted to hit him where it hurt, with the truth. She knew it, didn't want to believe it, but it was time to be set free. So many thoughts ran through her head. *The real Q has left the building and I, as soon as I get to the ladies room, I will be leaving as well. This is the most whack ass club I have ever been at because the owner has no soul.* She didn't want to return to the party; it was over...and she was an emotional wreck...this whole situation was beyond reasoning for her. *How was I going to get home?*

"You have *always* been in competition with me Q. And what for? I...actually...tried to put it aside for you. I compromised...you want to shine so damn much you scared of anyone else's light. It's sad. Deny it all you want, but you can do better, even if it's not with me. What you get from turning these, these ole rags-to-riches broads, project-hoes and mass murderers and shit into your lovers is beyond me!" Black tears were dripping all down her face, her dress and on her swinging hands. "Have some self-respect for goodness sakes. Needy ass women looking for a damn meal ticket, or in your case, the next victim should not be your type."

Quincy stopped in his tracks, with his back turned to Deon.

"I remember the first time you looked at me, before you knew I saw you wanted me. I remember the first time I let you fuck me. You loved every minute of it! Someone who can do stuff in bed that even makes your experienced ass blush."

"I never loved you," he said turning around to face her.

Her thoughts were multiplying by the second...back in the day, if she were an academic course, Q would have gotten an A...he studied her day and night. Almost choking on the bitter taste of her own consciousness, speechless, while so many thoughts continued to have recess in her head, Deon realized, he sounded, like he actually meant it. *Quincy. My Q. My first and only love.* Sounded like he...she swallowed hard, *actually meant it.*

Quincy continued. "What we had was less than love."

"You know you don't believe that," she pleaded.

Quincy shook his head. She didn't understand why he would say these things, after all that they had experienced together. She really wanted to go home. It was over.

"But you take your little...," Deon continued, running out of air.

"Have fun finding what you want!" Quincy said turning back around.

"You have fun running like a lil' bitch! 'Cause your little girlfriend you took to Jamaica, has a couple of reasons to make you sprint." Deon *had* to have the last...word, even if it killed her.

Quincy stopped in his tracks once more.

After a couple of seconds, he walked off. Flabbergasted, she was on to Plan B. She had seen Nadia go into the ladies room downstairs earlier so there was no telling where she was now. Deon was happy she had gotten her cell number from Sheila, a woman who really wanted to work at the salon a while back, but couldn't make the cut.

Once he was gone, she wiggled her way to the restroom, *finally*. The door was ajar due to a doorstop. She ran to the first stall. Normally one to squat in public restrooms, a bit germaphobic, all she could do was plop down on the public seat as her whole life drained out of her. Beyond hurt, and confused, after two minutes, of just sitting, she decided to get up and get her look together. *No loyalty...Love can't even save the day with dudes like that.*

She made her way to a mirror. Never had she looked so...ugly. Her eyes were holes of darkness and her nose was as crimson as Rudolf's. Ignoring the vibrating cell in her clutch, she looked at her tear-stained face.

The rest is history.

Part Two

Queen D Syndrome

Here Today...Gone
Tomorrow

To whom much is given, much is tested
– Kanye West, "Can't Tell Me Nothing"

THE very thought of him made her furious; hate filled her

heart. Now she was single-minded. Earlier, the crook in her neck wouldn't allow her to turn around to see more of the atmosphere, or lack thereof. With intense grit, her mind shifted and muscles in her poker face started to flex, but a frown suddenly formed as terror started to tease her eyes. The more she remembered about the past, the more frantic she felt. She used to be able to sink this stuff.

She put her hope in one man. Who would have thought that her perceived equal would have made her into a freaking statistic?

But I won't go down without a fight. Yes, they came, they saw, they almost conquered. He deceived, led me to believe that he was the answer. I held my breath, wanting to pass the test, I bombed it. I knew in my heart that something just wasn't right, but I didn't want to fight the feeling. Now, I fight for my life.

Officially dumpster diving in this clandestine sewage of schemes and dreams gone bad to rotten, digging for the piece of peace that was once mine. To get back to the top, I may have to crawl, but I refuse to lose! I have to get my mojo back!

She was determined.

Some guys used to think she sabotaged the relationship. If only they knew what she did - *her job*. She had a day job and she had a calling. Her day job was easy. Her calling was *real* work. It's a gift she didn't ask Santa for, that's for sure.

Although she stood still, her mind, like her at the salon, was working overtime. Energy was scarce, but questions on top of questions formed like never before. The pro at suppression, was realizing all the dirt she had vacuumed was resurfacing. Now flooded with even more alarming details, nostalgia hit hard. It seemed like just yesterday. This was no freak accident, this was a crime, and a highly personal one.

All of a sudden, the agony of defeat and the intensity of feeling forsaken far too many times started to work *for* her. She was so hot, it gradually melted the rest of the tautness.

The silent stranger in front of her watched as the mold started to break. Deon's joints were sent into sluggish activity, of course, she was not 100% Deon, but at least she could move parts of her body that seemed lifeless moments before. She knew she was getting somewhere, just slowly. She was thirsty and wanted food, but that could wait because she was practically starving for answers.

Eventually, she swallowed. Her throat was sore and her raspy voice was hoarser than normal, but not weak. "*Who?*" she nearly coughed up a lung. "Did...this...to...me?"

Deon watched the doll continue to stand there.

She came from a place where people stabbed, shot and even beat people to a bloody pulp, but that, *kicking* someone in the back so they could fall down the stairs, was to her, pretty...lame. *I'm not going out like that. Certainly not,* she promised.

Pushing past the paradoxical notion that she probably needed to lie down due to a throbbing lower back, she stood. She couldn't admit to herself that she was scared of this enemy called sleep and what it could do.

"Who?"

Pupil-to-pupil, his eyes seemed to stare right through Deon. Now able to move her neck a bit more, sheepishly, she scanned her surroundings only to find endless white space, beyond recognition. She figured, maybe this person before her didn't have plans, somewhere to be or better yet, people to see, but the sooner she got answers, the sooner she could get back to life. That fall landed her in what looked like a...hospital, the sick smell was stuck in her nostrils.

Beyond fuming, the emotion took over.

As a live victim, she felt like she was in two places at once. *And she was.* For now.

Still at a halt, the person looked right at Deon, as if they hadn't heard her hysterical cry.

"Look here dude...I asked you a simple question. *Who pushed me, damn it?*" He watched her right eye twitching. Her blood was rising and she felt like pushing...him! She couldn't stop her body, shaking fervently in the thin, hideous hospital gown. She looked down once more and examined the flimsy piece of polka dot material. The paper-thin outfit was barely there and itched her far from sensitive skin. She held the ends of the garment so the random wind wouldn't expose her. She knew she had to have lost consciousness at some point in time because she would have never let anyone put this on her. She shook her head. *Big mistake;* the slight gesture was not helpful. She held her hand over the part of her head that throbbed the most.

Reaching back in the corners of her mind to playback a scene did not do any good if answers were not given.

"Talk!" she grunted. He kept quiet.

She frowned and cleared her voice. "Do you have a mirror?"

He pointed to a full length mirror off to her right that she had not seen moments earlier. *Funny how he'll answer that question*, she thought. *I must really need one.*

"I hope no one sees me in this piece of crap." She made her way over. Her sexy shoes from the club made an echoey sound as they hit the marble floor. She saw a black robe on the left and a white robe hanging on the right side of the mirror. Didn't think much of them because when she saw herself, she gasped. Hair was wrapped up in a bandage - to her, an unfashionable turban. She knew it was wrapped to allow healing, but the pain or the shame that followed the fall seeped through the fabric. She scratched and patted the bandage around her head and wondered where her purse had wandered off to; she didn't trust anyone with her belongings. She closed her eyes, not wanting to have to ask another question, but she was about to. When she opened them, the man appeared beside her, on her left. The grave man stood. Still quiet as a mouse. From behind his back, he held her bff, her Louie and he slowly started handing it over. Just when she was starting to get used to the one-note facial expression he displayed, she witnessed the first sign of emotion on his face. She studied him a bit longer before grabbing it. When she finally had it in her hands, she hugged it to her chest and smiled. It was the only sense of comfort she had. Then, she reached in and felt for her cell. *"Where is it?"* she needed to check her doggie cam. Pepper, her poodle, was probably wondering where she was. Also she wanted to change the thermostat in the house and check social media. She also wanted to sneak in some calls since this stranger was acting so peculiar...She finally found it. "My phone is my life!" she kept thumping the screen. She frowned when she realized her phone was dead. Quickly, she perked up. "Oh, my charger! I need to get to it from my car, or my house."

"Rest your pretty little head. You need to come with me."

She couldn't help but grimace. Blinking quickly, she heard his distinct southern drawl that sounded like her folks deep down in New Orleans, Louisiana. Her parents are from the Boot. She was born and reared in Houston, but she would visit her grandparents at the Bed and Breakfast, *Good Morning, New Orleans* located in the French Quarter. Her grandmother was over operations. Deon looked at him closely but still saw a stranger.

"Where?"

"We are going to take a little trip down Memory Lane."

"In these stilettos?" She looked at her red bottoms and the red sores on her feet.

He smiled. "Look in your purse."

Reluctantly, she reached and found some slippers, some she didn't remember feeling before. "These aren't mine." Deon said, pulling out black velvety Mary Janes.

"These are ugly as hell," Deon continued.

"Slip them on because it's going to be a bumpy stroll," he said.

93

"Uhh no, not flats," she whined, "I wouldn't be caught dead in...flats. My head hurts."

"Well, you hit it pretty hard dear."

"Not because of that, but because of all this mystery. Is it really necessary? I want to know like right now! I deserve to know what happened to me last night."

"Yes you do. And in due time, you will know what you need. There aren't any...quick fixes around here."

Suddenly Deon felt relieved he was talking. She felt even more secure with the next thought that popped into her head; she remembered the last time she felt this discombobulated, there was a logical reason. Laughing out loud, wishing she had figured it out earlier, she said. "*Ohh, I get it! This*," she pointed, drawing an air circle, "this whole thing, this is a dream, isn't it? That is why *this* doesn't make sense," she shared while smiling. She started to violently shake herself, like she normally did when attempting to awaken from a nightmare...but it was taking a little too long. The man came over to stop her from increasing the damage.

"It's not that simple, my love. There are so many factors, so many stories, so many truths wrapped in lies. It takes time. We must start at the root."

Deon's eyes searched his. *Root*...she started wondering if he could see the grays she dyed black at the top of her head, but her blonde moment ended soon after, when she remembered the bandages. Deon got lost in his eyes, trying to figure if they were gray or hazel, just like hers. His lashes were thick and long. His formally gray skin was now alive and warm with copper.

"Look at it this way. Rest in knowing that there is one fate, one final fate, one robe to wear, and you my dear, need to use this time we will spend together wisely. You still have time to make the right moves."

The statement chilled Deon to the bone. *Final*? What was this guy talking about? Was he serious?

He was as serious as her condition.

"Why do you think you were targeted Deon?"

"How the hell would I know? That is a question I have. What are you good for anyway?"

She looked around hoping for some landmark and suddenly she heard a shrieking noise. A baby's cry stopped her from continuing the useless interrogation. The piercing scream started to grow so strongly, so profoundly, she could feel a kick inside her stomach, awakening something in her she never believed to be present.

She hadn't placed any puzzle pieces together and neither had he.

"I don't have *all* the answers, love."

"Yeah, I kind of figured that."

"If you give me a chance, I can at least help *you* sort through possibilities so you can figure out how *you* wound up...*here*. I must ask, do you have enemies?"

"Oh, so is this an investigation? Where is your badge, sir?" she laughed. "Enemies, I don't even know where to start with that one. I'm sure there are a handful. The more the merrier...just learned how to use my enemies as my footstools." He eyed the barefoot woman's hand and the stilettos she held.

"So you'd have to check the bottom of my stilettos for DNA."

He tried not to laugh.

She soon realized the part that her mind blocked out moments ago. What happened? "Oh my gosh...we need to find the stilettos that stabbed me in the back. That hurt!"

"Yes, we do, so please, continue."

She stood for a moment, not knowing where to begin. "Although Houston is big, it wants to be a small town...We know how small towns can be, right." Lifting her hands up, she stretched her body as well as she could.

"Do you think this was premeditated or just a spur of the moment type of attack?"

"Obviously, whoever did it wasn't so bright. Public place. My party. But then again, that is the perfect plan, if you can get away with it. Maybe they did it *for* the limelight. Maybe that was the whole point...to throw everyone off, appearing like an amateur. I really don't know. Nothing surprises me anymore." Deon frowned.

"You know, one person does come to mind more so than others. She was at the party. She has many enemies back home in Boston, but she came to Houston to wipe the slate clean. Her employment history is sketchy. She definitely wasn't there to celebrate *my* birthday. She was there to steal my man!"

His eyes lit up as Deon continued.

"The attacker is...probably...Nadia. She has motive. A single black female with a criminal record and a mysterious medical history. An off-the-grid mistress of disguise. Let's find Nadia Masters now!"

Deon was adamant about finding the woman who she hated with a vengeance. She had to have been involved.

"Okay, keep going...We are getting somewhere."

"Are we?" Deon totally needed to breathe. "What time is it?" To her, it felt like it was time for her and Ruby's routine cigarette break. She turned her attention back to the man before her. She looked around the foreign place again.

"Keep telling me your thoughts. We don't have that much time."

She frowned. "Says who?"

"I'll explain as soon as I can. But keep the thoughts coming before..."

Agitated, her hands were stiff and clamming up; she couldn't wait to get in a client's head. Hair is soothing to the skin, she thought. Instead, she felt *she* was being combed through, molded and shaped into this cheap, generic product.

The only psycho babble she needed was retail therapy. Rice Village, Montrose and River Oaks were calling her name. Memorial and the Galleria Mall. She wanted to take a trip to see what the Pearland, Sugar Land and The Woodlands stores had.

If I can't touch fashion, I need to see fashion. Even *Pinterest* would do right now. Her phone was an extension of herself, but it was cut off. Talk about torture. Her eyes were bored with bloodshot thoughts. They needed a muse. She answered the guy as best as she could.

"I was taken by surprise. Caught off guard. Nothing to hold on to. Just kicked in the back, *with a fucking stiletto*. How about that. I just know I was trying desperately not to fall hard of course. Instinct."

She blinked and her eyes started to wander. Not wanting to be looked at with tears welling up in her eyes, she noticed, she could hear another noise. It sounded like clunky jewelry. Like a bracelet being shaken by a madwoman. Nothing seemed to make sense. Her body was a ticking time bomb and only nicotine could stop the explosion.

"Who is this Deon?" a woman's voice came into Deon's ears, similar to an intercom she couldn't locate, since no walls were in sight. Where was the voice coming from? Deon, of course, couldn't understand. And was this a trick question, she wondered.

"Me! Who wants to know?" Deon looked up and around and even down to find no woman at all.

"But *who* are you?" the voice continued.

The guy in front of Deon rolled his moody eyes and looked, overpowered. Deon waited on him to speak.

"You heard it, too?" she asked.

He nodded.

"What is going on man? This is weird as hell."

The ominous woman's voice ruptured into a wicked laugh.

"Why can't you help me more?" Deon begged the silent guy. He just stood there. Her blood was bubbling when there was no answer. Nothing was getting done.

"My questions are simple enough to get answers."

"Okay, it is time to check out some videos, quickly. She's getting closer," he updated.

"Videos?" All of a sudden Deon frowned and looked closely at him. Was he for real? At a time like this, he *wants* to watch movies? She was appalled. "We better not be watching any freaky stuff," she warned.

He looked at her strangely. "Of course not."

"Well what are we watching then? I mean, do you have some type of itinerary for me? It better not be those Hallmark channel movies either...I can't stand those mushy stories. My niece, Autumn, is always gushing over them and the music makes it worse..."

She felt suffocated in obscurity. Movies moved people. Deon didn't want to feel *anymore*. She just wanted to do, retreat to work, make money then go home.

The injuries...the pain...the mysterious voice floating...the robot. One riddle too many. Styling clients was what she knew she was here on this earth for, not being a detective on her own ambiguous case. She needed to return to see what the salon girls were doing and most importantly, what they weren't. And this dude wanted to watch *videos*.

"I know you are a beast," said Deon's annoying android. "You don't make it easy for anyone. I know your track record. But we have some footage we need to go through if you don't mind."

"I do, actually. First of all, how else would Deon's Hair Divas stay on top if I wasted my time like this?" she refuted. Maybe you sit on your ass all day watching movies; maybe you don't have an idea of how to stand on your feet all day, working, styling, managing, creating, promoting, all that good stuff. Excuse me, I am not stopping for anyone, not even the person who has done this terrible thing to me." She stomped as she walked away.

Helpless and in need of a puff, she still had no idea who was responsible for this nightmare. Everything was such a blur, but she kept walking. Behind her, she heard a voice.

"And who is she...the voice?" Of course Deon was ignored.

"Just know that if you listen to me, you are in good hands and I won't let anything happen to you if it's the last thing I do. I just need you to trust me."

Trust?

Deon turned around. "I needed a laugh. I don't even know you. Plus, you seem like you..." Before she could finish, the man took the words literally out of her mouth. This man dropped his southern drawl to mimic her dialect perfectly. "...are out of this world and that is the last type of person to trust. And of all things, trust is the one thing I have never been good at, even with people I know..." He paused before continuing. Deon felt faint.

"What you did was impossible. It was like I was hearing myself, for the first time," she said.

"Need *you* say more?" said the creepy impersonator.

Deon looked around. Was that another recording? "How did you do that? How did you know...what I was about to say?"

"You may not...trust me. But I am trying to help you Deon. I'm not sure you know what you'll encounter if you turn your back on me. But at the end of the day, the choice is yours."

Deon looked around for cameras. "I'm not *famous*, famous, but I *am* national. Am I being *Punked*?"

"Okay," he shook his head. "You are in a toxic-free care center that is here to meet the needs of the person you have become."

Deon was at a loss for words now. She started to think about all of the drunks in her life. About all of the junkies she saw slip away.

"Now, I may drink and smoke, but I am not an addict. I have NEVER had a DUI or anything criminal. There is far more damage being done out there by others than by...me."

"Actually, you are quite blessed to be here."

"You could have fooled me."

"Please don't get defensive. This is not an issue of one thing in particular, but moderation is a needed factor right now. Unlike some people, you have a chance."

"Is this some type of punishment?"

"This is a process of recovery. You were hurt very badly. Your condition is critical and unstable. There is a chance that you can recover and it is my mission to help you do just that. There are different types of treatment. This is a bit experimental, of course. We will explore new methods in this toxic-free environment that will help you deal with inevitable toxic-filled environments."

"I don't need your twelve-step program, I need to get the hell out of here!"

"Yes, you do. And that is not up to me. There are some requirements, Deon, that you will need to meet to be considered cured."

Deon couldn't believe her ears, her eyes.

"One, you cannot associate with some of the people who are in the same situation. Two, you must break away from the substance that landed you here. And three, you must change some habits to help prevent relapse."

"Wow, this is the biggest joke of the century! You sure you're not on something?"

"Re-establishing yourself is the goal."

"I don't have the problem."

"If you don't think you have a problem, let's get the movie rolling. Shall we?"

Deon knew by the tone of his voice that she needed to brace herself. She did, as best as she could. Once again, the guy looked like he was not swindling her. *Uuughhh.*

"Deon, this is the story of your life." Suddenly, a projection screen dropped down from the sky: a still image appeared before the two, unveiling a scene from a hospital; the man smiled and said, "I got something better than 3D and Blu-Ray combined. Check this out." Then there was a small controller that appeared in his hands, like magic. She shook her head in disbelief. He made some corny move, like when basketball players dribble a ball behind their back. *Epic fail.* How lame this evening was going to be with this guy, she thought. But, she had to admit, he was kind of cute.

Before she knew it, the white surroundings dimmed to gray then to black. When her eyes adjusted, she could see him pressing buttons and then all of a sudden she could hear that same shrieking noise from earlier, one she dreaded daily. A baby's cry surround-sounded them. She quickly looked at the screen, buck-eyed.

"Hey, I never saw this video!" She was realizing she didn't know this guy's name. "How do you have this footage? What is this? *Nineteen Eighty-Four?* She looked around for Big Brother. I didn't give anyone the rights for my life to be made into a movie. You know that, right? Who do you work for?" she looked at him squarely.

"A gracious creative director whose files are open for our private viewing," he laughed and handed her a piece of paper. Deon snatched it then looked over at the man, convinced he was counterfeit.

"Deon, chill out for once in your life. This is not a battle."

She didn't know why he was trying to hold her captive in this digital voyage. "To whomever it may concern, you'll be hearing from my lawyer soon!" Then she looked back up at the screen, pouting.

"Are you done?" he asked, with that same cute smile. Deon rolled her eyes, trying to ignore the effect his pearly whites and perfect-size lips - not too big, not too small, were having on her and she finally looked at what she was handed. It was a dinner menu. The food options were scarce. She was never a soup, salad and sandwich kind of girl. She needed some meat.

"Are these supposed to be the options? I mean can a girl get crab, lobster, gumbo, even cracklin, or boudin or something?"

"Wow, you are something else. I'm sure that can be arranged though, but only for you."

He took the menu back then typed in the order.

Turning his attention back to the screen, he started with, "Now, this is only the beginning." He cautioned, "that is all we can do today. The rest must come shortly after, for the shadow to lift. Then we will look at the next section. And the next."

Deon was not listening. She was more concerned with what would be seen. Suppressed memories. There had been so many people in and out of her life, she had lost count herself. She cringed at the thought of reliving appalling early days that were far from playing dress up in mommy's clothes. Did she really need any more run-ins with all of the dudes she dated who were nothing but *temporary*? And all of the permanent enemies acquired along the way; people she had thought were friends were faint memories she wanted to keep in the back of her mind. Whoever the master controller is, fast forward *please*. Or just skip those chapters altogether, she thought.

"We are not going to go through my *whole* life, are we...*Self-reflection, isn't there an app for that?*

The guy's eyes widened, he started chuckling, holding his stomach, gasping for air...he looked like he was going to pee on himself, he was crying and laughing so hard.

"No, really?" I really didn't know what was so funny. "Thirty years is a loooong time, you know. *And technology is too advanced.*"

"Don't worry, you will have access to your own instruction manual on the D drive. That will help you make the best decisions along the way. Just let me do the rewinding."

"D drive...?"

"Yes, and it's quite Divine."

"I need to see it now! I'm not taking another step until I have a tangible explanation...I wish you had mentioned this earlier."

"Of course." He sighed and like a magician, all of a sudden *another* gizmo appeared. He handed her a wannabe iPad and led her to where she'd have access to this D drive. A PDF file of about 6000 pages - a handbook - appeared. "Thank God I am a speed reader." All types of questions ran through her head as she glanced at chapter titles and read as much as she could to try to get a grasp of what she was in for. After reading the main terms and conditions sectioned in the front, she felt overwhelmed. She wished someone, anyone, could bail her out at this point! Her revenue stream certainly could free her from almost anything, but her money didn't seem to matter here. She was in bondage, by something else. Whatever it was, she figured it probably would sell her out before helping her out. Her eyes invaded the space she was forced to be in.

"If I step any further, am I going to lose myself in this? Become reprogrammed?" Deon watched a lot of *Tron* and sci-fi growing up, and felt there were other worlds out there. Was she going to enter another universe beyond recognition? She was comfortable in the world she lived in.

He said nothing. She stood, bare-boned, with so much territory to cover and hopefully uncover. Shivering inside, she could only feel the warmth of him as he gently placed her hands in his. It settled her, for a second.

Deon couldn't make out the sound she was hearing. It sounded like chimes or...jewelry being shaken. Without any words, they entered her past, an old world. She clutched his hand for dear life, grateful that the humored and sturdy man didn't seem to mind. Like a dream, Deon could not really understand every detail as they stepped into a place that would not have been possible had she been awake.

They arrived. Despite funny feelings, they conspicuously entered the quaint, Memorial Hospital in Houston's Third Ward. Wednesday, January 3rd 1979. From another angle, she stood at attention, feeling privileged to be able to watch with a third eye. But she laughed. *I knew the beginning.* What scared her was the ending and not knowing whether it would fade to black or white. She wanted a drink.

The Apple of His Eye

*We are drowning in information and
starved for knowledge. – John Naisbiitt*

Hospitals made Deon edgy...Peering in the window, the

two stood outside the delivery room. The tour guide continued to
look at her with reassuring eyes. Something inside his gaze calmed
her, for the moment.

He slowly opened the door, and said, "An assignment is
given."

She tried to breathe...but not breathe in the smell of
"hospital." The nonchalant leader just kept on trudging along.

Thirty years ago yesterday, she saw someone who she
vaguely knew. She watched the little person, being dressed and
bundled up by the nurse and placed carefully in the nursery. "Look
at that. Is that supposed to be me?" she laughed.

The man beside her nodded. "Deondria Eliza DeVaulle" he
said proudly. "Welcome to the world!"

She looked over at him a bit alarmed. "Shhh!"

"They can't hear us. Or see us."

Deon rolled her eyes, disappointed. Was *this* the new
normal?

The up-close sight graced her eyes: a full, thick baby with slick baby hair that was adorned with a pink barrette.

"Now you saw me in my birthday suit, you even know my full name, but who in the world are you?"

He laughed and once again, she admired his pretty white teeth.

"Âme."

She knew a little French, but hadn't heard that before. "Come again?"

"Âme, rhyming with balm."

"Ahhh, I like that. I'm sure there's a meaning, huh."

"Of course, it's actually *soul* in French."

Deon nodded, storing the information in her name bank. "Names are important, but I know it is what you do with the name that really matters," she shared.

"True," he nodded.

"Like the name DeVaulle stems back to 18th century. The surname DuVall, which is French as well, within my family, changed a bit over time, closer to my dad's grandparent's generation. Boy, we are some proud Creoles."

Âme smiled; he looked a little strange, but Deon couldn't quite understand why, at that very moment.

110

"The name stops with me: the only living child and only girl. Josie was having a hard time having kids. The family remained lopsided, gender wise. Later, Autumn came along but for the most part, I grew up with mainly boy cousins my age. If my parents hadn't lost their boy, his name would have been Deondre."

"Sorry to hear about the loss."

Âme and Deon walked out into the hallway.

"Sometimes, being the miracle baby is hard," she said. Âme took her hand and led her to another part of the hospital. Deon was about to ask him for HIS full name, but she saw something that made her stop in her tracks.

Down the way, walking out of a delivery room was a woman with a head of soft, freshly pressed natural brassy brown strands Deon recognized as hair she used to play in as a kid. Deon picked up her pace to see if her eyes were playing tricks on her. Now, she was so close she could see the veins in the woman's thin skin, especially under her dark brown eyes. They made her unrecognizable to some extent, but yes, it was the then 25-year-old Josephine "*Josie*" Percy DeVaulle. Looked like she had been crying. Deon was concerned, but still in awe.

Even though Josie, a hairstylist who came from a long line of successful hairdressers in St. Lordes, New Orleans, would be the first to denounce sleeping in her make-up, Deon never understood how she, someone who grew up idolizing and watching her fashionista mom's every move, never saw her without it on her skin.

111

She saw it today. There was not a lick of it on her face at that moment. She must have sweated it off during labor, Deon figured. Her face, to the natural eye, was fresh. She had naturally arched eyebrows and rosy cheeks. Deon had forgotten the color of her lips because they were always painted. Without makeup, she was even more breathtaking, Deon thought, as she tried to keep up.

Deon remembered pictures of herself as a toddler with her mom, who rocked a Farrah Fawcett flip. And on church days, she did these twisted updos that were really neat and in vogue.

All of a sudden, a handsome man, then 31-year-old doctor Sylvester DeVaulle, called after Josie as he too walked out the same door and ran to catch up with his wife. "Daddy," she whispered with a smile. Deon knew that she may have been mommy's little doll, but she was really daddy's little girl. She wished she could get a hug from him at that very moment. He always made her feel safe, beautiful, and special.

At the time, the head-turning couple were newlyweds who had married just the year before. Deon wondered if they noticed her there now, out of place in this context. Probably not; they both looked distressed.

Both Josie and Sylvester were healers in their own right; both touched lives, both were business owners and their establishments stood as staples in the Houston community.

Sylvester finally stopped his wife and urged her to sit down in the nearest sitting area.

"We've got to," she said.

"I know," he agreed.

"She is not able. I don't want to see another child suffer."

"We can give her a good home. You'd be a wonderful mother."

Josie nodded.

"Did you see her? She is so beautiful. The daughter I always wanted. I just don't know how to do the rest of it."

"We will worry about the rest later. For now, we know what we have to do and that is what is best for the baby."

Deon frowned as she processed.

Âme walked over to Deon, not knowing what would happen next.

Deon looked up, speechless with terror in her eyes not wanting to ask another question.

In her physical state, Deon's adrenaline pushed her to run away from the scene and back to the room that she had seen the couple come out of moments earlier. She had to see for herself.

She burst through the door to see a woman, one who had been close to the family, too close for comfort. A woman who had had her battles with drugs, prostitution and Lord knows what else. A woman, no matter how many chances she was given, Deon never trusted after what she did to her...a child. A trusting child. An innocent child. This beautiful beast was supposed to be her...biological mother.

Certainly not!

Love Child

What's wrong with technology is that it's not connected in any real way with matters of the spirit and of the heart. And so it does blind, ugly things quite by accident and gets hated for that.
—Robert Pirsig

Deon felt dirty. She wouldn't believe such a lie.

Inconsolable, she managed to escape the emergency room. Pathetic would be the bestt way to illustrate the mush her formerly semi-fit physique was morphing into.

She knew that in due time, once she got a hold of her gym trainer, she'd look like the diva that she previously was. But to fully recover in the heart department, who could train her there?

This filthy woman! Deon shook her head in disbelief. *Heavens No!* It was too much to take a step further. She crumbled to the ground against a random wall. This is a cruel, cruel joke. *That trash...can't be my mom!* Deon didn't want to talk, so she didn't.

Âme came to her side, squatted beside her. "I will give you time, but we must continue the process. Take baby steps, but you must keep going."

Deon was mute as both of their backs rested against the wall. She wanted to die with the lie rather than live with *that* truth. Deon was in a trance or in trauma. Âme wasn't sure.

"We need to have the lies uncovered before your eyes, so you can come clean," he continued.

I can't do this. Don't want to, Deon admitted to herself. As if he read her mind, Âme promised, "Yes you can. I'm right here with you."

Deon was not coherent.

"Come on, buddy. There are a lot of people pulling for you right now. They want to see your eyes open," Âme begged.

They had so much ground to cover, but Âme figured they were going to have to get through this in a different way.

Deon looked like she had checked out. Âme was beyond concerned.

"Just remember, once you get a hold of all the dead things and poisonous things in your life and really put them to rest, you can truly live!"

Even though being in the scene helps the patient recover faster, he knew that may not work - he tried to give her the time she needed and then some, but he knew there was not much time to spare. He figured, rather than let her get weaker in the actual scene, it was time for her to sit and watch from the screen, some type of barrier.

He carefully picked up her limp body and carried her out of the hospital memory, the first lie uncovered. He got her to the nearest auditorium.

***

He sat her upright, hoping to see a quick change in her demeanor, but she was still a vegetable.

"Come on girl. Where is that fight I saw moments ago? Don't let the truth hurt you for too long. Come back please."

Nothing.

"The food is on it's way."

Still nothing. Deon had lost her appetite.

Suddenly, Âme's hands cradled hers. "You will never understand how much I need you."

His eyes pleaded with hers. His heart did the same. And Deon actually felt something she had never felt before. Somehow she had the strength to go a little bit further.

There was that Âme smile again.

"Here we go."

The screen showed a still shot of a new place - correction, an old place. Her old street. In front of her childhood home, were primary colored balloons that foreshadowed her room's color-scheme. *It probably scared the neighbors. Too much color in the almost all-white neighborhood,* she thought.

Time seemed lost in this place and space, but it had been at least an hour since she started following the man. Deon decided to make herself as comfortable as possible.

"Can we get some chairs, popcorn, and a white cherry slushie?"

He was relieved to hear her dominant voice re-emerge. The man laughed at her request. "Not much has changed from childhood, huh? I see you still running the show. I'll see what I can do."

With the screen sat at a pause, her dry mouth began to water as she saw the convenient cup-holders now holding drinks she requested. She finally noticed what else was there. She couldn't wait to get her hands on the big, round bowl of buttery popcorn that sat in the seats beside them; she was sure the fat would soon be sitting on her thighs. Based on what she saw in the mirror earlier, that wouldn't be a bad thing.

"Sweet!" Deon didn't hesitate. She started stuffing her face.

"Now don't tell about me getting you the popcorn; you could get me fired. But the sandwiches are on the way, okay."

Deon pinky swore. "You're an angel," she said as they continued to sit in what she considered pretty good, comfy seats, smack dead in the center of the movie screen, exactly where

Deon liked to sit when she'd see a film. Even though they were the only ones there, Deon still felt underdressed. She couldn't understand how this dude was magically putting them in places, but she wondered why he couldn't magically put her in normal clothes.

"Alright, I'm about to press play," he said. Simultaneously, the sound of a piece of jewelry seemed to shake sadistically then the screen showed a clip of Deon's family later that afternoon, after the delivery. Deon frowned at the noise.

"Wow, look at that ride! They don't make 'em like that anymore," Âme laughed as the car that carried the newborn and parents pulled into the driveway. "That's the Fox right?"

Although they were watching the past, the picture was a clear digital depiction.

Deon just sat solemnly in silence and she watched as the proud guardians brought her home to the posh Victorian-style neighborhood in River Oaks, Houston. She was desperately trying to not see the lie in them, but it was hard. How was it that she never knew she was not from Josie's womb? Why didn't they tell her the truth? She didn't want to find out like this, in front of a stranger. She just kept herself quiet, deep in thought, but also deep in repression, denial.

What dropped down from above was the answer to her stomach's prayers - comfort food. She devoured the juicy, succulent and utterly delicious crabcake sandwich; that lifted her spirits a tad bit.

Inside the happy home, a party was going on. The DeVaulle and Percy Clans were all ready to see baby Deon, the new addition. Music was playing, and although it was soon to be the end of disco as we know it, the household records from Donna Summer, Chic, Gloria Gaynor, The Bee Gees and Sister Sledge continued being played in heavy rotation.

Deon was jealous of the newborn. The newborn didn't know what she knew about her parents. And even the world around her. All she knew was love. Oh, to be held again.

After the unveiling, the baby was finally able to get to her first sanctuary, which was already meticulously decorated months before. Sylvester carefully carried her through the wooden paneled two-story home. For Deon, childhood represented three hard truths in life: 1. Perspective can be a deceiver. 2. Patterns can be piercing and 3. Some sign up for their jobs, others are chosen. Although many assumed she grew up with a silver spoon in her mouth, she actually grew up with golden shears in her hands.

Her grandmother, Ma'Dear, couldn't wait to get her hands on Deon, but Dad managed to have a moment with the baby, like he always did before handing her over to another fan. "Yes, Ma'dear she has all ten fingers and toes!" her dad reassured his mother-in-law. Like she had won the lottery, she was clapping; the baby had achieved the simplest form of normalcy!

"What a gift it is to be loved, Deon," said Âme.

Deon sat quietly, feeling left out of the experience. Now she wondered who her real dad was. It could be anyone, knowing how the soiled woman lived. She left the question alone, she just couldn't stomach the revelation, so she let her eyes settle on the pretty sights before her. Josie's beautiful sisters, Bianca, who was two years younger and Zoé, who was five years older, had gotten the room together for the expected baby boy, the one who never came.

"I remember I wanted a pink room. No girl I knew had primary color schemes," she shared with Âme. The room must have come in handy for the last minute decision to adopt, she figured. Lettered pillows were made. They spelled out Deon and they were pinned perfectly above the crib. Deon wondered if she had a different name prior to the switch?

"When I eventually got my way later on down the line, I found myself wanting to revert to something bolder anyway."

On the wall there was an air unit, blowing profusely.

Âme was grateful to have some conversation.

Zoé's daughter, Renée, was stuck being Deon's baby-sitter when the ladies went out. "Boy, was she a meanie," Deon said. "I guess I ruined her reign."

Josie, like her sisters, loved their *stories*. During the week, *Young and the Restless* and *Days of Our Lives* were watched religiously. "Don't let her miss *Dallas* or *Knots Landing* or she would have a fit!" She remembered the women getting all worked up over the drama. Deon only liked the big hair, the beat faces, the elaborate outfits and the lavish lifestyles they had. If she made an attempt to watch the idiot box, she had only a few favs back then: *Quantum Leap, Saved by the Bell* and *Star Trek.*

Josie rarely worked at the salon on *Soul Train* Saturdays, but the smell of cleaning products, heated pressing combs, eggs, ham, bacon, omelets, pancakes, and sausage were a normal aroma in the DeVaulle's huge kitchen, Deon's classroom. What Deon learned from the ladies could fit into three boxes: the good, the bad and the ugly. They would cook together fixing big meals for each wife to take home to her family. While they cooked, they danced. Mom's specialty was her casseroles. Zoé whipped up some of the best fluffy pancakes, from scratch. While the ladies got dolled up for a night out on the town they listened to zydeco. Deon pranced around in kiddy heels acting like she was on *Dynasty.* Her family knew how to party. Deon wanted to be just like them.

Before this experience, she would have said, "Our genes kept us Percy girls looking fit in our jeans," but now she had a hole in her pride. Deon was built like the curvy women in the family, she figured now, by coincidence. Mom did attempt some Jane Fonda, but it wasn't a real priority.

She would find the right time and place to ask who her father was, but her heart was still heavy with shock and disgust.

Who knows what Charmaine, her so-called-biological mother, was really coming from. She knew she was beautiful, but her life ended in such an ugly way. *Like mother, like daughter.* She pushed the thought out of her mind, disowned it and looked on.

Sylvester was the odd ball in the fam, a little square, but Deon never felt sorry for him; he was unflinching. He was always working at his doctor's office, but he let many Saturdays be for Deon and him as well. From him, she learned how to make quality time. Hanging with Dad was special. They stopped at *Marion's*, a round vintage-train car that had the best barbecue. They had the best link sandwiches known to man! Then afterward, he would go get his thick wavy hair cut by his brother. Deon liked being an interloper in the shop; hearing what the guys talked about was quite interesting.

Deon was not sure if wedlock or personal gridlock caused stagnation for her parents, or was it the prescription that created the monster?

In the swampy summers, she was sent to stay with Ma'dear in Louisiana, in what Deon called, a town of secrets, a third-degree burn waiting to happen. But it was the only time she really had fun. Ma'dear's home, an extension of her fearless and flamboyant personality, looked like a rainbow exploded and dropped muted watercolors: yellow, green, blue, orange onto the comfy cushions of the sofa and loveseats that surrounded the coffee tables. The accent pillows, lampshades and drapes weren't subtle either; they stick in her mind today. They were custom-made to fit the different rooms. The ceiling was a view in itself. Deon always sat wondering how someone managed to sprinkle gold dust on the wall. The chandelier was vintage *then*. But Ma'dear practically lived in the Bed and Breakfast, *Good Morning New Orleans,* where she worked diligently to keep things running. Deon was her little shadow at the hotel, her home away from home. Ma'dear's fostered busybodies: she was always hollering about "an idle mind is the devil's workshop." Her kids were either productive or faking it to keep her from giving them a task or two.

The bell hops were always cracking jokes. Year after year, they saw her grow up, right before their eyes. The hotel, itself, was such a treat and well after her childhood, she went to visit on her own. The extra tall doors and ceilings made her feel like a queen when she walked through the lobby, a human-sized jewelry box. Glass top tables and other reflective surfaces were all around. Deon loved roaming the claustrophobic streets, a true melting crockpot. The smell of Louisiana, the taste never leaves. Bourbon Street. The raunchy gentlemen stores...at every glance, the homeless man passed out outside of one. The buildings. The colors. The familiarity. The music. The *Essence* Festival.

NOLA was her second home.

Each room in the Bed and Breakfast had its own personality. Deon's room, 302, was a space PETA would have protested: the lambs, the wool rugs, the velvet, leopard print wallpapers were so different from her room at home, a color palette-less place.

***

There was that sound again, the sound of jewelry. Deon's eyes drifted to some snaggletooth faces playing in Louisa May Alcott Elementary's playground.

"Wow!" she pointed to the screen because she could no longer talk, she was laughing so hard.

"Now, who are they?" Âme asked.

"Monique, Val and Reece."

"I'm surprised you remember them."

"Back then, we were inseparable and were a close circle of four. We all lived on the same street, Cherry Grove."

Âme nodded.

"Look.at.us. This is a HOT mess. It is weird seeing our mini-mes." She had an urge to get out her phone to capture and share the moment but she remembered the many rules of this planet of privacy; her phone was dead and she despised *bootleggers*. So instead, she took it all in, naturally.

"I no longer have their numbers, especially after I moved. I tried to keep in contact, but when I found out from Monique that each of them were talking about me behind my back and seemed happy I was gone, I let it go. I really thought we would be friends to the end. But we were young." One was shown climbing up a tree; Deon and another were jumping from swings.

125

"Y'all were some rough little ones, huh?"

Deon smiled.

"All of us, except for MoMo." Monique was pictured. "She would sit under the gazebo with the teacher during recess. I heard she is an elementary school teacher now."

Âme's eyes squinted.

"I swear, she was a walking bag of broken bones. That girl was a magnet for the floor." Deon just shook her head as she remembered all the times she'd have to rally 'round and lend a hand. "We were always signing her casts, but I'm not sure what was worse...her breaking down or throwing up."

"You actually helped someone?"

"Well, in those days, yes. IT was natural.

We, as a class, had a routine. After lunch, while in single file, Rafeal would run and get the trash. I knew when to hold back her hair if she started to turn a shade of purple. As a class, we knew when to look away and hold our breaths. Thank God, the teachers and janitors knew how to clean up fast. None of us ever missed a beat. Please don't show those clips. My stomach is weak."

Âme clicked away.

"What happened there?" he asked Deon *as if she knew.*

Another day at recess, the kids were running rampant on the dusty playground. Oh, and the main attraction just happened to be Deon, in the sandbox; she had home-chick in a headlock.

"She must have asked for it," Deon said. "I rarely started something unless I had to."

"Who is she?"

"Tatiyana Lufkin."

"What did she do to you?"

Deon could remember, inside the house, her Barbie was rolling around in her hot pink Benz. And outside, Deon was fighting jealous broads in the neighborhood over her own pink Power Wheels. But this, this was a different fight.

"His name was Bobby. Bobby Cartwright. He sat by me in Mrs. Teagle's class. I mean, can I help that the boy felt compelled to buy me some confetti nails for Christmas; she had a fit. I couldn't handle her bullying me any longer, so I eventually had to shut that nonsense down. I was told, if someone hit me, hit them back."

"Did you have many fights?"

"Not sure. All I know is that I made friends quickly and lost them just as fast. I soon built a social shell to avoid them."

"Why is that?"

127

Deon shook my head. "I had business to take care of. Games were not a way of life."

Âme took a deep breath and showed another similar scene with a different girl.

"First of all, you don't mess with a girl's hair. That skank had the nerve to cut my hair when I was sitting, doing my work. My grandmother on my mother's side, the beautician, she would whoop me if I didn't whoop her ass."

"Maybe the girl needed the hair more than you."

Deon took a good look at him.

He smiled.

Deon rolled her eyes. "Anyway."

Once the fight was over, Âme and Deon gasped simultaneously. Dirty clothes, dust, sand and the hair that was left made Deon shake her head, feeling sorry for herself. "Oh, I don't want mother to see me like that," she said under her breath. "People think I am OCD, but they have not met Miss Josie." Outside of Josie's perfect expectations, she had something else – style. Some people are born with it; others had it beat into them at a young age. "If I could've gotten away with jeans and a tee, I would have, but...that was not the case. I had big stilettos to fill."

Âme was listening, but he was looking at something else in the scene.

"Look at little Tati. You really messed her up."

"She, of course, didn't get in trouble like I did. Plus, my teacher didn't really care for me, or my mom. She loved my dad though."

While Âme clicked the next chapter, all Deon could think about was how so many people were *impossible*. She had for a while taken a lot of crap off people, but early on, she decided she couldn't take the hate. She couldn't and wouldn't hate herself.

Now on the screen was a new scene and that same sound Deon was starting to despise.

Deon laughed. "Since being judged came early, I learned how to use it to my advantage to get money." Pictures of her as a seven-year old flashed across the screen. She wasn't your average seven-year old. All decked out in the full-fledge make up and Texas-size hair, center stage, Deon was in it to win it.

"Hi, my name is Deondria DeVaulle and I'm from Houston, Texas. When I grow up, I want to be a CEO of my own Fortune 500 Company." The audience gushed and smiled. On the stage, under all those lights, little Deon didn't play herself down. She was what she was - take it or leave it. Hate it or love it. She stood firmly, ready to take her place in the world. What she could observe, she could learn quickly. Her mind was very complex for a child. Simple minds held her back. Big ideas filled this little girl's head. She didn't know who whispered them to her. She just knew that if she didn't

129

act on them, they would explode. She took great pride in being greedy for knowledge.

Little Deon went on to sing a song from *Annie* and she nailed the interview question. Sylvester was front row and center at *every* single competition. His loud flat-handed claps in the crowd and booming chants of, "That's my baby!" was his norm; it pushed her.

"I didn't know you could sing," Âme said.

"I could carry a tune. I came from a musical family. Outside of being together, cooking, dancing and eating, the girls were the singers of the family and they were always working on music, performing locally and in the salon, getting dolled up for photo shoots. I just mimicked their confidence."

Deon smiled suddenly.

"Mother had the perfect soothing, soprano voice. She sounded nothing like how she talked; it was as if she borrowed someone's singing voice. Like mine, her voice was raspy and deeper, far from prissy."

Playing different roles came easily to Deon, a mimic, who didn't internalize her roles.

"Mom and I were inspired by the glamour of the studio era, black and white movies. We'd watch TCM...those women, Joan Crawford, Diane Carol, Dorothy Dandridge, Bette Davis, Marlene Dietrich, Ava Gardner, Lena Horne, Sophia Loren, Elizabeth Taylor,

Mae West and who could forget Marilyn. I practically knew every line of their household golden-age movies. There were so many divas. *Divas* I can respect; *drama queens*...I don't know about that."

Deon won *every* pageant she entered. *Little Miss Priss Texas* was where she retired her sash and earned her final crown, "I moved on out of the spotlight and started working behind the scenes, cooking up dreams." Deon knew that it was something about that spotlight that blinded her. She had other things she wanted to focus on: namely, building a beauty empire! Although good at numbers, not everything added up.

"I see money was your best friend," Âme concluded, as he saw the smile on her face when the camera closed in on a Miss Piggy calendar; names of neighbors, their orders and her deadlines for producing products were penciled in childish handwriting.

"My piggy bank was *obese*. I can remember my mom's brother; he'd call me Youngblood whenever he imparted his words of wisdom. Bruno, a barber, and shop owner, encouraged me to open up a bank account, to grow interest. He also told me to keep a stash of petty cash in my possession at all times. He didn't trust the government. He also taught me a lot about life and men - the low down dirty kind to avoid.

In the barber shop, she learned so much about how they play the girls that they were dating, *if the women let them*. Many did, but Deon promised to never let herself succumb to such a despicable thing. It was an eye-opening experience and she remembered feeling like love was a game you had to play in order to win.

From Uncle Bruno, a business man with a hustla's spirit, she also learned how to make cross 10 transactions. He knew how to make his work worth it and knew how to multiply his actions.

Neighbors were hooked on products Deon cooked up in a little factory. At the age of 8, the locals patronized her first venture, a Kool-nail stand inspired by the drink's bright colors. She was able to keep adding a hundred dollars to her account per week.

"Look at you." Ame watched the little girl neatly painting nails in her mother's salon while others waited to be next.

"They gave great tips!" Deon squealed.

"I see, so you said the living just ain't worth your time, but dead presidents sure held your attention, huh?"

"Are you trying to judge me too!"

Âme looked confused. "What? ME? No. Never..."

"I *used* to see the good in people, I really did, but when you've been used, it's hard to see. The people around you are important ingredients. I guess I learned the hard way." Deon had learned money brought in a lot of fair-weathered friends and foul-weathered ones too.

"*What* exactly?"

"That a recipe for success was determining who your true friends are. Like love, that term "friend" should not be used so loosely."

"True."

The story on screen moved right along.

"So, out with the bad and in with the...nothing?" he asked.

"It is what it is," Deon said.

A picture of Deon flashed across the screen. "Look at that S on your chest!"

Deon laughed as the screen showcased a time in her life when she started to embrace the skin she was in. She shut out any and every thing that made her feel bad about being her. She carried a secret like it was a million dollar question.

"I guess you didn't have the awkward phase like everyone else; you were just always stunning," Âme said.

Deon looked at him, trying not to blush. Like gumbo, the guys found her hard to resist; they tried to simmer her down, but she was strong, thick and mixed-up.

"Thanks, but beauty is in the eye of the beholder."

In high school, by default, she started making female friends when she entered into the cosmetology program, a sort of beauty sorority.

"It freed me to experiment with different looks."

Deon was pictured playing with food coloring. "What are you cooking there?"

"It's the ONLY reason I worked in the kitchen. There I am, making make-up products. You can make foundation colors."

You know blue people?"

"No, silly. Think of the color wheel. When you mix primary colors together, you get earth-toned hues. A lot of people paid big money for me to match them and create their own liquid base."

Âme laughed. "I will leave that up to you."

Back then, Deon's room had become the neighborhood salon.

"I offered my services at a reasonable price for kids my age. I would style doll heads, real heads, etc. Whatever made the customer happy."

Although she mimicked Josie's salon, there was one difference of course: salon talk. The ladies in Josie's salon had groomed her to marry well so she wouldn't have to work. But, she had a feeling that she may need to continue to take some notes on how to make her own way. After watching all the different stylists in Josie's salon, she picked up on a lot of hard truths.

"From what I heard from both the hair salon and the barber shop, love was a game." Deon swallowed hard. "For the most part, I wanted to take care of myself and my business. Have my own. No one could play with a woman who had her own shit, so I thought."

She shook her head with a smile.

"I kept my environment more focused on the individual and what made them who they were – not so much *relationship talk*. At least not on my end."

They watched the next shot: her with her parents walking into their Catholic church.

"You're a woman of faith?"

"We went to church occasionally. You know the main holidays, Easter, Halloween, Christmas. I never understood why. Half the people looked dead while there, including my parents. The other half acted mean as hell. I just remember questioning, *this* was an ideal? They had to be kidding."

Deon felt guilty about being a skeptic of spirituality. Slowly, but surely, the shame went away when she stopped going entirely. "Guys would invite me to their church. Most of them were Baptist. When I went, boy was it scary."

Âme looked confused.

"So many people hollering, shouting, jumping over stuff I didn't see. It just wasn't my thing."

Âme scratched his head.

"I guess life was like English class, a course I hated. There were so many philosophies, theories. It wasn't black and white. Right or wrong. It was too much talk in between." Deon narrated.

The next shot was of Deon's drool, which covered an assignment others continued to work rigorously to finish.

"Up all night in the lab huh?" Âme asked.

In the classroom, Deon liked the challenge and there wasn't enough of that. Science Fair projects and Robotics Team tournaments were the only things that really got her excited when it came to school. The straight A student was normally bored out of her mind, and was generally perceived as a brat.

"It's a shame how we descend. Quick-learners are punished by adults who dumb-down the kids."

Deon was in D hall after school on numerous occasions due to her inability to get with the program. That is where, since she was always done with her work, she caught up on all her sci-fi books.

"I literally wanted to cut the bullshit out of my life. I never had an escape."

"Did you date a lot Deon?"

"I dated in high school, but nothing serious, of course."

"Do you have someone in your life, Âme?"

Âme smiled. "I wish I could say that I do. My job makes it impossible for me to date – with the hours I work and all, plus when I meet women, they don't believe."

"Believe?"

The Dating Scene

*If you can get nothing better out of the world,
get a good dinner out of it at least.*
– Herman Melville

College was the escape. Work was the vacation. They both cradled Deon like nothing else could. Deon's first place off campus was ten minutes away from the University of Houston. Nothing fancy, but she made it that way. Visiting the family was hard. She was smelling secrets in the air instead of home-cooked food. She was seeing mis-matched clothing instead of picturesque ensembles on Josie. And more of a distant dad who was rarely at home. Over the weekends, she witnessed a house divided, which to her, was no home at all. She escaped. She vacationed.

"I wanted to ensure that whatever happened there, wouldn't happen to me. But details were missing. I wanted it to be a phase that our family was going through." Deon swallowed.

Deon's eyes were filled. So much emotion swept over her when she saw herself in the library, studying with a young man by the name of Quincy McKnight.

"Can we stop the tape?"

"Sorry dear, it doesn't work like that."

138

Deon wasn't sure how many lies she could take in one day's viewing. Like a kid on Halloween night, she thought she was getting candy, but she really got the kind with the needle stuck inside of it, *the kind that the news reporters warned us about in the 80s and 90s.*

"He was the only man I let trick me," Deon confessed. "No more, please."

Deon was dead-on, factoring Quincy out of the equations. She wanted to mind her own business – which is similar to how they met. The screen showed the two at a business conference at the George R. Brown Convention Center, Downtown.

Deon, after being in pitch mode for her future salon and day spa, found a cluster of tables off to the side of all the booths, which were pure madness. She sorted the stack of business cards she had collected at the Expo. She wrote details on each so that she could remember the different encounters before they became a pile of faceless, therefore pointless people.

Then all of a sudden, she heard a voice she would never forget.

"So this is where the party is...you worked the room!"

She turned to take a good look at her then, fellow college freshman.

"My name is Quincy McKnight and I..."

He gave his little spiel on how he wanted to be a realtor, one in the urban community, making homes affordable for the low to middle class. Help change the mentality of a people: focus on owning versus renting. Build housing that will allow more African-Americans to be able to attain the goal of home ownership. How he wanted to own and rent out several commercial properties in the city that could help bring in more black businesses...

"I took a good look at him. This was my first time actually 'seeing' him. And I had never seen anything like it. I knew many men, but he was different. Nothing about his talk was small. He wore passion in his eyes. I felt the fire inside of him inside of myself. This was exciting to me. It was what I needed to see, needed to feel. I needed to know."

Âme listened, but felt a bit uncomfortable.

Deon remembered. "I wanted to pull out my fine China for this Negro: he made me smile, inside and out." At the expo, she wanted to offer Q a seat; she was happy to talk business versus flirt, but this nagging feeling kept her from doing that.

Âme, though uncomfortable, stayed on his job.

"He wasn't that epic, larger-than-life figure initially. His maturity allowed him to become sexier with time. I'm a hard sell, but I was sold - his rugged, yet clean-cut, smooth swagger. His selective gaze could draw even the most bashful in. His silky baritone was music to my ears."

"Wow, you sound smitten. What did you admire most about him?"

"He was smart. I could sit and listen to him all day if there was enough time. He had the voice. A wealth of wisdom that could never go bankrupt. Homeboy was reading just about every philosopher, scholar, theorist you could think of; he could recite the most fitting quote in the heat of every moment. That boy loved anything Confucius said and he was quoting him every chance he got. His favorite was 'By three methods we may learn wisdom: first, by reflection, which is noblest: second, by imitation, which is easiest; and third, by experience, which is the bitterest.' A true student of life. He was the smartest person I know."

Âme blinked.

Although in the same undergrad program, Q and Deon never had classes together. They somehow ended up together though, in other ways.

"We both had a superhuman work-ethic, I am surprised we had time for each other."

She scratched her throat.

"He knew I worked out a lot. The closer we got, he didn't want me to go to the gym, I guess he didn't want me to be seen by others. He never said it, but when his boys were, I guess checking me out and going back and telling him about me, he started to offer to help me work out after and in between his practices."

"Practices?"

"He was a star athlete. He'd invite me to watch him play."

"How was he?"

"He shined on the field. Very fast. Very skilled. But I'm no cheerleader type. I had a lot of work to do, so we got into some spats about that. Time issues. But I must admit, some days were really tough to get through in college. Some days I had a lot on my mind, especially when coming from weekend visits with my family," Deon continued.

"The year I started working at a salon other than my mother's and the school's, we were a part of a study group that would meet on, I think, Thursday nights for the course of a semester. I remember one time we had a more relaxed study session, ordered pizza and had some drinks."

Deon was silent for a second.

"I was so embarrassed. I mean, I could be just sitting there. Everyone else could go on about their business or sit talking, not realizing I was on auto-pilot, but he would just have this radar."

Deon laughed, making Âme confused. There was another awkward silence that followed.

"I would get upset at any indication that I was not up to par and looked at him as an annoying father figure at times. He was always asking if I was okay, days that I really was far from okay."

142

Deon sat in silence. Âme saw her drifting to a secret place he felt he'd allow her to keep sacred. He knew. He knew what was inside of her, he knew it was dead, but it still was very much who Deon was.

She gently touched her stomach.

"I still wish I had listened to my gut feeling. He was a true gentlemen. Maybe too good to be true.

As much as Âme wanted her to stop talking about another guy, he knew it was helping her shadow to lift. She must continue revisiting such places in order to get out of this place.

"I didn't expect us to click. We were like night and day."

"How so?" he asked.

"Quincy grew up in the rougher part of South Park, got into the juvenile system early and got caught up. Misdemeanors followed, but he had such luck – unlike some of his boys, he turned it around in time to have a life worth living. Charisma carried him a long way, but his intellect kept him in places that were restricted."

"When invited to his childhood home, I didn't even realize how close we would get on that trip. There were so many coincidences. I hate coincidences."

"Why?"

"They are false starts."

"So what were some?"

"Nothing major, but for instance, we had the same exact numbers in both our childhood addresses, just different street names, neighborhood, of course - talk about weird."

"How was his family?"

"Testosterone city. The McKnights, a no-handshakes-just-hugs kind of family, were very cool. Quincy was the middle child among his four brothers."

She laughed.

"'Who is this beige Barbie?' his mom, Marie, had asked when we first met. Seeing his mother helped me to understand him even more. She had a glow about her, but she was always acting fascinated with other people. I was numb to hearing yellow-bone comments because color struck me everyday in some way. But she seemed to make me feel good, in the skin I was in."

Then came the sound of jewelry.

***

Soon, they were watching a new scene: Outside, Q and Deon a decade ago, walked down the street admiring the sidewalk art. *Deidra loves Quincy 4ever, Jackie luvs Que*...while walking with Q, Deon giggled at the sight that went on and on.

The block chronicled Q's love life. There were different variations, but he starred in every one.

"No one ever wrote my name in cement...They knew better," Deon said to Quincy.

"What do you mean?" Quincy asked her.

"They knew putting down something so permanent could come back to haunt them. I would never claim a man. There is no way to tell if he really loves you. You can't read people's hearts."

"You don't have to *read* people."

"You have to know the truth though. Most of these are lies."

"What?" Quincy looked offended, but he couldn't help but laugh.

"How many of these girls do you plan to spend eternity with? Just in general, in this fickle world, how many of the cement testaments reflect people who are still together, huh? Probably not even ten percent. Because you know why; it doesn't matter in the end. Especially since lust is for fools that think they are in love."

"Actually, at the end is where it matters the most. What is it that you want at the end?"

Deon stood in silence.

"I want to have a family of my own. I want *that* life – to be a wife and a mother."

Deon's words shocked him. He smiled. To him, she never seemed like she even thought about anything outside of work.

"I'm glad you are normal," Quincy added. "I was starting to worry."

Deon rolled her eyes. "What do you want? In the end."

"True love," Quincy said. Deon was shocked by *his* words.

"I agree with the *true* part," Deon said. The two walked on in silence for moments. They were reaching a nearby park. Hearing kids play. Loud bass in cars pass by, birds chirping. They found themselves on a rusted seesaw. Deon sat first. She looked at Q urging him to sit with her. He looked at her like she was crazy. "I'm not getting on that thing. You will fly." She laughed. "Just don't plop down on it silly."

"I don't know. I can't put my valuables in danger." Q said. Deon rolled her eyes.

He eased into a swing seat right beside it instead. He held his hand out to Deon, wanting her to come near. She slowly made her way. He gestured for her to come sit on his lap. As soon as they both were on the swing, the chain snapped. They plopped down. As the two made a loud thump, they could feel each other's laughter erupting, being that close. The two sat in the sand, still laughing, before moving to different corners of the sand box. Quincy looked around the park. "When I get to being a big name in this city, I am going to give money back to my community. Rebuild this park."

Deon felt in that moment in the sand, that she wanted to be a part of his dream. His dreams. She always felt a burst of energy when he talked about the future. He allowed her to dream. She smiled at him. She knew that whoever was going to be in his future was going to be a very lucky woman.

"Have you ever felt unloved although people say they love you?" Deon asked Q out the blue.

Quincy started, "I know it may be hard, but that is when faith comes in. You have to trust in something so abstract, something that can't even be proven, *in concrete*."

"I guess it would be nice to know that you were loved, for real," she said.

"When you trust love, you feel loved. So what kind of man are you into?"

"I don't want to talk about that in too much detail, but I will say, I don't want love to sneak up on me, I want to approve of it."

"Wow. That is different. All these girls want to do is get married."

Deon couldn't help but laugh and shake her head. She knew who was schooling them.

"My formula is to not factor marriage into the equation until I had a certain amount of money in the bank. Therefore, career is my focus and love is something that will happen in due time. Joint accounts can only work if the two have a net worth joining together," Deon said.

Quincy laughed as Deon started to shape some of the sand with her hands into what seemed to be a box.

"I want a guy to prove he is a man before I accept his marriage proposal. That is hard to prove in college. How do you know he can work, keep a job, if tough times come, get another job, stay in the game, not crumble?"

"I guess it depends on your definition of a man," Quincy said, as he broke a small stick in half and started poking holes in the sand with it.

Quincy seemed to want love. Nothing else. But Deon wondered how would anyone know true love if so many people played games.

"I don't like surprises, I like knowing what I am getting," Deon said forming more boxes around the other.

She continued. "I am pretty transparent. Maybe too much from what I hear, but I just feel that giving people the real deal is the best that you can do. Straight and no chasers, you know?"

The two kept the conversation flowing, but were not looking at each other.

"Do you think that it matters what kind of upbringing a person has?" Quincy asked.

"No, I think it matters what type of willpower he has. The world makes us all feel less than, if we let it."

"WE can agree to disagree," Q said.

"What?" she asked looking up.

"I just think love conquers all." Quincy said, as he looked over at her.

"Look at you, you are good with your hands," he said looking at the sand castle she built. "Queen D's castle?"

She laughed, getting up and dusting the sand off of her, like old times. "Something like that."

Quincy got up as well and did the same.

"Hopefully, your mom won't have a fit with us tracking all this dirt in."

Quincy frowned. "She raised a bunch of boys; she has seen worse."

Deon glanced at where Q had been sitting. She was shocked to see a heart with two initials: Q + D.

She was actually speechless for a second. "What were you doing over here?"

"Well, you said that I'd be a fool to write it in concrete, so I wrote it in the sand instead."

***

As the two were heading out, Quincy's mother pulled him aside to whisper. *It didn't matter since everyone could always*

149

hear her quiet voice. "I like that one, don't let her get away. She's good for you. She doesn't take any mess."

Deon smiled and thanked Mrs. McKnight once again for being so gracious and letting them walk in with sandy clothing.

On the ride home, one that was not far at all, Deon thought about how the two of them stood on common ground. She found that to be new, but deep down, she knew it wouldn't last. In fact, when they first met, in the pit of her stomach, she knew to stay away from him. But the challenge always got her going. The *no* always made her want to convert it into a *yes*. His surface didn't indicate anything. It was inviting and convincing. It was that feeling that she wished would go away so she could believe her eyes.

Âme watched. Puzzled. "So what happened to *you* guys?"

She knew she had never met anyone like him. They had so much in common; they were, maybe, even the same person, she sometimes thought. But it didn't matter because they were not good for one another; they were so caught up in their own world.

"We both immersed ourselves in a risky world. Both of our industries were *roll of the dice* type of jobs and we felt lucky to have a great start. Now, we just had to keep our winning streak. Failure was not an option and it seemed like we put each other in jeopardy."

"Never underestimate the ego," Âme said. "It conquers many."

***

Deon frowned when she heard the sound that kept changing the scene. Then the screen showed a wedding that took place years after graduation that changed all that was of a friendship. They had fallen out of contact, but then coincidences had them creeping back into each other's lives in 2008. Weddings.

"I didn't know the bride or the groom personally, I was just there to do my job."

The screen showed the scene.

"Dee, thank you so much. I, along with my wedding party, looked beautiful because of you. I wouldn't have wanted anyone else. Thanks for being here."

"Aww, the pleasure was all mine." Deon watched one of the other bridesmaids pull the bride to the dance floor while the bride excused herself. The deejay announced for all the bachelorettes to make their way to the floor in time for the bouquet toss. Beyonce's *Single Ladies* song chirped through the speakers.

Nauseated, she always knew she could use work as an excuse to dodge this bullet.

She told Ruby she was about to pack.

"Really, it was just getting fun...That cute guy keeps looking at ya."

Deon ignored her and left for the dressing room. Moments later, she was in the mirror, touching up her own make-up and hair. She started packing up beauty kits then Ruby walked in dancing.

"I swear this is my last one Ruby."

"Why do you say that? The bride looked as magnificent as the last. And the *last* and the *last* and the *last*."

"Don't get me wrong Ruby. I love being a beauty professional, but I never wanted to be a professional bridesmaid. The last *ones*, I was in. All these weddings. This one was a break."

"Well, all of your friends are married now so I doubt you would have to do another..."

She couldn't help but give Rue the infamous "evil eye".

"...I guess that really doesn't help, huh? Well, that tall, *chocolate* brother who kept looking at you is fine as wine. He looks just like the guy who was featured in the last issue of *Metropolis* mag as Houston's Most Eligible Bachelor. The Real Estate Man. Brother is banking. He's got commercial and residential properties all over the city.

She couldn't do anything but roll her eyes. Ruby was always outside of the hype, but today she was catching on!

"That *is* him. Eligible? I am not sure who gave him that title though?"

"Dee, you two are so funny. If I didn't know any better I would think that you two knew each other. Plus, if that is the man I read about, I know you both have probably run in the same circles once or twice. Now, that is the kind of brother you need to be with. Both of you being attractive and successful business owners."

"There you go, you said it best Ruby. There it is in a nutshell. One of the reasons why we can't be together."

"What? How do you know?"

"Trust me. I do." All of a sudden, Ruby's mouth made the perfect O.

"You two had something, didn't you? Well you two still got *something*. No wonder I got this weird vibe when I saw you two. Dee, you may *want* to check on him before we head out. You may *need* to before some of those vultures do."

"Uhh, that won't be necessary Ruby. There is something Deon *does not* do – and that is check on *anybody*. You know me better than that Rue. Plus, I got to get out of these clothes. I have been itching all day!"

"Alright boss, I will meet you downstairs. After I check on some fine *mens*, since you won't. Hey, somebody's got to do it."

Ruby took two of the make-up trunks out the door leaving Deon alone.

"Finally," she sighed. She stood in front of the mirror for a moment. A slow jam started to play.

She could overhear the man on the mic.

"Alright, here is the last song of the night. All you single ladies, grab one of these single brothers. All you lovely couples, hold on to each other," the deejay instructed.

She tuned out the song and swallowed hard as she grabbed the remaining make-up trunks. Before heading out, she couldn't help but stop to take a look at her reflection. Thoroughly, she examined her exterior, trying to find an answer to a question, as the song continued to play. She tried to drown out so much outside noise.

Then she heard a sound that jolted her. It was a voice.

"Hey beautiful...May I have the last dance? It is our song..."

When she turned to find Quincy waiting by the door doing his best Billy Dee Williams impersonation, she wanted to scream with joy, but she was torn between heart and mind.

He held out his hand to Deon. She stood contemplating. Maybe after being on top of my game, this was the season to let the heart run wild, she wondered.

***

The next day, after the impromptu reunion with Q, that bright Saturday morning, Deon walked into her lavish salon. Autumn was dusting around the front desk receptionist area. Sista Snow was consulting with a client interested in cornrows. Celestina was doing a blowout. Ruby was finishing up highlights. Deon was on cloud-nine.

"Look at you beaming...wow. I am nervous." Autumn ran to the front door to look up. "Is the sky falling?" Then she continued looking at the owner as if she were an alien.

"Looks like someone got some ass! She really got the glow," Snow insisted. Celestina agreed. "Doesn't she?! Alright mami, anyone we know?" Ruby blushed trying to hold her excitement. Deon gave her and the others the evil eye.

"Ladies...mind your business, please. Besides, when have you ever known me to share details about my life in the work place? Ruby, I need your assistance in my studio when you're done. I need you to shape up my layers a bit."

Moments later, Deon was sitting with a smock over her clothes.

"So..." Ruby tried to pry it out of her. Deon was all smiles. "We are meeting each other for coffee. Nothing major."

"Whatever! The way you were talking about him yesterday didn't seem like he could get you *anywhere*. Must have been *some* slow dance."

"We actually spent most of it talking. We both were avoiding catching up during the whole wedding festivities. But once we had our one-on-one, it was like all that nonsense melted away. He actually seems...different."

155

"Different in a good way or different in a *bad* way? Do tell!"

"I guess we will have to wait and see." It was so easy to smile when the thought of him crossed her mind. "Based on what he says, it's almost like I can't help but have a feeling that he is ready to settle down."

"He told you that?"

"No. No, not exactly. He brought up something from the past. Actually it stems from a silly pact we made in college."

Ruby looked at her blushing and luckily she didn't make a big deal about it. "We both are approaching 30, right. We always said if we weren't in a "serious" relationship by that age, we..." Deon couldn't bring herself to finish. She felt ridiculous. Like a school girl. And she was hoping that the information she shared wouldn't have her put her foot in her mouth. What if he was just...kidding, the whole time? There really wasn't any way to figure out other than seeing for herself, she figured.

"Well."

"We...would find each other and pretty much put all the game days aside...and be together. So it was weird. He sort of alluded to that the other night. So...you know."

"See, you were not a fan, but looks like he finally has come around," Ruby smiled.

Seeing such a scene made her feel like a fool. Deon was burning up inside – she never revisited a failed relationship. She was trying hard to forget Quincy altogether, but this universe was not letting her move on.

Then all of a sudden Deon was shocked to see scenes she was apprehensive about: scenes she thought they had passed up accidentally, scenes she suppressed so far back, she swore Âme couldn't find them.

"Hey, this happened in Middle School. I thought we were well past this."

"Well, looks like *you* weren't. This habit started then, but continued throughout high school. Even in college. Even recently."

Deon wanted to *booooo* the taboo subject. The physical scars now–a-days were covered up, even in the summer with make-up, tats and designer clothes, you name it. But in this place they were exposed, like her very soul.

No one could know. No one saw the wounds underneath all that material. They just thought she was a trend-setter.

"Okay, we can stop here, please. I mean, give a girl a break."

Deon had been a good sport, Âme figured, especially considering how she reacted to the news of her birth parent. He hoped she would handle some of the other revelations just as well.

157

Monitors shed light on many things, but they shed darkness, as well.

"Okay, we can get back to business tomorrow," he said.

Deon's eyes started to get heavy in the dark theatre.

Âme looked over at her and gave a warm smile. He knew she needed to get some rest, but he knew that the point they stopped at may open old wounds. He wished they could have dealt with it at that moment rather than put it off for another day. They were running out of precious time.

He gently touched her arm. She did need rest.

Something about his touch made her feel at home again. Deon saw a flicker of light in his eyes. He took all her trash out of her lap and signaled for her to follow him. She did, though wobbling here and there. He let her lean on him as they walked slowly away from the theatre. They approached an area where there was a twin bed.

"I have a queen at home," she said with a frown.

He soon tucked her into the comfy cot and before she knew it, she was out.

Beautiful Beasts

Without feelings of respect, what is there to distinguish men from beasts?
- Confucius

Sunday, January 4, 2009

The night was long.

"The devil is busy, but I am so glad we are busier doing God's work," Kyla said as her hospital shift came to a halt. Kyla felt she should stay the whole course, close to her ailing friend, Deon. After burning the midnight oil, dressed to the nines, her hubby, Reverend Hilton had made a trip to the hospital. After his visit and prayer, he was there to pick Kyla up in the early morning.

She had church in the morning. Two services. Her husband already had his sermon prepared, but he always liked going over his notes with his wife. They were centered around the Lord's Supper, the demise and empty rituals.

With one hour of some kind of sleep, the two were prepping for first communion Sunday at Mount Gerizim.

***

After hearing that there was a hole in Deon's back, Kennedy put on her sleuth suit and went back to the club where the nightmare occurred. She knew that Deon didn't just *fall* down. Now she just had to prove it.

***

What a rough night, Nadia thought, after being on a slight high from Q. Being around him was great, but the aftermath was always unsettling. It is still a reminder that they live in two different worlds, Nadia thought, as she went back to work. Nadia was happy to check in to her shift at a personal care home - she had the next week off. As she was helping to prepare food for the three ladies who were patients there, she thought to herself how she considered her own grandmother to be a wise woman, *but she hadn't met this one*. You can't be nice to everyone, Nadia thought, as Deon, someone who had gone out of her way to be a snob, treating people like she was Queen of the castle, invaded her mind. Nadia shook her head thinking about Deon. She made herself known to her. Minding her own business, Nadia failed to understand how so many people were in hers. So many tried to condemn her for something that they knew nothing about. Nadia shook her head, sometimes you meet your match, she thought.

Shark Tank

Perfection means not perfect actions in a perfect world, but
appropriate actions in an imperfect time.
– R.H. Blyth, student of Zen

Dreams always end on the part you need most. Deon was so desperate to find the piece that was missing, but suddenly she felt a different sensation: awakening to probing hands groping her breasts; she knew she didn't want any further contact because of their undeniable aggression. "I...I can't. Stop it."

Boy next door, I'm a *good listener* stuff. Wow, Âme, *really?* He had her fooled. *Certainly not cool!* Frowning, the hands were making their way to other places on her body. The closer they came, the more she felt engulfed in flames. Sticky skin...the violator's breath was hot and on her neck. She tensed up at the reality of what tainted the sensation. She liked Âme, but she still needed space after the last time she got close to a man. When she tried to turn, she was held...tighter. Gripped. She tried to break out of the possessive embrace.

"What...you know you like it," a woman's voice whispered.

Deon's eyes jumped as she jerked herself out from under this madwoman. "What the hell!" She knew that voice now. She kept hearing it over and over since this whole tragedy unfolded.

All she could see was a body, draped in a black cloak that didn't allow the face to be seen. That same robe, Deon saw hanging earlier by the mirror was on this woman. Deon looked down in utter shock when she realized she was...naked. She, for the first time wanted that ugly polka dot gown from earlier, or anything...just to shield her.

At that moment, she wanted to scream SECURITY, help break this up, tear apart the two that were going at it from the start. Her high self says walk, turn the other cheek. Be soft and spare. But her low says forget that made-for-TV, Kumbaya stuff; let bare hands handle the anger, the pain, the sheer disgust. Her soul cries out to get a hold of her. But the passionate, plentiful nature just wouldn't let that be. Peace is a foreign land. *She needed a passport.*

The lower half won when she started swinging. She hit the pervert in the face, grabbed the invader's neck and wasn't going to let go. She was taught, don't fight to hurt, fight to kill and that was her goal at this point.

She was not going to be violated, not as an adult! As she squeezed her neck, the woman's grip loosened.

The woman started to lose consciousness and her body was becoming limp each time Deon increased her grip. Then suddenly Deon felt a hand on her shoulder, pulling her off of this wicked one.

Âme frantically shouted, "Please stop. Both of you!"

162

"Hell no, this bitch tried me. Get off of me Âme!"

Âme used more force than Deon expected and pulled her off of the woman. The woman was still covered from head to toe, with that silly black cloth, but Deon could see her wrinkled hands touching her neck as she gasped for air. There, she had something that made Deon's mouth drop. Deon's charm bracelet from childhood – a gift that was stolen years ago, by the woman she had found, during this draining experience, to be her biological mother. Josie protected Deon, but the woman was so tricky. As a child, Deon was told that she was her aunt and Deon felt something was not right – that she was not safe until the woman died. She died on the streets. Deon never knew the details. She just knew she was safer now that the woman was gone. No more awkward visitations, molestation from her and others. Repression became her shield. Deon killed memories.

Seeing the bracelet brought them back to life.

The predator coughed for dear life.

"That is mine," Deon said as she continued to eye the bracelet. It was worth so much more than money. It was a gift from her maternal grandmother, before she passed away. The heirloom was stolen by this wayward woman who Josie and Sylvester later tried to protect Deon from, but somehow couldn't quite do it.

Then Deon turned to find Âme, a deer caught in *her* headlights. Mortified, Deon blushed and tried to cover as much of her trembling body as she could. Âme, apologetically, closed his eyes shut and turned his head quickly. "Let me get you some clothes. I am so sorry this happened."

The wicked woman was no longer choking, but now chuckling. Deon's eyes darted at her, "Evil never dies..." she said under her breath. Âme, before she knew it, was making his way back over, eyes closed and all. He held another thin cloth out for Deon to wrap herself in.

She kept her eyes on his lids while she tied the garment quickly; then her eyes caught the funniest sight. She tried not to laugh but he surely was rising to the occasion.

Snapping back in anger mode, Deon yelled at Âme "Who in the hell is this?" She walked over to the woman with a vengeance. "And why do YOU have this!" Deon was close, but couldn't even see the violator's face. She tried to grab the woman's arm to safely get her charm bracelet off without it breaking, but the unthinkable happened. The woman disappeared. Out of thin air. All that remained was her...laughter.

Suddenly, Deon heard the witch taunt her from a far-away place. "I'm your wake-up call."

Deon could hear the woman shaking the charms from the bracelet. She felt taken advantage of all over again. Her voice was in her head, appearing and disappearing, whenever it pleased. Who knew what else this woman was capable of doing?

Moments after the whole ordeal, Deon felt more confused: trying to process the place, the parents, the witch, the charms. Âme seemed to have read her mind and pushed her to pull out the notebook. "The answer is in the book *and* application," Deon started accessing as much as she could in the D drive. Her brain was on overload, but she kept filling it with more and more information.

As Deon searched, she heard the woman say, "Look at Mr. Hero! I never saw him run so fast for the others. I bet you wish he was there the night of the fall, huh?"

"Now I have about had it with all this crazy mess. I need answers!"

"I agree, let's get back to business, fast." Âme shared that they had more territory to cover and breakfast was on its way.

"Who came to my rescue anyway? Who called for the ambulance?" Âme looked as if Deon opened a can of...snakes. "Are you sure you are ready to visit that moment?"

"Sure she is," the woman interjected. "She's an adult. I can show her what she is asking for."

Âme looked upset.

"Luckily, it's not where you start, but where you end that matters," the woman's voice interjected. "Wouldn't you agree, Deon? Look at you, you are a prime example of a Cinderella story."

Nothing phased Deon anymore. She just stayed focused on moving closer to answers and everything kept getting more and more ambiguous.

"I think it's time for me to run the show," the woman said. Deon didn't trust her as far as she could throw her, but she did want to throw her, if she could find her. "I need to know. But only with Âme."

"This is not how the system works." Âme swallowed hard. "I wish I made the rules. I just follow them Deon. I can't control her. You picked one of her archives I can't access."

"Yep, he's right. It's my turn to show you around, booboo. Follow me if you really want to know what really matters now. She's a big girl now, Âme. We can fast forward."

Deon stood for a moment. Thoughts ran through her head: *Âme did have me wondering versus knowing. I really wasn't feeling the witch, but I could tolerate her to get what I wanted. But first things first.*

"Wait, who are you, really?" Deon asked.

She chuckled as if Deon should already know. "Your worst enemy," she snarled as she reappeared behind Deon. Deon frowned as she tried to get a good look at the woman.

"Oh really, why in the world would my enemy want to help me then? And why the hell are you all covered up in that mess? There are so many ways to wear black you know."

166

"You got that smart ass tongue from your real mom. And bitch, who died and made you fashion police?"

Deon rolled her eyes, "Don't act like you know me. I am not going anywhere with you until I get your name." She could hear her laughing whole-heartedly underneath all that fabric.

"Okay, okay, okay. You can call me Luci...for short."

Âme grabbed Deon's hands. "Just remember, I'm waiting for you, so we can finish what we started...Okay!" he held her hand tightly to reinforce his words. His hands were so warm in this cold place.

"Yeah, sure," Deon said.

"Deon, please don't stand me up," Âme begged.

"Awww, how sweet. Puppy love. Never saw you get like that."

Deon took a good look at Luci, wrapped up in the dark clothing. Then she took a good look at the man who was blushing and upset for some reason.

***

As the two women walked, Deon took a long look backward. Still Âme stood, growing smaller and smaller, at every step. Today, she was converted into a dead woman walking. She frowned. *I am still in this place. At least the dead can rest.*

As they walked, Deon couldn't believe that this woman still remained covered. Deon reminded herself that she needed...answers.

"Wow" said witchy poo. "So you worked all of your life, for *this*? What a way to show you some respect. I'm not a fan, but I give credit where it's due...You didn't deserve this. You won't believe what the people said. Who needs enemies with friends like yours." Deon knew this faceless coward was trying desperately to fan the flames. She was an enemy; Deon made a point not to respond.

But Deon felt she did make a sharp point, about working so hard and then this happening at such a crucial time. Deon must admit, it can be quite challenging defining success and her climb. There are so many unspoken truths. Upward mobility is not talk of the south. There were many flaunting degrees on top of degrees, but she believed class could not be bought. Many mind their manners, but southern hospitality can only get one so far up the corporate ladder. Plenty polite possums with sarcastic undertones survive, but don't necessarily thrive. That is why spoken lies are so much more, comforting. But Deon embraced the truth, no matter how much it hurt. That is why she continued to walk.

Deon could still hear the voice of her Paw Paw, a major gambler in the Boot, ringing in her ear, "In the south, it's not a game of tug-of-war. It's a game of push and shove. *Old* money pushes *new* money out." Even Uncle Bruno warned her, "Youngblood, hide your money."

168

Deon was not always happy with it, but she knew that a new day and a new set of rules were being played, not only in Houston, but in the world. Working in corporate America was the original goal and the reason she also studied Finance at U of H's Bauer College of Business. Her type A personality fueled this dream. But after working and rising successfully in a short period of time at two major oil and gas companies in the technology department, only to be cut down for one reason by both men and women, she had a light-bulb moment. In those two years, her superb work ethic was overshadowed by her physicality.

She tried to play her position, but she had never been good at acting, just mimicking. It either *is* or *isn't*. I was getting too close! Close to the top and closer to the edge, she thought.

But she was not going to let *this* ruin her appetite for success; success was in her blood.

They finally arrived in the theatre. Deon turned to look back. Âme was no longer in view.

They walked in. She didn't want to get too comfy, especially considering the witch and all her tricks. Deon stood close to the door, she didn't want popcorn. She didn't want anything but to get it over with.

Between Âme and Luci, hopefully, she could get clarity. She was trying to play the hand she was dealt.

Luci laughed and got comfy in her seat. Next thing Deon knew, they were hearing the emergency call and a frantic niece talking to the operator.

"911, what's the emergency?" asked the operator.

"My aunt has fallen down the stairs! She is bloody. Not responding to me..."

"What's the address of your emergency?

"We are at Club Sentinel in Houston off Main street – Please hurry!"

"How old is she?"

"30. Made 30 today. Are you on your way?"

"I do not want you to hang up...How much blood is it?"

"Jesus, a lot, it's a growing puddle of it...Are you on your way..."

So many things were taking place; it was hard to figure out what exactly was going on in the background.

Deon soon heard a man's voice. "Don't crowd her, move!"

"She's slipping in and out."

"How many steps did she fall down?"

Autumn tried to give an estimate over the sirens.

"Uh, Uh, uh, how many steps, guys?"

Another voice entered. "Everybody, move away from the body. Secure the property. Where is the woman?"

That was the end of the call.

Deon felt weak in the knees, being in shock for a minute. She hated that she was only able to listen to audio. But she could hear the panic in her niece's voice.

Poor Autumn, having to deal with that, Deon thought. She wanted to let her know she was okay and not to worry. But where was she, Deon wondered.

And how true was the statement of her being okay?

Deon soon heard another voice. The vampy voice. "Cell phone records are valuable, aren't they?" said the witch. "But I got something even better."

Deon wanted to SEE her kicker. Making no comment, she just stood there, wanting to be heard by those she loved. Wondering how she could get back there...to the scene of the crime. Fix the situation that had gone way wrong, or at least see who kicked her.

"Thanks. But, what else?"

The witch looked confused.

"What else you got?"

"What if I told you, I know who killed you."

Deon's throat started to constrict. *What?* Deon laughed. *Deon tried to scratch her head.* She could feel her forehead forming lines. "What in the hell are you talking about? How can I be dead when I'm here, talking with you?" The silence that followed was beyond awkward.

"Do you want to know or not?"

Shameless Plug

Deon was shaking her head so hard she felt that she

could bring on a concussion...Luci and Deon watched this lifeless, comatose figure, all hooked up to all these monitors and machines. *That cannot be me. Luci has got to be kidding!* Deon was panic stricken. "Bull shit!" All of a sudden Deon just felt the rage of reality hitting and hitting hard. Her uncontrollable screams erupted from her now fragile body. She took the notebook with the D drive that Âme had given her and threw it at the movie screen.

"Nooooo!?" Lights started flickering in the theatre as she screamed with fire in her lungs. "You lying bitch!" Shaking her head in disbelief, Deon freaked-out, ran out of that place in a flame of hysteria, determined to not let the lie engulf her.

"So soon? We were just having fun," Luci said under her breath. Deon felt outside of herself but she was going to run.

"You'll be back...especially if you want to know the truth."

Deon had tuned out the voice of the other woman. She felt light-headed at the thought of not being able to live life as she knew it...Vomit started to form in her throat; she was gagging as

173

she ran. She had had enough of these videos! She wanted her real life. *Why was this happening to me?* she cried. She wanted to be with her family. She needed them. These strangers...this strange place, were worse than the fall.

She couldn't escape the feeling, the propaganda - the emptiness of this hell hole.

She was trying to retrace her footsteps, knowing the open space was just that. She kept walking, not seeing anyone or anything. Just space. She was looking for Âme. She needed him.

After walking aimlessly, she suddenly felt a hand on her shoulder. "Hey, slow down, my dear."

She turned. What relief it was to see a familiar face. His fervent eyes secured her, temporarily. "I was looking for you Âme."

"Good, I found you. Lunch is on its way. Come on."

"Wait. Don't you have something to tell me?"

Âme stood, looking confused.

"That crazy woman back there, the one that has been spooking me out every other minute, told me that I was - dead!"

He blinked a couple of times before continuing.

"Bogus right!?"

He took a deep breath.

Deon stopped in her tracks to study his face – one that couldn't lie.

"Deon, in the natural realm, it seems that way. But the miracle is not easy to explain. That's why we have to hurry."

Deon couldn't hear him anymore. Her ears were deaf. All of a sudden, her body felt heavy and she lost her ability to stand. She felt the weight. Âme caught her in mid-fall. In his arms, her body went limp. Âme kept reassuring her with his calm voice and gentle touch, but she couldn't believe.

***

Suddenly, Deon could feel a glass of water being held to her dry, cracked lips. Sipping slowly, she regained some strength.

"Miracle? How is me being dead a miracle? You are just like everyone I meet."

"After the fall at the club, you were rushed to the hospital. Yes, the doctors did tell your family your condition. The miracle is the doctor never has the final say."

Wish this water was scotch, she quickly thought, but held her tongue, realizing more than likely that she was being watched from all angles, and possibly by angels. She now wanted to make the best impression.

Deon was quiet during lunch, deep in thought and mourning. *God have mercy on my soul.* She closed her eyes for a couple of seconds, trying not to let emotions take over – that was a no-no.

"*Why?* There are so many people who go after their dreams. So many people who find success in some aspect of life. From recess to now, why am I always a target? Fighting, clinging to life. Supported by a machine. Why am I in that situation?" Deon thought out loud.

"Don't give up, Deon. The enemy wants who he doesn't have. We still have some footage to go through, to get to the final evaluation - but if you need to rest, I can postpone it," Âme informed.

"How is footage going to save me? Keep me from dying? I am already dead – remember. What sense do you make?"

"The past presents the truth, and if you continue to face the truth like I told you earlier, once you get a hold of all the dead things and poisonous things in your life and really put them to rest, you will truly live."

Deon didn't know what to believe. But she wanted to live. Always.

"Well, you are certainly in the right place. The root of the issue is in these early chapters of your life."

"Are you insinuating that I am responsible for what happened to me? Âme, I didn't push *myself*." Âme gave her a weird look.

She grabbed him, desperately, "I need you with me, when I watch with her."

"I wish I could be there, but the rules are I can only access the past. She can access real time and some audio from the incident."

"How unfair is this system? Just like in the real world." She pouted. "Who is responsible for this nonsense?"

Âme's eyes widened as if to shush her. The lights flickered and soon they felt and heard something similar to a sonic boom. Deon's eyes amplified.

"We better hurry. Remember yesterday. The part we said we would return to?"

She nodded. "If getting through that helps me live, let's get back to business."

The two were back in the auditorium, alone, together watching a scene that went back to middle school, where Deon picked up a habit that sent her off to the Biel Mental Health facility. Returning to this truth was uncomfortable. It was a shameful time in Deon's life. A time when she was not quite as strong or accepting of self.

"My mom and dad were so hush-hush about the psychiatric ward, of course."

The reason for the entry was that the stylist found various uses for scissors - once she was found using them to cut into her flesh, her parents wanted her to get help, fast.

"They told people I went to Grandma's." She laughed, but Âme didn't. Âme looked at Deon after looking at the scars when they were new. She knew what he was thinking.

"But I never fantasized about killing myself; I hate those whimps. Even those ODers. Pain killers were all around. Dad supplied Mom with what she'd later abuse. I rejected that as well. I'd rather live and *feel* the pain, you know." She looked at him, as she shook her head. "Pain felt good to me."

He really felt so bad for her in that moment. Deon looked away, trying to avoid his concerned eyes. "I don't know how to feel good without it. The hurt was embraced like a friend, a real one." She continued. Âme listened closely.

"What would you say led you down this path though?"

"Just, I don't know, being misunderstood, maybe. I mean this was all the time. It became unbearable for me. No one was really on my side."

She shook her head. "I was always hated for something. I just wanted to feel loved."

Silence followed then she went on.

"I just got angry at myself, like others. I don't know what was going on in my head. It was like I shut my brain off. I felt a rush every time. Before I knew it, it was a habit, one that was easy to support."

"How did the treatment go?"

"Eventually, I returned to school. Being away from being able to make money made me never want to cut myself again." She stopped herself from laughing. "Now, I keep busy to stay out of trouble. I only use scissors to cut hair." Âme looked at her closely.

"Clean ones, of course," she reassured him.

She had never shared this part of her life with anyone. It was her secret, one of them. It was hard to keep eye contact with Âme. She was realizing and appreciating how it was easy to share with him. Was she glass before his eyes? she wondered. Was she making a fool of herself and he was just being polite, playing a role, doing a job? She could feel herself at his mercy. It made her a bit uneasy, yet freer than ever. The way Âme looked at her, as if he didn't seem to see her face made her feel listened to. Like what she had to say mattered too, like he was storing her words away. In a safe place.

"I'm sorry you had to experience that Deon."

"I brought it on myself. I just wasn't strong enough. I thought I was." Âme looked as if he couldn't relate, so he said nothing. Instead, he just stared at the woman he really cared about and wanted the best for.

She gently moved the hair out of her eyes. He stared at her, through her, for what felt like eternity.

"Your eyes...are really gorgeous."

She had heard that a lot, but it sounded different, coming from him. He didn't seem to say it as a come on to initiate a first date. It seemed more like a sincere observation.

She shook her head. "Thanks."

As she looked in his eyes, she wondered, how can she feel beautiful in such an ugly state. She didn't know, but she did. What was strange to her was...his eyes...not the color, but the placement were like hers. Her eyes were not symmetric. Her left eyebrow was raised higher than the right. So was his.

Âme interrupted her thoughts.

"Why do you cover them up? With those bangs? I see that on a lot of your looks from your 20s.

Decoding Deon was far from fun. Between Âme and Luci, these people were bringing up anything and everything Deon didn't want to resurface in this reality show from hell. There was no privacy, just piracy, she thought.

"Several reasons. I hate my widow's peak. The sun hurts my eyes. They are light in color and very, very sensitive. I guess my bangs are my shades, you know, the usual."

Âme sighed. He enjoyed talking to her, but time was ticking and every moment counted.

"We've uncovered a lot of lies but most importantly, a lot of truth. I'm proud of you for facing them head on. We are almost done with this part. Now here is where the D drive will really come in handy."

A Lucille Ball expression formed on Deon's face.

"Oh yeah, about that."

***

Luci waited in the theatre, knowing that she needed Deon more than Deon needed her. She knew she had failed as a mother and she knew that the least she could do was help her *biological* daughter out in some way, shape or form. But she battled, as she always did, to stay on the straight and narrow path.

IF the process of elimination was what Deon really wanted, Deon could have it, *but* she knew Deon needed to reclaim her birthright.

Whether she believed the truth, that was a whole other subject. Luci knew who was responsible for Deon's fall.

She knew she had caused Deon much grief and probably was the reason for some of the torment that she faced in middle school. She couldn't be trusted to be a mother, but she still wanted to be close to her – *but in the wrong way*. Coming back into her life, claiming to want to spend time with her daughter

181

turned out to be a scandal. She was angered by the DeVaulles lock and key type of parenting, once they realized Luci was not fit for visits and so on. She was angry at herself for not being able to keep her child. To have to give her up from the start. To settle for being called Aunt instead of mom. She knew she was wrong.

She knew she had a responsibility now, even in death, to be a guardian angel that didn't continue to torment Deon's already tormented soul.

She knew that if Deon made it past this phase, the reality she would face would be even harsher. So being loving was the least she could do at this point. Under the robe, tears rolled down her face.

***

Deon had a new notebook in her hand, courtesy of Âme. She knew what she needed to do with it before facing Luci again.

By trouble-shooting, she was getting somewhere, slowly, but surely. Deon wouldn't say she appreciated the nuances that had been thrust upon her in such a short period of time, but knowing her life was in danger, she wanted to meet them head on. She was going to make the most of the moments, as puzzling as they were, in hopes of soon piecing them together to form a big picture.

After completing steps in the notebook that would allow her to get closer to the end of installation, she knew what she had to do. Download the new protective software as soon as she could. "I think I'm ready to go back to see the rest now."

Âme nodded, understanding that she would be close to cracking her own case if she followed directions well. He just hoped that she would not crack or crash once she found out the truth.

Deon carefully walked herself back to the auditorium to face her demons. She opened the door, expecting to see Luci, but the woman in the black robe was nowhere to be found. She waited, sure to hear a wicked laugh or two, but as Deon came to the center of the room, she found something very dear to her instead.

Her charm bracelet Luci had on her wrist earlier was now there. Quickly reclaiming what was hers, Deon felt a sense of peace wash over her. She knew that the woman had no business wearing it in the first place, but at least she had the decency to give it back. She knew her so-called mother had stolen it years ago, among other things. She never thought she would see it again, especially since the woman she recently found to be her birth mother had died from overdosing when Deon made it to high school.

Deon didn't know what to do in the room that had the house lights on and no projection playing. Then she remembered the instruction manual and its directions on how to use it this time. Time alone. Time reflecting.

Deon sat there, not denying or suppressing, but instead, gathering her thoughts. Âme was not playing when he said she was in for a bumpy stroll: a journey, so close to home, yet so far away. A private paradox she couldn't welcome to stay. She appreciated its visit, yet she knew not to sit in it for too long. She would have to act soon.

She pushed play. A chapter title read *Discernment*. Projected on the screen was one blurred-out face and funny voice after the next. A litany of lies, doses of TMI and sweet symphonies of truth played out like a blockbuster to her soul.

Feeling Suspect

*The world is a looking-glass, and gives back
to every man the reflection of his own face.
– Williams Makepeace Thackeray*

Monday, January 5th, 2009

He never expected to fall for any woman, especially this woman who was a business woman first and beauty empress second.

At the hospital, Quincy sat knowing he messed up. Seemed like yesterday, but it was actually a month ago that they had a one-on-one at the mid-town gallery, Renazance Lounge. Why didn't he have the heart to tell Deon she still looked as beautiful as she did in college when he first fell in love with her? Instead, he got a rise out of making her vanilla skin grow bloody-red. The damage was done. He remembered the pact that he had thrown out there in college and knew that he had to answer to a woman who wouldn't take *no* as an answer. He couldn't do that; he couldn't go through with it.

There was a lot of inner turmoil that had toiled and turned him into this crying baby, sitting, helplessly, groping for the peaks the passionate pair had reached in the past.

That day, inner demons kept him from saying the truth each and every time – now, he knew, on this dreadful day, it may be too late.

In this city, she was as busy as he was making things happen. In a sadistic type of pleasure, he kept her waiting and waiting to hear what she wanted. He couldn't give her what she wanted.

In the nick-of-time, there she was, the other woman, his scapegoat. And a beautiful one at that...taken aback by his discovery and lost in its findings...a work of art so rich in composition, so unique in design and so perfect in execution...the flawless, well-sculpted structure was an innocent bystander in this scheme brought on by Q's biggest fear. He couldn't oppose the urge to examine every detail, every line and every curve up close and personally! He did what he did best, ran away when things got real. With tunnel vision, Quincy singled out Nadia Elaine Masters in the stark white exhibit hall across the way.

Punishing women sat like a second skin. Houston's Most Eligible Bachelor was not leaving his bachelor ways behind.

He could still see Deon whipping her silky long ebony tresses around, not sure of what to focus on in the crowded hall across the way, as he fixed his eyes on the Nubian Queen that stood so close, yet so far away, Nadia Masters.

A masterpiece! He answered to himself as he involuntarily left Deon more than mind-boggled at the table as he went after the stranger he wanted to become more familiar with.

After swiftly maneuvering himself through the zigzag pattern of tables, chairs and people like the agile football player he had been on the field, in a matter of seconds Quincy stepped into the exhibit hall. That was then.

***

...Now, Kennedy was frustrated and she wished she had a clone: one that could be at the hospital just in case the news changed, one way or another, and one that could be out there still looking for clues to who kicked Deon. She was happy to at least know that her hunch was right. After the nurses informed them more about the examined hole in Deon's back, some things came to Kennedy's mind.

Once Kennedy could break away from Kyla's prayer circle, she opened her phone. Tons of messages were sent about the accident. Kennedy bypassed them and opened her latest project proposal that she was scheduled to send today, but before the incident. She postponed it. Her dream of casting Deon was going down the drain. It was weird seeing the information...information that was ready to be used before this horrible ordeal. Deon was one of a kind and Kennedy knew that even though she could look for another Bachelorette, there would never be one like Deon.

Suddenly, call-screening Kennedy saw an unsaved number coming in. Moments later, a voicemail was left by gossip connoisseur, Gabby. She said it was urgent. Kennedy returned the call outside.

***

Sheila didn't have a lot of free time, but most of it went to social media. Still flooded with details on Deon's fall, her eyes were glued to the screen filled with updates. Suddenly she got an IM from Romeo.

"I wish it didn't have to be this way, but karma is a bigger bitch than Deon," he said. Sheila hesitated before replying. Although hurt, she was not into being hurtful. Words, she knew you couldn't retract them. She knew how hurtful they could be. Four months earlier, Sheila had had a hell of a morning, that was for sure. Prepared for weeks for the interview, her youngest out of three children had come down with something Sheila was still trying to treat. Sheila was rarely late, and usually five minutes early. She pleaded with Deon.

Sheila could see her whole dream becoming a nightmare.

"Ma'am, I can explain the situation," Sheila expressed whole-heartedly that day, the day that seemed like yesterday since it was a day that kept playing in Sheila's head.

"A situation that I don't want to hear," Deon said, closing her eyes as she eased on her shades.

188

Sheila swallowed hard as she watched Deon pull out a carton of Marlboro cigarettes.

"Honey, you're alive. The only excuse I would have accepted was if you were dead, or something of that nature," she said in her pitchy voice that had become harsher over time.

Desperately, Sheila continued to stand, wanting to explain, but Deon pulled out her lighter.

Deon held her index finger over her lip. "You have said enough," she snapped as she lit her cigarette then stuffed the box back into her purse. More words were said, basically to put Sheila in her place. Sheila held her tongue.

"I'm always on top," Deon snapped.

Sheila frowned at the woman who stared at her directly through her dark shades.

"Out of respect for Romeo, I gave you an interview. But baby girl, I advise you to get on top of your game." Deon put the cigarette in her mouth and started to walk off.

Though she was a bitch, what happened to Deon was something Sheila wouldn't wish on her worst enemy.

Burned Bridges

Their words bled on the screen. She came from the school

of if you fail the test, there were no retakes. Windows of
opportunity close. She did not want him to win if it involved her
losing. Underwhelmed with life itself, she wanted to be away from
a group that: 1. Doesn't understand her 2. Doesn't support her 3.
Makes her feel lifeless. She watched hours of footage, of no-nos.
lame fame-chasers. mean wanna-be-mack-daddys. real mack
daddys. retired mack daddys. more no-nos. boundary pushers.
emotion disregarders. the disengaged. the disappointed. the
distanced, yet all in your business. After all the footage was
watched, Deon did the only thing she could do.

Laugh. What's a diva to do? Keep on keeping on. *To all my
critics - I'll show you where you can shove it.* What did these
people know about her? None of them had walked in her stilettos.
She was who she was. She was a nobody who became somebody
and she wasn't going back. She was going forward. She was not
making any apologies for being desperate to bloom. She
bloomed where she was planted instead of died where the
daggers lie. The desire to be great produced the hate that killed

her. She could live with that truth. Deon tried to remain calm, cool and collected. She knew the rules, but she wondered, who were these people? She could count her friends on one hand.

***

A three-day hold in this treatment facility made Deon's dark days take on a whole new meaning. Determined to overcome the addiction of darkness and come clean, she knew who she was and she knew who she wasn't. I'm not a playette or a perfect angel. I am a real woman. I want to feel special, not random. Not like an afterthought, a plaything, a game piece, a challenge and not even a catch. *I am NOT going to sleep in this place*, Deon thought, fighting to keep her eyes open. She was convinced that Kyla would be proud of her, putting in all this reading of the word and all. Deon missed the people in her life. As she watched more and more, she read more and more, she saw some of the scriptures Kyla recited glibly at any given moment to try to keep a hold on *us sinners*. There were detectives, there were doctors and then there was the D drive. *Thank God for the D Drive*, she thought. She felt she was getting somewhere. Boy did monitors shed light on many things. One thing is the notebook's battery needed to be recharged. Deon, with all her might, tried to keep going. Her eyes were getting heavy...she feared sleep. It was a strange place to be in. Superstitions set in, making her feel uneasy and she didn't want to miss a beat. Didn't want to be violated. The room was foggy, the light was faint. Soon she was back at a place she knew all too well. In those moments of truth...Deon looked in the mirror, fighting to recognize herself. She was panicking to find human quality.

> Did I really want to come back to life, back to reality? A world where there is all access but no penetration. Less and less human infiltration? A world where people talk behind my back and smile in my face? – Hell yeah! I have work to do. I have a great family. I got a future husband to get to know. I have a future family to be taught by an existing one. Fuck my haters. Uh, scratch that. "Bless" them. I'll even try praying for them later today, - baby steps, remember...but for now, I had one thing I was putting my all into. I was going to do all I could to see the light. Change does not come without a cost. In spite of all doubt, I was seeing things, more clearly, one puzzle piece at a time. Life did count. As precious it is, I don't always know what to do with it, but I sure as hell know I'm not doing it with hate! Love was the answer. Was all fair in love? No, but **it's not my time to go.** Pushing. No longer can my spirit dwindle. Or my fight grow faint on this journey. I must remember to rekindle the love you have for me. A narrow door – ahead. I am pushing. Reverse this curse! From treasure to trash and back to treasure again! So soon I can say, I dealt with my dirt, soon I can say it's time to come clean, clear the air, let the good air in. Soon, (I hear more voices, but a different kind.) Voices that give me chills. Not from haters either. Not from death. But from a faint voice, a beautiful life, one that vibrated my soul.

***

"We stand here today, God, asking that your will be done, but selfishly, we ask that you please factor in our prayers, our want for our friend to return to a healthy state. We are praying for a full, 100% recovery." As Kyla stood, leading a group of friends and family in prayer outside the room, her voice was like fire: rising and rising, getting hotter and hotter with conviction.

Part Three

Queen D Syndrome

Time Tells

Forgive your enemies but never forget their names. –JFK

I just miss seeing her eyes. I don't know what I'll do if I don't see them again," a sleep-deprived Josie cried inside Deon's hospital room.

"Josie, don't talk like that," her sisters said as they came over to comfort her. Josie was in her own world, talking out loud.

"Open your eyes, baby! Please, it's momma. Open your eyes. Deondria."

Still pushing through, with all her might, as if it were the last, Deon mustered up enough strength to grunt. She realized that she did something that made Josie happy, so she kept trying.

"Look, she squeezed my hand!" Josie jumped out of her seat, but still held on tightly.

Cries of joy filled the room, as the touchdown was scored by the former vegetable-like figure.

"Look, she's smiling!" one of her aunts said. Deon was glad she could hear, because she was lost.

"Oh my God, she opened her eyes! She opened her eyes! Nurse!"

Like myth to reality, Deon had never been so happy. She didn't care what the state of Black marriage was. She was alive! She didn't care about the pessimistic studies and evidence. She was alive! She didn't care about her mom lying about her birth. She was alive! She didn't care that Nadia was the apple of Q's eye – well, maybe she did, but she cared more about the fact that she had another chance at this thing called life, and she sure as heck was not into wasting any seconds worrying about something out of her control.

After moments, and more moments, Deon was trying to fix her words to say something, but nothing connected until now. Deon couldn't see anything and moving was ambitious, so she tried it. *My sight. What happened to my sight?*

She could feel people watching her and her eyes were watering as she realized, no sign of light, just darkness. *Please don't let me come back like this.* She wasn't aware of all of the terms.

A week later...

"The first 48 hours are crucial. Make sure she is not by herself," Deon heard someone say to her family as she was being put into a white robe then lifted by her dad into a wheelchair.

"Of course," Josie said.

"She needs plenty of rest."

197

Oh no, I don't, Deon thought to herself.

"But she shouldn't be taking sleeping pills," the physician continued. Deon's sight was now blurry, but the doctor encouraged them that if it didn't improve in three days, they would need to return.

"She may experience headache, nausea, and even vomiting."

Sylvester nodded sympathetically.

"Stressful situations need to be avoided. No contact sports for at least four weeks. No work until she has completely recovered.

Deon's heart sank.

Josie patted her back. "Of course."

Deon knew driving was off limits, but that didn't suck as much as the not being able to work.

"Most importantly, she needs to avoid any stress."

"Please return if she loses consciousness or feeling in the body. Even if drowsiness or dizziness occurs. If you see leakage from the body. IF the eye sight is still blurry."

Deon respected the doctor, but she wasn't planning on returning. "No alcohol. No caffeine in the diet," they added. Deon rolled her eyes, "of course," she thought with a laugh. *No life.*

"Right now, all we have to work on is making sure that she heals 100%. That is not just focusing on one area. She survived a traumatic fall and skull injury. It takes time...She is lucky to be alive."

"Blessed, doctor, blessed!"

***

Returning home was bitter-sweet. Yes, Deon was grateful to be alive, but she was not blind to the reality of how hard it was going to be to get this Humpty Dumpty back together again. Taking it easy was hard and a bit frustrating to her. Sitting there in the bed overwhelmed her. It reminded her of being confined. Then she felt weird just lying there because she knew there was work to be done, money to be made and bills to be paid. She would get tired, but she would have a hard time actually sleeping.

"I know next week that I will be able to actually do something," she said. She was not trying to make matters worse though. She was following their orders, keeping record of all symptoms.

They pulled up to what was dubbed her castle. As she was carried inside the house full of mirrors, she knew she didn't need one to tell her how awful she looked.

***

Waking up was excruciatingly painful. She remembered watching old people rise in the morning. How much pain it seemed they were in was a bit unbelievable, but she now knew

199

what every second of that effort meant. It took her more than a moment to sit up. It took several people to help her ease into a sitting position. It took even longer to stand up. Her family was there, waiting to guide her. So was a physical therapist. She was to begin the sessions the next week.

Crutches

My love is like a band-aid;
my memory helps it stick.
– Deon DeVaulle

Two weeks later

"I don't want that thing..."

Deon said, continuing to sit at the mirror of her bedroom vanity. Her master sanctuary was a bit schizo, unlike the rest of the home – it had no signature colors, just random décor that showcased her Texas roots and bohemian, handcrafted pottery work that she had gotten through travel and DIY practices. She was Miss Fix It...IKEA supplied her with many home projects, finished and unfinished.

Her family, already dressed in crème and purple, stood behind her, concerned at her inability to understand that she was not in any shape to walk on her own yet. Though postponed, the wedding at her home was still on. And it happened to be today.

They laughed, but Deon was serious. She shook her head as she finished screwing the antique pearl earring in her ear. "No canes for this 30-year-young woman." She was determined to walk down the aisle, which happened to be stairs, without one.

"We just don't want you falling again, sweetie."

Deon didn't either. The dead horse was beat. She could feel the hole in her back, a constant reminder of the night that changed her life forever – she didn't need much else. To her, a lesson learned was valuable, so valuable that on the tag, there is no price.

"I understand, but I don't want that thing," she said eyeing the stick.

Deon's doctor had stated that she was making an astonishing recovery and how her case shows how the brain's competence to restore some functions after significant injury is uncanny, but Deon still had a long road ahead.

Quincy was outside of the door, overhearing what he didn't want to barge in on. He was anxious to get to her. When some of the family started to clear the room, he knew it was time.

At the sight of him, many of the women smiled, spoke and he greeted them.

He peeked in to see that Deon was not alone. Her mother still stood, wondering what to do next with the defiance. At the sight, the mom turned, but Deon stayed looking in the mirror adding finishing touches.

Quincy felt uncomfortable, but he had to talk to her. She had been hard to talk to since she had been admitted and released from the hospital, of course.

Her mother seemed confused, but smiled through the confusion. She excused herself, but informed Deon she would be back shortly. Deon continued to not see the man.

Quincy didn't know what to say or do as he watched Deon sit as her own guard.

Peace after pain is what she was requesting. She didn't want to retaliate - (that is a miracle). She was able to think straight - *a living testimony that one can change for the better.*

"Deon, you are one fine looking specimen."

Deon stood in silence, looking in the mirror. She tried to focus on pinning her hair neatly into the side bun, the look of the bridal party. This was the first one she was in where she didn't do the make-up for the bridal party.

"I came because I need to talk to you about something. Something I have been putting off and putting off and now I know, time is of the essence." He looked for permission and got nothing. He walked back to the door and looked outside of it before slowly closing it. Deon didn't want to be on Q's emotional roller coaster any more. She was not going to start a new trend of dealing with dudes she was so over. "I can't go back." Deon slowly reasoned.

"Okay, don't worry, we will go forward," he insisted.

Deon sat.

"I know and I understand I have been a real jerk lately. I know none of the stuff is adding up to you. I felt awful, but I thought it was best if I let you go because I love you. You don't know the whole story. You deserve better. I didn't want to hurt you."

Deon laughed. He paused and looked more serious than ever. To Deon, he even looked pitiful, something she was not used to seeing on his face.

He swallowed before continuing. He wasn't sure how much detail to disclose.

"Deon, I have a disease."

All kind of thoughts ran through Deon's head. She thought the worse, wondered if she should ask what kind. He continued.

"I recently found out and I am coming to terms with it and I wasn't sure how to deal with it, let alone let people in on it. So I didn't. Since it didn't affect you and your health, I really didn't want you to know."

Deon didn't want to believe her ears. IT all came together, his sudden distance, his irrational behavior, his wanting to let go. She understood the strange behavior, but she wished this was not his reality. She wouldn't wish that on her own enemy. It crushed her. "Are you okay?"

"I am taking it one day at a time."

All of a sudden she frowned. "When...did this happen or when did you find out?"

"Last year. So I know what I brought up years ago and I know we were getting closer to that time. You were not going crazy; I was, with all my emotions. I knew what I wanted...I knew you didn't sign up for me like this. I didn't want to endanger you and I knew I didn't want to let you down. I didn't want you to deal with it. Period. I didn't want to tell you because I knew you would..."

"I would what?"

Quincy didn't finish. "I wouldn't blame you if you...changed how you saw me." Deon stopped, looking in the mirror and turned to stand up slowly. She faced him. She touched his gentle face.

"Quincy, I love you regardless. Nothing can change that. I am so, so sorry that this is your reality. I appreciate you letting me know. Letting me put my mind at ease. Because I knew you better than that."

Deon was grateful that Quincy tried to protect her in some warped way.

"I hope you are okay." Then suddenly, Deon started to experience déjà vu in such an acute way she had to sit back down as she cradled her stomach; she felt something she couldn't believe.

She had a secret too.

Money & Power Curves

Knowledge conquered by labor becomes a possession
- a property entirely our own.
- Samuel Smiles

March was here. It was Monday morning, an off day,

but a work day for the owner. Once Deon's sight got sharp enough to see details; the global nomad was on the computer a lot, trying to catch up. In no time, she was continuing her studies to get her MBA at Rice University, and she was back to work only to find business was no longer where it used to be. Sister Snow and Celestina had quit; their stations were empty. Their two week notices were not sent. Only a flustered Ruby stood amidst two vacant chairs when Deon arrived.

Ruby didn't have the heart to tell her when it initially happened in February, but she knew keeping it a secret wouldn't be great either, considering how much money was lost per day. Luckily, the salon still made money through products, Ruby's customers and loyalty. Ruby was booked solid trying to also take care of the other women's clients who wanted to stay.

"Where is the liquor?" Deon asked.

"You can't drink yet," Ruby insisted.

"No, to pour in memory of these dead bitches."

The two ladies laughed.

Deon knew she would need to hire new girls, and this time, *boys* fast. She'd have to get the energy from somewhere. But for now, she was just going to let it all be. She was tired of dealing with people who didn't want to be around her. They may be hard to replace skill wise, but to her, the attitude wouldn't be missed. She did still have her Saturday girls: loyal clients Kennedy, Kyla, Autumn and more. She could only hope for the best.

As they poured in memory of the old salon, Deon shouted, "No nigga formed against me shall prosper."

Ruby knew the old Deon was coming back, slowly, but surely.

She had been doing so well, physically, but she still did feel overwhelmed and overburdened.

Moments later, the two ladies started working on separate projects. Deon was looking through records which were in a disarray.

"You okay?" Ruby asked.

Deon wasn't.

"When does it end? This threat, this nightmare?" Deon replied. She didn't want to deal with all of it; rebuilding her salon, paying bills on top of medical bills, not being able to move her own hand the way she used to. She was scared she was losing her magic after almost losing her life.

"I just wanted to get through life." The anger was still there inside of her. It never left; it just died down a bit. She was mad alright, mad at the world. The unfairness. But she was driven by madness. She worked through the madness to mask the mounting pain as she climbed the corporate ladder. Her mind had always been on her grind. But some things were different now. Her heart was smart, but she ignored it. It was trying to tell her more than she wanted to hear.

"It is funny how many educated fools are out there with more degrees than a thermometer," Deon said out of the blue.

"What made you say that?" Ruby said laughing.

Deon was always in it for the money and never understood people who worked for free....who ever volunteered. Everything she did centered around money and making more of it.

Deon shook her head as she started to ramble. "I just wonder was it all worth it? All the sacrifices."

Ruby was sympathetic. "Of course!"

"I just don't know. I feel I have always been held to a higher standard and I never had a problem with that. But dropping the ball is too much for me. It feels like some people are allowed to be more human than others, to make more mistakes and not be judged as harshly. Can get away with more.

Everything I thought that mattered, doesn't matter right now. I guess I feel that if you are going to flaunt something in life, flaunt common sense, because not a lot of people possess that," Deon finally said, trying to make sense of her frustration.

Ruby looked closely at Deon. "God didn't send you to fight your wolves. Time for a break," Ruby insisted.

They both looked at each other nodding.

Ruby, out of habit, almost grabbed her cigarette, but Deon had that sad look on her face. She was trying to do right. She didn't want to take any chances.

"Oh yeah, what replaces that?"

"Nothing," said Deon pouted. For now the tube will do. She grabbed the remote. She turned on the flat screen television. And there was Dr. Lynne sharing her expertise on some talk show. "The Shadow psychology, Carl Jung's proposal was that the 'Unconscious mind consists of forbidden feelings, primitive instincts and repressed desires.' Interaction can take place. He wrote 'the less aware a person is of shadow, the darker it is.'"

"I guess Kennedy left you alone about the dating show."

Deon turned the channel. The ten o'clock news made both of them stop in their tracks – Deon's heart stopped for a second. The photo of Gabby, the gossip girl at the party, sat to the right of the screen. The headline read: Gossip Columnist Found Dead in her apartment.

***

Kennedy was trying to track down the woman with the lethal stiletto. She needed to talk to Deon who may still be in danger.

She needed to talk to Deon fast. But she hadn't been answering her phone. She had been in a different zone, far from her old self.

***

"You look great as always. Even after all this."

Meeting up with Romeo came at a great time. He had called to check on the diva, but instead, he came to the house with a get-well jokey card that could help lift her spirits.

Deon slowly sat after walking him inside the home.

"Now where is everyone?"

"They let me have a break from them. I needed it."

"I know you can't drink *drink* yet, so I will make you a Shirley Temple. I am glad to see you're getting back to yourself."

"I know. It has been such a journey."

"So what happened?"

Deon sat for a moment then shook her head.

"I really cannot remember everything. There still remain unanswered questions. I wish you were able to see it. I remember the party was so live...I really was having a good time. It just took a turn."

"I heard...but you know you always got to go straight to the horse's mouth before you start to speculate."

"Heard what?"

"That you were drunk and fell. But I know you better than that. I am so glad you are okay. We don't have to talk about it. So what do you plan to do with yourself?"

Deon rolled her eyes. "Just trying to take it easy."

After a couple of sips, Romeo could see Deon becoming a little drowsy.

Deon asked about his boo. Romeo shared that things were the same ole same ole thing.

"How are the men in your life?" he asked.

"Q and I got back together like we said we would."

Romeo looked like he had seen a ghost.

"Really?"

Deon watched how shocked he was. *She hated her lie.*

"You don't sound too happy."

"Well, I just remember him treating you like crap that night."

Deon smiled. "Hmmm...Interesting. I thought you weren't there, remember. How would you know that? No one knew that except for...you know." She looked at Romeo closely.

"What? What are you talking about?"

"You know exactly what I am talking about Romeo."

"What did I do to you that was so bad? What did Gabby do to you? Take pictures of what she saw? Pictures you never knew were taken...of you that night."

Romeo's betrayal was beyond unbelievable. He was a dirty thief that looked clean, but had sticky fingers.

"You were in drag that night, weren't you? At my party. I must admit, you looked good too. You are very photogenic. Either that or that Canon Rebel is a damn good camera."

"What the hell are you talking about?"

"I'm talking about how you give drag queens a bad name! They are going to be pissed at your disloyalty. You know some of our friends would be so mad to find out how you get down. WE were supposed have each other's back. You kicked me in mine and had me falling down the stairs. And that fall hurt like hell!"

All of a sudden, Deon couldn't continue to talk. He looked at her drink and smiled as she slowly slumped over, passing out."

Romeo watched Deon pass out.

"You always were a selfish bitch. You never think about anyone else but yourself. All these years, I have begged you in one way or another, to do this show or do this project. You decline." He said under his breath.

All of a sudden, Romeo pulled out a small prescription bottle. He popped off the top and let two little capsules fall beside the half empty drink. He started gathering his things.

"Not this time, Romeo," Kennedy said coming from behind a door with a picture that Gabby had taken of Romeo right before the kick and an audio recorder that was still recording, in her left.

Deon, grateful for dumbass criminals, decent acting skills, and a few loyal friends, eased back up from her slump right in time to see Romeo looking as though he had seen *another* ghost.

Who's Who

Buy the truth, and sell it not: also wisdom and instruction, and understanding.
- Proverbs 23:23

Sunday, January 3, 2010

2 am

It felt like the first day of school, when you can't wait to see who your teacher is and the make up of the class. The new year had already begun; a new age still hadn't broken in and a new way to celebrate her 31st birthday was in effect.

Deon needed to be out the door in an hour. Months before, she had made preparations to leave, but she just hadn't locked down a destination. After some careful planning, she knew where to really experience a digital detox.

Already packed, the designer duds stayed home, some white tanks, long sleeved collar shirts and painted on jeans were her vacation uniform. Her cell was only brought in case of an emergency.

As she slid on her boots, she found it eerily easy to travel light. Although Deon had been reprogrammed and denial was of

214

yesterday, Deon still didn't have peace. Still something tugged at her antsy soul.

The bangs were no longer bangs - they grew out shortly after her discharge from the hospital. During recovery, a year–long process, she didn't let anyone touch, let alone cut, her hair. So now, her mane was longer, no set style. The black dye, faded, uncovering her sandy brown tresses and gray streaks here and there.

Her sight had returned to its norm and wanting nothing to block her view, she brushed her long strands up into a ponytail, creating a high-fashion bun in seconds.

She could look at herself. She had a hold on Deon – the one before she was rudely interrupted...before the parent swap...before the affair with money...the viral vanity...the party...now she had to *move*. She had to *do*.

But in order to *do*, she needed inspiration and Pinterest wasn't cutting it anymore. The 31 year old forgave herself for not being able to do all she planned to by the age of 30; like in business, failures come before success. She also accepted that many frogs had been kissed, and the fact that her Prince Charming still wasn't in the picture. She had to realize that she was not Superwoman; she had a human longing. A place far away, but near and dear was a necessity.

She clutched her paintbrush, vowing to not misuse it; she was going global. To find her muse. With a Bible and her

French/English dictionary in her purse, she turned off all the lights in the home, turned on the alarm and was off to Bush Intercontinental Airport without telling a soul. Yes, a note on the front porch, just in case anyone were to really care, was written in French. *She needed as much practice as she could get.*

So many people had been in her head, she had to clear the space. With no travel companions - just a blank sketchbook – she was going back to the drawing board. She wasn't taking any more guilt trips. Instead, she was escaping to the best places money could buy. Paris, as a wise beauty icon once said: *Paris is always a good idea.*

***

The luxurious, yet raw two-hundred-year-old hotel made the birthday girl forget about the ten-hour flight. The internet pics didn't do Hotel de Renee justice - a boutique hotel not too far from Rue des Francs-Bourgeois street and The Seine.

She was relieved that the flight had been manageable; baggage claim at Charles de Gaulle airport was not a hassle, US dollars were easily exchanged for euros, and the taxi ride was actually smooth. Deon let out a sigh once she reached her room, 518.

It was 7:52pm. Once she opened the door, she stopped dead in her tracks, letting her bags fall by the door as it closed. In awe of the view, she smiled. With the gilded mirrors and crystal dangling chandeliers, it was a place fit for a queen. She twirled

216

around in the center of the room for a second. The opulent high ceilings and crown molding had Deon feeling like she had stumbled onto the set of a Golden Age movie. Her penthouse suite possessed the sweetest sophistication; it was such a pure, ornate space: a royal blue, green, and gold fantasy.

The lavish bathroom was a retreat in itself. The vanity was out of this world. The living room was majestic. There, Deon could open the French doors of Paris. She walked out onto the terrace. She stood, taking it all in. The lights were starting to glow; the drizzly winter produced a silver sky that Deon liked. This place was magic, and she could get engulfed in the aesthetically-pleasing color palette, but most importantly, the love affair with the city.

Her stomach reminded her that she needed to get a move on. She zipped up her heavy-lined coat. She knew she'd enjoy the room even more on a full stomach. She wanted to forget room service and get out and about in the 42 degree weather. While hunting some great French cuisine in the capital, she was sure she was going to look like an anxious tourist.

She and her mother had traveled to Paris during the summer of '92. The obvious: the Eiffel Tower, which was beautiful at night, Notre Dame, and of course the famous river, The Seine, galleries and gardens were all taken in back then.

Although still picturesque, things looked a lot different as an adult visiting Paris, she thought, as she walked through the slushy streets.

The weather was a bit nippy, but being from Houston, weather can never deter anyone from having a good time.

Thirsty, she wandered into Café Belle.

"Bonjour"

"Bonjour"

As she took off her gloves, the waiter brought over a menu and also offered her favorite. She loved her a good bottle of red. Soon, she ordered The Loire. As the warmth filled her, she was well past working up an appetite. She ordered the moules mariniere and enjoyed the french bread while she waited. She sat back, wrapping herself in the weather, her sketch pad lay right by the centerpiece on the table. She couldn't remember the last time she ate alone...*this should be...interesting.*

The food came and it looked so delicious that Deon did not want to devour it, but she would. She started sinking her teeth into the tender cuts, but saw a sight that made her squint. Out the window, and from a distance, she saw someone who made her twist her head all kind of ways to see if that was the guy that she thought it was. She was not the only American floating around. *Mercy, mercy me!*

Her body, by instinct, jumped out of her seat and ran out the door of the café.

"Hey! hey!!!" She ran after him, leaving her food at the table. She wanted to tell him how thankful she was for everything that he did for her while in the twilight zone called recovery. Once she caught up with him, she hit him on his back.

A bit confused, he turned and looked beyond her mind-boggled. His face mirrored hers for seconds before she heard a word from his mouth.

"Mademoiselle?"

Deon was now alarmed when French came out of his mouth. She didn't know what he...said after that. A thick French accent, and this whole realization had her now blushing with embarrassment. Wow, if only he knew he looked so much like him, he would know she wasn't over-reacting or a crazy American.

"I am so sorry, I don't know too much French. She started to play charades with her words: I thought you were a guy...I once knew."

Burying her face in her hands, she began to walk away quickly, that hoping the café didn't call the police on her for leaving without paying – jail in another country was always tricky.

***

She stepped into the steaming hot water, water that she didn't know was scorching hot. Quickly, she sat on the rim of the sleek, white claw-foot tub to keep from falling in any further or falling out on the cold, black and white tiny tiled floor.

She had had a long day – and it was time to unwind. Her mind was even playing tricks on her. She swore she knew the guy, but...since the accident, she still wasn't herself, but she was grateful for the self she had left.

After playing around with the dials, she finally got the temperature warm enough to where she could actually sit in it. Sitting on the rim of the tub was a rubber ducky, an expensive one at that. It came with a message: *choices determine who we are.*

She sat in the tub as the bubbles formed around her, relaxing her body. *Wow, I want one of these at home.* She leaned back and relaxed as much as her common sense allowed. She draped her hands outside of the tub to keep from sinking too far into the water. NOW she understood how some people drowned while in these vintage style tubs. It was easy to be lulled into complete relaxation.

She took the milky soap and towel and cleansed her body. She lifted her leg and smoothed the soap over the word tattooed on her body - success. Unfortunately, there were secrets to it.

She never told Quincy about their baby. In fact, she had never told any one. The miscarriage – the year of graduation – was something she felt she should take to the grave. She was ashamed as she wiped up the remnants of her future on the salon bathroom floor that she worked at at the time. Just like that. Like a simple spill. A life was over, really even before it began. It was a scary moment that she wished she didn't have to go through alone. But she did.

Who knows what Q would have done, said, or thought. She chose to keep the secret, not the baby. Sacrifice was synonymous with success, but evidently, so were secrets...

Deon exhaled. Secrets to success were not always good. She was going to do more sharing in the future. Hopefully, it wouldn't take another tragic moment to push her to do so. Although she could live with some secrets, she refused to live with any new ones.

Her definition of success needed to change because she had.

Although money used to be her BFF, nowadays, she was becoming her own. It seemed like the best way to spend precious time, redefining this thing called life.

***

She sank into the firm, full-sized bed. The dark room soon glowed as the moonlight from the round top windows peeked through, like eyes watching over her. She was so comfortable that she didn't want to see the sun.

***

Early morning came and Deon was ready for day two in Paris. Heading out, she didn't plan on going on a shopping spree, but she knew she couldn't go to Paris without at least getting something. Rue des Francs-Bourgeois was a block away, for goodness sakes. But something stopped her in her tracks – an envelope lay under the door.

***

Deon walked past the many boutiques, she wished to take a piece of Paris back home with her.

Life was like a charm bracelet...a collection of symbols...linked together. Beautiful it is, but heavy and cluttered, nonetheless.

Some people want to see how far they can pull you, but I pushed myself too far. Loaded myself down with objects. I had to let go of the chain itself in order to officially break the ties that bind, she thought.

She thought about how the world had told her she was cursed, but being single was a gift. One she would embrace. Down the line, she had heard from many men that her brutal honesty helped a lot of them grow up. She didn't even know she was doing her civic duty through dating.

Even though she felt her dating days were pointless, and all in vain, she learned from past guys that she was valuable to them in some way - she made them a better person, for the next woman of course. Deon laughed at the irony.

No matter the scale of the trip, and all the fancy objects she could buy, and bring back with her...she was the souvenir.

In life, everything has a price. She paid it, but she couldn't deny the perks that came with the trip.

She was about to head into a boutique that caught her eye when all of a sudden, she was alerted by a man shouting, "Ma'am! Wait up. Please..."

Deon turned to see the handsome man with the familiar face. The one from last night. Soon they were face to face. What was strange to her was...his eyes...not the color, but the placement was like hers. Her eyes were not symmetric. Her left eyebrow is raised higher than the right. So was his.

"I left you a note."

That would be something - come to Paris to pick up another crazy, Deon nodded, but she was confused as to how the note got there. How did he know where to leave it, or get someone else to? She was hoping the guy was not a stalker who followed her.

"What is your accent?"

"No, no. I do know English. I'm from here, but I live in America."

Deon was still all frowns, but she was taken aback by the man's smile.

"You ran off before I could talk to you. How about I take you to lunch since we missed breakfast. You know to chat. It's not everyday that you find an American as beautiful as you in Paris."

This guy looked just like...*she couldn't remember*...his name, she couldn't remember his name; that was unlike her.

"Mark." He held out his hand. "I'm here on assignment for my technology students at the charter school I work at. I received a grant to continue research for my studies."

She stood for a moment and shook his hand. He felt so familiar.

"I'm Deon."

He blinked and then almost choked.

"No!"

"Yes."

"Deon as in Deondria?"

Deon looked a little suspicious. Mark started to chuckle to himself. "This can't be! I knew you were special." He shook his head. He then looked closer at her eyes. "This is fate."

She felt a number of things but all she could do at this point was to laugh. The guy sounded crazier than she felt.

"This is not a coincidence, like I thought last night. You wouldn't believe me if I told you. Let's just say, we have a lot to talk about over lunch."

Deon felt like analyzing those things. Then she stopped herself. In such a charming setting, what an adventure this would be. She was 30 when she was 21. She was tired of the old her. She guessed now she could actually be 21. She can actually breathe a little. Live a little. Overthink only just a little. Feel a whole lot more. For goodness sake, let the good air in!

Day three in Paris was spent with Deon and Mark getting to know each other.

***

Once home, she and her new-found friend, Mark, found out they had way more in common than they could have ever expected. Yes, they both made the Dean's List in high school and college, but when Mark invited her over to his apartment and showed her his book, she felt faint?

This guy she had never met, spoken to, or knew since Adam had highlighted her name years ago because it was something about her picture that spoke to him.

He didn't go into detail about why, he just said, "You were the girl...of my dreams, literally."

Mark showed Deon his notebook of sketches; sketches, his vivid imagination had prompted. Deon was astonished by how close his heroine favored her. She was surprised she looked much like the Super shero he had created.

225

More Than a Good Idea

*If you think in terms of a year, plant a seed;
if in terms of ten years, plant trees; if in terms of 100 years, teach
the people. – Confucius*

Friday, January 3, 2015

After Mark's sweet and sincere introduction, Deon hugged him before she stepped to the podium in a new space in the salon among tons of smiling and chanting guests; she took a deep breath and took her time. Sharing her feelings was new for her, especially to a crowd like this one - but she knew it was a new day and this was a part of her new life. Telling the truth on the other hand, came naturally.

"Fairy tales, those doggone fairytales and dumb-ass reality shows landed me in this abyss of illusion. I grew up in a castle made of quicksand. My culture produced a crown of sorts, one blinged-out tiara after the next and I certainly wore each proudly, unaware of how each later fashioned a classic case of claustrophobia…and a permanent dent in my forehead."

They laughed. So did she.

"Oh how the cookie crumbles, especially when a corset is so tightly drawn, you can't even breathe."

226

There was more laughter and head nods.

"Breathe...Breathe...Breathe! I wanted desperately to do that...but that can be hard when your heart stops. You realized how short life is.

As a kid, I never feared flying, I feared falling. The same lucid vision would wake me up in cold sweats, each and every time. But this time, it was no dream. It happened.

The sad truth is that in life, although many grabbed my attention, few grabbed my hand to pull me up. Instead, I was pushed to the limit, and finding my footing was nearly impossible.

I had always had a high tolerance for pain, but this was beyond me. Depleted may be the best word to express how it felt to not be able to do what my mind commanded. Being in a coma, coming out of the coma, recovering, all are parts of a miracle's domino effect.

"I knew my body could bounce back as soon as I got a hold of Zac, my trainer; he's amazing. Thanks for being here."

She pointed him out.

"Even my physical therapist. Thanks for coming out for this occasion."

There was applause for both.

The night of my fall was sketchy, and I was waiting for the pieces to fall into place, not for me to fall down the freaking stairs!

Even when a little birdie let the cat out of the bag about my surprise party.

Autumn blushed.

"The event still lived up to its name. When I hit the Galleria Mall earlier that day for the latest red bottoms, the last thing I expected to do was hit rock bottom at the club later that night. Maybe it was because my mind was somewhere else...on all the men in my life."

Deon smiled at her husband of two years, her soul mate, a man she was grateful to have in her life, one that had her undivided attention. Mark's smile was always her heart's medicine. It settled her down.

"But I fell so hard and so low it took everything in me to get up. Now, I was standing, but it was costing me."

In life, everything has a price. I paid it, but I couldn't deny the perks that came with the trip...and fall.

A smile formed. A feeling she never knew, peace was what she possessed. She, for the first time in her adult life, felt whole. The dress, the make-up didn't do it. Man's acceptance didn't either. She accepted herself.

You don't have to fall down the stairs. You don't have to go to Paris. You can self-reflect in the comfort of your own home, your own bedroom, anywhere. That is what we have to do – take a good look at ourselves, inside and out in the most authentic way.

She was handed a huge pair of scissors. The ribbon was about to be cut.

The salon had a new face. Changes had occurred in the salon. Sheila and two more skilled stylists were now on board along with a great receptionist. Deon had allowed the salon to also become more community-centered. Instead of adding on a spa, she added a wellness center. On a regular basis, Autumn, Kyla and a few social workers worked to bring women's health awareness programs into the shop. *The Soul of the Salon* was a sanctuary.

Kennedy, who was also in attendance, capturing the event live, accepted Deon's "no" for the show. But she was grateful Deon didn't turn down an opportunity to work with the show as a producer for three seasons. Kennedy was actually cast as the original bachelorette for the *Most Eligible Bachelorette* show.

And thanks to Deon and Mark, as of January 2015, if women need self-reflection, *there is an app for that!*

The end,
for now

Queen D Syndrome

Micole Williams

5 Year Anniversary
Special Edition

Toxic Ties Trilogy:
Queen D Syndrome
Volume 1

232

Reader's Guide

1. What universe does Deon occupy after her big fall? What details inform these ideas?
2. How does Deon's upbringing and environment shape her friendships and relationships?
3. What is Deon's biggest wrongdoing? Biggest success?
4. How rich do you think Deon is? What has influenced this lifestyle?
5. Throughout the story, is Deon a victim or a villain? What shapes your opinion?
6. Is Âme a spiritual or mystical figure?
7. What societal constructs bind or define Deon?
8. What are your feelings about her relationship with Quincy and how it has transpired over time?
9. How do you characterize the author's writing style?
10. How does the ending close a chapter in Deon's life while opening up a new one?

About the Author

Micole Williams is a native
Houston, Texan who is the author of the satirical
romantic series, *Tangled Web of True Love Tales* and
creator, director and producer of the indie short film
series under the same title. She enjoys what she calls
being "lit for life" which entails working as a high school
English Language Arts teacher while writing for various
online magazines. This is her second book.

Visit her at www.micolewilliams.com and

check out her other books and media arts

projects!

www.ingramcontent.com/pod-product-compliance
Lightning Source LLC
Chambersburg PA
CBHW020552020726
47494CB00006B/2030